FRAGILE BEINGS

NEW PROTECTORATE STORIES: VOLUME ONE

ABIGAIL KELLY

Author's Note

The theme of this volume is *fragility* and how, despite our strengths, we are all vulnerable in our own ways. That said, your comfort as a reader is important to me. For those that wish to peruse them, a list of content warnings for each novella has been placed in the back of this book. Flip to the final page to find it.

~Abigail

For my patrons,
in honor of your generosity, humor,
and good taste.

#376

FATE CAN'T BE CONTAINED.

CHAPTER ONE

MADAM MILLIE'S MAGIC SHOPPE WAS, BY ANY STRETCH of the imagination, the single worst purveyor of consumer goods the world had ever seen. At least, it was the worst that Charlotte had ever seen — and she'd seen quite a number of terrible things since her kidnapping.

It wasn't like the hapless shoppers who wandered through Millie's jingling doors could hear Charlotte and take her warnings to heart, no matter how she howled or banged on the glass of her prison. She could have gotten stark naked and bellowed to the high heavens and no patron would have been the wiser.

If any of the curious non-magical — *arrant,* more precisely — customers could hear her, Charlotte could have told them that, no, those over-priced crystals wouldn't do one's energy any good. Or that, if one didn't have a lick of Foresight, the stacks of tarot cards were about as useful in predicting the future as reading the smears left by roadkill on a street.

She couldn't tell the tourists that the sigils on the cheap silver amulets were nonsense, nor could she warn the teens that they were wasting their allowances loaded on their implanted IDs on bootleg fey-made goods that would give them rashes before it did anything close to what Millie claimed. She couldn't tell them that the shop was a front for something far, far more nefarious than poor quality goods and services.

If you wanted real magic, real divination, real curses, real sigilwork, the shopkeeper wouldn't help you find it. She was one of those arrant humans who enjoyed playing at being a witch, but loved turning a quick buck more. Nothing in Millie's would do the trick — nothing except the people trapped in glass prisons on a shelf behind the counter.

Person, not people, Charlotte reminded herself. *All the others have been sold, remember?*

Most of Millie's customers were the hapless, magically uneducated sort, but not all of them. Some were the kind that came looking for the real, super-duper illegal stuff. Millie didn't make a mint off of her bundles of dried weeds and glass crystals, after all. That was a front for her real business: *m-siphons.*

Charlotte planted herself on the wee granite pebble that served as her only furniture and watched as another arrant woman forked over fifty bucks for a bundle of something that looked vaguely mystical, but Charlotte knew came from a dime store up the street.

She tapped her foot on the mossy ground of her cage, grimly fascinated by how easy it was for Millie to swindle people. Honestly, the more unscrupulous fey could take a page out of her book.

She didn't begrudge anyone taking comfort in whatever rituals they needed, but Charlotte had long lost patience with the mix of ignorant shoppers looking to spend their cash on nonsense and the unscrupulous folk who thought buying trapped fey for spellwork was anything less than barbaric.

Millie was saying something to the woman, using that same breathy voice she always affected whenever a gullible shopper walked through her door, but Charlotte could never quite make the words out. The glass that held her captive was just too thick, or perhaps it was part of the sigilwork that held her in there. Either way, she could never make a single word out.

It wasn't like it took ears to figure out what Millie did, though. Charlotte's eyes still worked perfectly.

Bored by the familiar charade, Charlotte kicked her feet in the air and examined her toes. She'd worn shoes once — nice heels with pointed toes and dainty little ankle straps — but after three hundred and seventy-six days in a terrarium-turned-prison, it just didn't seem necessary. Most of what she once stubbornly clung onto from her old life remained in a little bundle beneath the fern that filled up most of the globe. Still, she kept on the slinky silver jumpsuit she wore the night that rat bastard feyrunner drugged her in an alley.

Charlotte propped her hands behind her back and hoisted herself up to glare at the warped image of the beast that stole her life.

No, Millie she wasn't the feyrunner who initially snatched Charlotte off the street, but she was the one who paid him and kept her there, a product on a shelf, to be used as a magical battery for some two-bit sigilworker lacking the right *oomf.*

Charlotte scowled, watching as Millie meandered about the store, puttering around with her sausage fingers and her mumu and her non-prescription glasses.

Tempest break her, she thought for the thousandth time. *If I weren't so terrified of being left in this jar to rot, I'd be begging Grim to drag her to the underworld already.*

When the arrant shopkeeper passed out of her limited field of view, Charlotte slipped off of her pebble and retreated into the relative privacy of the lush fern that took up most of the space in the terrarium. She collapsed onto her bed, a thing composed mostly of moss and flower petals that, thanks to the stasis spells that kept Charlotte unchanged, remained unwilted. She stared up through the leafy canopy.

The sunlight filtering in through the shop's windows made

the air within the terrarium humid, but it was slightly cooler in her little nest. The familiar scents of moist earth, forget-me-nots, and water were a comforting balm to her senses.

As far as jails went, the terrarium wasn't the worst. Charlotte could have been trapped in a teapot, or a locket, or a repurposed coffee can, or a glovebox. Overall, the terrarium was kind of nice, if you could get past the crippling isolation and boredom.

Charlotte turned on her side and pillowed her arm beneath her head, trying to tune out the dull sounds of the ridiculous chanting Millie called music that wormed its way through the glass. Mostly Charlotte tried not to let the boredom consume her by spending every hour of the day critiquing her captor and her livelihood, but sometimes sleeping was the only way to get through it.

As usual, she dreamed of her parents.

They were the nicest pair of arrants one could ever find, and she used to hate them for it. Being a Changeling wasn't easy. They raised her like an arrant, knowing full-well that puberty would smack her in the face with acne and arcane magical abilities.

Being a Changeling meant watching her friends go through trauma like boy drama and periods and weird, chunky foundation while Charlotte lost the ability to lie, ate everything in sight, graduated from an A cup to a whopping B cup, grew a ridiculous pair of glassy, basically useless wings, and developed the insatiable need to *fiddle* with things.

The worst, by far, was the glowing. Every time she felt anything beyond low-level apathy, she'd light up like some damn glowbug, telling all the world that she wasn't as normal as she was supposed to be.

Her parents never asked her to *be* normal, but Charlotte grew up surrounded by normal arrant kids in a normal human neighborhood of the Elvish Protectorate. Her parents wanted to give her a good life there.

They just didn't think about the particulars when they made

a deal with the local fey covey. It must have seemed easy enough:
A baby to raise, with only a contract that stipulated Charlotte
would be turned over to her covey in the event that she mani-
fested any "significant ability" by the age of sixteen to worry
about. Her parents had their wish fulfilled and her biological
family got rid of an unwanted bastard with minimum fuss.
Win-win.

Except she never did show signs of a "significant ability", and
all her human parents got was a moody teen who took to yelling
when her ability to tell a convincing fib went out the window.

In the three hundred and seventy-six days she spent trapped in
the terrarium, Charlotte had ample time to reflect on her kind,
bumbling parents. She couldn't exactly fault them for wanting a
kid — not when the result was a pretty good life, all things
considered.

Sure, most people didn't go deep into the forest during a new
moon with a bowl of cream and a baby blanket, ready to make a
deal with the higher-ups of the local covey. Adoption was a thing.
So was a fertility specialist. And surrogacy, for that matter.

But most people didn't have the history her mother's family
did, one rife with old magic and fey deals, so perhaps Charlotte
could cut them some slack. It wasn't like she was the first
Changeling in the family, after all. She was just the only one
dumb enough to get caught.

Charlotte, her short black hair mussed from her fitful nap and her
nose pressed against the glass of her cage, blinked hard several
times to focus the image through the warped glass. It was a small
mercy that Millie put her up on a high shelf. If she weren't able to
watch the old cow every day, Charlotte was sure she would have
gone insane already.

Or maybe she already had, and that was why she could very

clearly see a demon standing there amidst the curling incense smoke and buffoonery. He towered over Millie. Even through the glass, Charlotte could see the grand sweep of his antlers, the shock of deep black sclera around irises of shining bronze, and the way the air fizzled slightly around him, as if his humanoid shape was ever-so-slight... off.

Dressed in a simple white long-sleeve with his chestnut hair swept back neatly between his antlers, the demon looked exactly like the kind of person who shouldn't wander into Millie's misbegotten trash heap.

Which meant bad things for Charlotte.

The last time someone came in who actually *looked* like they knew what they were doing, the terrarium next to hers ended up going in a suitcase and out the door, off to a fate she couldn't contemplate without spiraling into a dread so deep, there was no clawing her way out of it.

Charlotte tried to get a good look at Millie, but it was impossible from that angle. Her stomach twisted into knots. *There's no one else left.*

Obviously, she didn't relish the idea of spending eternity trapped in stasis on Millie's shelf, but Charlotte didn't exactly look forward to being sold to a stranger, either. Better the enemy she knew, right?

It did occur to her that the demon could be there to buy something, but what a demon could want from a woman with the magical ability of an old shoe was beyond her. Perhaps he was there to kill Millie and drag her corpse into the woods for the mites to eat; an old-timey sacrifice the god Blight would *probably* appreciate.

That sounded pretty great, if one ignored the fact that Charlotte was still trapped in a jar and would remain that way until someone released the seal on the stasis spell holding her captive.

Charlotte was all for Millie's untimely demise. Just not when it meant she might be tossed in a dumpster when the cleaners came to clear the shop out.

Pressing herself as close to the glass as possible, she strained to listen as Millie gave the demon her usual spiel. It didn't last long. One muttered sentence from the demon — who had a voice so deep it reverberated through the glass of her prison with rich bass notes — and the hand-waving ceased.

She watched, beginning to sweat in earnest, as Millie's demeanor changed. Her usually warm, slightly slouched posture vanished. It was replaced by a stiffness that Charlotte knew well.

They're negotiating, she realized, stomach knotting up. *Please don't be for me.*

But what else could it be? There was, as far as Charlotte knew, nothing else of any real worth in Millie's shop. Only the m-siphons, cleverly disguised as decorative terrariums, could bring in clientèle like a demon in.

And there were no more m-siphons left except the one holding her captive.

Charlotte lurched up and away from the glass. Her feet sank into the rich soil and springy moss as she paced, raking her fingers through her short hair until it stood on end. All around her, the demon's baritone rumbled with menace.

What could she do? *Nothing.*

There was no escaping the terrarium. She tried a hundred different ways, but whoever laid the sigilwork on the damn thing was no slouch and she lacked any sort of real magical skill that might have helped her. Charlotte rarely got over a C in magical extracurriculars. Her sigilwork was basically chicken scratch. She couldn't even properly *fly.*

I went to college and got a degree in communications! I am not cut out for any of this!

But she couldn't just sit there, doing nothing, as her fate was decided behind the dusty counter of Millie's tourist trap front for hawking illegal goods. Charlotte was a woman of action if not any recognizable ability.

Scrambling into the heart of the fern, Charlotte only half-listened to the sound of Millie's voice raising as she climbed the sturdiest of the stems. The view was a little bit better the higher she went, but she couldn't go terribly far without the fern flopping over. Gripping the stem with white-knuckled fingers and toes, Charlotte craned her neck just in time to see Millie hit the floor, a strange, dark mass rippling around her slumped form.

Charlotte's stomach seized as panic overtook her. Yes, she wanted to see Millie get her just desserts, but not when the person dishing it out might have even worse plans for *her.*

The demon wasted no time stepping over Millie's prone form sprawled on the grimy mat behind the counter to approach the nearly empty shelf Charlotte's prison called home.

No, no, no! She threw herself down from the fern and into her nest to land with a wheeze in the moss below. Frantically covering herself with hunks of greenery and silky flower petals in the vain hope that he wouldn't see her and know just how valuable she was, Charlotte hunkered down into the shadows and squeezed her eyes shut.

The light filtering through her eyelids changed — he must have blocked out the light from the windows — and that voice filtered through the glass again, so deep she could feel it humming in her molars. Tucking herself into a tight ball, she covered her ears and refused to look. It didn't matter that she was curious about seeing a demon up close for the first time.

He was stealing her, just like the feyrunner did, just like Millie did.

The best case scenario was that he hooked her up to a low-level generator for the rest of eternity. The worst involved being sucked dry of all energy until even the stasis spell couldn't keep up, leaving her mummified corpse to molder in the lush soil of her green prison.

The jarring sense of her world heaving forced Charlotte to open her eyes. Her stomach roiled as the demon's fist closed around the tiny glass jar, wreathing her world in darkness. The feeling of her prison moving wasn't something she'd forgotten, but it had been so long that Charlotte wasn't prepared for the motion sickness that came when the demon pulled her off of the shelf and began to walk.

"Don't drop me," she croaked, digging her fingers into the moss like it might steady her heaving world. "Don't you drop me, you jackass!"

Not that she knew what would happen if he did, exactly, but the likelihood was high that it would kill her. A drop from that height onto the floor would surely shatter the glass, but it would probably also break her body.

Charlotte gritted her teeth as the swaying, heaving movement seemed to go on forever. Her world became nothing but darkness and endless nausea. The smell of moist, upturned soil clung to the back of her throat and inside of her nose. The moss, once a comfortable place to take refuge from her captivity, crumbled under her grip.

A flash of light broke through the shadows to blind her. Charlotte threw up an arm to shield her eyes as light — real sunlight of deep orange and butter yellow and that particular lavender of a summer sunset — burst through the swaying leaves of the fern.

She choked on tears, at once overwhelmed with joy and horrified by what it meant to see the outside world again after so long. It didn't last long, though. The demon was merely adjusting his grip as he opened the door of his truck. Charlotte had only a moment to bask in the light before he popped the glove compartment box open and shoved her prison inside.

Domhnall wiped his sweaty palms on his thighs, told himself to buck the fuck up, and pulled his truck away from the curb outside of *Millie's Magic Shoppe* at a totally normal, non-suspicious speed.

He might not have been so worried about being seen if his truck didn't stand out so much. Large, well-loved, and splattered with a thick layer of dried on mud, his vehicle stood out starkly amongst the zippy little m-enhanced town cars that filled United Washington's streets. Not that he fit in much better out of the truck, of course. With his height and his antlers, there was no way for him to go incognito. Even in a place like the New Zone, where all the races were welcome to start fresh — for the right price — could a demon walk the streets unnoticed.

That was why he normally stuck to the forest and his own little homestead on the border of the Orclind. No one except his clan bothered him there, and the wildlife he looked after for the Iron Chain didn't think twice about his unusual heritage. The orcs that passed through didn't either, for that matter. Not that he saw them much.

But he didn't see anyone much, which was why he was so viscerally uncomfortable with this little quest his Matriarch sent him on.

Damn prophetess, he swore, tightening his grip on the steering wheel. *I love the woman, but this was too much.*

But one simply didn't say *no* to the Matriarch of a demon clan, let alone a prophetess. Amongst the superstitious demons, that was considered the worst kind of insult and the quickest way to bring down Blight's hand on them all. Dom had no patience for superstition, but he had even less for the inevitable fallout that would occur if his family found out he didn't do as his Nan asked.

Sighing heavily, Dom checked his rearview mirror for pursuers, but wasn't surprised to find no suspicious vehicles tailing him as he wound his way back to the small motel he called home since he arrived in the New Zone. *Millie's Magic Shoppe* might have traded in the most illegal and vile merchandise, but it wasn't exactly a high tech criminal enterprise. There was no back-up coming to hunt him and the stolen merchandise down.

Still, he didn't breathe any easier until he pulled into the parking space in front of his rented room. The run-down motel was on the very edge of the sprawling city and nestled into a small wooded area — the only reason he was able to tolerate being so close to the city at all.

It was dark by the time he pressed his thumb to the keypad to turn off the truck. Dom sat back in his seat for several long moments, his amber eyes fixed on the middle distance as he considered just what in Blight's name he was doing.

Find the shop. Find the terrarium. Find your fate. His Nan's words stuck like a bur in his mind. There was little else to go on, aside from a hastily scribbled address she penned while in one of her trances. It seemed like a hassle, but easy enough.

Except when he walked into the shop, Dom knew it wasn't so simple. Magic hummed in the air — bright and sharp on his tongue, like cold, fresh citrus. Not from the aging proprietress, but the shelf behind her.

M-siphons.

One m-siphon. One small, globe-like terrarium. A pretty trinket disguising a prison that kept a living, breathing creature locked away for the use of another. A wildly illegal item sitting pretty on a shelf, out for all the world to see. A crime so vile it made his skin crawl just to think about it.

Cursing under his breath, Dom fiddled with the latch on the glove compartment and tried to rein in the urge to hunt the arrant woman who ran the tourist trap down. The desire to rescue whomever was trapped in the m-siphon meant he only knocked her out, but the animal in him demanded more.

Demons already had a bad reputation, so what would be the harm of a little bloodletting? Surely it wouldn't even begin to scratch the surface of what the woman really deserved.

Gnashing his fangs, Dom sucked in a deep breath through his nose. *Calm. Help the victim first. That's why Nan sent you.*

He reached into the glove compartment to gently extract the small, palm-sized globe. A *zing* of magic coursed through his palm and up his arm, sending a rush of goosebumps over his body. The glass was warmer than a real terrarium would be — almost hot, with a prickly energy humming through it.

Whoever was locked away in the globe had magic that fizzled across his senses in ways that made his inner animal perk up, hackles raising. It was a rushing, wild sort of energy that made his heart beat faster and the skin around the base of his antlers tighten.

Shaking his head, Dom cupped the m-siphon against his chest and got out of his truck. Gravel crunched under his steel-toed boots as he stomped back to his little room in the blue-black shadows of the summer evening.

Annoyingly bright lights buzzed overhead, tucked into the awning that stretched over the row of motel rooms. They dimmed slightly when Dom stepped close to his door and fished for his key. The shadows that were an inherent part of him, the wildness of a dark woodland and all its most vicious creatures, coveted that light and reached for it on instinct.

Demons came in all shapes and sizes, from all over the world — Dom's clan originally hailed from the northernmost edge of Siberia, for instance — but it was that inner shadow, that very real hunger for the light that made them all the same.

It also made them pariahs for most of history. Blight, the god of disease and all forested places, blessed demons with their many gifts, but no one wanted to get too close to his chosen people.

Stepping into the modest motel room, Dom kicked the door shut with his heel and turned on the lights with his free hand. There wasn't much to be said about the room itself. He wasn't one for luxury, so he didn't care that the feed screen didn't turn on, or that the sheets were scratchy. His antlers fit through the door and the water in the shower ran hot. That was all he needed.

And if the two rooms on either side of him quickly emptied out as soon as their occupants saw who checked in next door, it only bothered him a little.

Ignoring the way the dull yellow light flickered when he passed beneath it, Dom sank onto the edge of the large bed and examined the m-siphon in his hands.

Aside from knowing what they were and having a rough idea of how they worked, he had no idea what one did with the things, or how to go about dismantling one. A cursory search on his phone provided nothing useful aside from a series of articles detailing the stories of rescued victims and the havoc a sigilworker could wreak with one at their disposal.

There was no information on how to release the stasis spell that kept the person within it captive, only the clear warning that, should a person come across a stray m-siphon, they should call the authorities.

Dom gently turned the globe around in his palms and brought it up to his face so he could peer through the thick, slightly warped glass. Would he be able to see the person inside?

There was nothing. Not even a hint of movement. If Dom couldn't feel the magic coursing through his body, he would have been fooled into thinking it was just a cute little terrarium full of dirt, pebbles, tiny blue flowers, and a lush green fern.

Smoothing the pads of his callused thumbs over the warm glass, he eyed the deceptively normal-looking cork that sealed the terrarium from the outside world. Tiny sigils had been seared into it — totally incomprehensible to someone like him, who only barely passed the state required sigil classes in middle school and who had the wrong sort of magical pathways to use them properly anyway.

Was there some sort of lock? A magically reinforced barrier that would burn his hand to a crisp if he tried to uncork the thing?

Dom grunted, not exactly enthused by the idea. He was no stranger to pain, but if he could avoid being cursed or permanently losing the use of one hand, he'd rather do that.

"Can't break the glass, though, can I?" His gaze dropped to watch the progress of a droplet of condensation as it slid down the inner curve of the globe. Was that a flash of silver he saw as it disappeared behind the fern? He squinted, trying to make out the shape that—

A leg.

It absolutely *was* a leg. Tiny, half buried under moss and leaves and flower petals, but with all his jostling, the person trapped in the m-siphon had to scramble to stay hidden beneath the fern. Dom only caught the flash of a slim ankle and a metallic silver pant leg before it was gone again.

"Fuck this," he grunted, his blood coursing hot and furious. He wasn't the most sociable demon in the world, no, but he was a compassionate one. He couldn't bear unjust suffering. Whether it was an animal caught in an illegal snare or a person locked away in a quaint little prison didn't matter. He wouldn't let it go on.

Gritting his fangs, Dom prepared himself for pain as he pressed his thumb against the side of the cork. The zap of magic that singed him wasn't exactly comfortable, but it was also a lot milder than he anticipated when he pushed the cork up and out.

The cork resisted for only a moment before it gave way with a loud *pop!* It flew across the room to ricochet off a generic black and white photograph before landing somewhere on the cheap carpet.

The scent of green things, of rich soil and bright citrus, permeated the room. Dom sucked in a deep breath as he held the terrarium out, as far from his body as possible. His inner animal, already roused by all the magic in the air, turned its full attention to the source of the scent — recognizing the smell of home and something far more tantalizing.

Dom watched, confused by the feeling of recognition and the sight of smoke curling from the open mouth of the globe. The smoke carried that scent of citrus and clean, soft skin. A woman's smell.

He had only a moment to consider that before two things happened: The glass began to crack, and the shadows that were the very root of his soul *lunged.*

What happened after that was chaos.

The light overhead popped and went out. The terrarium shattered in his hands, exploding in an arc of glass and soil. The air appeared to crumple in on itself, twisting and scrunching in front of him before snapping back into place — this time with a fully-grown, very pissed off woman where there once was nothing. She was small, decked out in a silver jumpsuit streaked with dirt, and howling with rage. Dom's shadows, always more calm than most demons his age, burst outward to coil themselves around her in the split second it took for her to appear on the motel floor.

He watched, too shocked to do much else, as his shadows moved around her, holding her captive as she struggled to kick them off. The more she moved, the more shadows joined in, creeping from under the bed, the darkened bathroom, inside the drawers of the generic dresser that stood next to the bed.

It wasn't a violent hold. It wasn't meant to harm at all. It was instinct — the ingrained impulse to snap up his mate and keep her close, to let his darkness seep into her skin until every demon this side of the Atlantic and beyond knew she belonged to him and him alone.

Oh, fucking— My fate, my ass! His Nan didn't send him on some ridiculous quest to save a trapped fey. She sent him out to bring home a *mate.*

Dom lurched up from the bed to throw himself down beside his struggling mate. His hands shook as he tried to soothe her, to calm her so that he could in turn calm himself. The more distressed she became, the more his shadows would react to a threat that didn't exist.

No wonder his shadows reacted like they did, he thought, daring to crawl across the filthy, glass-strewn floor to where his mate was trying and failing to tear herself free. She was so small; so very *fey,* with her short black hair and fine bone structure. Even covered in dirt and spitting fury at him, she looked like spun glass.

"Hush, hush now," he crooned, like he would for one of the many animals he rescued and rehabilitated every year. "You're safe, little one. You're safe with—"

"Let me *go!*" His mate twisted her body sharply to one side and made to stand, shadows clinging to her like great, silken scarves. Dom moved to help her up, suddenly hyper-aware of all the glass on the ground, of her small bare feet and hands, but he misjudged both his shadows' ability to hold onto a slippery fey and said fey's desperation to be free.

Seeing him near, she whipped her head round to hiss at him, eyes lit with rage, and slammed one of those wee feet directly into his nose.

CHAPTER TWO

JULY 2044 - A MOTEL ROOM ON THE EDGE OF THE NEUTRAL ZONE

THEY STARED AT ONE ANOTHER FROM ACROSS THE room.

Dom pressed a wadded up ball of toilet paper against his nose and breathed through his mouth, his eyes locked on his mate. She sat on the floor, her back pressed against the flimsy motel door, and glared back at him. A slim band of darkness clung to her right ankle — a tether of shadow that stretched across the cheap carpet straight to his heart.

His little fey had calmed down some since she damn near shattered his nose, but she still refused to speak to him. Trying to give her space and seem as non-threatening as a demon could, Dom leaned against the doorway to the pint-sized bathroom and attempted to get his nose to stop bleeding.

"You've got quite a kick," he noted, his low voice nasally.

His mate's glare intensified. There was a very faint glow to her skin, a pulsing light that made the animal in him want to curl around her and soak up the warmth of it, the vitality of it. Not that he *would*, of course. Not when she looked like she was ready to spit nails at him if he so much as stepped out of the doorway. But he wanted to.

Dom pulled the bloody toilet paper away from his nose. Testing the aching bridge with his fingers, he grimaced. The bleeding was done, thank Blight, but he'd have a nasty bruise in the morning. He supposed he was lucky she didn't shatter the bone, though.

Turning to throw the bloody paper into the trash, he scrubbed his fingers through the hair between his antlers and said, for the fourth time, "I'm not going to hurt you, fey. If you would just tell me your name, maybe we could tal—"

"Why would I want to talk to someone who's keeping me captive?" Her voice was scratchy from disuse and pitched to convey all the fury she kept in that pint-sized body. To illustrate her point, his mate jerked her leg. He could feel the ripples in his shadow, the living pool of darkness inside him, and its absolute unwillingness to let her go.

"I told you, it's not intentional." Dom stepped back into the bathroom to fill a tiny glass with water from the tap. He didn't like the raspiness of her voice. Concern beat at him. What were the physical side effects of staying in stasis? Was she starving? Dehydrated? Just how long had she been trapped in that fucking globe, anyway?

He hated not having the answers to those questions almost as much as he hated the fact that she stubbornly refused to tell him her name. She'd rather snarl and spit at him like a wounded animal.

His mate was a fierce little thing. While the demon in him admired that, the man found her stubbornness deeply frustrating. He wasn't used to being gentle with people on a good day, let alone *now*.

Taking in a deep breath, he slowly walked across the room, arm outstretched so she knew he was only entering her space to deliver her water. When she stiffened anyway, those big dark eyes narrowing suspiciously, he scowled.

"Drink some water," Dom muttered, crouching down in front of her.

"Tell me what you want with me and then maybe I'll drink it."

And *this* was why he mostly preferred being alone. Dom had no patience for her ridiculous refusal of something as simple as a glass of water. Yes, he was a demon. Yes, she'd been in captivity for the gods knew how long. And yes, he could allow that things didn't start out on the right foot, but it was a glass of fucking *water*, not a damn grenade.

Growling, he set the glass down by her bare foot before dropping back onto his ass. "I *told* you," he rumbled, "I'm not going to hurt you. I'm your mate. That—" he gestured toward the shadow curled lovingly around her ankle "—is an instinctive response I can't control. If you were a demon, I'd have your shadow on me right now, too."

For protection. For the identification of family. For bonding. The sharing of shadows was a mark of ownership and community. Dom would wear her shadow proudly, if only she had one to give him.

"Uh-huh." His mate eyed him up and down critically as she pulled her legs in toward her chest, away from him. He fought the urge to squirm under her obvious appraisal. The animal in him wanted to preen, to impress, but the man would sooner eat his own boots than puff himself up for inspection.

"I don't want a mate who buys m-siphons— Sorry! *Steals* m-siphons — and then does whatever the fuck this is." She jiggled her foot at him again. "So I *hope* you're lying."

He nudged the glass of water an inch closer. "Drink, woman. I can hear your damn throat scratching from here." Dom watched her eye the glass warily, her throat moving with a hard swallow. A strike of sympathy cut through some of his annoyance. With her dirt streaked cheeks, rumpled hair, and curled up limbs, she looked like she expected the worst at any moment. He didn't want to be the worst anything. He wanted to be *hers*.

Gentling his voice as much as he was able, Dom coaxed, "You drink and I'll tell you why I was in that shop. Why I took you. And then maybe I can order us some food and we can talk about the rest."

Her head snapped up. Dark eyes framed by long, sooty lashes fixed on his face. "Food?"

Dom's whole body tightened when she leaned forward, her lips parting just enough for him to glimpse the tiniest fangs and the tip of a rosy tongue. "Yes, food," he answered, gruffer than he meant to. "Are you hungry?"

He watched her dirty little fingers curl against the threadbare carpet. When that pink tongue swept out to lick her lips, he tried to remember what it was like to breathe.

"I'm *starving.*"

He didn't like that. He wasn't much of a dater and he definitely wasn't known for his charm, but Dom could feed a woman. He *wanted* to feed her.

Fishing around in his pocket, he pulled out his cell phone. "Tell me what you want and I'll get it for you." When he got no direction, Dom glanced up from the screen to find his mate staring at his phone, her eyes wet and her fangs pressed hard into her full lower lip. A heavy stone of dread dropped in his stomach. "What? What's wrong? Are you hurt? Do you need—"

"Can I call my parents?" Her voice was thick, strangely lacking in venom.

Dom closed his eyes, cursing himself to the underworld and back. "Yes, of course. I'm sorry I didn't think that you might have someone you would need to..." He didn't hesitate to hand her the phone.

Her eyes widened like she was surprised he actually agreed, but she didn't miss a second in snatching it from his grasp.

For several long moments, she merely held the phone in her hands, her eyes locked on the call screen, almost like she expected him to snatch it away if she dared to move. Little rectangles of light reflected in the tears that gathered in her lashes.

Dom clenched his hands against his jean clad thighs and resisted the urge to reach out to her. All around the room, shadows rippled. They wanted to be near her, too. Everything in him, everything he was and all that he could be, yearned for this strange little woman — to comfort, to keep safe, to know.

He wasn't a demon who dreamed of matehood. As a teenager he fought in the final battles of the last Great War. Not even old enough to have his full antlers in, to have even gone through his first rut, and he participated in some of the single bloodiest, most pointless engagements of a grinding, devastating war.

He didn't come out of it dreaming of a family. He didn't come out of it dreaming at all.

When the dust cleared and the Peace Charter was signed, all he wanted was peace, quiet, and solitude. Taking up a post as a junior ranger for the Iron Chain forestry service was the perfect thing for him. Moving up through the ranks until he could have his own swath of wild territory to look after was the only thing he was truly proud of.

And then he got kicked in the face by a little fey woman in a silver jumpsuit.

As Dom watched her type a number onto the digital keypad with shaking fingers, he finally understood why so many left the war and went hunting for their mates — or whatever their race's equivalent was.

He didn't know her and she seemed to know instinctively which buttons to press, but when he looked at his little fey mate, Dom felt *right*. The world didn't seem so overwhelming or nefarious. It didn't threaten to move out from under him when he wasn't looking. Everything was stable. Centered. Focused on *her*.

And he sure as fuck didn't like it when the new center of his universe cried.

Dom watched helplessly as she raised the phone to her ear and held her breath. He knew that he should leave her to her call in peace, but he couldn't seem to move from his spot on the floor.

Even if he knew it wasn't true, the idea that his mate *might* need him rooted him to the spot.

He did his best to tune out most of the phone call. Not that he wasn't interested, but it was the only privacy he was capable of giving her under the circumstances.

His mate curled her free arm around her knees and buried her face against her thighs, the phone pressed tight to her ear as she explained where she'd been, that she was alright, that she missed her parents and needed to know they were okay. He tried not to listen to the words, but he felt every hitch of her breath, every watery syllable, every shaky exhale like hard fists in his gut — over and over.

It wasn't until he picked up the words *"go home"* and *"flight"* that Dom tuned back in, his velvety ears twitching. "You're in the New Zone," he told her when she paused to look at him.

"I'm in the damn *New Zone?* No, no. If that's right, there's no point in trying to— Mom, it's the New Zone. No one calls the authorities here!" His mate shook her head, the short strands of her black hair sticking out even more. Disbelief pinched the skin between her brows. "Mom, can you get me a flight— What do you mean there are no flights in or out of the EVP right now?"

Dom winced. "There's an embargo on travel to the EVP for the next six weeks."

She stared at him like he was a madman. "Why in the world— Mom, no, slow down. Just explain it. No, don't hand the phone to Dad!"

Her mother's tinny voice rose and fell on the other side of the line. With each word, his mate's expression grew more and more incredulous. He couldn't blame her. The news of Delilah Solbourne's abdication in favor of her much younger brother, Theodore Solbourne, shocked everyone.

Every territory was on edge, wondering what the new Sovereign would do, what the reaction of the Five Families that ruled the Elvish Protectorate would be. The elves were a blood-thirsty lot — power hungry, insular, and hierarchy-focused to a fault. If ever there was a perfect time for someone to challenge the Solbournes for the Sovereignty, it would be now, when the power was settling into the hands of an untried boy.

The fear of civil war in one of the wealthiest territories of the UTA sent a wave of panicked immigrants out into the New Zone, seeking sanctuary before the bloodshed began. Those were the people who remembered the reign of Mad Thaddeus, who helped plunge the world into the Great War all those decades ago and who, rumor had it, was finally struck down by his own cold-blooded daughter.

But the ensuing panic meant that the New Zone couldn't handle so many new residents at once. To stem the flow, the government put a temporary freeze on all flights to and from the EVP. As it stood, there was no violence yet, but the news was only a week old. There was plenty of time for those people now stranded in the territory to fall victim to an elvish power play.

"You're not going back there." The words were out of his mouth before he could stop them, but he didn't care if he sounded overbearing. He knew what elvish violence looked like. He knew what kind of bloodshed his mate could waltz into, what it would look like when she was turned into nothing but ribbons of fey flesh and shattered bone. "I'll drive you anywhere you want to go, little one, but until I know for sure that the elves aren't going to start burning each other in their beds again, or tearing each other and anyone who gets in their way limb from limb, I'm not letting you step foot in the EVP."

"Mom, I'm going to figure it out. Let me call you back in a little while, okay?" His mate slowly lowered the phone, her thumb pressed against the *end call* button despite the way her mother continued to speak on the other end of the line. His mate kept her eyes locked with his.

In a surprisingly civil tone, she said, "Thank you for letting me call my parents."

Dom shifted uncomfortably. "Of course. I would never keep you from—"

"But you *are* going to take me back to the EVP," she continued, her stare unblinking, her expression hardening. "You will, or I'll find some other way to see my parents."

The skin around the base of his antlers tightened. Memories of fighting for his life against elves who just wouldn't *stay down* made his hackles rise. Old scars, long healed and gone, itched below the surface of his skin. There was no way he'd let his mate walk into elvish territory when they could start tearing out each other's throats at any moment.

Planting his palms on the floor, he leaned forward to growl, "Like fuck you will."

She nodded once, precisely, before reaching down to pick up the glass of water. His mate drained it in one long swallow. Swiping her palm across her mouth, she sent him a mulish look. "I will. Are you going to try and stop me, Mr. I-Am-Not-The-Bad-Guy?"

Dom reached forward to pluck the phone out of her hand. She made an indignant noise and grabbed at it, but he had a significant height — and therefore reach — advantage over her. Holding it out of her reach, he huffed a hard breath out of his nose. "I'm not holding you prisoner. I'm your *mate*. You really think I'm going to take you into danger? We'll find some other way for you to see your parents." He eyed her flushed cheeks and bared fangs thoughtfully. "They're fey. They've got a covey, right? I'm sure your parents—"

His little mate struck him with her foot again, this time right in the kidney.

Seeing as he weighed three times as much as she did, the kick didn't actually hurt him when she wasn't aiming for uninsulated bone. That didn't mean he *liked* his mate striking him, though.

Dom snatched her foot before she could pull it back. His fingers, huge compared to her fragile build, curled all the way around it. "Stop hitting me, little wildcat," he snapped. "Mates don't do that."

She tried to tug her foot free of his grasp, a cute little hiss sneaking out from between her tiny fangs, but Dom held fast. He wasn't about to let her get another shot in, for one, and he liked the feeling of her smooth skin under his fingers. Of course, he'd rather be petting her than restraining her, but if she only gave him the one option, he wasn't fool enough to refuse her.

His mate bared her tiny fangs again. Somewhere behind her, a low buzzing picked up — a distinctly and befuddlingly fey sound. "My parents are arrant, asshole," she seethed.

Dom blinked owlishly. "How is that possible?"

His mate glowered at him, but it was hard to take her seriously when she had one foot in the air and dirt streaked across her skin like a wild thing. The buzzing tickled his ears, too, and it took him a moment to place exactly where it could be coming from. Not her chest, surely, and he was fairly certain she didn't have a rattle hiding anywhere.

It's her wings, he realized with a small start. Dom leaned slightly to one side to peek at the glassy petals of her small, vestigial wings as they shook with what he presumed was fury. *My mate has tiny little wings. Huh. Cute.*

When she caught him looking, his mate made an outraged sound and announced, "I'm a Changeling, okay?"

A Changeling? Dom's grip slackened, allowing her to yank her leg out of his hold. He stared at his fierce little mate with wide eyes. *My mate's a Changeling.*

It was the polite way of saying she was an abandoned child raised by parents outside of her race. It was a succinct title that proclaimed, in a word, that her covey didn't want her, so they probably shoved her at the nearest arrant couple, forever sandwiching her between two worlds. There was nothing inherently *wrong* with that position, but there was a reason so many people pitied Changelings. In a world as terribly fractured as theirs, they just never seemed to *fit.*

Dom's chest ached as he watched his mate curl up into herself against the door, her cheeks flushed and her eyebrows lowered in a defiant look, as if she expected him to say something cruel.

As if he could ever be cruel to the one person who made the world seem less overwhelming, less intent on causing him pain.

"I'm sorry. I shouldn't have assumed." He scrubbed a palm over his day-old stubble. *Gods,* he just wanted to be good at this, good to *her.* Too bad he was a surly recluse who preferred wounded animals to people and lost whatever charm he might have had in a bloody cornfield a hundred years ago. "I'm messing everything up. I'm not good with people."

"I just want to see my parents." The sight of her lower lip wobbling made his nerves fizzle. "I don't care about what else is going on in the world. I just want to get out of this place and go *home.*"

"Okay," he rasped, fighting the compulsion to stroke her hair, to nuzzle her throat, to soothe her in the way his people did. He'd do anything to make that wounded look in her eyes disappear. "Okay. We'll figure it out. But not right this second."

She shot him a watery, narrow-eyed look. "Why not now?"

"Because you're hungry, tired, and adjusting to being outside of a fucking terrarium for the first time in gods know how long." Dom slowly shifted, moving inch by inch, until he was sitting beside her, his back pressed against the door jamb. She tensed, but only her eyes moved as she tracked his movements. "Here." He held his phone between them. "Let's get some food in you. Then we'll talk about how you can see your parents."

When she didn't immediately take the phone from his loose grip, he tipped it in her direction. "Go on. Choose anything you want."

Her fingers were dirty, smeared with dark soil and bits of crushed greenery, but they were also fine-boned, with claws buffed to a high shine. He liked the way she moved, how she twisted her wrist and took his phone from him with delicate, graceful fingers. He liked it even more when she bit her lip and looked up at him through her wet lashes, a little of her wariness fading into something soft, almost hopeful.

"Thanks." Her voice cracked, the hard edge of desperation

blunted as she breathed out a long, shuddering breath. Cradling the phone with two hands, she swallowed hard before adding, "I'm Charlotte, by the way."

Charlotte. A strong name for a fierce little fey. His mate, *Charlotte.*

He smiled, showing off his own set of fangs — larger and duller than hers, meant for crushing rather than tearing, but fearsome in their own way. "Domhnall," he answered. "But you can call me Dom."

~

Charlotte was woman enough to admit when she'd made a misjudgment. Not aloud, obviously, but within the privacy of her mind? Sure, she could admit it.

Inhaling her third slice of gooey cheese pizza, she surreptitiously eyed the demon sitting in the tiny wooden chair by the equally under-sized table by the window. He kept his brawny arms crossed over his chest and his eyebrows pushed low over his amber-on-black eyes, but despite his surly attitude, he'd actually been pretty nice.

She still thought he earned the kick to his nose, though.

Charlotte sat cross-legged in the center of the motel bed, a huge box of half-eaten pizza in her lap. It was late, but she was too wired to try and rest. All she wanted to do was eat and eat and stare at the handsome demon who insisted he only meant to keep her safe.

My mate, she thought, squinting at him over the top of the pizza box. *I don't know how I feel about that.*

It wasn't that she didn't believe him, necessarily, but that she found the entire concept so deeply unnerving that she couldn't process it all at once. The world outside the terrarium felt huge and overwhelming. The air felt different on her skin. The politics of her home territory had changed overnight. She felt her wings buzz and shake every time Dom came within a foot of her, making her bones vibrate with the need to shift just a little bit closer, to entice in the way the fey were famous for.

It was all too much, too fast.

Charlotte swallowed her last bite of crust and reached for another slice, her desire to experience food bigger than her actual hunger. "So," she began, "you gonna tell me why you stole an m-siphon, or…"

Dom shifted in his seat. The chair squealed under his bulk as he leaned backward, his gaze locked on her. She watched, fascinated, as his antlers cast moving shadows on the plain wall behind him.

Actual moving shadows. They rippled in unnatural ways, as if Dom's presence brought every dark corner and shadow to life. Maybe it did. Charlotte knew next to nothing about demons, after all. They didn't like cities, and she spent all her life in some of the most populated places in the EVP. She knew weres and shifters and the occasional vampire or two, sure, but demons were about as rare as nymphs or selkies.

Only, demons have a bit of a reputation, don't they?

Not that she put any stock in that sort of thing. The fey had a reputation, too. They were known for being swindlers, as free with their bodies as they were with their deceptions. People looked at the fey and saw people to party with, but to watch carefully. They saw good craftspeople and designers, but also marked them as generally untrustworthy and undateable.

If anyone had a healthy disdain for caustic superstition and rumor, it was Charlotte, who wore the twin, suffocating mantles of both *fey* and *Changeling*.

"My grandmother is the Matriarch of my clan." Dom's voice was a gravelly thing — all pleasant roughness and hard edges that made all the soft things in her sit up and take notice. "She's also a prophetess. She told me where I needed to be, but not why." He shook his head. "I had no idea that woman was selling m-siphons until I walked in. Guess I should have suspected something, being in the New Zone, but…" He shrugged.

Charlotte took a slow, greasy bite and swallowed before reply-ing, "And you knew I was your mate then?"

"No. I knew it when I opened the terrarium." He tilted his head toward the dirty floor. The glass was gone, because he *"would not have her cutting her defenseless feet"* on his watch, but there was nothing they could do about the soil smeared into the scratchy fibers of the carpet without a vacuum or a Met to cast a simple cleaning spell. Neither had the right technical chops for that sort of spellwork, so the dirt remained.

"What does that mean for you, exactly?" Charlotte pressed the lid of the pizza box down a little, making it easier to see the hulking demon who seemed to swallow up half the motel room. "Like, I get what it *means,* but all I want right now is to go home and see my parents. What do *you* want out of this?"

Dom uncrossed his arms to press his palms against his thighs. Little spots of black blood stood out starkly against the fabric of his plain white shirt. In a no-nonsense voice, he answered, "I want you."

Charlotte let out a gusty sigh and wiggled her half-eaten slice at him. "Yeah, see, that's not an answer. I *know* you want me. That's what mates do. What I want to know is what your plan is. You gonna date me? You gonna throw me in the back of your truck and lock me away in some basement until I agree to hold your hand? I don't know how any of this works for demons. Give me something to go on here."

Truthfully, she wasn't even really sure what *fey* did when they found their mates, only that they didn't have a preference for monogamy and tended to go through several in a lifetime. Charlotte only ever received a cursory education about her fey-specific anatomy and bodily changes, but she'd tuned most of that out in middle school out of pure adolescent stubbornness and no shortage of spite. The *wing* thing, though, she remembered.

She watched, unsurprised, as Dom's expression darkened with indignation. "I told you I am going to help you see your parents.

I'm also going to make sure you're safe. I am *not* going to lock you up, for Blight's sake. What exactly do you think mates *do?*"

Charlotte swallowed her last bite before she took a swig of cheap, artificial-tasting lemonade. *Tough talker, invoking Blight's name like that.* Even she felt a little hesitance saying it aloud, and she wasn't much for religion even in the worst of times. "I was raised by arrants, remember?" She untucked one of her legs to shake her bare foot at him. "No humans do this weird shadow thing! And fey don't, either. I have no idea what any of this entails!"

Not to say she hated the little anklet of pure, condensed shadow now that she'd calmed down some, but Charlotte knew for certain that she'd never heard of any race doing something like what demons apparently did when they found their matches. She knew orcs had some weird hormonal shit that involved nests and gifts and things. Shifters courted ruthlessly until their mates agreed to a union. Dragons *chose.* Elves... well, no one really knew what elves did, but Charlotte had interacted with enough in their capital city to suspect it was something intense.

Fey, though.

Fey didn't keep lifelong partners. They found a person they liked. They sang their mating song. They enticed with their glow. Instinct drove them to a frenzy that sparked hot and burned fast. Charlotte wasn't sure what part of that was nature and what was nurture, but she wasn't particularly interested in an endless string of quick relationships. She'd always wanted someone to call her own, to be her home, to accept the weirdness of her dual natures.

Maybe that was why her wings and her glow had never reacted in the fey way to a potential partner. Maybe, deep down, she did want a mate. A *permanent* one.

Too bad Dom had terrible timing. Before her captivity, she might have thrown herself at him. After? Charlotte wasn't about to do *anything* hasty.

Dom stood up slowly from his chair. He walked with huge, deliberate strides to cross the distance between them. Looming over the foot of the bed, he asked, "And what do the fey do when they find their mates, hm?"

Oh, he's awfully pretty.

Charlotte craned her neck to stare up at him, her heart thumping out a staccato beat in her chest. Her wings — usually neatly folded, useless things — buzzed against her shoulder blades with the mating song. Cheeks darkening with a blush, she answered, "We have our own weird shit."

"Like what?"

She pushed the cooling pizza box off her lap. Why was it hard to look him in the eye all of a sudden? "Why should I tell you if you won't explain to me exactly what the weird shadow thing is for?"

Dom pressed a knee into the mattress and leaned forward, edging into Charlotte's space. The mattress dipped under his much greater weight. "It's how demons identify who belongs to what clan." His voice dropped an octave. It blended with the cadence of her humming wings, creating a smooth, sensual song. "Every shadow has its own unique... fingerprint, you could say. That fingerprint belongs to the individual demon, but a part of it belongs to a clan, too."

He leaned closer. One hand, huge and deeply tanned, reached out to trace the shape of the shadow banded around her ankle. The tips of his fingers skimmed it, sending a tingle of magic over her skin and up her spine. A lick of pure heat skated across every nerve.

Oh, she thought, shocked by the intensity of such a simple touch.

"This," he continued, gaze lowered to where his shadow curled around her delicate bone, "marks you as being part of my clan. As being mine." He swallowed hard. In her periphery, shadows pressed closer, creeping slowly across the floors to brush the cheap bedskirt. "My shadows belong to me and move at my command, but they also have a mind of their own. They recognized you as my mate, that you were in distress, and acted accordingly. Now I'll always know where you are, if you need me, because you will always carry a piece of me with you."

Charlotte held her breath as he curled his fingers around her ankle. The shadows licked up and around his hand before melting into his skin and back out again. They were a part of him, clearly, but also not. An extension of him, but independent, much like her wings were.

His palm and fingers were callused but warm; the feeling of his magic — dark, wild, like a force of nature barely restrained — made her breaths shorten. She got the peculiar sense that Dom was bigger than his physical form let on. He was packed tightly, all compressed darkness and wild, animal hunger leashed; his power wound into a coil ready to spring at any moment.

In that moment, she understood three things: First, that Domhnall was far, far more dangerous than she initially assessed. Second, that he was no threat to her. And third, that she *desperately* wanted his hands on her.

How long had it been since she had any contact with another soul? Charlotte knew the pitiful answer: three hundred and seventy-six days. Not since the night she was snatched away from her small birthday party at her favorite bar in the city. Not since the feyrunner drugged her and spelled her into that mossy prison.

The feeling of Dom's skin against hers, the rich, earthy smell of him in her lungs, the way he *looked* at her, like he couldn't tear his eyes away, like he wanted to *consume* her, made everything in her scream for more.

She watched as his chest expanded with deep breaths, as his eyelids dropped to a sultry half-mast. His lips parted to reveal a glimpse of long, blunt fangs. Dom skimmed his hand up her calf, under the leg of her stupid silver jumpsuit, and whispered, "You're *glowing.*"

"Fuck." Charlotte pulled her leg back, out of his reach, and jumped off of the bed, her heart in her throat. "That's not— godsdamn it!" She looked down at her bare arms with considerable disgust and more than a little mortification. He was right. Her glow had taken on a new but unmistakable pulsing beat.

Was it not enough that her wings wouldn't stop making that *stupid* noise? Now she had to light up like a fucking glow stick?

She couldn't meet his eye, but Charlotte could see Dom staring at her with open wonder through the fringe of her eyelashes. "Do you... Is it pulsing in time with your *heartbeat?*"

Closing her eyes, Charlotte prayed for patience and a reprieve from the ceaseless humiliation of being what she was. "Yes," she gritted out.

"Do you always do that?"

"Only when I'm feeling strong emotions." Raking her fingers through her spiky hair, she was doubly annoyed to find several tiny leaves knotted into the strands. It wasn't totally a lie, so the words slipped out with minimum discomfort. She *did* glow when she felt strong emotions. Charlotte just chose not to explain that the throbbing beat was new. "It's not— it's just fey shit, okay? Ignore it."

"Why?"

Charlotte opened her eyes to glare at him. "Why *what?*"

"Why should I ignore it?" Dom took a step closer, one hand raised as if he meant to stroke her some more. Charlotte bobbed and weaved until she was clear of his long reach, her back toward the open bathroom door.

"Because it's embarrassing," she answered. "It's *always* embarrassing."

"It's *beautiful.*" Dom straightened to his full, impressive height. Putting his hands on his hips, he added, "Why don't you think so?"

"Yeah, no, I am not getting into my childhood trauma with you right now, demon." Charlotte turned toward the bathroom before he could see the way her blush had spread from her cheeks to her chest. "Thanks for the pizza, but I'm going to take my first shower in over a year and—"

"Your wings."

She made the mistake of peeking over her shoulder. Dom stood in the same spot, his head was tilted to one side and those amber-on-black eyes narrowed contemplatively as he examined her back. "Your wings are moving. I thought they were supposed to be vestigial."

"They move when they want to," she snapped back, defensive on behalf of her silly little wings. "Under certain specific circumstances, a fey's wings can even sing."

Like when our bodies recognize a compatible partner, she silently finished. Charlotte was not about to explain that, though. She barely understood the complexities of the mating song, of the pattern her glow had taken on — both meant to entice and bring a fey partner to a frenzy, but something she'd never actually experienced before. There was no way she was going to attempt to explain something so embarrassing and deeply private to the demon she'd just met.

Especially not when he looked at her like he *knew.*

Discomfited and embarrassed, Charlotte fled to the relative safety of the tiny bathroom. But not even the rush of running water or the whir of the overhead fan could cover the sound of her song.

And no matter how she scrubbed or how hot the water was, Dom's shadow clung her skin — as gentle and insistent as a stubborn man's kiss.

CHAPTER THREE

*JULY 2044 - ON A ROAD LEADING OUT OF THE
NEUTRAL ZONE*

"SULKING WON'T HELP."

"I'm not sulking." Charlotte pulled her legs in close to her
chest and leaned her temple against the cool glass of the passenger
side window. She would have liked to relish her freedom, but a
thorny knot of disappointment and frustration took up all the
space in her chest where relief could have grown.

It took root there the previous evening after another long
phone call with her parents that ended with more than a few tears
of frustration. It bloomed in full during the night, when she slept
on the motel bed — so luxurious, yet so foreign after a year in
captivity — and Dom silently took the floor, his steady breathing
overly loud in the quiet. It only got worse as her first day of
freedom wore on.

Before setting out from United Washington proper, they
stopped at a small department store to get her something other
than her slinky silver jumpsuit to wear. Luckily her implanted ID
still worked just fine, so she didn't need to rely on Dom to take
care of her any more than strictly necessary — even if he did

bristle a little when she insisted on paying for her small bundle of necessities *and* their quick, greasy breakfast at the diner next to the store.

But she wasn't yet comfortable with the whole "mates take care of each other" spiel he tried to give her, so she ignored him. And continued to do so.

Dom was quiet for a while as they sped away from UW toward the border of the New Zone, the engine of his huge truck rumbling like the chest of a dragon. But for someone who claimed to like quiet and solitude as much as he did, Dom couldn't seem to hold his tongue for long.

"Your mother was right," he insisted, filling up the cabin with the low, bone-rattling rumble of his voice. "There's nothing wrong with waiting a few more weeks until the travel ban lifts to go home. We'll spend some time at my cabin, and when the political situation cools down, I'll take you to them. Or they can come to us."

"A few more weeks?" Charlotte curled her nails into the outer seams of her new jeans. She staunchly refused to look at him. "I lost a year of my life to that damn jar. Don't you tell me that a few weeks is nothing to be upset about, demon."

"I'm not saying there's nothing to be upset about." Dom's shadow rippled around her ankle. It tightened and loosened in a pulsing wave, as if it sought to soothe her even when its demon host wouldn't or didn't know how to. "I know a year is a long time. I only fought in the Great War for a year, and it made me the man I am today — good and bad. I get that time is precious, believe me."

Charlotte finally turned her head to peer at him from under the hood of her baby pink sweatshirt. Dom drove confidently, with one huge hand on the steering wheel and his other arm draped over the center console, his fingers loosely curled by the cup holder. He was handsome in profile, but in the way that all wild things had a beauty to their harshness.

His brows were heavy. His nose was a hard edge sticking out

from between high, rounded cheekbones. His lips were surprisingly soft-looking when he wasn't scowling, but that happened so rarely, she had little time to appreciate them. His antlers were large, creating a sort of crown around the sides of his head, his ears were gently pointed and covered in soft, velvety fur. Pair all of that with his blunted fangs and his huge build, and Dom was a visual force to be reckoned with.

Just the sight of him made her wings buzz louder, but Charlotte was grateful that the demon had decided to politely ignore her song after she made it clear it embarrassed her. Not that Charlotte thought he'd drop it forever, though. She got the feeling that her demon was a patient sort of man. No doubt he would end up demanding answers soon enough.

And what will I say? 'Don't worry about it, it's just my mating song. Does it do anything for you? Because I'm *horny as all get out.'* Charlotte cringed just thinking about it. She shifted in her seat, trying to alleviate the small but growing ache between her legs.

"What I meant was that a few weeks resting in my cabin won't feel like a year of captivity. It'll give you time to relax and get your head on straight before you see them again," he continued, oblivious to the humiliating thoughts circling her mind like love-drunk, horny cicadas. "Besides, it'll give your parents peace of mind. They were relieved when I said I'd take care of you until the ban lifts, right?"

Charlotte grunted. "Yes, because my parents are incredibly romantic, open-minded arrant hippies who think mating means instant, undying love and devotion."

An hour post-breakfast phone call with her parents and she was still bitter that they'd taken to Dom, a demon they didn't know, so quickly. One would think that having their daughter kidnapped and held prisoner for a year would make them *more* wary of strangers, not less, but they were trusting to a fault even still.

There were, of course, worse flaws to have. And even though it smarted that they didn't agree with her half-cocked plan to smuggle herself into the EVP, she also didn't believe Dom meant her any harm.

Knowing that the only way forward involved sucking up her frustration, Charlotte sighed and decided a subject change was in order. Wiggling around in her seat until her back was to the door and her bare toes were pressed against the edge of the console, Charlotte gave his arm a small nudge with her heel. "So how old are you, anyway? I mean, if you fought in the War."

Dom didn't take his eyes off the road as he covered the tops of both of her feet with one hand. His palm was deliciously warm and rough. *He told me he works in forestry,* she recalled, both surprised and a little worried by the way that simple, platonic touch made her skin heat up. *I wonder if that's why his hands are so callused.*

She'd never had much of a preference for rough, I-work-with-my-hands-and-drive-ten-foot-high-trucks men before, but she was starting to see the appeal.

"Does it matter?" His usual scowl deepened. Grip tightening on her feet, he gruffly added, "Your feet are cold. You should put your shoes and socks back on."

"I got used to not wearing shoes," she explained. Charlotte wiggled her toes. "And don't dodge the question."

Sighing, her demon began to slowly rub the delicate bones of the tops of her feet when he answered, "I fought in the war when I was eighteen."

She tried to run the math in her head, but Charlotte had never been very good with numbers. "So you're... what? Two hundred?"

Dom shot her a withering glare out of the corner of his eye. "I'm one hundred and forty-six, glowbug."

Charlotte sputtered. "Don't call me *glowbug!*"

"Why not? You glow and you've got those pretty wings." He shrugged his powerful shoulders. "It fits." Dom paused long enough to grip her feet with a little more force. A warning rumble shook the air and made a home for itself in her bones.

"Don't kick me while I'm driving, glowbug. I can feel you about to try."

She lifted her upper lip to show him her fangs, small and pin-sharp as they were. "The kids who bullied me in middle school used to call me that." Although it wasn't the worst nickname they gave her, it still carried a weight to it that bothered her.

"All the more reason to take it back and make it your own, don't you think?" Apparently no longer worried she was going to aim for his antlers this time, Dom let go of her foot to cover her knee with his palm. He shot her an intense look from under the shadow of his drawn brows. "I'll stop if it really upsets you, Charlotte, but I like the name."

"Why?"

He answered immediately, without even a hint of teasing. "Because you remind me of a firefly. You're pretty and small and light up the darkness. I want to cup you in my hands and keep you close. Is that so bad?"

Heat suffused her cheeks. The low buzzing of her wings grew just a touch louder in the confined space. "That's... not so bad, I guess," she muttered, trying to hide the smile that wanted to break out across her face.

Gods, but it was nice to talk to someone again. To flirt? It was a godsdamned luxury. Even the conversation of a surly old demon was better than her own circular thoughts. *Much* better, actually.

"What should I call you, then?" She fiddled with the draw-string of her hoodie, her stomach tightening into a pleasantly anxious little knot the longer she looked at him. "How's *old man* sound?"

"I am not old," he insisted. "I'm only just hitting my prime. Demons live an average of four hundred years."

"You're old compared to me. I'm twenty-six."

The car jerked sharply, nearly going over the line before the tech in the engine realigned it automatically. Charlotte braced herself against the door and sent the demon an outraged look. "Watch the road!"

"You're only *twenty-six?*" Dom's eyes darted between the road and her face. His whole head might have moved, too, if there wasn't the danger of his antlers catching on the roof.

Charlotte settled back down into her seat — properly this time, so that if he did manage to override the self-correcting controls, the seatbelt might actually help her out.

"Yes," she answered, sniffing with displeasure. "Something wrong with that?"

Dom shook his head slowly, but the way he blew out a breath and stared hard at the road sent a different message. "No, I just... that's young. Awfully young."

A shiver of real anxiety, not the flirtation-induced kind, slid down her spine. In a voice full of forced nonchalance, she asked, "Your *mate* too young for you now?"

The band of shadow around her ankle gave a sharp, proprietary squeeze. *"No."*

"Then what's the problem?"

"It's not a problem," he insisted. Dom's hand found its way back to her knee. The old Charlotte might have raised an eyebrow at his handsiness, but the woman who emerged from a year in captivity relished every little touch. It reminded her that she wasn't alone anymore.

Besides, she *liked* it when he touched her.

Stranger or not, a base part of her recognized that Dom was *right.* He was solid. He was steady.

Dom was grumpy and taciturn, sure, but he also didn't think twice about promising to drive her across the UTA. He made sure she was comfortable and said over and over again that he only wanted to help her. He even gave her his dish of blueberries at breakfast, no questions asked, when he caught her eyeing them with envy. And sometimes, when he thought she wasn't looking, Charlotte caught him staring at her like she was the center of his whole world.

The loneliest part of her, born into every Changeling and cultivated in her captivity, craved that sort of focused attention and obvious desire. If it had its way, she would have grabbed him by the antlers and kissed him silly already — just to feel, to hold and be held, to *touch*.

Too bad for him Charlotte had a lifetime of experience ruthlessly quenching her desire for kinship. *Maybe* she would see where their relationship would go, but she wasn't about to make any hasty decisions, no matter what her fey nature and biology demanded.

When the silence stretched dangerously close to awkwardness, Charlotte cleared her throat and admitted, "I was taken the night of my twenty-fifth birthday, you know."

Dom's fingers clenched on her knee. He let out a slow breath before he replied, "That's awful, glowbug."

"That's why I was wearing that stupid jumpsuit." She licked her lips and struggled with the impulse to grab his hand for only a handful of seconds before giving in to the urge. If Dom was surprised by the way she clutched his big, callused hand between both of hers like a damn lifeline, he didn't show it. He simply curled his big fingers around hers, no questions asked.

"I was going to a bar in the city with some work friends — no one I was really close to, but people to hang out with, you know? Thought we could have a good time, maybe meet some people." She shrugged. None of them were really *friends*, but she'd always struggled to make those sorts of connections. Just having people around who didn't look at her askance was enough. It had to be.

She chuckled wryly. "Thought I might even meet a guy that wouldn't ask about my wings on the first date."

"I bet you had no trouble meeting men," he huffed.

Charlotte was flattered by the assumption, but that didn't mean he was right. "Not really. I wasn't all that social, but it was my birthday and I wanted to have fun." Feeling suddenly trapped, she pushed her hood off and stared at the greenery on the side of the road, desperately trying to remind herself that she was not in locked away in her prison, staring desperately through warped glass. "When I went outside to take a call from a friend who was running late, the feyrunner grabbed me, pulled me into an alley, and that was that."

She shuddered. That gross, stinky alley was the last view of the outside world she got before the terrarium; before endless, numbing solitude.

Dom untangled their hands just long enough to tentatively settle his palm on the back of her neck. In a low, firm voice, he told her, "You will never be held against your will again, Charlotte." He gave her nape a light squeeze. "You have my shadow, remember? No matter where you go, no matter what happens, I'll always be there to help you. You're not alone anymore."

Charlotte blinked away the prickle of tears. Was it silly to believe him? Maybe, but she desperately wanted to. Any sort of reassurance she wasn't dreaming this, that she would never be put back in her prison, was welcome.

"Your shadow would keep us connected even if I got put back in an m-siphon?" Her voice was annoyingly thready, but she needed to know the answer. For her peace of mind, for that anxiousness that insisted she could be snatched and thrown back in her humid little prison at any moment. She *needed* to know that someone would find her.

Dom held her gaze for as long as he could before turning his attention back to the road. "Yes, it would. My shadow isn't just magic, Charlotte. It's my *soul.*"

She blinked rapidly. "Your... Are you saying you have a little bit of your soul circling my ankle right now?"

A small smile quirked the corner of his lush mouth, turning a face of hard angles into something softer, something handsome enough to make her breath catch and her wings sing. "Yes. Does that scare you?"

After a year of being alone, believing she'd be reduced to a husk and then to a moldering corpse in a jar? No, it really didn't. Charlotte wasn't about to look a gift horse in the mouth, no matter how surly, antlered, or callused he was.

"As long as you promise to never let anyone put me in a jar

again, you can get as weird as you want with your soul, old man."
She grinned. Just a little bit of her fear loosened, but it was
enough to make breathing easier. "Besides, it could be worse. You
could be a dragon or something."

Dom arched a heavy brow. "Have a problem with dragons?"

"Oh, *every* girl knows to avoid dating a dragon," she smartly
replied, a little bit of her pre-captivity personality shining
through. "One day they're the most fun, playful guys, and then
the next — *poof!* They're roaring, possessive, territorial, big-ass
lizards."

No one was really sure what triggered the change in dragons,
but there absolutely was one. She'd lived in the city long enough
to meet a handful of the brilliantly colored, horned race, and
knew that they underwent a monumental shift in personality
when they *"chose"*.

The problem was that dragons didn't have a single mate
predestined by the gods — or chemicals or whomever one wanted
to blame. Like the fey, they had multiple possible partners, and
that meant enticing the one you wanted and fighting for the right
to be their choice. The worst case scenario involved a dragon
choosing someone that already had multiple interested parties.
Dragons were infamous for their implacability and their sheer,
single-minded determination to win a mate — no matter the cost.
Taking out rivals in whatever way they deemed necessary was a
point of pride for dragons and one of the many reasons the other
races kept a wary eye on any dragonblooded romantic partners.

One of Charlotte's favorite fairytales involved three dragons,
all from different clans, fighting for a single human mate. It was
only in adulthood that she learned the real story it was based on
ended with two of the dragons ruthlessly murdered by their rival,
their corpses thrust onto pikes, displayed for all the world to see
and know that the victor would tolerate no challenge to his claim.

Dom snorted. "Dragons aren't fun to be around when they've
decided on a mate, no."

"Are demons much better?" Charlotte sent him a curious

look. "The fey don't really have any customs around courtship — they're not partial to monogamy — so I'm in the dark here."

No, they just had the mating song and the frenzy, the instinctive change in behavior triggered by the presence of a compatible mate. The fey usually went through many partners in their lives, many frenzies, and the products of those frantic couplings created people like Charlotte — unwanted, untalented Changelings.

"Demons respect matehood." He sighed, and there was a wealth of old feeling in it. "Maybe too much. I know many demons who've run off into the world, hoping to find their mates before even *thinking* of what else there could be in life."

"You don't sound terribly enthused by the idea."

Dom lightly massaged her nape before sending her a quick, apologetic look. "I wasn't. I like being alone. Always have." He paused, shoulders bunching, before quietly admitting, "But... I like you. Seems obvious to me now that my life will be better for having you in it." He cleared his throat, clearly uncomfortable with his own admission. "Do I think those demons should get to know themselves a little before they go handing their shadows to anyone who asks? Yeah. Do I get *why* we chase mates now? Looking at you— *being* with you, I get it."

Charlotte's toes curled against the rough carpet. Her heartbeat thudded in her ears; her glow pulsed in time, lighting up the skin of her hands and face. "You don't even know me," she rasped, suddenly terrified that this big, earnest demon wouldn't feel so sweetly toward her when he figured out she wasn't anything special or noteworthy or—

"Don't care." Dom slid the pad of his roughened thumb over the corner of her jaw. It was a small, chaste caress, but it lit up her blood like nothing before it. "You're my mate. We have centuries to get to know one another." A flash of amber was her only indication that he peeked at her out of the corner of his eye when he added, "If you'll have me, of course."

Warmth bloomed in her stomach. "Well, maybe we could go on a few dates and—"

The truck swerved sharply to the right, nearly pulling over onto the shoulder before it self-corrected. Dom swore and removed his hand from the back of her neck to clutch the steering wheel.

"What's wrong?" Charlotte craned her neck to see if they swerved around some debris or roadkill.

Dom let loose a low, terrifying rumble. It wasn't quite a growl, but it wasn't a noise like any she'd ever heard, either. It came from deep within his chest to fill the entire cab, raising the thin hair on her arms beneath the sleeves of her sweatshirt.

He turned his head just enough to glare at the rear view mirror. "We're being followed."

Dom swore as the big, dented SUV tried to drive them onto the shoulder again. This part of the New Zone was largely unpopulated wilderness broken up by long stretches of highway. There were no walls or bumpers to keep cars from going off the roads and into the low drainage ditches overgrown with greenery. This far away from UW, they were one of only a handful of cars on the road, too.

If they'd been in anything except his sturdy work truck, they would already be in a ditch.

Pressing his forearm back against his mate's chest, Dom firmly held her in place against her seat as he swerved out of the way of the tan vehicle — which must have been either old or heavily tinkered with. No untouched or modern vehicle could move that dangerously on a road with even the most basic m-grid. It would stop automatically to avoid a collision; something this car obviously had no intention of doing.

Dom ground his teeth together. A hot flare of protective rage roiled the shadows under his skin, pressing them close to the surface — to fight, to get his mate to safety, to avenge her for the wrongs done.

He wasn't a violent man, but he *was* a demon. Like elves and orcs and dragons, his people had their own code of justice. Humans liked to pretend that everyone that even vaguely looked like them were civilized, but that was something they needed to think in order to sleep well at night.

The truth was that when you had a population comprised of individuals that could rip up trees with one hand, slit a throat with a claw, bend shadows to their will, claim a territory with might and tooth and fire alone, justice needed to be swift and brutal. The havoc that could be wreaked by a single rogue individual was immense. The bloodshed could be extreme. Mates and children could be lost.

No one would lay a hand on his mate again. Everything in Dom rebelled against the idea. Every bloodthirsty instinct, dormant since his bleak days in the war, roared to the surface.

He could feel Charlotte's heart beating fast as a hummingbird's against his forearm. Her voice was tight when she asked, "Do you think they're after me?"

Dom grunted an affirmative. He wouldn't lie to her. There wasn't any point.

Little, clawless fingers dug into his forearm. "What are we going to do?"

"They're trying to keep us from crossing the border into the Draakonriik." Dom reluctantly pried his arm away from her so he could grip the wheel with two hands. Keeping an eye on the vehicle moving aggressively in the rear view mirror, he quickly ran through the only options available to them. "We could try to outrun them, but we still have a good hundred miles before we hit the border."

Unfortunately, this far out there were few places for one to lose a pursuer — probably why they were being targeted now, instead of in the city. The road to the border was long and straight, with no cities in which to get lost. His truck couldn't outpace their SUV, so speed wasn't an option. Besides, they were clearly desperate to stop him from crossing the border and willing to do whatever it took to make that possible.

They clearly had *some* sense. No criminal in their right mind would pull a stunt like this in the Draakonriik. The New Zone was functionally lawless. As soon as they crossed the border, they would be in dragon territory — and subject to dragon justice.

Dom swerved to avoid another attempt to run them into the overgrown ditch, a calm sort of fury settling into his bones. The people who took his mate and imprisoned her would not give up the chase. It was a mistake he intended to use against them.

Eyeing a deserted rest stop area not too far ahead, Dom laid a hand on Charlotte's knee and gave her a quick, reassuring squeeze. "We won't make it to the border, so I have to end this before one of us does something stupid and we get into a wreck. Do you trust me?"

"Trust you?" He took his eyes off the road for a split second, just in time to see Charlotte looking at him like he'd grown another set of antlers. "I don't even know you!"

"Doesn't matter," he gritted out. "Do you *trust me?*"

Dom was a sensible demon. He understood that he was asking a lot from a creature who didn't have the same instinctive connection that he did, who was as mistreated as she was. But he also hoped she might feel *something*, some sort of innate understanding that he meant her no harm and that he would lay down his life for her without hesitation.

"What are you going to do?" Charlotte twisted around to peer out through the back window. "What's your plan? Why do I need to trust you? Are you going to—"

He blindly reached for her shoulder to push her back into the proper position. "Sit *down!* If we get in a wreck, your seatbelt won't do you any damn good with you twisted around like that."

She hissed at him — a high, almost whine-like sound from between her sharp little fangs. "Well, tell me what you're going to do, then!"

"I'm going to take care of the problem." He didn't bother signalling his turn before taking a sharp right off of the road and into the parking lot of the bare bones rest stop. Gravel crunched under his tires, then the tires of the SUV that swerved to block the exit.

Throwing his truck in park, Dom took precious time to unbuckle his seat belt and turn to his mate. She was gaping at him with open confusion and no small amount of fear, her usually rosy cheeks pale.

He could hear the sound of a car door opening, but he ignored it in favor of clasping the back of Charlotte's neck, drawing her close, and planting an impulsive, hasty kiss to her slack mouth.

It was only a moment. A handful of seconds at most, but it was the best kiss he'd ever had and the only one that mattered.

She tasted like tart citrus and fresh honey. Her lips were smooth, warm. The hands that grasped the front of his shirt and clutched, pulling him as close as the console between them would allow, were eager and greedy. He could only linger there for a moment, but Dom wanted to stay more than he wanted anything else in his long life.

Charlotte was just leaning into him, her lips parting on a soft sigh that went straight to his cock, when Dom forced himself to pull away. Cupping the side of her head, he stared into her eyes and grated, "Don't you fucking move out of this truck, you hear me? Close your eyes and count to one hundred. I'll be back before you get to eighty."

She blinked owlishly, her lips parted and flushed a delectable berry red. "What? Why should I close my eyes?"

"Because," he replied, moving to open his door, "you don't need to see what I'm going to do to these people, glowbug."

Chapter Four

July 2044 - At a rest stop on the edge of the Neutral Zone

Of course, Charlotte didn't listen. For one thing, she wasn't about to let Dom fight her battles for her. For another, the idea of sitting in the car, her hands over her eyes and her head between her knees while her kidnappers stood a few feet away made her stomach heave.

She couldn't just *sit*. She couldn't wait and hope that Dom would fix this for her. She needed to see them with her own eyes, to fight if she had to. They stole everything from her once. Charlotte wasn't about to lay down and let them do it twice.

Shoving her bare feet into her shoes, she scrambled to unlock her door and follow Dom out.

The air was stiflingly hot and humid outside of the truck, but Charlotte barely noticed it. She didn't register the bite of gravel under the thin soles of her flats, or the way sweat dewed along her spine under the fabric of her hoodie and t-shirt. The sound of shouting — an unfamiliar, hoarse voice mixing with the one she recognized as Millie's — made her breaths shorten. Her heartbeat drummed in her ears and her hands shook as she threw herself out of the truck and headfirst into the nightmare she had only just escaped.

They won't put me back in there, she swore to herself.

It didn't matter that her prison wasn't that bad. They stole her *life.* They reduced her to nothing but a battery to be sucked dry — like she was less than a person, less than an intelligent being with hopes and dreams and people that loved her. She couldn't go back to the isolation of her imprisonment. She *wouldn't.*

Charlotte hung on by a thread before Dom rescued her. Being forced back into the crippling loneliness of a life as an m-siphon *now?* It would break her.

And no matter what Dom said or what she suspected he was capable of, she wasn't about to let him square off with her kidnappers alone.

Blood rushing with adrenaline and fear and no small amount of rage, Charlotte bared her fangs and ran headlong around the side of the truck just as the unmistakable whine of a bolt gun filled the rest stop.

Charlotte choked on humid air as she slid to a stop in the gravel, one hand snapping out to skim across the hot metal of the hood of Dom's hulking truck. She stumbled around to the driver's side. *Don't be dead. Don't be dead. Don'tbedeaddon'tbe-deaddon't—*

Feyrunners were notoriously vicious. They were legendary for shooting down anyone who threatened their extremely profitable business. It didn't matter that Charlotte suspected she was caught by some two-bit low-life, not any sort of criminal genius or massive enterprise. Even the lowliest, most ill-connected feyrunner would go to any lengths to get their stolen product back.

The idea that Dom, her surly demon who only wanted to see her to safety, might bleed out in the parking lot of a shitty rest stop *because of her* was so unacceptable, it made her blood actually *fizz* with fury.

Charlotte charged around the side of the truck, ready to do *something*, but skidded to a halt at the sight that greeted her.

The SUV was parked haphazardly, its doors flung open. Crouched against it was the unmistakable form of Millie, dressed in her familiar uniform of a long, swishy skirt and her oversized glasses. She cowered against the grill of the vehicle, her lined face slackened with horror and her glasses askew on her nose. Not three feet from her, a still-humming bolt gun lay in the gravel.

It took Charlotte only a moment to figure out what had her one-time jailer so terrified.

Well that's... She blinked hard several times in quick succession, as if that might make the image of Dom — not the Dom she knew, but unmistakably *him* — strangling the life out of a man make sense.

No, she thought, gaping at Dom's back. *Not strangling. I don't have a word for what he's doing right now.*

That was partly because she didn't have a word for what *Dom* was just then. The man she looked at was not the man who cupped the back of her neck and drew her in for a toe-curling kiss. He was... something else.

Demons were intimidating on the best of days. She knew they came in a myriad of forms, with many different characteristics based on region and what clan they belonged to. Charlotte thought she understood the breadth of Dom's differences, more or less, in the day and night they'd spent together.

Sure, he was the size of a house, had funky amber-on-black eyes, and sported a set of antlers, but he was still a *man*. He had a harsh set of features not helped by his habit of scowling, but when it came down to it, he didn't look or act any different than the dozens and dozens of sapient beings who roamed Burden's Earth.

At least, that's what she thought.

Sometime between his leaving the truck and her following, Dom had transformed into something that made every fine hair and every survival instinct stand at attention. He stood between the vehicles, his back to her and his legs spread in a solid stance.

She recognized the washed out black of his t-shirt and his faded working jeans. She recognized his scuffed work boots.

What she didn't recognize was the rest of him.

"How did you track her?" The voice was rough, the words grated out from somewhere in the mass of shadows and writhing, hungry darkness that made up Dom's form. She couldn't see his face from where she stood. She wasn't even sure he still *had* a face.

The feyrunner — *her* feyrunner, she realized with a start — struggled against those twisting tentacles of shadow wrapped around him. They coiled mercilessly around his limbs, his bobbing throat, and wrenched his head back with a grip in his gelled hair. The feyrunner's face, handsome and familiar through the haze of fear and drugs that distorted her memories, began to turn a terrible shade of puce.

He thrashed against Dom's hold, his features twisted with malice. The feyrunner didn't have claws with which to fight, but he raked his nails against the living darkness that held him all the same. "Fuck you, dem—"

"Answer the question." Dom dragged the feyrunner closer and lifted the smaller man clear off of his feet to bring them nose to nose. *"How did you track my mate?"*

Charlotte tried to breathe normally, but couldn't manage it. *Oh, gods. They put something in me.* Cold terror trickled into her veins. "You *chipped* me?"

Dom went rigid. The shadows holding the feyrunner clamped hard at the same time that the delicate circlet around her ankle contracted, a pulse of pure power against the delicate bones of her ankle. Her demon swung his head in her direction.

"Charlotte!" It was a gruff reprimand bitten off of the tip of his tongue. And yes, he *did* have a tongue. It was just... different.

It was different because *everything* about Dom was different. In this form, his rugged but handsome features were swathed in shadow, distorted and rearranged until they made a ghoulish mask with a jagged opening for a mouth and two endless black pits for eyes. Only the tiniest sparks of amber remained in those black sockets — two winks of sinister flame in the face of a monster.

Even his antlers were bigger. They arched up and over his head in jagged spikes that flickered in the hot sun. It was as if every part of Dom had been amplified, brutalized, torn open to reveal the core of every vicious beast that roamed the dark mashed into one being.

It was fucking terrifying.

It was also *incredibly* hot.

For a long moment, all Charlotte could do was stare at his terrible, moving visage and try to reconcile it with the man who picked up every tiny shard of glass on the motel room floor with his bare hands so she wouldn't hurt herself. They were, somehow, the same being.

Somewhere far away, her wings buzzed hard through the gaps in the back of her hoodie — calling out to him without a hint of self-consciousness or fear. *Come closer,* her wings sang. *Come get me.*

"*Get back in the truck,*" Dom grated, breaking the spell that held her frozen against the door.

Charlotte gave her brain and her desperate loins a hard internal shake before she straightened her shoulders and took a purposeful step forward. A low rumble filled the parking lot — a hair-raising, nearly inaudible sound that immediately quieted all the bugs and low creatures stirring in the surrounding greenery. "Don't you growl at me," she huffed. "Did you really think I was going to stay in the truck while you handled things for me?"

Dom's big, rippling form shifted to keep his bulk between her and the suspended feyrunner. "*Char—*"

"Shush." She stepped beside him and, ignoring the now much louder growling coming from the center of his chest, she gave his side a small pat. Charlotte gave him a good once-over before training her eyes on Millie, who appeared to be about half a step away from a heart attack. "Did I hear a bolt gun go off? Are you okay?"

"I'm fine." As soon as she was close enough, coils of shadow extended from Dom to curl around her waist, her shoulders, and her thighs. They didn't have a weight to them, but she *felt* the power of them, the brush of raw magic against her senses as he drew her in close.

It was hard to discern emotion when nothing about his face was human, but Charlotte got the sense that her demon was deeply annoyed with her when he continued, *"I didn't want you to see this."*

"What? My well-earned revenge? What didn't you think I'd like about that?" She turned her attention to the struggling feyrunner. "Did I hear something about tracking?" Charlotte clenched her fists so hard, her small claws bit into her palms. "It wasn't enough that you stole my life and imprisoned me for over a year. You *put something in me, too?!"*

She didn't realize that she'd taken a step forward, her anger rising and crashing in a furious tide, until Dom's shadows pulled her back with a firm yank. *"Too close,"* he bit out.

"You're *lucky* he's holding me here, asshole." Charlotte strained against her bonds, every injustice Millie and the feyrunner had committed against her a vicious bite in her hide. "You *both* are lucky! Do you have any idea what it's like to be trapped alone in a fucking jar for that long? Do you know what that kind of isolation can do to a person?"

It could shatter them. It *did* shatter them. Charlotte wasn't immune to the damage isolation could wreak. She was just barely strong enough to keep putting all those broken pieces together every time she fell apart.

But those poor people who were spelled into windowless containers, who were chucked into drawers or locked in safes — those who were used so relentlessly for magic that it drained their very marrow — those were the people she lay awake at night thinking about.

These people... Millie and the feyrunner, they didn't care about any of that. It was probably pure happenstance that Charlotte got lucky enough to be in a lush little prison. It wasn't like they cared about being humane, or what it would do to the psyches of the people they trapped. They were a thousand times more monstrous than she or Dom could ever be.

And Charlotte wanted them to *hurt* for it.

Leaning hard against the insistent pressure of Dom's shadows, she continued, "What did you put in me? A chip? A tracker? What was the plan? Sell me off and then steal me back when my owner wasn't looking?" She made a wordless, outraged sound. "Gods, you both are the fucking *worst!*"

The feyrunner gurgled as his eyes roved madly around the parking lot. They briefly landed on the discarded gun, bulged, and then swung back to Millie. He made another choked sound and flailed one arm in the direction of the gun. *"Mil— Get—"*

"Marc, I-I don't know how to— you said this would be easy! I *told* you he was a demon but you didn't listen!" Millie fell back onto her hands in the gravel and began to crab walk backwards, toward the SUV. Her glasses, already barely hanging on to the tip of her nose, fell off and bounced off of her thigh to land in the dust and crushed rock. "I'm not the one who shoots people, Marc! I'm not gonna stay and get strangled by a fucking demon!"

"Do not move." Dom turned his head to regard the fleeing shopkeeper. He pinned her with his terrifying stare, freezing her in place against the filthy tire of her vehicle. *"You are going to answer my mate's questions. Now."*

"I don't do that side of the business," she cried, throwing up her dusty hands. "I just sell the things and Marc does all the other — he's the one who makes the product!"

"Makes the *product?*" Charlotte hissed out an expletive from between her fangs. "We're *people,* you two-bit feyrunner trash!"

Millie gave Charlotte a bug-eyed look of pure, unfiltered derision. "It's not my fault you got caught. It's a predator eat predator world out there, fey! You can't blame me for doing what I need to survive in this world. Do you have any idea what it's like out there for us arrants? We have to fight to keep up with all you m-types every godsdamned day!"

"You're working with a witch! What kind of arrant solidarity is that?" Charlotte gestured sharply to the dangling feyrunner, whose eyes continued to dart between the arguing women with increasing desperation.

"So?" Millie jerked herself into a more upright position and slowly pulled herself up against the side of the SUV. She sniffed hard, like all of this was somehow everyone else's fault. Even though she managed to mask most of her fear, her hands still shook when she smoothed them down her thighs. "We work with the tools we're given." She cast her struggling companion a withering look. "Even sigilworkers who don't know when to let merchandise *go.*"

Charlotte gaped at the shopkeeper. "That is the most ridiculous thing I've ever—"

Millie dove for the gun and several things happened at once: Dom snapped the neck of the feyrunner and tossed him aside like an old rag, Millie skidded through the gravel to grasp the gun, and Charlotte lurched out of Dom's hold to meet her just as her fizzing, popping blood *exploded.*

The struggle over the charged bolt gun was brief and brutal. They tangled in the gravel, a snarling, screeching knot of limbs fighting over a slim, matte black bolt gun. Millie's finger curled around the trigger just as the skin of the forearms under Charlotte's hands began to burn.

The whine of the bolt releasing came in the same instant that Millie started to scream.

Dom watched his mate slump to one side in slow motion.

He'd seen people die. Of course he had. You didn't fight in the Great War for any length of time without witnessing Grim take her tithe — or being the one to hand it to her. It never got easier, and even after over a century, he still thought about rotting, gaping corpses in open fields and the animalistic rush of ending a life before his opponent could do the same to him.

Death wasn't easy. It wasn't clean. It wasn't always cruel, and Grim wasn't a goddess to fear, but it could be senseless. It left its mark on the living even when it was kind.

Dom wasn't a demon that ever reveled in death or violence, not any more than his nature forced him to, but in the seconds that encompassed Millie's mad dash for the bolt gun — a weapon that would struggle to take down a demon even half his age — and it going off, he came to a new understanding with the white-robed goddess.

Without a thought, he ended one wasted life and in the same breath prayed for the safety of another. *Not her,* he thought, dropping to his knees to catch his mate before she fell into the gravel. *Not her. Not when I just found her.*

"*No, no,*" he rasped, gathering Charlotte into his lap. His hands, his *real* hands, with their elongated claws of compressed shadow, stroked her hair and skimmed down her front, looking for the wound. Charlotte wheezed and clutched at her chest, her eyes wide as she struggled to draw in air.

"*Let me see.*" His voice was a raw growl from deep in his chest, almost incomprehensible. Cold panic made him frantic as he tried to support his mate's weight and peel her hands away from her chest at the same time. "*You have to let me see, glowbug,*" he urged. "*Let me help.*"

Dom wrapped one arm around her back, mindful of her delicate wings, and used his other hand to firmly pull her hands away from her sternum. He held his breath, disregarding the funny, almost uncomfortable tingle that singed his palm.

His mind raced ahead of him, wondering how quickly he could get her to a med center or a local healer, so fast it took him a moment to understand what he was looking at.

Charlotte's chest heaved with stuttering inhales, but where he expected to find the gaping, cauterized wound of a bolt blast, all he saw was a swath of inky black. A breastplate of moving, opaque shadow had adhered itself to her baby pink hoodie, saving her from a ghastly wound.

Dom felt everything in him, every cell and every shadow and every bit of his soul, shudder. He couldn't cry in this form, but he still felt his throat close, first with the cold grip of terror, then with the vice of pure relief.

She's okay.

"*Thank you,*" he muttered to Grim, to Glory, to Blight himself — it didn't matter who saved his mate. He was grateful. He was *more* than grateful.

Dom dragged her against his chest and let his shadows curl around her however they wanted to as he stroked her back, encouraging her to take deep breaths. "*That's right. Breathe, glowbug. Breathe. You just had the wind knocked out of you. You're okay. Breathe for me, glowbug.*"

The feeling of her arms coming around his chest, her small hands curling into the fabric of his t-shirt over his shoulder blades, made him sag forward with relief. She was okay. His mate was fine. He'd taken care of the threat and nothing would *ever—*

Dom lifted his head to search for Millie, his arms and shadows contracting hard around Charlotte's slim back. A menacing growl built in his chest at the sight of the woman lying a few feet away, but it died almost as soon as it began.

He huffed out a surprised breath. *Ah, no wonder my hand tingled.*

Millie lay twitching on the ground, the exposed skin of her arms already turning the blue-green, sickly yellow, and black shades of putrefaction. He watched her convulse, her back arching as her mouth opened in a silent, agonized scream.

Dom glanced down at the crown of Charlotte's head with renewed respect. His defenseless little Changeling wasn't so helpless after all. Wee feet and fangs she might have, but it appeared she'd hidden a rare — and profoundly dangerous — magical skill.

My mate's a poisoncraft, he realized. Dom puffed up a little, his spine straightening with no small amount of pride. *Hot damn.*

He'd never encountered one before, but he'd heard of them. Poisoncrafts were an extremely rare subclass of alchemic m-types. Alchemic types were people who were naturally suited to turning physical substances into whatever their specialties were, with the most common being crystalcrafts. The least common crafts involves specific chemical specialties, and most ended up working in the pharmaceutical industry at a young age.

But poisoncrafts were a subclass within a subclass; highly dangerous and sought after folk who could, with only a touch, create the most complex and unique chemical mixtures in the world. Dom had once read that some poisoncrafts went into bespoke perfume creation — and that their work went for hundreds of thousands of dollars a piece. But others simply disappeared; snapped up by the governments of their territories to work on things that would make the average person's stomach turn.

Did Charlotte know? He peered down at her speculatively. No, he didn't think so. If she'd known, his little wildcat would have tried to douse him first thing. Not that it would have done anything lasting, of course. Demons were made of sturdier stuff than most other races realized. Only prolonged exposure to even the most caustic or perfectly biologically tailored poisons would take him down.

That was part of the reason so many demons managed to come out of the war alive, while other races suffered so many losses. The witches, healers in particular, still hadn't recovered to their pre-war levels.

Dom wondered how his wee Changeling would feel about the discovery of such a coveted ability. He wasn't one for prestige or chasing luxury. He liked his quiet life and his woods and his mate. But if she wanted to pursue a career as some high profile perfumer or other, he'd support her.

Before all that, though, he needed to get her away from this rest stop. He didn't worry about authorities coming after them — the few that existed in the outskirts of the New Zone could be easily dealt with — but he wouldn't feel secure in her safety until they were over the border and out of reach of any backup her kidnappers might have had.

Not that I think they had much, if any, he thought, eyeing the cooling corpse of the feyrunner dispassionately. No sophisticated outfit came to retrieve stolen cargo with a single bolt gun. *Especially* when they were going up against a demon, mated, and in his prime.

With that thought in mind, Dom turned his gaze back to Millie just as she let out her last creaking breath, the skin of her face and strained neck a pallid, mottled green. The whites of her eyes, fully exposed as she stared sightlessly out toward the treeline, were a deep yellow.

It's a predator eat predator world indeed, he thought. Too bad Millie overestimated just how much she could chew when she took on his mate.

With both the threats now fully out of commission, Dom forced his form back into his other shape. One was not better or more natural than the other, necessarily, but navigating the wider world was easier when people didn't flee at the mere sight of him.

A cold shiver of dread worked its way down his spine as most of his shadows curled inward, retreating to the solid core within him. Would Charlotte fear him now that she'd seen his other shape? She didn't hesitate before, but she was also flush with adrenaline and anger. When that wore off, would she look at him as her mate, or as a monster?

After a moment of terrible doubt, Dom decided it was a problem for later.

Gently rearranging her so he had one arm looped under her knees, he stood up from his crouch. "Let's get out of here and find a place to hunker down on the other side of the border, hm?" He rumbled a soothing purr for her. "Everything will be fine. I've got you."

Charlotte nodded against the side of his neck. Her little claws pricked at the skin of his back through the tiny holes she made in his t-shirt. Her voice was muffled when she asked, "What about Millie?"

Dom hesitated, one boot lifted in a frozen step toward his truck. His first instinct was to lie, but he wasn't a liar. He was a direct sort of demon, even when it bit him in the ass. And besides, he wasn't about to start lying to his mate twenty-four hours after finding her. She could handle the truth.

"She's dead, glowbug."

"What?" Charlotte wheezed, whipping her head around to peer at the twisted form on the ground. A high, shocked sound left her throat. "Did *I* do that?"

Dom amped up his rumbling purr and turned away from the grisly scene. Charlotte craned her neck to try and keep Millie in her view, but he broke her line of sight when he circled the truck and tucked her into the passenger's seat. He was strapping her seatbelt across her lap when she asked, voice warbling, "What about the bodies? Won't someone care that there are two dead people in the parking lot?"

Clicking the mechanism in place, he pulled back enough to look his mate in the eye. She was pale and shaken, but her eyes were clear. No shock, then. She was just rattled by the adrenaline drop and the knowledge that she'd killed a person.

Mindful of the small scrapes on her cheeks, Dom cupped her jaw with both of his hands and assured her, "You're safe, glowbug. They're gone. As soon as we leave here, some creatures you don't want to think about too hard are going to melt out of the woods and do what they do best. The bodies will be gone in a couple hours."

Well, he inwardly amended, *maybe not Millie.* The scavengers and beasts of the woods had noses for fouled food, after all.

Not that it mattered. In the New Zone, people died and disappeared every day. In the same way anyone could come into the neutral territory to make a new start, it was the perfect place to disappear unnoticed. Even if he wasn't confident the world was better off without the likes of Millie and her feyrunner companion, Dom was certain no one in any position of authority would think to look for them once a body was discovered.

Rumor was that the Syndicate, the interconnected and often feuding web of vampire clans, were the real power behind the New Zone. They weren't exactly saints themselves, and if push came to shove, Dom knew that a vampire would understand his need to protect his mate at all costs. They weren't a forgiving race, but they were just as viciously possessive of their beloved *anchors* as demons were of their mates.

But he didn't need to say all that to his shaken mate. Dom was a rough sort, but even he knew that some things you just kept to yourself.

Stroking her cheekbones with the pads of his thumbs, he asked, "You gonna be okay until we can find a place to stay the night? We still have a drive ahead of us."

Charlotte stared at him with wide, dark eyes. Her lips, soft and plush in ways he would stay up at night thinking about, trembled for only a moment before they pursed with determination. "Yes," she answered, firmer than he expected her to. "I-I think so. Just... just don't leave me alone for a while, okay? I don't want to be alone anymore."

His fierce little mate knew how to hurt him. Dom swallowed hard, recalling the things she said to the feyrunner, all that raw pain in her voice. *My mate has been alone too long.*

He'd see to it that she never felt that kind of pain again.

Stroking her short black hair back behind the small points of her ears, he said, "I'm yours, glowbug. I'm not going anywhere."

She dipped her head silently, and he knew instinctively what it was she asked for. Cupping the sides of her face, he leaned forward to press a lingering kiss to her forehead. "You're safe." He whispered it against her skin one more time, just for good measure. "I'm here. They're gone."

Her voice was a naked rasp when she asked, "But what about the tracker?"

Dom slipped one hand down to massage the back of her neck. "We'll figure that out when we're over the border. You heard what she said, right? The feyrunner was a sigilworker. My bet is they went low-cost, low-tech, and just put a rudimentary tracking sigil on you somewhere. We just have to find it."

Her nod was jerky. Dom lingered there, crouched half in the truck and half out, for as long as he could before he began to feel the press of instinct again. *Get her safe.*

That was his priority. Get her over the border, then get her home to his territory, where he could...

Well, he wasn't entirely sure what he'd do yet, but letting her out of his sight wasn't an option.

Pressing one last firm kiss to her temple, he regretfully untangled his fingers from the silky strands of her hair before rising to close the door. His skin prickled as he circled the truck to climb into the driver's side.

Scanning the tangled woods ringing the edge of the rest stop, he knew without actually seeing anything that the creatures within watched him, just waiting for their departure so they could descend on the bodies left behind. The man in him didn't feel any remorse for what they'd done, and the animal didn't either.

He protected his mate. Now the natural order of these things would follow. The world would go on, as it always did, and hopefully be a tiny bit less cruel for the loss of two people who cared so little about the lives of others.

Chapter Five

July 2044 - A motel room just inside the border of the Draakonriik

Dom stared at the closed bathroom door. He sat on the edge of their motel bed, his boots planted firmly on the cheap carpet and his elbows braced on his knees. He'd maintained that position since his mate disappeared into the bathroom a half hour ago.

Everything in him, every instinct, held itself in perfect silence as he waited for any sign that she would reappear. As the minutes ticked by, his nerves stretched until they threatened to snap.

She said she wanted a shower, he firmly reminded himself. *You can't bust in there just because she's taking a long time.*

But he couldn't stop himself from worrying. Charlotte had been quiet since their encounter with her captors. He'd only known her for two days, but already he felt attuned to her, as if every instinct he possessed was made for her and her alone. It ate at him that he *knew* Charlotte was in distress and yet he could not figure out how to help her.

Demons were tactile. If she were a demon, he wouldn't think

twice about hauling her into his lap and holding her close so the rumble of his throaty purr and his warmth could soothe her.

But his wee, perfect mate was not a demon. She was fey, and she was dealing with some extremely heavy shit. He didn't know the first thing about soothing her and that knowledge made his skin tighten with shame.

A demon who doesn't know how to comfort his mate. It was galling.

Dom stood up from the bed, the sudden loss of his considerable weight making the springs squeal, and moved to stand in front of the door. He braced his hands on his hips and glared at the wood.

He would be damned if he went down in history as the first demon to let his mate suffer alone. Demons didn't *do* that. They looked after their mates. No one was more devoted than a demon. No one was more committed to the happiness of a mate than a demon. There were whole folktales written about the lengths a demon would go to please a mate.

But there he was, shaming his clan by just standing there, waiting for her to come to *him.*

The only reason I don't know how to help her is because I haven't had the chance to learn yet, he decided. It was time to remedy that.

Feeling the disapproving stare of every one of his ancestors prickling the back of his neck, Dom dragged a huge breath in before he raised his fist to knock on the door.

"Charlotte," he called, knowing she would hear him. The shower had stopped running fifteen minutes ago. When he got no response, he stepped closer to the door and lowered his voice. "Glowbug, open up. I need to see you."

He closed his eyes, wincing. *Didn't mean to say that.*

What he meant to say was, *"Are you okay?"* Or even, *"Do you need me?"* But what came out of his mouth was a pitiful plea. Dom rested his forehead against the door and swallowed a groan.

Yeah, he needed to see her like he needed to breathe oxygen or drink water, but he didn't need to be so *obvious* about it.

Dom opened his mouth to elaborate on why he wanted to see her — to check on her *and* satisfy the frothing animal in him that lived for every scrap of attention it could get from her — but the door opened before he could get the words out. Righting himself with a small jerk, he gripped the door jamb with one hand and peered down at his little mate.

She stood in the doorway. The fresh scents of body wash, steam, and *her* billowed out around her to smack him in the face. Dom leaned back automatically, the muscles of his stomach tightening at the sight of her standing there in nothing but a thin sleep shirt and some dangerously brief shorts.

His blood rushed south so fast he felt momentarily lightheaded. *Sweet Tempest, my mate has the prettiest fucking legs I've ever seen.*

Not that *all* of her wasn't beautiful, of course, but Dom had a special appreciation for her long, smooth calves and supple thighs. He pressed his palms flat against his pockets to quell the urge to run them over every delicious inch of her. It didn't stop the way his pulse pounded in his ears, though, nor the ache of his erection pressing hard against his fly.

"I can't find it."

Dom's eyes snapped up from their inspection of her creamy skin, his instincts prickling at the subdued whisper. "What?"

"The sigil. I can't find it." Charlotte shifted in place, her bare feet shuffling against the linoleum floor of the bathroom. She refused to meet his eye. "I was looking to see if I could find it, but..."

"Oh." Dom swallowed hard. The shame of not knowing how to soothe her was compounded with the guilt he felt for ogling her when she so clearly needed caring for, not a demon lusting after her.

Lifting his hand to cup her cheek, he said, "You should have told me. I'm here to help you, Charlotte."

"It feels personal," she admitted. Charlotte closed her eyes and tilted her head into his hand. Her lower lip trembled when she added, "They must have put it on me when I was passed out, and I had it all this time without knowing, and I just—" She cut herself off.

"It's violating." Dom slid his palm around to the back of her neck. Using his gentle grip, he drew her in slowly, ready to release her at the first sign that she might not want to be held.

But Charlotte didn't tense up or step away. She opened her eyes to look up at him as she cleared the doorway. The expression in her gaze was heartbreakingly bruised. Dom felt a familiar flush of rage in his blood, roiling in his shadows, but forced it away.

Her tormentors were dead. He and his mate were safely in dragon territory. He wouldn't let anything happen to her again, even if he had to devote the rest of his godsdamned life to make it happen. The anger, rightfully earned as it was, didn't serve either of them. It wouldn't fix Charlotte's pain, nor would it help him understand how to care for her.

What his mate needed was comfort. She needed reassurance. She needed *him.*

Dom drew her in close. Gently pressing her cheek against his chest, he curled his arms around her and bent his neck to plant a kiss on the crown of her damp head. Charlotte might not have been a demon, but she melted into him all the same.

Her little claws curled into his back when she whispered, "Yeah, it is."

He rubbed his lips against the silk of her hair, back and forth. All of his senses focused on her: how she felt in his arms, the sound of her breathing, the smell of her skin, the low buzz of her wings, the feeling of his shadow, an extension of himself, coiled around her ankle. Everything worth having rested in his arms.

"You're safe," he whispered. "I promise you'll never have anything to fear again, Charlotte."

"Because I've got a big old demon to protect me?"

It was a half-hearted tease, but Dom didn't take it as a joke.

"Yes." He pulled back just enough to slip a knuckle under her chin. Tilting her face up so he could look her in the eyes, he said, "I'm *your* old demon, Charlotte, and there's no being on this Earth who loves or protects more fiercely than a demon. You'll always be safe with me."

Charlotte stared up at him for several long seconds, her lips parted with surprise. "What if I don't want a mate?"

Everything in him tensed. Dom breathed through his nose and tried, in vain, to get his erratic heartbeat back under control. "Then..." He cleared his throat. "Then that's your choice. But I'm not going to give up, not unless you tell me to, and I'm not going to stop looking after you."

He couldn't. He didn't *want* to. Being with Charlotte, no matter how she aggravated him or forced him out of his comfort zone, made Dom feel *alive.* It had been so long since he felt that way that he'd forgotten just how lonely he was, just how lost he felt in a world that didn't see him as anything more than a bad omen or a causality of a brutal conflict.

Charlotte gave his world purpose and vivid color. Even if she never let anything progress between them, he would still feel that way. Even if she said no to being his mate, he would care for her with everything he had.

Because he belonged to her. His fate, aimless since he was just a bloodied boy on a battlefield, belonged to her.

That didn't mean he was a pushover, though. He'd fight for her. He'd back off if that's what she really wanted, but until then, he'd do everything in his power to prove they were meant to be together.

His arms tightened around her just as a coil of shadow seeped from his skin to snake around her waist, an instinctive response to the acute fear of watching her walk away from him.

"Charlotte," he grated out, "I understand that being mated to a demon probably isn't how you saw your life going. I'll even understand if you're scared of me. Especially after what you saw today— After seeing what I *am,* but I swear, I can make you happy. If you'd just give me a chance, I could—"

He was silenced by Charlotte stretching up onto her tiptoes to press a swift, gentle kiss to his lips. Just a peck. No more than a tantalizing brush of petal-soft skin and warm, sweet breath.

Dom felt her begin to pull away, her intent to give him a quick peck all too clear, but he didn't let her go. He couldn't. Following her retreat, he wrapped his hands around her waist and bent over to deepen the kiss. He traced the seam of her mouth with the tip of his tongue, matching the rhythm of his stroking thumbs moving over the delicate bones of her ribs.

He was gentle but insistent. Determined. *Open up for me,* he silently urged her. *Let me in.*

Dom wanted everything from Charlotte. Everything she had to give. Every touch, every flaw, every breath, every tear. He wanted to cup her in his hands and keep her with him always, if only he could convince her to give in to him.

Charlotte gasped and clutched the side of his neck for support as he slowly dragged his tongue against her lower lip in a sensual caress. When her little pink tongue darted out to meet his, Dom shuddered with equal parts relief and pleasure.

Gods, but she tastes like every wild and beautiful thing.

She tasted *alive;* like light and sweet, fresh water and berries straight from the forest. He wanted to taste every inch of her — once, twice, a thousand times. It would never be enough.

Dom felt the sharp bite of her claws as he began to walk them back towards the wall. Keeping one hand on her waist, he slid the other up to cup her jaw and tilt her head back, allowing him to kiss her with everything he had. Charlotte, for all that she was a small thing, gave as good as she got.

She stretched up to meet him and, using her grip on him as leverage, kissed Dom with a wild energy that burned him. Pin-sharp fangs nipped. Quick, flirty touches of her tongue set his blood ablaze. The sounds she made were soft, breathy, and made desire a hot, heavy thing in him.

Dom felt the scrape of her sharp little fangs against his lower lip all the way down to his cock. It sizzled across every nerve, a shock of pain-pleasure that made him want to get his itchy hands on every perfect part of her.

He took two more steps to press her back against the wall. The hand on her waist slid down to skim the elastic band of her sleep shorts. "Glowbug," he breathed against her mouth, "let me touch you. Let me show you what I can give you."

Charlotte made a soft noise in the back of her throat. Her hand moved down from his neck to rake at his chest. "Dom, I..." Her voice was a husky whisper, barely audible over their harsh breathing.

Unwilling to let her start over-thinking things, he slipped his fingers under the hem of her shirt to feather them over the soft warmth of her stomach. Her muscles fluttered under his exploratory touch. "You don't have to commit to anything. You don't even have to *do* anything." He trailed his lips down over her cheek to skim the length of her throat. Speaking into the luxurious softness of her skin, he said, "Just let me show you how good it can be, glowbug. Let me take away your worries for a little while."

Charlotte's chest rose and fell fast. He could feel her pulse thudding hard against his lips, but Dom didn't push her. Instead, he gently skimmed the sensitive skin of her lower stomach with his callused fingers, coaxing her, and lavished her throat with attention.

He waited patiently. When she tilted her head to give him better access, he knew he'd won. Dom pressed a triumphant kiss to the base of her glowing throat. "Okay," she breathed, "okay."

The animal in him wanted to crow with success, but Dom didn't waste any time doing that. Rumbling his approval, he moved his head back up to kiss her several more times, his tongue and blunt fangs used to their fullest capacity. While she melted into him with a whimper that made his cock press against the denim of his jeans with increasing discomfort, Dom slowly, *slowly* slid his fingers past the waistband of her shorts.

Her skin was so smooth, so gorgeously soft, that he struggled to compare it to anything he knew. Charlotte was wrought in silk and velvet and sweet, perfumed things — everything he wasn't and never knew he wanted until it was *there,* begging for him to touch and taste and keep as his own.

When he passed his fingers through soft curls and even softer skin, wet and waiting for him, Dom let out a harsh groan. "Fuck me," he hissed, skimming the pads of his fingers against her petal-soft flesh. "So godsdamn warm and ready for me. Perfect."

Charlotte's claws bit into the skin of his pectoral muscle. Her legs spread a little wider as he began to drag his fingers back and forth. When Dom lifted his head just enough to gauge her reaction, he found her head tilted back, her cheeks flushed, and her expression heavy-lidded. His mouth went painfully dry.

"Perfect. You're perfect, Charlotte." With just a thought, his shadows moved to pull her shorts down around her ankles. She stepped out of them without looking down, her gaze locked on his face as he stroked her. "Look at you," he rasped, "so pretty and small and mine. There's nothing I wouldn't do for you, glow-bug." Dom's free hand curled around her chin, holding her jaw captive as he slid his tongue along the parted seam of her lips, unable to keep himself from tasting her again and again. *"Gods,* I want to kiss every fucking inch of you."

"Dom." It was a whimper and a reprimand rolled into the sweetest sound he'd ever heard.

"Yes, glowbug?" He ran the tip of his nose down the length of hers as he continued to tease her with soft touches. "What do you want?"

Charlotte panted. Her hips began to slowly rock into his hand, but he didn't increase his pace or pressure. He moved with her, negating the effect until she gave up with a strangled cry. "Dom, *please.* I thought you were supposed to..."

He smiled down at her, the scent of her desire and the sight of her rocking into his hand almost too much to handle at once. "I told you I'd make you feel good," he answered, "I didn't say I wouldn't torture you a little first, though."

She huffed, but when he pressed his slick fingers firmly against her clitoris for just a moment, it turned into a gasp. He switched back to gentle petting almost immediately, making her squirm with frustration. "Dom!"

"What, glowbug?" He slipped two fingers down, teasing the hot, pulsing core that begged for his attention. "What do you want?"

Charlotte made an incoherent noise and pulled at his shirt, her head dropping back against the wall with a dull *thunk*.

Dom pressed a series of soft kisses to her pliant mouth. In between each one, he asked, "What do you need, glowbug? Do you want my fingers? Or do you want me to kiss you like I *really* want to?"

She said something, but Dom didn't want her to whisper it. He wanted to hear her *say* it. "Louder, glowbug," he told her. "Tell me what you want."

"Kisses," she gasped out. "I want kisses."

Dom was not a demon who needed to be told twice. In less than a second, he was on his knees before her. Charlotte squeaked with surprise when he slung one of her legs over his shoulder. Forced onto her tiptoes, she reached for his antlers to keep her balance as he buried his head between her thighs.

She wobbled, but when his tongue slicked across her skin, Charlotte leaned into him with a breathy moan. The sound of it burrowed under his skin, driving him forward, pushing him to prove just how far a demon was willing to go for his mate.

It didn't take long for Charlotte's orgasm to catch up to her, but Dom wasn't finished when she began to tense. Staring up the length of her body, he sucked hard on her clitoris just as he thrust two fingers inside her.

"*Ah!*" Charlotte's back bowed as her skin pulsed with wave after wave of light. The hot muscles around his fingers contracted hard, pulsing in time with the glow that was so unique to his mate. He curled his fingers as he pumped them in and out, prolonging the pleasure as much as he could.

Gorgeous, he thought, watching her ride out an orgasm he refused to let die. *My mate is so godsdamned beautiful.*

She was fierce and fragile and so full of life, he could hardly imagine returning to an existence where she was not the center of his world. He didn't *want* to imagine it.

Finally, Charlotte slumped against the wall, the leg bearing her weight shaking with strain. Dom reluctantly pulled away from her and eased her other leg down from over his shoulder. He didn't let it go right away, though. No, first he pressed a hot kiss to her inner thigh. When he felt her muscle bunch and relax under his lips, he pulled back to skim his callused palms over her backside and her silky thighs.

"I never want to stop touching you," he whispered. "I'm so fucking hungry for you, Charlotte."

He watched her lashes flutter against the tops of her cheeks as she caught her breath. "Is that what I have to look forward to if I agree to be your mate?"

Dom gently nipped at the soft skin of her stomach. "Yes. And more."

A loud buzzing sound reverberated through the wall. Dom stroked his hands upward, over the swell of her backside, to touch the base of her wings as they hummed. Even folded against the wall, they wanted to move.

"What does it mean when your wings do this?" Dom peered up at her. He had a sneaking suspicion that he already knew, but he wanted to hear it from her own mouth.

Charlotte threaded her fingers through his hair, her expression sated. In a thick voice, she answered, "It's the fey mating song. It's supposed to attract a partner and whip them into a frenzy."

Satisfaction was a roar in his blood. *My mate wants me.*

Gods, the knowledge that Charlotte wanted him was heady.

Dom traced the ridges where her wings connected to her shoulders with a possessive touch. "Are you singing for me, glowbug?"

Her pupils were huge. Her lips were a ripe, berry red. Her nipples were stiff under the thin material of her sleep shirt. Charlotte looked thoroughly loved and ready for more. He thought she was beautiful before, but Dom knew that *this* Charlotte was the one who would take his breath away for centuries to come.

Her voice was husky when she answered, "Yes."

Dom flicked his tongue out to taste the sweet, slightly salty flavor of her skin. "Am I the only one?"

He didn't know why he asked. Dom vividly remembered her saying that fey weren't generally monogamous. But he had a gut feeling, and he *wanted* to know. It didn't really matter if she sang for others, but if he happened to be the only one? Dom sure as shit wanted to know about it.

Charlotte's pink cheeks flushed hotter. She licked her lips before answering, "You're the only one."

His fingers dug into the notches between her ribs. "And you can't lie."

"I can't."

Dom pressed a hard kiss to the bow of her hipbone. "Gods help me, glowbug, I won't ever get enough of you."

She shuddered. In a small voice, she asked, "How do you know that? We only just met."

Rising slowly to his feet, Dom circled his arms around her middle to bring her in close. "Because," he told her gruffly, "I've waited my whole damn life for you."

Charlotte leaned her cheek against her kneecaps and let out a long, shuddering sigh.

They sat against the flimsy headboard of the motel bed. Dom was behind her, his big, surprisingly deft fingers skating over her bare back. At regular intervals, he would slip his hands around to brush her sensitive nipples, to trace the dip of her belly button, as if he sought to memorize every soft slope. His muscled thighs hemmed her in, but she didn't mind the feeling of being trapped when it was her demon doing the trapping.

My demon, she thought, drowsy in the post-orgasm, post-burgers and french fry dinner haze.

He was hers. She didn't need him to wreck her whole world, sexually speaking, and then follow it up by ordering her an extra large milkshake for her to know Dom was a demon she wanted to keep around. She'd known it from the moment Millie reached for the bolt gun, and she knew it even when she asked him what would happen if she didn't choose him, just to know that if she needed him to let her go, he would.

He killed for me.

Maybe that thought should have horrified her, but Charlotte couldn't muster the moral fortitude for it. Death was a fact of the world they lived in — a certain necessary brutality that could only be hidden beneath the thinnest of veneers. A human might have balked at a mate killing someone right before their eyes, but Charlotte wasn't human.

She was fey, and even her kind respected a certain amount of targeted ruthlessness. Besides, what could she say? It wasn't like she was guiltless.

Charlotte closed her eyes and tried to banish the memory of Millie's grotesquely mottled face from her mind.

I did that, she thought. *I did that.*

Knowing that she took a life wasn't easy. Knowing that she didn't *care* that she took Millie's life was... troubling.

In the grand scheme of things, did Millie's actions in life balance out against the sin of Charlotte murdering her without remorse? The answer to that question was too big for her, but Charlotte was adult enough to understand that some things just *were.* There was no going back, anyway.

Dom's fingertips danced along the dips and swells of her bare back. They moved from freckle to freckle, skimmed the hard ridges that connected her wings to her shoulder blades, and traced the bumps of her spine.

They didn't bother turning the feed screen on. They didn't need extra noise, or the buffer of an entertainment feed. They were content, just the two of them, in the quiet of the motel room.

"I can't go back to the EVP," she confessed into that soft quiet.

Dom pressed a kiss to her shoulder. She felt the velvety texture of his antlers brush her temple when he asked, "Why not?"

"Because of the contract." Charlotte turned her head to peer at him from under the fringe of her lashes. "My adoption stipulated that I was to be turned over to the covey if I showed any significant magical ability. If I go back, I'll have to go to the covey or my parents will be found in breach of contract."

And no one wanted to end up on the wrong side of a contract with a pissed off covey. *No one.*

Dom planted his big palms on either side of her waist and drew Charlotte back against his chest. Uncoiling her arms from around her legs, she let him wrap her up in his warmth. With his arms banded tightly around her chest, he rumbled, "I thought most Changeling contracts ran out at sixteen."

Charlotte leaned her head into the crook of his neck. "Mine did, but there's a stipulation for specific abilities. It's so rare that it almost never matters, but..."

"Poisoncraft is one of those abilities."

"Yes."

"What would happen if you went back?" He nuzzled the side of her head. Dom couldn't seem to get enough of touching her now that she'd made her interest clear.

Charlotte let her eyes drift shut. "I'd have to tell them. If I got caught hiding my abilities, that would also be in breach of the contract. My parents would suffer for that too. So if I *did* go back and I *did* tell them, I would be compelled to live with the covey for a minimum of two years."

"You'd be trapped again."

She grimaced. The idea of being trapped again, even metaphorically, made her gorge rise. Charlotte couldn't be trapped again; not by the covey that never cared about her, not in a relationship, *nothing.* "Yes."

And the likelihood that they would be willing to let such a lucrative ability slip through their claws after the two years were up? Slim to none. Fey were known for their craftiness for a reason. They would find a way to keep her there forever.

"Then you won't go back." Dom said it so matter-of-factly, as if it was the simplest thing in the world.

Charlotte moved forward a little, giving herself space to turn her head to look at him. "But where will I go, then? I have no job. No family aside from my parents. I have nothing and no one outside of the EVP who I can ask for help. What am I supposed to do now?"

"You don't have nothing and no one." Dom squeezed her tighter. His eyebrows lowered, casting his expression into a look of dark intensity. "You have a mate. You have a clan. You are not alone, glowbug. Not anymore."

She blinked hard, the prickle of tears insistent, and skimmed her knuckles over his bent knee. "You mean that?"

"Yes."

"What happens if you find out I'm annoying? Or incredibly high maintenance?"

Dom cracked a tiny, breathtaking smile. "I already know those things."

Charlotte hissed and gave his knee a tiny pinch. "I am *not* high maintenance!"

"Well, then we have nothing to worry about." He pressed a soft kiss to her brow. "You are perfect for me. I'm going to try every day to be perfect for you. You just have to agree to be my mate, glowbug. Nothing else matters."

She swallowed hard around the lump in her throat. "Do I have to give you an answer right now?"

Could she give him an answer?

Charlotte knew in some part of her mind that this thing — *them* — was an inevitability. She also knew that Dom belonged to her. She saw it in his eyes; felt it in the way he held her. The possessive, lonely core of her soul craved that, *loved* that.

But she had also been a prisoner for over a year, and a shard of fear remained lodged in her heart. What if she said yes, but in six months he discovered he didn't actually want her? What if she freaked out because she felt trapped? What if this was all a fucked up dream her isolated, broken mind tricked her into thinking was real?

It *would* be something her mind would conjure, wouldn't it? Millie and the feyrunner dead. Her parents healthy and waiting for her. An incredibly rare magical ability sprung from nowhere. A handsome, grumpy, possessive demon that wanted nothing more than to pet her and make her happy?

Charlotte felt cold sweat dew along her hairline. Panic was a raw ache in her throat. *What if all of this slips away from me?*

"Shh, glowbug." Dom stroked her bare arms. His calluses scraped against her skin, sending delicious bolts of friction across her nerves. "It's okay. I am not going to pressure you."

Charlotte curled her fingers into Dom's corded forearms and bent forward. She tried to catch her breath, but it was hard to find the oxygen when panic sucked up all the air in her lungs.

"I just— I'm so afraid that none of this is real and that I'm going to wake up in the m-siphon any minute," she babbled, finally letting loose the torrent of emotion that she'd held at bay since her release. "And even if this is all real and I'm free and Millie is dead and I have you, what if I mess it up? What if I'm not what you want? What if—"

Charlotte dug her claws into Dom's forearm, her chest seizing. "You said that I probably didn't see my life turning out with me mated to a demon, but Dom, I can't imagine you *not* in my life. And that's so fucking scary. When Millie went for the bolt gun, the only thing I could think of was you and what would happen if I lost you and I *just can't do it.*"

Dom pressed his lips against the nape of her neck. His arms were a tight band around her chest — almost *too* tight — but she welcomed it. The squeeze grounded her. It reminded her that he had to be real, that he had to want her. She couldn't have conjured him from her imagination, and he wouldn't hold her like he worried she would disappear if he *didn't* want her.

Right?

"Charlotte." His voice was a hard rasp. "Breathe for me. It's okay. You're safe. I'm here. It's okay to feel this way. I'd be scared too, if I were you."

"But what if I *lose you?*" The words tumbled out of her, end over end, each one sliding into the next until they were barely understandable.

But they were the truth. That was what she feared. Losing Dom, this big, earnest demon who looked at her with those soft eyes, made Charlotte's gut churn. She'd always wanted to belong, but she had never wanted to belong *to* someone as much as she wanted to belong to Dom. He was just... right. A solid presence that drew her in, made her feel like she was finally, finally home.

"You won't lose me." His lips moved against her nape, tickling the silky hair there. A little electric prickle bit at the sensitive skin. "You can't. I'm yours, Charlotte. Even if you take a hundred years to decide to be with me, I'll still be yours."

Her voice was thick when she asked, "You promise?"

"I'll swear it to any god you ask me to, glowbug. Even Blight himself." Dom pulled back a little. Cold air rushed in to kiss the heated skin of her nape. He shifted slightly behind her and let out a low, hair-raising rumble. "Ah. Glowbug, I think I might have finally found the sigil."

Charlotte's head snapped up so fast she nearly broke his nose. Dom cursed and ducked to the side as she craned her neck, trying to see her back. "What? Where?"

"Easy, you wee wildcat." Unwinding his arms from around her middle, Dom carefully brushed away the short hair at her nape. "It's here. Just under your hair."

Charlotte's heart jumped into her throat. "Can you remove it?"

His big hands squeezed her shoulders. In a low voice, he answered, "I can. I can use my shadows to... Do you trust me?"

This time, she didn't have to think about it. "Yes."

Dom let out an appreciative rumble that made a home for itself in her chest, easing some of her barbed anxiety. "That's my mate. Just keep that thought in your brain, okay?"

Charlotte tried to look at him over her shoulder without moving too much, her stomach dropping. "Why?"

"Because," he replied, sighing heavily, "this is going to hurt."

Chapter Six

THE TRIP BACK TO HIS CABIN TOOK FOUR DAYS. IT didn't have to take quite so long, but Dom was loath to put his mate under more stress than was absolutely necessary. Besides, he liked spending time with her. Every minute they spent in the truck or in motel rooms, Dom felt a little closer to her, a little more certain that she wouldn't walk out of his life the moment she was able.

So he stretched the trip out, just because he could.

After the horrible night in the motel by the border, when he had to pin Charlotte down to cut out the tattooed sigil on the back of her neck with a blade of compressed shadow, they passed through the carefully portioned countryside of the Draakonriik without incident. The road was smooth and perfectly maintained, something Dom was grateful for when he worried that every bump might jostle his mate's bandaged neck.

But Charlotte didn't seem to care. That first day on the road, she held his hand and stared out of her window, watching the dark shapes of dragons and jets soaring overhead as they put a healthy distance between them and the New Zone. She was quiet, but that wasn't surprising. His mate needed to process all that had happened to her. That would take more than a single night in his arms to accomplish.

Occasionally, a terrifying rumble would rattle the body of the truck, but that didn't bother her. It bothered *him,* but that was because he'd been under dragonfire more than once in his life, and the idea of bringing Charlotte close to an aggressive dragon guarding his roost made the hair on the back of his neck stand up.

When he asked her why the sounds of dragons fighting over territory — or the gods only knew what else, as combative as those scaly bastards were — didn't frighten her, Charlotte merely shrugged and answered, "Dragons do a lot of business in the EVP. When I worked for BriTech's marketing department, I met a few. They're scary, but once you've seen one do a presentation in front of a room full of bored corporate stooges, a little bit of the shine comes off."

And so the trip went. They wound through the Draakonriik slowly, making stops to see landmarks and stretch their legs, before they passed over the border into the Orclind. Conversation ebbed and flowed naturally between them. Every day, Dom was relieved to see his mate take on a little more sparkle, a little more sass. It was a relief when she started to bicker with him over little things like the audio feed frequency, what was the proper way to make popcorn, or whether shoes should be worn in the house. The nightmare of her captivity had begun its slow fade, helped along by the certainty that Millie and the feyrunner were nothing but picked over bones far behind her.

He didn't press her for an answer about staying by his side, but rather took a more persuasive tactic: demonstration. Dom did everything in his power to show her that he could be a good mate, even if he could never be perfect.

Every day, he sought to learn more about her and share himself in return. He wasn't a particularly open demon, but when she told him something about her life, he did his best to reciprocate. He was awkward, of course. Always had been. Speaking about his clan wasn't hard, but his year in the war was markedly less pleasant. He told her, though, because he needed her to know and because she looked at him with such honest yearning that it unwound him.

When they weren't driving, he carefully chose their meals so she would always have something she wanted. He thought it was a good tactic, too, until she picked up on what he was doing and demanded that he also get what *he* wanted. It might have annoyed him, if only her concern for his needs didn't make his chest tighten with an uncomfortable surge of affection.

However, his favorite part of the trip across the UTA was not their shared laughter at her embarrassing stories from middle school, or the sight of her staring misty-eyed at the sunset streaking over the plains. It wasn't even the moments when he caught her staring at his profile, her eyes wide and soft.

It was the evenings.

Every night, they retired to a rented room together. And every night, he coaxed his Changeling into long, drugging kisses until the sound of her wings singing for him filled the room. He liked to tease her until her skin flashed with that impatient glow, telling him without words how desperate she was for his stroking fingers and eager mouth.

Dom was very careful to always make it about her pleasure, not his. Even when she reached for him, a question in her eyes, he insisted. Not because he didn't want her touch — *desperately* — but because he had his demon pride to think of. Above all things, winning and caring for his mate took precedence.

Despite the tension that pulled all his muscles taut and made his cock ache, he didn't want to give her the impression that he wanted to *take* from her; not when she was just finding her footing again, and definitely not when there was still a lingering fear in her that he might just disappear when she wasn't looking.

It was a war to win her trust, and every night he won another battle. Every time she reached for him first, it was a win. Every stolen kiss at a stoplight or in the booth of a restaurant was a victory. Every morning that he woke up to her little claws curled possessively into his chest was a boon.

For the first time in his life, Dom felt like he was living for more than the safety of solitude. He lived for every soft puff of her breath in his ear and every bright smile she flashed his way. Never was he more proud, more assured of his place and his worth, than when his mate grabbed his hand without thinking — a reflex that spoke of just how far she'd come in the days since her release.

It was good timing, too.

As they neared the Coeur d'Alene Forest, a quarter of which was his assigned territory, Dom began to feel more than the usual sexual tension raking across his nerves.

They had just passed a large caravan of orcs, a family unit moving from one settlement to another in the annual migration, and were moving into the land that bordered his home when he finally thought to count the days until August.

Three. Three days.

Dom's knuckles bleached white as he adjusted his grip on the steering wheel. No wonder it had gotten harder and harder to restrain himself when he pleasured Charlotte. It was in the drowsy days of summer, when the heat began to tip over into the chill of autumn, that his kind went into rut.

Normally, that wasn't a problem for him. He rarely saw other people, so his increased aggression and constant, painful arousal wasn't an issue. Like all beings who had a mating season, he learned to *deal*. Dom typically worked out more, saw people less, and took care of the rest with his hand.

But the solution that had so far served him well was useless now.

He had a mate. He had a mate who would be staying with him for the foreseeable future, and if he didn't scare her off, he might even be lucky enough to keep her forever.

Once he realized what was happening, Dom struggled to block out the way drawing her scent into his nose made his skin tighten over his bones, or how his cock throbbed in his too-tight jeans. The presence of his near-constant erection suddenly made more sense. He couldn't decide if it was a miracle that he'd finally found his mate just in time for this year's rut or if it was a disaster in the making.

He shot a glance at her from the corner of his eye. Sweat gathered along his spine as he watched her fiddle with a plastic bottle of what was once orange juice. Since the discovery of her gift, Charlotte had taken to experimenting with liquids, trying to understand where her talents were.

So far, she'd managed to turn milk into yogurt and cola into an acid so corrosive, it nearly burned a hole clean through the floor of the truck. He wasn't sure what she was going for this time, but he could tell she was only half paying attention. Most of her focus was on the audio feed coming through the speakers of the truck.

"...indispensable. While I understand the public's concern that I am too inexperienced to take the seat, I assure you that I am not." Theodore Solbourne's smooth voice filled the car. His address, streamed live from the Solbourne Tower on Treasure Island, came in crystal clear. *"I have the support of not only my sister, but the Five Families, who, after a small amount of debate, voted to approve her abdication. The travel ban was put in place not as a means to control the transfer of power, as some have suggested, but to quell mass panic. It will be lifted in five weeks, at which point I am certain the public will be comfortable with having me as their new Sovereign."*

Charlotte turned the bottle of orange juice end over end, the contents sloshing back and forth, as she listened to the young man who had taken over power in her home territory. Her gaze was distant, but she didn't seem terribly worried. Dom still didn't trust that there wouldn't be violence in the Protectorate, but as each day crept by with no hint of bloodshed, even he had begun to loosen up.

"Furthermore," the sovereign continued, *"it is my intention to see the Protectorate enter into a new and more cooperative age. To*

that end, I will be sending my sister, the former sovereign, to a new post as our delegate in the United Territories and Allies Congress. From this position, she will speak for the Protectorate in matters related to other territories and—"

Dom flicked his finger against the console, turning off the audio feed. He was too tightly strung to listen to an elf go on about cooperation and delegates and all the other political machinations that went into keeping the threadbare tapestry of the UTA strung together.

He felt Charlotte's eyes scanning his profile as he guided his truck into the forest he called home. They weren't far out now, less than a half hour, but the minutes were beginning to feel longer, more painful. How had he gone this long without noticing the build up of tension, that bubbling spring of testosterone and arousal that made all demons so very volatile at this time? He was normally good at spotting the signs of the rut, but Dom had been so focused on Charlotte that he let the most sensitive time of the year sneak up on him.

A soft hand stroked the corded muscle of his forearm. Immediately, every nerve in his body came alive; each one hyper-aware of his mate and her proximity. His shadows writhed under his skin, eager for the taste and touch of her. His lust wasn't helped by the fact that he *knew* how sweet she was on his tongue, how pliant she could be under his hands. The memories of their nights together slammed into him as one entity.

Fuck. He tried to breathe through the pounding lust in his veins, but it was almost impossible. It was as if his realization had unlocked the gate holding back the flush of hormones and instinct.

"What's wrong, Dom?"

He swallowed hard, but his throat was too dry to form words properly, so Dom ended up having to clear his throat before he could speak. "I just remembered something."

When he didn't immediately continue, Charlotte let out a

long sigh. "...Are you gonna tell me, or are you going to let my anxiety speculate?"

Dom blew out a huge breath. Staring hard at the road that wound ever-deeper into the forest, he answered, "August is in a few days."

"Uh-huh." He watched her move out of the corner of his eye. Charlotte shifted in her seat to peer at him, the constant movement of the bottle in her hands stilling. "What? Are you going back to school or something?"

"No." Dom lowered his window, hoping that the scents of home and fresh air would help alleviate some of the tension currently threatening to snap his bones. "No," he began again. "It's *August*. It's the demon mating season."

There was a beat of silence, broken only by the rumble of the engine and the rush of wind through his window, before Charlotte let out a long, *"Oh."*

A flush stole up the back of his neck and into his ears, darkening his deep bronze skin. "Okay," she said, "so... what happens?"

Dom looked away from the road just long enough to send her an exasperated look. "What do you think happens, glowbug? I'll be hard as a fucking rock for two straight months. The rut makes us want to do two things: fight and fuck. Not necessarily in that order."

It was satisfying to watch her face turn bright pink, but only for a moment. Hadn't he gone out of his way to make her comfortable, to not push her? Guilt and hormone-fueled frustration stabbed at him.

Dom let out a long breath. "I'm sorry. I didn't mean to— I'm just tense. Normally I do everything I can to avoid people when the rut hits, but with everything else, I just *forgot* about the damn thing."

And what grown-ass demon forgot about such a basic part of their biological clock? Dom would have been humiliated, but he allowed himself the tiniest shred of grace. Given the circumstances, he thought he could be forgiven for the oversight.

My Nan sent me on a quest and I found my mate trapped in a jar on the other side of the country. Not exactly my usual routine.

Before Charlotte could respond, as he knew she was about to, he continued, "Listen, I know that we are... that things are going well for us." He snuck a panicked look at her. *Fuck.* "I mean, *I* think things are going well. But I don't want to pressure you into anything, and the rut can be intense, so if you want to stay with another member of the clan while I ride it out, I'll understand. The ban will be lifted around the time the rut ends, so your parents can come visit you there or at my cabin, if you come back."

Gods, why did I just say that?

Yeah, he could ride it out, but it would be approximately a thousand times worse now that he knew who his mate was, what she tasted and smelled like, and *where* she would be. He'd never heard of a mated demon being separated from his partner during a rut. Would he even be able to stop himself from tracking her down? Or would the worst of the season finally crush his will and force him to seek her out for relief?

But he couldn't do that. Not if it would scare her. A mate was patient, attentive. They didn't crawl on their hands and knees to beg for sexual release when their partner clearly wasn't ready for that kind of intimacy yet.

Just the thought of being separated from her during such a desperate time, and after just finding her, made the muscles of Dom's abdomen clench hard. Everything in him rebelled at the prospect of letting her go.

He would do it. He *had* to do it. Never, ever would he put Charlotte in a position where she felt trapped or unable to say no to something she wasn't ready for. Even if he had to suffer in the worst kind of agony for two months, he would do it. Without question, he would do it.

"I'm not doing that."

Dom was so surprised, he nearly let go of the wheel. Swearing under his breath, he corrected his hands before replying, "Glow-bug, I don't want you to feel pressured into—"

Little claws curled into the muscle of his forearm. A shiver of pure need rippled down his spine. His mate loved to sink her little claws into his flesh when she wanted him, and he'd grown to anticipate the sharp bite of them. A prick of claw usually meant pleasure was soon to follow. *"Dom, I want to."*

He averted his eyes back to the road. They were so close to home, and the prospect of having her in his cabin, surrounded by his scent, willing to give herself to him in all the ways his imagination could conjure, made every second of the trip seem longer.

If he hadn't been driving, Dom would have closed his eyes and sucked in a deep breath. Casting her a warning look instead, he said, "It's intense. I won't be able to hold back like I have been. I'll need to— You know. I'll need you again and again and again. But... I don't want to do anything you'll be uncomfortable with, Charlotte. I can't hurt you. I *won't.*"

A low buzzing began to fill the car. Dom clenched his fingers on the wheel as what little blood was left in his brain rushed below his belt. Not wanting to crash the truck, he forced himself to keep his eyes firmly on the road.

The sound of a plastic bottle being placed in a cup holder was his only warning before a soft, familiar hand skimmed the length of his tense thigh. "Dom." Charlotte's voice was husky, but held a distinct note of exasperation that was so endearingly *her,* it made his chest ache. "You sweet, ridiculously thoughtful demon. I'm your mate, remember? I'm supposed to be here for you, not let you suffer."

The prick of her claws through the tough denim of his jeans made his heart slam against his ribs. Her voice dropped into a rough whisper when she added, "Besides, there is not one thing about what you described that I don't want."

Dom groaned. Unable to stop himself from touching her, he dropped his right hand to grasp her thigh. His much bigger palm swallowed it up, allowing him to curl his fingers around the supple muscle of her inner thigh, tantalizingly close to the blazing heat radiating from between her legs.

Gods, when she spread her legs like that, he could smell how much she wanted him, how badly his mate *needed* him. It was enough to make his hormone-saturated head spin.

He grated her name out from between clenched teeth, half warning and half moan. *"Charlotte..."*

Charlotte covered his hand with her own and guided it up to brush the seam that ran down her center. "Yes, Dom?"

He turned his head to hold her gaze. "We're not going to make it to the cabin."

⌒

Charlotte held her breath as Dom pressed down on the accelerator, his left hand fisted around the wheel and his right cupping her between the legs with a possessiveness that made everything in her melt and tense up at the same time.

The forest outside was lush and green, with fir and pine trees standing tall enough to block out the sun. The air wasn't quite as cool, the trees not as majestic as the redwoods she was used to seeing in the EVP, but the scenery had a certain roughness to it that reminded her of Dom. Not that she was paying much attention to the flora just then, though.

No, all of her attention was on her mate, who looked about ready to come out of his skin.

Charlotte wasn't blind. Of course she noticed that he seemed to get a little more tense every day, but she had attributed it to the fact that he seemed dead-set on getting her to his home. Dom explained to her that he felt on edge when they were outside of his territory. It wasn't just because he was a solitary sort of man, but because instinct made her safety his top priority. Getting her back to where he *knew* she'd be safe was his sole focus.

That made her feel good in ways she couldn't really describe.

A part of her had agonized over whether she would begin to feel trapped under the intensity of his focus, his concern, but as the days passed, Charlotte settled.

No, she didn't feel trapped. She felt loved. Cared for. Secure in the knowledge that nothing would ever take away her right to choose, her right to *live,* again. Dom would never let that happen.

So when he suggested she leave him to suffer through the demon mating season alone, of course she balked. He'd done everything in his power to take care of her since he freed her from her prison. She wasn't about to abandon him the moment he needed something in return. Plenty of beings went through mating seasons, anyway. It wasn't a big deal.

Besides, she wasn't lying when she said nothing about what he told her sounded bad. It actually sounded really, really good.

Of course, she loved it when Dom touched her. Charlotte had never felt more special than when he spent hours stroking her skin with his fingertips, as if he couldn't believe he was allowed to touch her. But a girl had certain needs, and when he kept forgoing his turn to be petted and tasted and loved, she grew increasingly exasperated.

So it was well past time for *her* to do a little taking care of her mate. Charlotte had a feeling she'd enjoy it, too.

Dom pushed the truck well past what she assumed the speeding limit was, but there was no m-grid this deep into the wilderness to stop him. Not that she cared. The feeling of speed, the way he flexed his fingers against the seam of her jeans, all of it had her heart pounding. Excitement and desire mingled to bubble in her veins.

She barely noticed when he made a sharp right onto a dirt road, the tires of his truck squealing as they left the pavement. Charlotte only caught a glimpse of a quaint, golden cabin nestled amongst the trees at the end of a long driveway before he slammed the truck to a stop by what looked like an old woodshed.

They were still some ways from the cabin, but Dom didn't seem to care. Unbuckling his seatbelt with one hand, he curled the fingers of his free hand into her hair to pull her into a brutal, hungry kiss.

It was all Charlotte could do to hold on. She reached up to cup his jaw, her fingertips skating over skin roughened with stubble, and let out a surprised squeak when he slid his tongue into her mouth. Dom was normally a coaxer, a long, gentle kisser. This frenzy was new.

Or maybe he's just been holding back, Charlotte realized with a jolt. She'd gotten so used to the way Dom lavished her with attention that she never thought to question whether he was actually toning his intensity *down* for her.

Glory save me.

Charlotte squeezed her thighs together to alleviate a little bit of the pounding ache between her legs. Of course he noticed the movement immediately.

Dom pulled back with a low rumble. His expression was frenzied, his lips glossy and his cheekbones stained with dark color. Charlotte could feel his hungry gaze raking across her skin in time with the possessive pulsing of the shadow coiled so lovingly around her ankle.

"Out of the truck, glowbug."

Charlotte swallowed hard. For a second, she sat frozen, her wings buzzing so loud she couldn't hear her own thoughts. When she didn't immediately follow his command, Dom pressed another bruising kiss to her lips. *"Out,"* he rasped against her mouth.

A *zing* of pure arousal snapped down her spine, as sharp and hot as a lightning strike. Charlotte didn't waste any more time. Unbuckling herself with shaking fingers, she hurried out of the truck.

The air was hot and dry outside. The faint hint of dust and pine filled her lungs as she gasped for air. Somewhere far away, she thought she heard the rush of water. The forest pressed in close around them, nearly swallowing the sun bleached woodshed and the narrow driveway Dom parked so haphazardly in the middle of.

She didn't have time to get her bearings, though. She didn't even have time to properly shut the door.

Seconds after her bare feet made contact with the dusty driveway, Dom was on her. Hoisting her against the side of his truck, wrapped her legs around his hips and *devoured* her.

His big, callused hands wrapped around her waist as he ground himself against her, his hips moving with a rhythm that made her toes curl. She dug her claws into his shoulders and hung on for dear life as her mate finally let himself take what he wanted.

The hot, dry air, the blazing warmth radiating off of her demon, the feeling of sweet friction as he ground his straining erection against the seam of her jeans... Charlotte tore her mouth away from his to gasp, trying in vain to catch her breath as Dom slid his hands under her backside and staggered away from the truck.

She made a sound of surprise and wrapped her arms around his neck. "Where are we going? Into the cabin?"

"No. Too far." Dom's voice was a gravelly rumble against her jaw. His lips moved restlessly along the curve before he found her ear. Giving her earlobe a sharp nip, he grunted, "Forest. Shadows. Safe."

Before she could really process what he was trying to tell her, Dom stumbled off the driveway and into the treeline. Immediately, the heat lessened. Cool shadows brushed her in ways that might have felt unnatural a week ago, but now felt an awful lot like coming home.

Her heart beat a staccato rhythm as Dom dropped to his knees on the forest floor. His hands and shadows went to work removing her clothing, desperation in every jerky movement. Seams tore and buttons flew, but she didn't care. Her skin flashed with each strike of her heartbeat, calling to him to ease the furious lust that made her squirm in his lap.

Somehow, he was even less careful with his own clothing. Dom tore at his shirt and jeans, shucked his heavy work boots, and all but destroyed his underwear. Charlotte watched him move with a dry mouth, her eyes glued to the play of muscles under his deep bronze skin and the way his shadows writhed, pushing out and retreating, as if they couldn't decide which form he should take when they joined.

There was a certain headiness to seeing someone as steady and reliable as Dom absolutely *lose it.*

Charlotte sat back on her knees to admire him. Of course, she'd had the privilege of seeing him shirtless before, but he'd been so careful about holding himself back that she was denied seeing *everything.*

"Gods," she whispered, blinking hard, like clearing her vision might make Dom more real, less beautiful.

He was thickly built, with ropes of muscle that were not the perfectly sculpted kind that came with a gym membership, but the slabs of pure strength built from years of hard work and outdoor activity. His skin was a beautiful dark gold, liberally sprinkled with hair that led the eye down to thick thighs and an erection that made her breath freeze in her lungs.

Gorgeous there, too. Not that Charlotte had ever really thought about the relative beauty of penises before, but there was no denying a perfect specimen when it was inches from her.

He was hard, flushed, and ready for her. His cock bobbed against the flat plain of his abdomen, the tip glistening with pre-come, when he crawled toward her. Shadows flickered around him, *through him,* and the sight of his most primal form breaking loose as he advanced on her made Charlotte unspeakably needy.

Shadows curled around her ankles. She didn't fight them when they spread her legs for him. Nothing in her wanted to fight him, *this.* Charlotte submitted to the press of them; the strange, electric sensation of his shadows stroking her nipples as he dropped down to bury his face between her legs.

Her wings *sang* as he wrenched a hard orgasm from her with his teeth and tongue and insistent, sucking pulls. Nothing about it was gentle or coaxing. It was intense, almost brutal. She didn't feel the bite of rocks or pine needles under her naked skin. She didn't feel anything other than being consumed by him.

Charlotte was still blinking away spots when Dom let loose a bone-chilling rumble, grabbed her waist with both hands, and flipped her over. Pine needles and forest debris clung to her sweaty back. A sharp pebble bit into her left knee. Her wings vibrated too violently for Dom to properly cage her in, but Charlotte didn't care.

When he surged inside her with one hard thrust, stretching her with a delicious burn, she melted into the forest floor. Her claws curled into the dirt and small, scrubby plants. It might have reminded her uncomfortably of her time in the terrarium if Dom weren't there, the center of her whole universe, breaking her apart and putting her back together again with each brutal thrust.

She tried to breathe, to meet his rhythm, but she couldn't manage it. All she could do was let him sweep her away into something so intense, she could barely process it.

Pleasure and discomfort mingled, an ebb and flow that was as unpredictable as it was exciting. When he picked up speed, his movements jagged and so deep she could feel him in her damn lungs, Charlotte felt the change come over him.

The hands pressing bruises in her waist got bigger, the blunt nails sharpening into claws of living shadow. She could feel the air change behind her. Could feel him change *inside* her, and her entire world narrowed into the space between their bodies as he took and took and *took.*

Shadows pulled her legs wider. They stroked over every inch of her. They stroked her aching nipples and scraped against her scalp. They kissed her lips and found every sensitive patch of skin. They slid downward to lick against the slick skin where they were joined and made her cry out hoarsely. As Dom angled his hips *just right,* Charlotte let out a broken cry and convulsed around him, her skin flashing in time with her thundering pulse.

Dom followed her over with a tearing sort of growl that sent goosebumps prickling over every inch of her skin. Sinking his claws into the flesh of her hips with just enough pressure to hurt but not injure, he surged forward one last time before locking them together to spill inside her.

She sagged into the forest floor, her ears ringing and her muscles gone liquid. Charlotte lost all ability to comprehend time as she waited for her post-orgasm glow to fade and for reality to return. Hadn't they just been in his truck? It felt like another lifetime, like she was another woman.

Reality didn't return, though. As soon as she began to come around again, Dom was there, his big hands stroking her back and sides with blatant ownership. Still buried to the hilt, he rolled his hips once, twice, and rasped, "You okay, glowbug?"

It was all she could do to pillow her cheek on her forearm and turn her head to peer over her shoulder. Dom was on his knees behind her, his head lifted proudly in the air, antlers a striking shape against the shadowy trees; half man and half shadow. *Good gods,* she thought, her muscles giving an involuntary squeeze. She watched his expression change when he felt the rippling pressure and let out a sigh of pure admiration. *He's the hottest fucking demon in the world.*

Her voice was raw when she answered, "Yeah. Gods, yeah. I'm... I'm *great.*"

She watched Dom bend over to place a warm, reverent kiss between her wings. They didn't buzz quite so loudly as before, but with his touch, they gave it a college try. "Good," he whispered against her skin, "because I'm not done with you yet."

Charlotte blinked at him. "But... *how?*" She squirmed a little. He was huge and heavy in her yet, and she could swear that she felt his thundering heartbeat through their connection. "Didn't you finish?"

Dom scraped his teeth against the sensitive line of her spine. His huff of laughter was dark and deep, sending a thrill of anticipation through her core. "This is just the start, glowbug."

In what felt like the blink of an eye, he had her repositioned on her back. One strong arm was a band across her spine, carefully keeping her delicate wings from being crushed against the forest floor, as he dragged his mouth against hers in a deep kiss.

She shuddered, the new angle providing an immediate and almost overwhelming stimulation. "Did you say this would go on for *two months?*"

Dom slicked his tongue against her lower lip before he bothered to reply. "Two months." His amber-on-black eyes lifted to pin her with a hard, hungry look. "This is barely the start. You think you can handle it?"

Charlotte swallowed. Desire was a low-burning fire in the pit of her stomach, growing stronger with every second that passed. Reaching up to curl her fingers around the base of his antlers, she dragged his mouth back to hers. "I don't know," she mumbled, "but I'm not a godsdamned quitter."

EPILOGUE

SEPTEMBER 2044 - COEUR D'ALENE FOREST, THE ORCLIND

THE WANING DAYS OF SUMMER PASSED IN A HAZE OF golden light and ceaseless desire. Dom worried that the rut would be too much for her — he hadn't, after all, had a mate to think about before — but his wee Chageling took it in stride, and for that he was immensely grateful. Things were easier with her. The aggression didn't build up until he wanted to lash out at anyone and everything, and when the lust became too much, she was there to ease that terrible pressure with an enthusiasm that made him feel like the luckiest demon in the world.

It was an exhausting two months, but it was a deeply pleasurable time. The rut was always hard, but with her, it felt *almost* normal. He couldn't remember being more content than he was when he came home from patrolling his territory to find his mate experimenting with her craft, or waking up with the sunlight streaming across her naked form, curled up in the safety of his arms, or when he slid into the tight heat of her body and listened to her gasp out his name.

They slotted into one another's lives like they were always

meant to be there. He even grew to like it when she sassed him, and he *knew* she loved him when she began to smile through her exasperation. Arguments ended with hard, needy kisses, so he tended to pick fights more than was probably necessary.

Dom didn't know how he'd ever lived without the sound of her padding barefoot around the property. He couldn't fathom a life in which he didn't wake up to the sight of her, or fall asleep knowing she was safe under his guard.

When her parents did eventually come for their tearful reunion, the travel ban having been lifted as promised, Dom felt so settled in their life that he didn't bat an eye when they asked about her return to the EVP.

Charlotte loved her parents, even when it was clear they didn't entirely understand their daughter. He knew it hurt her to tell them that she would not be returning home with them, but he also knew that she was certain in her choice to stay by his side. She'd told him as much a month after their arrival at the cabin.

He didn't tell her that he'd already figured it out. No one who clutched that tightly in their sleep would leave their mate. And if he was privately smug about the fact that Charlotte didn't even consider moving into one of the apartments the clan owned in the nearby town of Kellogg to have some space after the intensity of the rut, Dom didn't feel too bad about it.

He'd won his mate, he *loved* his mate, and he'd be damned before he let himself take her for granted.

Dom didn't even mind it when his clan decided it was time to meet the new member and descended on his cabin with food, drinks, and purely demon lack of boundaries.

Charlotte's parents clearly loved every second of the party thrown in their honor. Despite being as average as arrants could get, they didn't even blink when they were handed a baby with soft nubs for antlers, or when a good natured brawl broke out between two hot-headed juveniles over the last of the barbeque. They were good people. The clan took to them immediately, even when they both ended up getting too drunk to do much more than fall asleep on his couch.

Dom wasn't one for the big gatherings his clan liked to throw, but he endured it without complaint when Charlotte was welcomed with open arms. Half the clan *oo-ed* and *ah-ed* over her pretty wings, and the other half let out loud whoops of admiration when she turned a glass of wine into a poison so intensely volatile, it melted the glass.

He didn't even mind it when his Nan gave him one of her usual tight hugs, cuffed one of his antlers like he was still a kid, and smugly asked, "Didn't I say you'd find your fate, boy?"

Dom cracked a smile and pulled his mate in until she was curled against his side. One of Charlotte's sneaky little hands slid under the back of his shirt to tease the base of his spine as he grinned down at her. "Yeah. You did, Nan. Thanks for the tip."

Charlotte winked at him before turning her blazing smile on his Nan. "I've got no complaints. Although maybe next time, you could give the poor soul a little more to go on?"

His Nan, a weathered demon who'd seen ages pass and whole generations come into being, gave his mate a light tap under her chin. Her eyes, butter yellow on deep black, sparkled with mischief when she answered, "Foresight isn't always clear, little bug."

Dom shook his head. "You also like to make trouble."

"Worked out well enough for you, didn't it?" She clicked her tongue and glanced over to where a fire raged in his stone-lined fire pit. His cousins mingled, their shadows rolling happily together in the flickering light of the fire, and sipped from an odd assortment of beer bottles. Someone was telling a story with more enthusiasm than skill, but none of the tipsy demons seemed to care. They tossed their antlered heads back and roared with laughter.

Dom followed his Nan's gaze. Smiling ruefully, he asked, "Who's next?"

She shot him an innocent look and straightened her spine.

Even ancient, his Matriarch towered over him. There was no lost strength in her spine, no slow grind of age. She was old, but with her mate still living and her health holding, she would be the unquestioned leader of the clan for many, many years to come. Grateful to her in more ways than he could ever say, Dom prayed for more years after that. As far as he was concerned, his Nan had earned the right to godsdamned immortality.

"Now," she drawled, giving Charlotte's cheek a pat before turning to walk away, "where would be the fun in telling you that?"

Dom pulled Charlotte into his chest, giving in to the need to have her close. A grin stretched across his face. "You're right. It's more fun not knowing."

His mate snorted. A small finger jabbed him in the kidney. "Is it?"

"Yeah," he answered, stooping to press his lips to the crown of her head, "it makes the happy ending that much sweeter."

THE END

ASTRAY

A DRAGON'S KISS BURNS COLD.

CHAPTER ONE

DECEMBER 2044 - THE ELVISH PROTECTORATE

PALOMA SLAMMED THE DOOR OF HER TRUCK AND swore.

Pressing her thumb against the ignition switch, she studiously ignored the familiar faces wandering out into the packed dirt parking lot in front of *The Shack,* the unofficial town hall. She could feel their familiar gazes on her through the shatter-proof glass of her windshield, but she couldn't bear to make eye contact with any of the people she'd known her entire life. She gritted her teeth and tried, with limited success, to block out the sounds of their continued muttering.

Paloma grew up with most of them. She babysat for them. Her eighth grade teacher sat beside her in a folding chair and raised a wrinkled arm to vote *yes.* Looking at them now, Paloma wasn't sure she actually knew *any* of them.

The town she'd been a part of and the people she'd known her whole life wanted to execute a dragon without warning or even an *attempt* at something less deadly. They wanted to end a life because they felt threatened by a shadow that had only barely brushed their mountaintop.

And it was Paloma's fault.

Tears blurred her vision as she backed out of the parking lot and onto the only road the tiny, scattered mountain town could boast.

When she spotted the blip on one of her monitors two days prior, she had no idea that she would be responsible for the death of an innocent being. As an aerial researcher, she only did her job: watch the skies and monitor her sensitive equipment's readings for abnormalities in energy buildup that could lead to devastating weather patterns and other, more specific m-phenomena. Spotting the dragon was a surprise. They normally flew so high that most ground-based monitors couldn't pick up their flight patterns, but her equipment — specially designed by her late father and perfected by Paloma — managed to catch a glimpse of them.

That wasn't immediate cause for concern, of course. Dragons could and often did fly wherever they liked. The high peaks of the Sierras were not strangers to the passing dragon shadow. But it was rare enough that Paloma noted it. All day, she watched that little blip on her screen get closer and closer. She let herself imagine what it would be like to be capable of that kind of freedom as she waited for the dragon to sail overhead — on their way to wherever they needed to be, great leathery wings outstretched to catch the air currents.

Except, they didn't continue on their way.

She watched, dread knotting her stomach, as the blip circled back around before making jagged, irregular movements around the surrounding peaks. Over and over again, the blip sailed from mountain to mountain in an ever-tightening circle around the tiny town far below Paloma's home and research station.

The tell-tale mark of a rogue dragon.

Of course Paloma was concerned. A rogue dragon was dangerous to themselves as well as others. Dragons were beings of immense size and strength, with a capacity for destruction that rivaled any machine of war the modern age could conceive of. She had to report the sighting to the town and their single, ancient Patrol officer, just in case the dragon decided it was the perfect place for its roost — a decision that would result in the violent eviction of every single individual currently occupying it.

She didn't just worry about the town, though. Paloma's heart ached for the lost, circling dragon.

Paloma was just a scientist. An arrant with no magical ability and no experience with dragonhandling, she did what she was supposed to do: she passed her information along to the mayor and town council. Surely there was a way to help a rogue, right? She knew next to nothing about dragons or how to help them. There had to be *someone* they could call.

Bunch of godsdamned cowards, she seethed, wiping furiously at her stinging eyes as she wound her way through the darkness and up the mountain she'd called home her entire life.

The town's solution to the problem was not to seek help in subduing and rehabilitating the rogue. The people she'd grown up with, spooked by the tension of the recent political upheavals in San Francisco, voted to call in Patrol at the first sight of the dragon.

They didn't want to help the rogue. They wanted to call in the elvish authorities — who would not hesitate for even a *moment* to execute a being who hadn't done a thing wrong.

Paloma didn't blame Patrol, necessarily. They were tasked with the safety of the territory, and in a world so full of beings capable of so much harm, they had to be ready to defend that safety with ruthless efficiency at a moment's notice. Wars had been started over less than a dragon's flight over a small town, after all. And with Delilah Solbourne's recent abdication in favor of her brother, rumors of a takeover from another powerful faction flew.

Theodore Solbourne, the newest sovereign of the Protectorate, had done his best to squelch those rumors, but Paloma knew anything could be taken as a challenge to his authority. If a rogue dragon sighting was called in and the sovereign's people didn't act immediately to protect his citizens, it could turn into a political nightmare — all the more reason for Patrol to handle her dragon with brutal efficiency.

But this was the modern age. Paloma had to believe that there were other ways to handle a lost soul, circling endlessly in the frigid air, than a swift execution.

Too bad the town refused to listen to her.

No matter how loudly she argued that there was no evidence the dragon intended to threaten the town, she was unanimously outvoted. The mayor — Old Jack, owner of *The Shack* and all-around ass — promised to call Patrol in the morning.

Bile crept up the back of Paloma's throat. She'd watched that man's two dogs for pocket money as a kid. Shit, she'd even briefly dated his son in high school. To see him so easily condemn a creature — a sapient being with thoughts and feelings and family and a *soul* to death without so much as a blink? It was like she'd stepped into some awful alternate reality where everyone she thought she knew turned out to be a monster in disguise.

It was a long drive back up the mountain to her home. Paloma stewed in her helpless anger the entire way.

It was her fault that the dragon now had a sword poised against its throat, intentionally or not, and the fact burned inside of her like corrosive acid. Their death would be on her hands. The thought made her want to pull over and heave up her dinner along the side of the road.

There was no way she could sit and watch as the town called in a Patrol squad to take down the rogue. She couldn't do it. She *refused* to do it.

The road under her truck's tires was a black blade of asphalt, so narrow in some places that the sturdy pines lining the road seemed to lean over it, creating a cage of jagged teeth in the dark. She'd made the trip hundreds of times in her life, but never had she pushed her truck to move quite so fast, to take the hair-pin turns or serpentine path up to her cliffside home with so much urgency.

Paloma knew she didn't have much time before the dragon appeared on the horizon. Her phone beeped with an alert every time it picked up on the dragon's presence within the bounds of her surveillance — and those beeps were getting more frequent, the time between them shrinking. Her fingers spasmed on the steering wheel every time another one cut through the silence.

It would only be a matter of hours before Patrol appeared. If she wanted to save the rogue, she had to try tonight.

She *would* do it tonight. There was no other choice.

Paloma was no expert on dragons. She'd never even met one. The small town she'd more or less grown up in was home to a couple witches, a tight-knit were pack, a lone shifter or two, and a vampire who rarely ventured off of his remote, sprawling property but never failed to fund school plays and town initiatives when politely asked. The rest of the town was like her: arrant. Born without the right pathways to channel magic of any kind, they made their way in the world as best they could.

The EVP was home to the second largest population of arrants in the United Territories and Allies because it was — at least since the execution of its last mad Sovereign — the safest territory. Arrants didn't have to worry about being muscled out of their homes or their livelihoods by those bigger and more magically inclined when the iron-fisted EVP government kept things running smoothly and relatively fairly.

Paloma grew up in a peaceful era under the brittle truce left in the wake of the Great War, but her father hadn't. A quiet man of great intellect, he'd retreated to the jagged mountains of the Sierras after his time in the intelligence branch of the EVP army ended. He raised Paloma at the remote research station he'd built from scratch, and she'd never had much inclination to leave. The only time she'd spent away from home were the miserable, blurry years she'd spent in college.

If she met a dragon during her studies, Paloma couldn't recall it. She tested into a highly specialized and selective program in the du Soleil Center for Magical Research in Los Angeles. Of the fifteen students in her year, only four graduated. The intensity of her studies and the size of her classes hadn't allowed her any time to explore the city or meet new people. What she knew of the world beyond her mountain came from books and educational feeds.

Normally, she didn't mind that. She liked her life. She felt privileged to be the steward of her own little slice of wooded territory, to spend her days satisfying her intellectual curiosity and furthering her field of study.

Sure, she got lonely sometimes. After her father passed, she had to grapple with his sudden absence from her life. For all that they'd been a small family, they *were* a family. Without his quiet muttering and the patter of his footsteps in the next room, Paloma finally began to grasp the downsides of her isolation. She'd even begun to entertain the terrifying idea of starting her own family. Her father had raised her on his own, and since she had few chances to meet a romantic partner in her day to day life, she'd finally settled on doing the same.

She knew she was inexperienced in most normal life things and usually it didn't trouble her. Paloma did things in her own time and in her own way. It just never occurred to her that she wouldn't have the luxury of time to do that.

Her truck was barely parked before Paloma threw herself out of it. Boots crunching in the gravel, she hustled toward the house. The floodlights fixed to her front porch cast the driveway and yard in an eerie glow that worked to scare off both the magical and non-magical predators slinking in the shadows of the forest.

The area around the front of her home was cleared for both equipment and fire safety. In the half-moon of land that radiated around her porch, she'd cultivated a healthy garden — dormant for the winter — and lovingly tended a small flock of chickens in a hutch, already latched for the night.

The back of her home wasn't quite so hospitable — mostly because it clung to the edge of a sheer cliff overlooking a dizzying gorge. A strip of pale blue snaked along the bottom of that gorge, a ribbon of the icy Sacramento River. During the day, she could stand on the overhanging deck and take in the surrounding peaks, snow-topped in the winter and vivid green the rest of the year, and at night she could taste the crispness of the thin air and gaze at the soft bruise of the Milky Way.

It was beautiful, but it was also terrifying. The wind whipping through the gorge could sweep a person off their feet if they weren't careful, and the sheer drop on the other side of the railing was enough to give even the heartiest soul vertigo.

Paloma was used to it, but even she treaded carefully along the deck on bad weather days. With the high winds, she could rarely put any sort of furniture out there besides an old iron fire pit, so she didn't spend more than a few moments a week out on the wrap-around deck her father so painstakingly built.

Paloma craned her neck to scan the familiar skies. Her lips thinned.

Dragons were nearly impossible to spot in the daylight, but they were entirely invisible at night. The reflective bellies and undersides of their wings made them stealth predators, while their unique physiology allowed them to fly at altitudes no other living being could survive. If it wasn't for her equipment, Paloma might never have seen the dragon at all.

It would have been better for the dragon if she hadn't, but Paloma couldn't change the past. She'd made this mess, and she was damn well going to fix it.

How, though... She hadn't made it that far yet.

Paloma's mind raced, sifting through every scrap of information she had about dragons at lightning speed as she threw open the front door to her home. She didn't bother stripping off her down jacket or pulling off her knit beanie as she flew down the hall and flung open the door to her lab.

The glow of razor-thin screens lit the darkened room with an eerie blue light. Servers blinked with tiny LEDs and machines hummed a low, soothing song for her from their positions against the walls. A stainless steel workbench took pride of place in the center of the room, its reflective surface covered in bits of machinery and coiled wiring. A rolling cabinet of tools sat next to her scratched wooden stool, while her father's seat stood across the bench, in the exact place he'd left it the day his heart failed.

For the first time in three years, Paloma did not skim her fingertips over the wooden seat as she passed it, recalling the decades he'd spent hunched on the stool, his nose buried in smoldering circuitry.

Hurrying to the bank of screens along the far wall, she braced one hand on the edge of the desk and waved her other over the large trackpad. Immediately, the computers came to life. A projected keyboard flickered into being next to her half empty mug of coffee from that morning.

Her phone beeped another alert in her pocket, but she didn't need it. Scanning the screens, Paloma felt her heart drop to her knees.

"Godsdamn it," she breathed, throat constricting hard around the words.

She hadn't exactly held out a lot of hope that the dragon would miraculously alter its course and turn around, but she had *some*.

The data didn't lie, though. The dragon's course hadn't changed. Its jagged, tightening circles around the mountain were closer than ever. It also appeared that the dragon's altitude had dropped considerably. If it had been daylight, Paloma suspected that anyone within fifty miles would be able to catch the telltale flicker of light and the terrifying, swooping shadow now.

The dragon was looking for a place to land.

Paloma gripped the edge of her desk with fingers gone stark white. She lowered her head and squeezed her eyes shut, willing her brain to *think*. There had to be a way to save the dragon. She was a genius, wasn't she? There had to be some scrap of information she'd absorbed over the years that would help her. Help *them*.

The idea of calling the Draakonriik embassy in San Francisco came to mind. They would know what to do about a rogue, right? The Draakonriik was dragon territory. It was run by the fiercest, most terrifyingly attractive dragon in the world: Taevas Aždaja, Isand of the Draakonriik and Lord of the Dragonclans. Surely the dragons would know how to deal *non-lethally* with one of their own.

Her phone buzzed in her pocket.

Except, the dragon doesn't have that kind of time.

Even if she were able to get in touch with the embassy, and even *if* they were able to assemble a crew to take down the dragon, there was no way they would get there in time. Patrol remained on call for just this sort of thing at all times. They would probably use an emergency m-gate, a magical tear in space that took an incredible amount of energy to produce, and have a bolt in the dragon's brain in less than an hour.

They wouldn't ask questions and they wouldn't show mercy. Not everyone in Patrol was elvish, but most of Command was. Elves didn't *do* mercy. If you were a threat, you were extinguished. End of story.

So calling the embassy was out. What other options did she have?

Paloma lifted her head and opened her eyes to stare at the innocuous red triangle moving slowly across her screen. Her chest ached. What could one arrant woman do to save the life of a being so beyond her reach?

Even a low-level witch, a brightling, might have tried to telepathically connect with the rogue. A harpy could have flown to meet it at a lower altitude. An elf would have had the resources to get in contact with help. Even a damn demoness would have a clan around to figure it out with her.

Paloma had never felt lacking before. Being an arrant wasn't a bad thing. Millions of people were just like her. No, she wasn't born with the right m-paths for magic. It was nothing more than a quirk of genetics; the hand fate dealt. The goddess Glory hadn't blessed her or any of the other arrants out there, leaving them to Craft's whims. She wasn't religious, but even she thought it was a little unfair that her people were left under the care of the trickster god.

Sure, life wasn't always easy or fair when you went up against people who could move mountains with their thoughts.

But then again, the world wasn't exactly kind to those people, either.

She reached out to press her fingertips against the cool glass of the screen, tracing the path of the dragon headed her way. The poor being was probably exhausted and lost, looking endlessly for a place to land and rest their wings. Because of Paloma, the moment their clawed feet landed, they would be executed. Her eyes stung. The satellite image and its digital overlay blurred.

The dragon would die because of her fuck-up. *Just because they needed a place to rest.*

Paloma jerked her hand back from the screen with a cry. "Craft's ass!" She slammed her palms onto the desk three times in quick succession, her breaths excited puffs. "Holy shit! Shit!"

The dragon needed a place to *land.* If she could lure it to her cliffside *before* dawn, no one in the town below would know that the dragon was even there.

Of course, she wasn't foolish enough to think the dragon would *never* be seen, but it could buy them both time. If they weren't that bad off, she might even be able to coax them into shifting. Even she knew that communicating with dragons was much, much easier when they wore their humanoid shapes.

But how did one draw the attention of a dragon? She couldn't risk any sort of siren, since sound traveled for miles around. Normally she would use the electrical storm warning system, but that would draw the town's attention directly to her and her dragon.

Paloma wracked her brain, trying to think of any way to draw the dragon's gaze to her research station that wouldn't immediately alert the town.

What could possibly get a dragon's attention?

Dragons were known for two things: their love of wealth and fire. Paloma didn't exactly have a big pile of gold to flash at a moment's notice, but she *did* have fire.

Heart pounding, her thoughts snapped to the old metal fire pit, unused since her father's passing, on the deck. Normal fire might do the trick, but with the dragon still so far out, she didn't want to take the chance. If she really wanted to get the dragon's attention, she had to make them think there was another dragon nearby.

If her dragon really was considering setting up a roost nearby, they would be compelled to investigate any evidence that another dragon was within their chosen territory.

Dragon fire was easy enough to fake. Hollywood did it all the time for entertainment feeds. Back in school, one of her professors moonlighted as a stunt tech on sets. He regaled her requisite chemistry class with his chemical misadventures — and taught them all the easy trick to faking the color of dragonfire.

No one but a dragon could *really* make it, of course, but Paloma didn't need to. She just needed the dragon's attention.

It was pure luck that she had just the thing to make that happen.

It was well past midnight by the time Paloma got the fire roaring in the pit. The air was frigid, but blessedly windless. Her breath fogged up in front of her as she made a dozen trips to and from the woodshed, piling one seasoned log on top of another in the huge iron bowl of the pit.

The fire grew and grew, spitting smoke and flames into the air. Great curls of blue-gray smoke swept upward before fading into the velvet black of the night sky. Standing too close to the flames made her sweat under the layers of her down jacket, but Paloma didn't stop to unzip it. The dragon was closing in on her side of the mountain. If she missed this chance, they would swerve around to the opposite side — where the town would see them silhouetted against the rising sun.

So she added more logs to the fire and ignored the sweat gathering between her breasts or beading along her hairline. She didn't think about how her cheeks stung with a combination of bitter cold and blazing heat. Paloma built the fire until the pit could take no more.

And then she added the copper chloride.

She kept a few pounds of it around for the lab for a myriad of things, but only really used it in small doses. Tonight, she dumped the entire bag of red-brown dust on the fire and watched, heart in her throat, as the roaring flames changed from gold to vivid, *dragon* blue with a hiss and crackle.

Tossing the empty bag aside, Paloma raced over to the metal railing. The fire's heat burned through her clothing to sear her back, but she didn't care. Her eyes darted over the familiar shapes of the surrounding mountains, searching. In her pocket, her phone buzzed again and again.

"Come on," she whispered. *"Come on.* I know you have to see it!"

She only hoped the dragon was close enough to be interested. The blue flames would only last for a maximum of fifteen minutes. If the dragon lost interest before then, the flames would sputter and turn back to their natural yellow and red. Without more copper chloride, Paloma would have no other way of safely getting the dragon's attention.

The skin of her palms burned with cold as she curled her fingers over the freezing metal of the railing. Paloma wasn't a pious person. She didn't make a habit of praying to any of the gods, but she shot a prayer out into the universe anyway.

Please, let this work.

The minutes dragged. Her muscles locked, cramping with the

force of her tension as the blue flames flickered behind her. The longer she stood there staring at the endless black of the night, the worse she felt. *Come on,* she silently begged the dragon. *You have to see the flames. Why aren't you here yet?*

Tears pressed hard against the backs of her eyes.

Gods, she just... she *couldn't* be responsible for another person's death. Not being able to help her father as he died on the ground next to their generator was one trauma too many. Paloma didn't think she could take the guilt of knowing she'd doomed someone else to a senseless death.

Her phone buzzed constantly. She could feel it in her front pocket, the alerts pinging so close together they could no longer be distinguished from one another. The dragon had to be close, but even when she squinted hard, she couldn't make out anything. She scanned the sky anyway, taking in great sweeps of sparkling stars, until she caught a flicker of movement.

She held her breath. Was that a shape blocking out some of those stars, or was she just seeing things? Paloma leaned over the railing, trying to get closer, but of course it didn't help. Stars flickered on their own, didn't they? Surely, if there was a dragon close enough to—

A faint whistle echoed through the gorge, bouncing off of ancient granite walls weathered by time and the slow drag of glaciers, half a second before a huge blast of cold air nearly sent her toppling backward into the flames.

Paloma staggered backward but kept her whiteknuckled grip on the railing as the massive shape of a dragon swept up from *under* the deck and over her head, wings beating hard enough to send her hair into a wild disarray. Sparks and smoke filled the air, disorienting her as she twisted around to try to keep the dragon in sight.

There was that low whistle again. It was a haunting sound, almost birdlike, and not at all what she expected from a rogue. Weren't dragons famous for roaring?

And *why,* of all the things she could fixate on, was she thinking about the sounds the dragon made?

There was a *dragon* circling her *house!*

Paloma stared, gobsmacked, as the dragon swooped low over her property again and again. She couldn't quite make out their face, but she could see the underside of their huge, leathery wings and their reflective belly, the blue flames of her fire flickering against the metallic skin of the purest black. The vague shape of deadly claws curled close to the belly made her palms sweat with the sudden realization that, while her plan was certainly a success, it was also woefully incomplete.

Great, I've got the dragon's attention, she thought, watching with mounting panic as the dragon landed in a crouch on the reinforced roof of her home with a long, low whistle. A huge head lowered over the lip of her gutter to peer at her. Eyes of blazing crimson — almost too bright, like artificially colored candy or a ruby struck by light — pinned her in place against the railing.

Now what?

Chapter Two

Artem breathed deep. His huge lungs burned with the change in air temperature. The smells of the ground — the sharp bite of pine, the satisfying burn of smoke mingling with the crisp scent of cold mountain water — were at once familiar and strange. He couldn't rightly recall when he'd smelled them last. Had it been weeks? Months?

His mind was muddied. Thoughts that had once flowed with the clarity of the river far below now swirled in dark eddies. He wasn't insane. His reason, his identity, remained. Artem was fully aware of what had happened to him: the *roaming sickness* had taken his ingrained sense of direction and turned it against him.

All dragons felt the instinctive urge to find a roost of their own — a high place that afforded them a view of their territory, that they could fortify and fill with a mate and offspring. It was deeply embedded in the same part of their brains that controlled their sense of direction, which was itself attuned to the magnetic field that encircled the Earth.

It wasn't abnormal for a dragon to fly from the family roost on the cusp of adulthood, compelled by those twining instincts to find their own direction, their own place. But occasionally, that compulsion went into overdrive.

Artem wasn't a boy. He was nearly seventy, and he'd never had a problem with his roaming instinct before. When he felt stifled by life in his clan's stronghold on Drummond Island, he flew. Usually, he returned to his clan after a few weeks of bitter cold flight, his instincts settled once more.

Not this time, though.

When he set out from the Dragon Roost after a raucous dinner with his cousins to celebrate his little sister's completion of her mandatory military service, he didn't feel any different than normal. A fearless launch off of his balcony, a mid-air shift, and he was off, wings outstretched to catch the air.

But time blurred after that. At some point, he'd lost track of it altogether. The need to *go* was a slow, steady drumbeat in his mind, drowning out every other need. It usually faded quietly into the background after a few days of hard flight, but as the days passed, Artem felt it only grow stronger.

Go. Find a roost. Go. Find a roost. Go! Find a roost!

The mantra circled endlessly, pushing out every other thought or base need. He couldn't remember the last time he ate, or slept. By the time he began to circle the snow-topped peaks of the Sierras, he could barely hold his wings up to catch the air.

Dragons were made to fly for weeks on end, their bodies built to go long distances with neither rest nor sustenance, but Artem knew the roaming sickness had pushed him beyond his body's limits. He had to land. If he didn't, he would eventually fall — the most humiliating death a dragon could imagine.

It didn't matter that he was aware enough to understand landing would spell his death. Rogue dragons were dangerous and prone to bouts of territorial rage. Even his own clan would have used force to subdue him in his current state. The fact that he was in *elf* territory meant there would be no mercy. They would not subdue him and try to beat the sickness out of him, as his clan would. As soon as he touched down, his life would end.

Desperate, hungry, and exhausted, Artem was barely coherent enough to feel the grief of his reality. It was there, a shadow pressing against the edges of his mind, but unable to reach him. All he knew was the pain in his exhausted wings. The ache of his empty belly. The relentless pounding in his head.

The lonely, broken call of his soul. *Go. Find a roost.*

Home, his instincts urged. *Find a home.*

That might have been possible in the Draakonriik. He could have found a roost there, perhaps on a craggy peak of the Smoky Mountains, where he could build a fine roost for himself and his Chosen. But with his sense of direction so snarled in instinct, he'd veered far off course and into the Elvish Protectorate. If he picked a roost there, without first getting the proper permissions from the EVP government, he would be shot on sight.

No one wanted a rogue dragon in their territory, after all.

Too bad he didn't have the strength to haul himself back across the continent. At the rate he was going, Artem would either land in the Sierras or he would fall into them.

What was more humiliating: falling from the sky or having a bolt put through his brain?

No self-respecting dragon would accept either. Dragons were meant to die one of two ways — in combat or in the arms of their Chosen at a ripe old age, with offspring flourishing in the world, carrying on his clan's legacy. Falling from the sky was a humiliation akin to slipping and dying in a godsdamned shower. An elf putting a plasma bolt in his brain was only half a step up from that. Neither was acceptable to a dragon such as Artem, a man in his prime and cousin of the greatest dragon alive, Taevas Aždaja.

The choice loomed larger in his head as he circled the icy peaks of the Sierras, his instinct fixating on the jagged shapes of granite cliffs and sharp, brittle pine trees far below. As night fell, his wings shuddered, pain lancing up through the nerves and delicate muscle as he fought to maintain his altitude.

It was no use. He was falling. Instinct might have compelled him to cross whole oceans, but that didn't mean his body could actually do so. A dragon was the most powerful creature on Burden's Earth, but even they needed rest.

The flicker of dragonfire in the distance was... Artem didn't have a word to describe the relief he felt when he spotted it. Not once did he think of rescue, of help. He thought only of ending his torment.

No dragon who roosted in this high paradise would suffer a rogue to land in its territory. No dragon would ask questions first. They would simply act. If a rogue dropped out of the sky to threaten their roost, they would defend it with tooth and claw.

Better to die that way than to hit the ground like a diseased bird. It was the first clear thought he'd had that day.

Artem pushed himself forward, toward the beacon of dragonfire that should have warned him away, not drawn him closer. No sane creature would approach another dragon's roost uninvited — especially one who clearly had a Chosen. As he swept down into the gorge below the roost, Artem could smell the sweet fragrance of a woman on the frigid air.

Human, his exhausted mind supplied. Yes, this was exactly what he needed. A dragon with a human mate would be even more vicious. Humans were so very fragile, lacking in sharp teeth or claws or a protective dual form. The dragons he knew with human mates were nearly driven to madness with the protective urge to coddle them.

It worked perfectly for Artem, who had no intention of dying a sad, whimpering death.

To die under another dragon's claws was vastly preferable to a rabid animal's execution. And if he felt a sharp twang of envy in his scaled breast for this lucky creature, with such a fine roost and a mate to safekeep, Artem didn't dwell on it. His chance to have both went out the window the moment the sickness pushed him out of the Draakonriik.

Still, he sucked in a burning breath when he swooped up and over the deck of the dwelling that clung to the cliffside. The woman's scent was thick around the roost. It cut through the sharp pine and the scent of burning wood to sear a path down his throat.

Oranges and vanilla. That's what he smelled. Like a sweet treat to enjoy on a hot day, she called to him over the din of scrambled instinct and exhaustion.

Immediately, Artem's focus snapped back to him. Lifting a shuddering wing, he gritted his fangs and wheeled around to glide up the wall of the gorge. Something niggled at the back of his mind, but he couldn't place it. Some missing piece that made his instincts bristle as he shot up over the deck of the dwelling.

...and straight through a thick cloud of that mouthwatering scent. Fresh and delicious, it clung to the roof of his mouth as he flew over the deck to circle the painfully small dwelling.

Without thinking, a crooning whistle escaped his throat. It was a courting call — one he'd never felt compelled to use before. Startled, Artem thrust out a wing and hauled himself back over the property, surprised and unsettled to be allowed so close.

Where was the dragon? What kind of protector would allow a rogue so near their roost? Their *Chosen?* One that smelled so deliciously edible as she did should have been squirreled away at the first sight of a wing on the horizon. Everything about her spelled out softness, delicacy, the need for protection.

Artem banked hard to land, legs spread, on the roof of the dwelling. Even with his clouded mind and his confusion, he knew enough to spread his considerable weight out, keeping any damage to the roof minimal.

He wanted a fight, sure, but he didn't want to lay waste to a woman's home. Not when she smelled so very soft and delicious and—

Mateless.

Artem shifted on the roof to peer down at the deck, his ruby eyes fixed on the slight form clinging to a metal railing below. It took him several long seconds to figure out what he was seeing.

A woman, swaddled in a down coat, stood on the other side of a roaring fire pit. The flames were dragon blue, but up close, any dragon worth his claws would see that it was regular fire chemically tinted. The heat radiating off of it was a dead giveaway. Dragonfire didn't burn hot. It was ice cold.

Artem blinked slowly, his clear, secondary lid closing over his eyes twice before he could register exactly what his instincts were telling him. *No dragon.*

His lungs heaved. Every muscle cramped and trembled as he clung onto the roof of the woman's home. Artem barely noticed.

No dragon. No mate.

He scrambled forward to lean his huge body over the roof, bringing his horned head closer to the little woman staring up at him with wide eyes. The blue flame of her fire cast strange shadows across her dusky skin and large, dark eyes. Long dark hair fluffed out from beneath her knit beanie to fall around her shoulders in a tangled mass. Her eyebrows were arched high with surprise, her full lips parted to reveal a hint of pink tongue and pearly white teeth.

Her arms were stretched back, fingers curled tight around the railing, but she didn't quail before the predator perched on her roof. He watched her throat work as she swallowed thickly.

Another crooning whistle escaped his parched throat. This time, he didn't try to stifle it. Lowering his head a bit more, he ignored the flames licking at the underside of his chin as he prowled forward, leaving only his hind legs and tail coiled around her roof.

She had such a soft face; all smooth tanned skin and curving lines. Heart-shaped and lovely, she looked like a woman made for a lush roost full of silk and sunlight and rich food.

Instincts prickling in a building wave, Artem braced his forelegs on either side of the fire and swung his head left and right. Surely he was wrong. There had to be another dragon. Fake fire or no, there was no way a delicious little creature like her — perched on the edge of a perfect roosting cliff, no less! — could be without a mate.

The idea made every muscle in his aching body tense. Aggression coiled like a spring in his belly. A rumble rolled up his throat as flame, icy and more destructive than any other on the Earth, licked at the inside of his mouth.

What kind of dragon would leave her unprotected? There was no telltale ash marking around the property. No mingled scents. Adding insult to injury, the dwelling was *woefully* inadequate for a Chosen such as her.

Worse than all of that, of course, was the fact that she had been left to fend for herself against a *rogue.*

Gods only knew what might have happened to her if he were anyone else. Artem had enough of his mind left to understand that *he* wasn't exactly safe for her either, but the longer he stared at her, the clearer his mind became. For the first time in weeks, his instincts began to untangle themselves; settling into a low, insistent thrum in the back of his mind.

Assured that there was, inexplicably, no dragon coming to her rescue, Artem turned his gaze back to her. She'd eased backward far enough to put her spine against the railing, her dark eyes leveled on his snout. He was so fixated on admiring her face that it took him a moment to realize she was speaking to him.

"...s'okay," she whispered hoarsely. "Everything's okay. Just... just stay calm and everything will be fine. Isn't that right, dragon? We can be friends. Just keep things nice and calm."

He wasn't sure if she was speaking to him or to herself, but he liked the sound of her voice regardless. It was as soft as she looked.

Letting out another courting whistle, the only response he could manage in this form, Artem stretched his neck to carefully nudge her shoulder. *Away from the railing,* he mentally urged. In his state, he couldn't dive fast enough to catch her if she tumbled over the edge.

He felt her flinch when he carefully pinched the shoulder of her jacket between his teeth, tugging her away from the metal rail. Making a startled *eep,* she stumbled forward and directly against his snout.

"Sorry, sorry!" she gasped.

Artem whistled for her again and carefully pulled his head back. He kept the bulk of his body over the roaring fire, just in case she stumbled again. Biting back a hiss of pain, he slowly folded his abused wings against his back. Exhaustion was a dark ring around the edges of his vision, creeping closer every second. He would collapse soon, and that meant he would probably wake up to the barrel of a bolt gun pressed against his forehead, but he didn't care. Suddenly all that mattered to his bruised mind was the soft, delicious scent and voice of this strange little woman.

Crooning a low note, he forced his legs and tail down from the roof to land on the wide, wrap-around deck — perhaps the only feature of the dwelling he approved of. It was much larger than the house itself, but only just big enough to fit his bulk. Not quite what he would classify as a dragon's perch, but close enough.

As soon as his claws hit the wood, Artem's legs buckled under him. Every muscle shuddered with terrible, agonizing cramps as his body finally allowed itself to relax.

He let out a pained chuffing noise, the only kind of complaint he could manage, and listed slightly to one side. His chest rose and fell with rapid panting breaths. Bracing his great, horned head on his foreclaw, Artem watched his lovely human from under half-lowered eyelids and willed himself to stay awake for a few moments more, to endure the pain for as long as he could.

"Oh, you poor thing," she breathed, wariness melting out of her expression. Artem's heart seized when she dropped to her knees in front of him. Her face, cast into shadow by the flames at her back but still perfectly visible to his predator's eyes, was full of concern. "I wish I knew how to help you."

He managed an appreciative whistle. Even in his muddled state, Artem wasn't sure he'd ever heard of such a vulnerable creature going out of their way to help a rogue dragon before. Most sane beings would have run in the opposite direction as soon as his shadow passed over their heads.

But his human didn't run. Reaching out, she dared to press

one soft palm against the thick scales covering his cheek. He wished he had the strength to lean into her touch.

"It's okay." She skimmed the curve below his eye with the tips of her fingers. A featherlight touch that made everything in his exhausted soul keen. "You're safe here, dragon. No one will hurt you, and you can stay as long as you need to. Just don't fly off tomorrow morning, okay? If anyone sees you..." She trailed off, but he didn't need her to finish. He knew what awaited him in the light of day.

Curling her hand into a fist, she withdrew from him to glance over her shoulder. The fire spat sparks into the air as the flames flickered from vivid blue, to sickly green, to their natural yellow. Letting out a shaky sigh, she sat back on her heels and rubbed her face.

Artem wanted to croon for her again, to soothe her anxieties away like a good mate should, but he couldn't manage it. It was all he could do to settle into a more comfortable position as sleep crept in on him from all sides. Normally, he would have coiled his tail around her and held her against his chest as he slept, keeping her safe against his heart, but that would have to wait until his muscles stopped spasming.

For the first time in ages, his mind settled into a quiet stillness.

She lured me here, he realized, full of wonder as he watched her stand and put out the fire with a bucket of water. He breathed deep one more time, just to assure himself of what he already knew. There were no other scents in the vicinity, old or new. *This is her roost. There is no mate to watch over her; no one to protect her. She made her own dragonfire to call me to her side.*

Artem felt a rattling purr bubble up from the center of his chest as his eyes slid closed. The snarl of instinct smoothed out into a single, perfect thread connecting his heart to hers.

She Chose me.

～

Paloma slumped next to the hissing remains of the fire, her heart a thundering beat in her chest. She stared at the dragon currently sprawled across her deck with the distant expression of someone just realizing they are in way over their head.

On one hand, she was deeply relieved that her plan worked. On the other, she had no godsdamned clue what she was supposed to do now.

The dragon was a huge, dark shape barely illuminated by the glowing coals in the fire pit. Slumped to one side, he lay half curled around her house, his great, spiked tail between her and the sliding glass door.

Bracing her palms on her knees, Paloma tried to get her thoughts in order. *The horns mean male,* she noted, eyeing the vicious-looking spikes that fanned out around her dragon's head. Her stomach knotted up with a sudden burst of nerves. Didn't people talk about women staying away from male dragons? Wasn't that a common joke on entertainment feeds? She couldn't recall why. *I guess I'll find out why when he shifts.*

She curled her fingers into the denim covering her thighs. *If he can shift. One step at a time, I guess.*

With her limited knowledge of dragons, she struggled to piece together anymore information from his appearance alone. Since the dragon was about the size of a large SUV and had a full set of horns, she guessed he was an adult. Aside from those two basic observations, she really had nothing to go on.

The fact that the poor creature was clearly exhausted was the only obvious thing about him. The dragon's chest rose and fell rapidly. His eyes, those terrifying ruby-red globes that were bigger than her fists, flickered behind tough, scaly eyelids. His wings were folded haphazardly against his back, as if the dragon was too exhausted to even tuck them away properly before he lost consciousness.

Paloma swallowed hard. Sympathy for the poor, lost dragon made her throat tighten. She just wished there was something she could *do* for him.

A fixer by nature, she thrived on problem solving and caretaking. All her life, she'd played the caretaker and the companion to her softhearted father. It never felt like a burden, but helped hone her natural inclination toward showing affection with acts of care. To not know how to help the dragon who so clearly needed some care made her want to pull her hair out.

Frustrated and cold now that the fire was extinguished, Paloma levered herself up onto her feet. She carefully stepped around the dragon's twitching claw to very, very slowly throw her leg over the spiked tail blocking her way back into the house. She held her breath, eyes flicking toward the prone dragon, before easing herself over the danger zone.

Her fingers were so cold they barely managed to flip the latch on the sliding door. She peeked over her shoulder, worried that her fumbling would wake the massive creature on her deck. There was no movement, though. Nothing besides that worrisome twitching and the sound of huge, gulping breaths being pushed out of a long snout.

Sliding the door aside inch by slow inch, she opened it just enough to slide through the gap before closing it in the same way.

Standing in the warm darkness of her home, Paloma stared out through the glass.

There's a dragon on my deck.

Not just any dragon. A *rogue* dragon. A dangerous, unpredictable being who needed help that she couldn't provide and wouldn't get from anyone in the EVP. A massive, clawed beast that could breathe ice-cold fire or swallow her in one bite.

She pressed a shaking hand against her galloping heart, her eyes glued to the shadowed form of the dragon. Perhaps she should have been afraid, but she wasn't. After all, if the dragon wanted to lash out, wouldn't he have done so already? Besides, she knew the signs of a creature in pain. She'd had enough pets and rehabilitated enough wild animals in her life to know the sounds, the way they moved. Her dragon wasn't aggressive — he was just lost, hurt, and exhausted.

And if the dragon was dangerous... well, that was something she would just have to find out in the morning.

Letting out a shaky exhale, she momentarily wondered if she could risk sneaking back out to cover the dragon in a few blankets — or twelve — but begrudgingly dismissed the idea. If a dragon could fly at the same altitude as an m-jet, they could survive a December night on her deck.

She didn't *like* it, obviously, but the risk of disturbing the dragon's much needed rest outweighed her nagging need to care for him.

Paloma reluctantly stepped away from the door and turned to make her way to her bedroom. Grabbing a fistful of her knit beanie, she pulled it off as she walked down the dark hallway that once separated her half of the house from her father's. A man who believed in autonomy and privacy, he'd built the home so that she had her own little wing, complete with a microscopic sitting area and her own bathroom.

The home was built out of an old miner's shack, but only the kitchen retained any of the bones from that original structure — mainly in the rustic beams and old slate floor that, despite being a bitch and a half to clean, Paloma loved. Being part research station, part home, and part shack, it wasn't the most cohesive structure in terms of design, but she couldn't imagine living anywhere else.

Up until tonight, she couldn't imagine having a massive, fully grown dragon on her deck, either.

Shaking her head, Paloma closed her bedroom door with the heel of her boot. The lights came on automatically, casting her old, much loved furniture in a soft golden glow. After a long day sitting in front of her screens, she preferred the gentle warmth to the harsh brightness of a cold light.

Paloma shucked her thick jacket and began preparing for bed. There wasn't much else she could do, but a part of her felt the strangeness of doing something so mundane when a dragon lay just on the other side of her wall. Her mind whirred out of control even as she slipped into a comfortable pair of sleep pants and a soft nightshirt.

Sliding under her covers, Paloma passed her hand over the panel on the wall by her bed. The room plunged into the familiar blue-black darkness of a winter night.

She stared at the ceiling for several long moments. Would she hear the dragon if they moved? Would she wake up to find a huge, ruby eye staring at her through her half-parted curtains? Would she wake up to her home burning down around her?

Paloma twisted onto her side, her hands curled under her pillow. Drawing her knees up to her chest, she squeezed her eyes shut and imagined the huge creature outside, the poor lost soul she had nearly condemned to death. Would they be alright out there all night? She had to think so, but worry bit at her all the same.

She turned onto her other side. The house seemed terribly quiet. Even when she strained to listen, all she could hear was the faint whirring of fans and the whistle of wind through the trees. No growling. No hard, pained breathing. No crackle of fire. It was like the dragon wasn't even there.

A spike of alarm sliced through her.

Sitting up abruptly, Paloma scrambled onto her knees to peer out the window over her bed. A portion of the deck wrapped around the outside wall of her bedroom, giving her a partial view of the gorge and the mountains beyond it. Paloma scanned the darkness, looking for a sign that the dragon hadn't slipped silently into the night when she wasn't looking.

Squinting hard, she was just able to make out the vague shape of a spiked tail.

Breathing a gusty sigh, she sank back down into her twisted blankets. It gnawed at her, this inability to *do* anything for the dragon. She couldn't help him, and if the dragon got it into his head to fly off in the morning, there was nothing she could do to prevent it.

Paloma swallowed the bitter taste of helplessness in the back

of her throat. Pulling her blankets up over her shoulders, she tried
to find some comfort in the fact that she'd done everything she
could for the dragon. If he stayed, she'd figure out how to do
more. If he didn't...

That, like so much of life outside of her lab, was beyond her
control.

Chapter Three

The sunrise over the Sierras woke her from a
fitful sleep.

Paloma came to wakefulness slowly. The warmth of her bed,
the soft rasp of her breathing, and the golden light filtering
through her eyelids were familiar morning visitors. She'd woken
up the same way nearly her entire life — always the first one up,
since her father tended to work late into the night. Never one to
need an alarm clock, she woke at first light, her mind already
abuzz with the list of things that needed to be done that day.

That list started with feeding herself and her small flock of
chickens before it shifted to tasks revolving solely around her
research. Paloma's days followed a ritual of routine that soothed
her overactive mind. Her weeks blended together, broken up only
by her regular trips to town for groceries and a stop at *The Shack*.

This morning felt no different than any other since her
father's passing: quiet, drowsy, and lonely.

Paloma rubbed her cheek against the smooth fabric of her
pillowcase, her mind already churning with all the tasks she'd have
to complete by the end of the day, a stream of data spilling across
the back of her mind to supply her with an endless to-do list. *Get
up, feed the chickens, make coffee, check the readings on radar 5,*

submit data from last week to PWS, replace the cooling coil in sonic transmitter 12, make sure the generator isn't malfunctioning again, maybe eat something if I have time, see if the dragon is still within range—

Paloma bolted upright.

Suddenly wide awake, she threw off her covers to scramble onto her knees. Curling her fingers around the edge of her headboard, she nearly pressed her nose against the cold glass of her window, looking for any hint that the previous night wasn't some stress-related lucid dream. Or worse.

Paloma pushed her mussed hair out of her eyes. The sun was bright, casting a glow of butter yellow and fiery pink across her frosted deck. Beyond the gorge, the sun lit the snow-capped mountains with candy colored flames. It was a gorgeous Sierra sunrise, full of saturated color and the promise of a new day, but its beauty slid right past Paloma.

The dragon's gone.

Her stomach sank as she scanned what she could see of the deck from her window. She had only been able to make out the vague shape of the dragon's tail the previous night, but in the light of day, she expected to be able to see much more of the huge creature parked on her deck.

Except there was nothing. Only strange dark shapes on the planks hinted at where the dragon once was — his great body shielding the wood from the glittering film of frost that settled on the other parts of the deck overnight.

Chest seizing, Paloma sank back down onto her haunches and dropped her forehead against the wooden headboard.

Of course she hadn't dreamed it. There was a dragon there, but now he was gone — probably flying right over the town as she sat there, unknowingly sealing his fate as the mayor called in Patrol to do their bloody work.

"Fuck!" She hurled a pillow across the room. It smacked into her standing mirror, sending the scarves and knit hats of varying colors draped over it flying, only to fall into a pitiful heap on the floor.

Pressing the heels of her hands into her stinging eyes, Paloma tried to breathe through the frustration that threatened to sear her from the inside out. It didn't matter that she knew there was nothing she could do to prevent it. One couldn't very well chain a dragon to a post, let alone command it to stay in one place. They were sapient beings with their own iron wills. If the roaming dragon wanted to go, he would.

That didn't make it any easier to swallow, though.

Pushing at her eyes until she saw spots, Paloma tried to work through the anti-anxiety mantra her therapist gave her after the death of her father.

"This is beyond your control," she breathed, voice raspy with sleep and emotion. "You did everything you could. This is beyond your control. You did everything you could. This is beyond your *fucking* control, Polly."

No matter how many times she said it, no matter how often she used her childhood nickname to anchor herself, she still felt the band of guilt tightening around her throat, squeezing the air out of her. The dragon was going to die and it was her fault.

Paloma sat in the center of her rumpled bed for several long minutes. The fate of the dragon picked at the wound her father's sudden death left on her heart with a ruthlessness that stunned her. If she'd acted sooner, been smarter, maybe she could have stopped both.

But it was too late.

Shoulders slumped, she forced herself to crawl out of bed. Her misery was acute, but what could she do about it? Nothing. Life went on, relentless and unfair; so too did she.

The chickens would be eager to get out and pick at the frosted grass around the front of the house, and of course, there was work to be done. No matter what, there was *always* work to be done.

Shrugging on a thick robe, she didn't bother tying it closed as she shuffled out of her bedroom and towards the front door. She scrubbed at her tired, stinging eyes. The weight of bitter grief pressed on her until it felt like every step took extra effort.

Eventually she made it to the door. Shoving her socked feet into her old rubber work boots, she barely even grimaced as she pulled the front door open and was greeted by a blast of cold morning air. Her robe and pajamas were no match for the weather, but that was fine. Once she let the chickens out, she would retreat back into the house to lick her wounds over a cup of hot coffee and a screen of data.

The gravel lining the path to the chicken coop crunched under the soles of her boots. Ducking her head against the icy breeze, Paloma didn't pay any attention to the familiar surroundings of her front yard as she made a beeline for the coop, half-hidden by the side of the house.

She was so lost in thought, her insides tangled up with frustration and grief and that persistent ache of loneliness, that she nearly squashed one of her beloved hens under her boot.

Paloma staggered backward and slipped in the loose gravel as she tried to step over the chicken, who absolutely *should* have still been in her nesting box. Tinker, a puffy black ball of sass and vinegar, squawked indignantly as she narrowly avoided Paloma's stomping gait.

"Gods! What in the *world...*" Clutching a fistful of her sleep shirt, Paloma tried to calm her racing heart. Her eyes flicked left and right to take in the sight of not just Tinker waltzing around the yard, but her other hens out and about, happily pecking at the grass and weeds. She blinked several times in quick succession. Had she forgotten to latch the hutch?

No, that wasn't possible, she hadn't made that mistake in years; not since a bobcat got into the hutch and killed three of her girls in one night. Paloma shook her head, aghast, as she rounded the corner. Tinker followed in her wake, pecking at the turned up gravel marking her footsteps. "I'm sorry, sweetheart," Paloma muttered, glancing down at the hen. "I can't believe I put you and the girls at risk like that. I won't—"

"Good morning!"

Paloma's head snapped up. She staggered to a halt as her gaze fixed on the man standing next to the open door of the hutch, one very content chicken tucked into the crook of his elbow.

Sunlight slanted over the roof of the house to gild a body of pure, dragonfired muscle. It glanced off of reflective skin so red, it reminded her of freshly crushed raspberries — a color so saturated it almost looked fake. A crown of horns held back a messy mop of dark red hair, highlighting a face of sharp angles and even sharper teeth. Those teeth were on full display as the man grinned widely, one corded arm lifted in an exuberant wave. When he moved his arm, the light moved across his skin in a strange, rippling pattern: candy red to midnight blue, back and forth, highlighting the outline of a circular tattoo on his bicep.

As if all of that wasn't enough of a shock, he was also absolutely, completely naked.

Paloma stood frozen on the path and stared. And *stared.*

"Good morning," the dragon crooned once more, dropping his hand to stroke the chicken tucked into his elbow. Only when he lowered his arm did she notice the leathery wings folded against his back. Wicked talons crowned the tops of each wing.

That's... my dragon, she thought, trying to match the sight with the exhausted creature she left on her deck the previous night. *That's my dragon.* Her eyes dropped involuntarily when something swayed out from behind his back. A tail, spiked at the end, curled around one muscled thigh.

Paloma's eyes snapped up, her face flushing. *Had it right the first time. Definitely male.*

The dragon didn't seem even a little bit concerned with his nudity. That shouldn't have surprised her, considering it was really only humans and elves who fussed about modesty, but she didn't exactly expect her lost dragon to show up as a naked man, either, so she thought she could be forgiven.

The dragon clicked his tongue and murmured something to the hen in his arms — Wendy, she realized, and one of her older

Rhode Island Reds — before he gently deposited her on the ground. Wendy hopped off, wings flapping, to join the other girls in their hunt through the weeds.

"I hope you don't mind, but I heard them scratching around and thought I could save you the trouble." He flashed her a wide, white grin. "Did you sleep well? I tried not to wake you."

The dragon sauntered closer. His feet were shaped differently than hers: in his bipedal form, the five toes were split, the sole arched high like the foot of a bird's for ease of gripping and take-off. The sharp claws on the ends of his toes crunched in the gravel, but with the way his weight was distributed, he moved much more quietly than she did.

Paloma swallowed. Why was she so flustered? It was a damn miracle that he was still around. It was a good thing. She just... didn't really think her plan through. Getting the dragon to her home and then keeping him there until she figured out a way to help him seemed impossible enough. She didn't consider the fact that he was a person, too, and that she might have to deal with a huge, naked man in her yard for her trouble.

"I'm sorry," she finally croaked, aware that she'd done nothing but stare at him for some time. "I'm just surprised to see you here. I thought you'd gone. And that you'd be..." She gestured vaguely toward him.

"I couldn't leave if I tried. My wings will need a lot of recovery time before I can attempt another flight. That, and I didn't feel like walking down a mountain." His tone was wry and his expression lacked any of the haughty pride she might have expected from a dragon. While she didn't know much about them personally, she knew enough from feeds and general cultural osmosis to get the impression that dragons leaned toward cockiness rather than easy vulnerability.

"I see." Paloma's eyes flickered back and forth, landing for a moment on all that fine red skin before jumping away again. She didn't *want* to ogle him, but what could she do? Human eyes were naturally drawn to bright, saturated colors.

And he was terribly, terribly pretty.

Paloma felt her cheeks heat and desperately hoped he would credit her blush to the biting cold. She had a tendency to be awkward around strangers, but usually she could at least manage to *look* at them. She could hardly look at the dragon without her stomach dropping in a low, excited swoop.

Unnerved, she twisted her hands into the material of her robe. "Well, uh..." The words died on her lips when his tail snaked out from behind his thigh once more, this time daring to brush the spiked end against the rubber toe of her boot. Jumping at the unexpected contact, Paloma's eyes darted back up to meet his.

The dragon cocked his head to one side. His ruby eyes were fixed on her face. A slow smile curled at the corners of his full lips, effectively knocking any rational thought from her mind. "You have a very fine roost," he told her in a voice that was all deep baritone rumble.

Paloma flicked her gaze around the yard before bringing it back to the dragon. "I... yes?"

The dragon didn't blink much. Those ruby eyes were locked on her face, their slit pupils expanding and contracting in a way she found deeply unsettling, as if they wished to capture every micro-expression, every changeable shadow created by the sunrise. "Very fine," he repeated, flicking his claws over his shoulder in a careless, expansive gesture, "but your dwelling needs work."

Paloma frowned. "My dwelling? You mean my house?" She glanced over her shoulder at the home she'd grown up in, the place that was a mish-mash of lab and home and old mining shack, where all her memories and all her love found purchase. "What's wrong with it?"

"It should be bigger." Paloma turned her head back around just in time to see the dragon puff up, his broad shoulders straightening as his wings flexed behind his back. "It should be nicer, with bigger windows and stone walls that can withstand the weather at this altitude. Your deck should be reinforced to take more weight, and there will need to be a nesting wing added."

"What? I'm sorry, that's— Who do you think you are?" When she finally started to process what he was saying, Paloma bristled, all her sympathy for the rogue withering under his frank assessment of her home. Yeah, she struggled to keep some parts of it up to snuff on her own, but it wasn't *that* bad. The roof needed to be replaced, but who had the time for that sort of thing? At any rate, it still kept out the worst of the weather.

And I don't even want to know what the fuck a nesting wing is!

"You can't just stand there and judge my house!" She pushed her chin out and narrowed her eyes. "It's not like it's your problem, anyway! It's perfectly fine as it is."

The dragon made a soft whistling sound in the back of his throat and raised his hands in a small gesture of surrender. "I don't mean to offend, sweet treat. I only mean to point out how I will improve things. A fine roost like this deserves a fine dwelling to match it. Now that it's mine, I'll see it done." He tilted his head to one side, considering his words as he gazed over her shoulder. "It is much too small for me and any offspring. Don't worry, I'll have it taken care of so it doesn't trouble you."

"Did you just call me *sweet treat?*" She stared at the cords of his neck for three seconds, trying to comprehend what he was saying. "Wait, did you... this isn't *your* roost!"

The dragon made a *tsk*ing sound and raised his arms over his head. Grasping his elbows, he stretched, shamelessly showing off all that stunning dragon skin and muscle. Even his wings got in on the act. They peeked out from behind him; strong bone and flexible muscle moving to hint at just how massive his wingspan must be.

Even indignant and more than a little alarmed, Paloma struggled to keep her eyes on his face as he casually answered, "It is now."

A stiff breeze whipped up from the gorge to tangle her robe around her legs. Tugging the sides close to her body, Paloma sputtered, "No, no, that's not why I— Listen, you *are* the dragon that landed on my deck last night, right? The lost one?"

The dragon shot her another dazzling grin. It was all fang and boyish dimples. With his long, deep red hair that curled around his nape and his easy smile, he looked more like he belonged in a dragon-centric boyband than in her yard.

Spreading his arms out wide, he answered, "That's me! Your rogue, Artem Aždaja, at your service."

"Artem." Paloma cleared her throat. "Right, okay. Artem, look— I think you might have gotten the wrong impression about why I..." She trailed off, struggling to think of a way to phrase what she'd done the previous night without sounding out of her mind.

"You lured me here," he finished for her, "with your fake drag-onfire. I don't remember a lot, but I remember *that.*" His grin faded into something sharper, hungrier. "You chose me."

"I did lure you here, yes. But I didn't..." Suddenly keenly aware of the fact that she *had* invited a strange dragon to her home without considering the fact that there was a man beneath the scales, Paloma shifted nervously from foot to foot. "I was just trying to help you." She swallowed. Eyes skittering across the yard, she continued in a more subdued voice, "The town was going to call Patrol if you crossed the ridge. I couldn't let that happen."

She caught Artem's shrug out of the corner of her eye. "I figured." His fangs flashed with another grin. His chest puffed up, and there was a note of admiration in his voice when he said, "Very, very clever, sweet treat. Not many people know how to make dragonfire."

Another stiff breeze threw Paloma's hair into her face. Pushing it back impatiently, she took a wary half-step back. "Then why would you think—"

She let out a small shriek when one of Artem's wings shot out from behind him. The deadly claw at the top nearly grazed her cheek as he curled the flexible membrane around her shoulder, effectively blocking out the worst of the bitter wind.

"You're cold." Artem gave her back a nudge, spurring her into movement as she did her best to avoid making contact with his claws. "We can discuss this inside your small dwelling."

"I don't know if I should let you in my house," she replied, quick-stepping out of Artem's personal space. "I don't know you, for one thing, and for another, you're *naked.*" She eyed his easy smile with distrust. "And you seem fine enough to me."

"Yes, and I am very impressive, I know." The dragon didn't seem the least bit perturbed by her evasive maneuver. Easy expression unchanged, he artfully used his tail to halt her retreat. Yipping with surprise, Paloma backed up several feet. Artem followed her easily, his red eyes gleaming with humor. "I will give you two very good reasons to let me in, sweet treat."

"And what are those?" Paloma's heels hit the low step below her front door. Jumping with surprise, she realized that Artem had somehow managed to corral her back up the path.

Prowling closer, he extended one clawed hand to skim a lock of her windswept hair back over her robed shoulder. "First, I am not... quite recovered from the sickness," he began, a hard-edged look of consternation briefly taking the place of his cheerfulness. "I will need to eat a great deal very soon to regain the strength I've lost in the time I've been roaming. And then I will probably collapse again." He paused. "I will most likely sleep for several days."

She blanched, recalling the poor dragon's labored breathing the night before, and how his wings shook with strain as he struggled to fold them against his back. *This* dragon seemed whole and hale, but when she cast her eye down across his torso, Paloma was chagrinned to notice the way his wings vibrated faintly against his back and the very, very fine tremors that made his hands shake as he stroked another stray lock of her hair.

Before she could ask any questions, he casually continued, "And the second reason is that, should you leave me out here to sleep on your stoop, I have no plans to go away. When we set our minds to something, a dragon doesn't give up. Ever. Haven't you ever heard the story of the three dragon kings?"

Paloma rasped, "No. I don't know anything about dragons."

A sly smile curled the corners of his lips up. "You'll learn."

In hindsight, perhaps forcing himself to shift the moment he regained consciousness wasn't his wisest idea, but he didn't regret it. Being able to speak with his Chosen, to touch the silk of her hair, to feel her gaze skating over his naked skin, were luxuries he'd suffer for a thousand times over.

Artem pushed the pain in his body to the back of his mind. It was terrible, but it was nothing he hadn't felt before. The Draakonriik military required every fit dragon to serve in its elite Draakon unit for at least five years. The training he'd received for that, and all the ways he'd pushed his body in defense of the Draakonriik since, were not so far off from how he felt then, sitting at the strange, pockmarked kitchen table in his mate's pitiful little dwelling.

He did his best to cover his dismay as he swept his gaze around the room. Not even his more recent training for diplomatic service helped him completely hide it, though. What kind of home *was* this? It looked like someone had slapped three separate homes together with glue and tape — and none of them were great before the ill-thought out surgery.

While his mate seemed perfectly content, if nervous, as she fluttered around her strange little kitchen with its exposed sink and ancient *gas range,* Artem was appalled. A dwelling was *essential* to family life. It was a dragon's pride, his most treasured possession, because it was where his mate and offspring were kept safe and comfortable.

To watch his mate fiddle with the knob on a gas appliance that went out of use nearly a hundred years ago made every instinct in him rumble with discontent. Under normal circumstances, he might have stormed up to her, swept her off her feet, and demanded she stay in a hotel with him until the proper arrangements could be made to renovate their dwelling, but such things were currently beyond him.

Effectively pinned to his creaky wooden chair by muscle spasms that made spots float across his vision every few minutes, he could only frown. And plan.

His thoughts weren't entirely clear yet, but they were getting there. He knew that there were many important things he needed to do, like call his cousin to let him know what had happened, where he was, and that he would be settling down to roost with his mate in the EVP, whether the elves wanted him there or not. His parents would want to know what happened to him, and his loyalty to the Draakonriik meant he never wanted them to waste resources looking for him if it wasn't absolutely necessary. Before the sickness, all that truly mattered to Artem was the 'Riik and the clan.

But that was before he met *her.*

Taevas sought to give him a diplomatic position somewhere in the UTA, citing Artem's ability to "charm anyone, living or dead" as his qualifications, but those ambitions would have to wait. Mates came first. Once decided on, *Chosen,* they became the core of a dragon's life. A dragon's heart. Taevas, while unmated himself, would understand.

But calling his cousin would have to wait until he didn't feel as though his stomach was turning itself inside out. Preferably, it could wait until he'd slept for a week straight *and* successfully wooed his Chosen, too.

Slowly leaning his upper body onto his folded forearms in what he hoped looked like a casual move and not the desperate need to lay down that it was, Artem watched her from under half-lidded eyes. He didn't want to sleep. No matter how badly he needed the recovery time, all Artem wanted to do was drink in the sight of her and learn every little thing he could. Dragons were acquisitive and territorial by nature, so Artem didn't question the way his instinct tied his heart to hers so quickly. Once a dragon Chose, there was no going back. He couldn't even imagine it. He didn't want to.

So pretty, he thought, chest expanding with a rush of warmth. *So sweet smelling. I can't wait to find out if she tastes more like oranges or vanilla.*

"Do you eat eggs?"

He tracked her as she hustled toward the table with a pitcher of water and a thick, bubbled glass. Her hair was a mess from the wind and she still had her dirty rubber boots on, but Artem hadn't been so struck by the sight of something since his very first flight. Like seeing that first sunrise burst over a glittering horizon from high in the air, the sight and smell and sound of her burned a place for her and her alone in his mind.

"Yes," he answered, stomach cramping hard at the mention of food. He desperately needed those calories. Back home, he would have eaten pack after pack of perfectly designed protein gels to replenish his fat stores, but eggs would work. "Dragons will eat most things."

She set the glass down next to his right elbow before filling it with water from the pitcher, a fanciful ceramic number with colorful painted chickens and flowers around the bottom. "Right, okay. Um, I'll make eggs and pancakes. How many do you want?"

Briefly eyeing the pitcher, he breathed deeply. "As much as you can make." Catching her baffled look, he continued, "I haven't eaten in longer than I can remember. I need to replenish my stores before I sleep again, or else I might fall into a coma." He grimaced. "I *will* fall into a coma."

Her fingers clenched around the pitcher's handle as her face went ghostly pale. "That can happen?"

"Yes." He shrugged. "It's not uncommon for a soldier to fly for so long that when they land, they never wake up again. Haven't you ever heard of Marathon, the dragon who flew so hard and fast that he died after delivering a message to his king?"

"I guess, but I never..." Letting go of the pitcher so abruptly water nearly sloshed over the edge, she turned to head back to the kitchen, a stark, determined look on her face. "I'll make breakfast quick, then. Luckily we have a *lot* of eggs."

"Wait!" Before she could leave him, Artem gently grabbed her wrist. She was warm and silky smooth beneath his palm. "Wait, you haven't told me your name yet."

She stared down at him for a beat, lips parted with surprise. "Oh, I'm Paloma. Dr. Paloma Contreras."

"Doctor?" Artem leaned forward as much as his muscles would allow. "Doctor of what?"

"Electric field and m-weather phenomena," she answered. Her gaze flicked down to where he still held her wrist before moving around the home. "This house is mostly built as a research station. I monitor the atmosphere for signs of electric storms and m-weather, but my main focus is spotting spontaneous sapient manifestations."

Artem released her wrist slowly, but only so he could drag the pads of his fingers down the silky underside to briefly brush her palm. "Ah," he sighed, more certain than ever that he'd made the right choice. "I knew you were smart."

He watched, delighted, as her cheeks flushed. "I should go make those eggs."

This time, he let her go, but not without regret. Reaching for the pitcher of water rather than the glass, he turned her name over in his head again and again as he brought it to his lips for a long pull. *Paloma Contreras. Dr. Paloma Contreras. Paloma, my mate. Paloma Contreras-Aždaja. My mate, the* doctor.

It had an awfully nice ring to it.

Chapter Four

PALOMA TRIED TO FOCUS ON THE SCREEN IN FRONT OF her, but it was a losing battle. She hadn't been able to focus on much of anything since Artem waltzed, naked and glorious, into her house.

She glanced at the glowing numbers in the corner of her screen. By her count, he'd been asleep for twelve hours.

It was late and she was beginning to feel the strain of sitting in front of her screens for so long, but Paloma hesitated to go to bed. She wasn't sure she *could*. No one besides herself and her father had slept in the house since she stopped having sleepovers. It was strange knowing that there was someone else in her space, breathing her air, using her blankets, after so long.

It's not bad, she allowed, staring blankly at a readout of m-signatures gathering over the Sacramento delta. Normally she might feel a small thrill at the sight, her intellectual curiosity drowning out any physical discomfort she might feel, but not at that moment. Paloma's mind wandered back to the dragon in her living room. *Definitely not bad. Just... weird. Like I didn't notice how empty the house was until he got here.*

She felt like she could hear him even when she knew that was impossible. There was no way she could pick up on the rustle of blankets all the way across the house, or smell the distinct, crisp scent of him through a closed door. Logically, she knew that. But it sure felt like she could.

Sighing, Paloma pushed back from her desk, the wheels of her old chair squealing, and rubbed her tired eyes. It had been a long, tense day, and she needed rest.

The Protectorate Weather Service could wait a few more hours for her report. Not that they really cared about the fluctuations in rainfall or tamer atmospheric phenomena. They really only wanted to hear about one thing: spontaneous sapience.

That was the reason she got the funding she did, and why the PWS was so quick to snap her up after she got her doctorate. Paloma was an expert in the study of m-weather and sapient events. So far, she'd managed to locate three different hot spots before touchdown — an unparalleled success rate.

Squinting at the cluster of numbers and vivid, hot pink lines on her screen, she made a mental note to keep an eye on the movement of the cluster headed inland over the delta. It wasn't worth worrying about yet, since m-weather happened in pockets all the time, but if it merged with another cluster on its way toward the Sierras, she'd need to get on the phone with the Spot Unit so they could intercept it.

A spontaneous eruption of magic, in *just* the right conditions, could create breathtaking new life. It could also destroy whole cities if it wasn't wrangled away from a population center in time.

After what happened to San Francisco in 1906, no one took chances with that sort of thing.

Still, it wasn't worth worrying about yet. There was no immediate danger of a merge with another cluster, so she felt confident enough leaving it for the night. She would just have to check on it again in the morning. So long as her emergency alert didn't go off, of course.

Powering down her screens, she crept back through the house, straining to hear any hint that he was awake. Of course, Artem warned her that he could sleep for days at a time, but she struggled to imagine it. A day seemed reasonable enough, especially when she could see the way he flagged as the minutes ticked by over breakfast, but *days?*

Carefully closing her bedroom door, she leaned against it for several long moments. Not for the first time that day, Paloma wondered what exactly she had gotten herself into.

Sure, Artem seemed nice enough, but she got the uneasy feeling that she'd made a mistake somewhere. The proprietary way Artem viewed her home raised her hackles, but the way he looked at *her*...

I've definitely missed something.

Finger combing her hair back from her flushed cheeks, Paloma nervously edged away from the door to change into her pajamas. All the while, her eyes flicked back to the door. Did she feel safe sleeping with a strange man in her home? The door wouldn't stop a human, let alone a *dragon.*

But Artem doesn't seem dangerous. Paloma scowled. *That's ridiculous. Of course he's dangerous. He can turn into a SUV-sized dragon at any time!*

Except, she had trouble picturing him trying to hurt her. The more she tried to imagine it, the harder it became. Artem's blazing smile, the glimmer of humor in his eyes — all of it put her at ease. Would someone dangerous really smile like he did? Would they say thank you for breakfast? Would they look at her like she hung the moon?

She didn't know. Worse than her general social inexperience, she felt her lack of understanding was somehow tied to her ignorance regarding dragons. It was galling.

Pulling one of her father's old sweatshirts over her head, Paloma padded over to her nightstand to pick up her old tablet. The right corner was cracked, and the back had been pried off and resealed so many times it was more dented than her ancient truck, but just like every piece of tech in the house, it ran beautifully.

She sat on the edge of her bed and, with a furtive glance at the door, typed her query into the search bar: *Dragons + roaming.*

Chewing the edge of her thumbnail, she scrolled through the results with a critical eye. There were several hits, including a few academic articles on the subject of *Magnetic Directional Dysfunction,* which she quickly realized was the technical term for what Artem called the *roaming sickness.*

Huh. Paloma blinked several times as she absorbed the information scrolling across her screen.

A rogue dragon suffers from MDD, or the sudden misalignment of the part of the brain that interprets their visualization of the Earth's magnetic field.

She read on, her brow furrowing as she processed exactly what Artem suffered from. The misalignment led to a cascade of internal misfirings, including the instinct to find home. Dragons were ten times more likely to go rogue if they didn't have an established roost. Neurologists connected that number with the ability to then circumvent the misalignment, effectively resetting the dragon's sense of direction with the roost as their starting point.

Paloma frowned, recalling what Artem said about her "roost". Had he somehow fixated on her home and used it to restart his dragon homing beacon? If so, what exactly did that mean for her?

The more she read, the more the sinking feeling churned in her gut.

According to the experts, there were two ways for a dragon to be free of MDD: either they died of exhaustion or they settled on a roost.

Slowly lowering her tablet to her lap, Paloma turned her head to stare at the door. No, she didn't *like* the way he talked about her home like he owned it, but she didn't think he actually meant to stay. The way the article described it, it sounded like a dragon picking a roost was a *permanent* sort of thing.

There was no way he could really mean that he thought of her home as *his* now. That wasn't how the world worked.

It wasn't just some empty cliffside. It was where she'd grown up. It was where she worked, looking after huge sections of the

West Coast with her radar and the data only she truly knew how to interpret. What was he going to do? Kick her out?

Paloma jumped from article to article, her dread growing into bigger, tighter knots of unease. *Dragons: The Definitive Acquisitive History* didn't soothe her worries at all. Neither did the markedly less academic article *Caught in Claws: How One Man Found Himself Mated Before He Even Knew Her Name!*

The more she dug, the more she found: lists of tips for dealing with domineering dragon partners; guides to spotting the signs of a dragon's *Choosing;* a surfeit of pieces detailing the gruesome reports of just what could happen to someone who trespassed on a dragon's territory.

And countless posts, some of them satirical but many of them serious, about what to do if you suddenly found yourself in the crosshairs of an unmated dragon.

The thread binding everything together? *Dragons want, dragons take. End of story.*

Outright panicking now, Paloma quickly scrolled back to the article on MDD, looking for any hint that her fear might be unfounded.

...the dragon's need to roost takes precedence over all things, including eating, sleeping, and drinking. Even when the dragon is not suffering from MDD, many feel the compulsion to find one soon after puberty. It is a deeply personal as well as instinctive decision with much cultural significance related but not limited to the drive to mate and procreate.

The alignment isn't easily undone. For non-MDD sufferers, it is a great source of cultural stigma to "give up" a roost — statistically, one in three dragons report getting into a life-threatening altercation over a roost at least once in their lifetimes — but for those afflicted with MDD, losing a roost has more severe consequences. After losing a roost, a dragon previously recovered from MDD is 88% more likely to regress than those who don't.

Paloma wheezed.

Setting her tablet on the bed, she stood up and began to pace. *88% more likely to regress?*

What did that mean? That if Artem decided he wanted to stay, she couldn't kick him out for fear that he'd go back to flying until his wings gave out? That couldn't possibly be right.

Was she glad that she'd saved Artem from being shot down by a Patrol sniper? Yes. Did she wholeheartedly reject the idea that he now claimed her land as his own? Also yes.

She fisted her hair and pulled, hoping the sharp sting at her temples would help ground her as she tried to sort through her panic. She didn't know what to do. Her need to take care of her land, her father's legacy, butted up against her desire to keep Artem safe. *She* was the one who inadvertently turned Patrol on him, after all, and *she* was the one who lured him to her home. It wasn't his fault she found herself with either an unwanted roommate or a very large, very scary landlord who could kick her out at any moment.

Her only hope was that he didn't *actually* think of her land as his roost. Maybe if she found him another place to stay, perhaps on a nearby ridge or closer to the Empire Estate. Surely, Harlan Bounds wouldn't mind a dragon for a neighbor. He hardly ever left his estate anyway. Besides, being a vampire and only active at night, he and Artem would probably never even see each other. There were *plenty* of good mountaintops around. Artem didn't really need hers, right?

But if he does, he could go right back to roaming. Paloma's stomach knotted up with a painful, anxious feeling. Would dooming him to that existence be any different than calling in Patrol herself?

"Just talk to him," she muttered, stopping in front of her door. "Go see if he's awake and talk it out. If you can find him a new roost, it's an easy fix. Don't stress. Stay calm."

Disregarding the fact that it was well past the time any day-dwelling creature would still be up, Paloma slipped out of her bedroom and tiptoed down the darkened hall to the living room.

Peering around the corner, she found Artem exactly as she'd left him: sprawled in a heap of blankets and pillows on the floor between her worn couch and her feed screen.

She offered him her father's bedroom, despite the distinct twinge of discomfort it gave her, but he refused. After eating two dozen eggs and at least twice that number of pancakes — not to mention three full pitchers of water — he asked for her help building a temporary nest in her living room. Although she thought it was a strange request before, Paloma could see why he refused a normal bed.

Even with every spare bit of bedding and all the pillows except for the old, flattened one she left on her bed, it was barely enough to fit him.

Artem stretched out across the cushions on his stomach, a throw blanket haphazardly draped across his lower back and thighs. His wings were spread out on either side, each finely wrought bone and inch of his tissue-thin membrane gilded by the moonlight spilling through the living room windows.

He had one of her pillows bunched up under his arm and pressed close to his face, his nose buried as deep as it could go. With one leg hitched up, he revealed a muscled thigh and a swath of smooth skin. Her eyes traveled the length of him involuntarily, tracing the path of bone and muscle, cataloging the differences between them. Aside from his huge, claw-tipped wings and strange, talon-like feet, he wasn't too different from a human man.

A beautiful, beautiful human man, posed like a melancholic spirit in a Renaissance painting.

A flicker of movement out of the corner of her eye made her jump. Artem's tail snaked across the pillows to curl around a bunched section of a blanket and began to drag it closer. Before it could pull the blanket close enough to touch his side, it released its grip with a strange little rattle. She watched, fascinated, as his tail did it again and again, going in different directions, clearly seeking something that wasn't there.

Maybe it's a dragon-related sleep thing? Like dogs running in their dreams.

Drawn in by curiosity and the still driving need to talk to him, Paloma crept out from the hallway to stand beside the couch. She curled her fingers into her palms. Was it weird to watch her... guest sleep? Definitely. Could she stop? Paloma rocked back on her heels, a strange sensation of heaviness settling in her stomach.

She *needed* to talk to him, but she also just wanted to look at him. It was strange and exciting having someone else in her space. Of course, it helped that he was nice to look at. Artem was gorgeous. Every line of his body was finely made, and his confidence in his skin fed the curious part of her that wanted to look her fill until she understood what made him so alluring. If he didn't care if she looked, was it still wrong?

Of course it was. She knew she should leave. He clearly wasn't waking up any time soon, and she would rather be caught dead than standing there mooning after him in the dark. She wasn't the most social being in the world, but even she knew a normal, apparently well-adjusted person like Artem would think that was weird.

Shifting to creep backwards and think about her recent life choices in the privacy of her room, Paloma barely stifled a shriek when something wrapped around her ankle.

Gripping the back of the couch to steady herself, she looked down to find not a shadow monster or a skeletal hand wrapped around her ankle like her overactive imagination feared, but Artem's tail. The spiked end rested harmlessly on the floor, while the smooth portion looped possessively around her, trapping her there.

Pressing her hand against her chest to try and calm her pounding heart, Paloma slowly lifted her foot, attempting to very gently shake it off. Instead of loosening its grip, like she hoped, it only coiled tighter and higher up her leg. She silently cursed her choice to wear sleep shorts to bed rather than her usual flannel pants.

The smooth glide of his skin against hers sent a tremor down her spine. It had been a very long time since a man touched her. Despite not really missing it, Paloma was suddenly keenly aware of how potent even glancing skin contact could be.

She stared at the sight of his tail curled around her calf with wide eyes. Dragons were dichromatic. At night, Artem's ruby red skin shifted to a blue so deep, it was almost black. Only when the moonlight glanced off of him did she catch a hint of that vivid red once more.

The image of his dark tail coiled around her bare leg was startlingly erotic. The feeling of it squeezing gently was even moreso.

Gotta go! Right now, Polly! Paloma licked her lips. Opening and closing her hands, she struggled to think of a way to extract herself from his grip that didn't involve touching his tail or waking him up.

She held her breath for several long seconds, hoping that if she stood very, very still, Artem would let her go like one of the pillows.

But he didn't let her go. If anything, he only tightened his hold on her. Paloma watched with dawning horror as the muscles bracketing Artem's spine bunched, sending ripples of movement down the length of his back. It was a hypnotic sight, but she couldn't appreciate it. Half a second later, his tail flexed, attempting to pull her closer to the nest on the floor with clear purpose.

Without meaning to, she let out a small gurgle of alarm as she tried to resist the gentle pull. It didn't let up, though. The more she fought it, the more his tail flexed, as if it took her resistance personally.

If I try to shake it off, he wakes up. If I keep standing here, it might give up, or it might wake him up anyway. There was no good choice. Either way, it appeared her chances of getting away with sneaking back to her room unnoticed were slim to none. And what could she say when he woke up?

Sorry, I was just getting a glass of water and just happened to step in tail-swiping range. The kitchen was on the opposite side of the room. There was no way he would buy it.

Making a strangled noise, Paloma was forced to let Artem pull her half a step closer to the nest.

Artem lay slightly on his side. From this angle, she could see that his face wasn't completely buried in her pillow. She could make out one eye and the corner of his mouth under a fall of deep red curls. Her heart lurched. Were all dragons so beautiful, or was it just him?

She thought the dragons she'd seen in photos and on feeds were pretty, sure, but she'd never been *struck* by a face before.

The feeling of soft fabric under her bare toes snapped Paloma's focus back to her unfortunate situation. She stared down at where she stood, now firmly *in the nest,* if still on the outer edge, and raised her arms in a useless gesture of pure panic. She eyed the dozing dragon with an amazed sort of wariness. How had he not woken up yet? Most predator races were incredibly light sleepers, and she hadn't exactly been quiet.

Her chest tightened. *He must have been exhausted. To sleep this long and still not wake up? He needs his rest.* She scowled at the tail wrapped around her leg. *If only he'd let me leave him in peace!*

Hazarding a step back with her untethered foot, she attempted to lean as far away from Artem and his sleeping space as much as she was able.

It might have worked, if only Artem's clawed hand hadn't shot out to wrap around her calf, effectively freezing her in place.

"Where are you going, treat?" His sleepy voice was a deep, throaty rumble. Overly loud in the quiet of the night, it rattled through her bones and left her feeling weak-kneed and unsettled. One ruby eye stared up at her with a drowsy look of pure possessiveness.

Asleep, he was beautiful. *Awake,* stretched out and drowsy, with all his fascinating dragon skin on display, he was breathtaking.

Paloma swallowed hard. "I'm sorry," she whispered, hoping her voice didn't come out as a squeak. "I was just thinking about talking to you because I read something— I mean, I saw you were sleeping and I was going to leave but—"

But what? She stayed to admire him because he looked like every lush sexual fantasy come to life?

Artem's fingers skated up the back of her leg, tracing the contour of her calf and the strong tendons behind her knees. Each stroke of his fingers sent a rush of warmth through her blood.

"My sweet treat," he sighed, turning so he was laying more on his side. The wing closest to her folded inward slightly. It brushed her legs as it lifted just enough to reveal the soft, cushioned place beside him — and a considerable amount of skin for her to look at. His tail tugged her gently, urging her closer. "Come lay in the nest with me."

Paloma did her best to keep her eyes up and away from all the naked skin she had the mad urge to touch, just once. Just to know what it felt like to run her hands over a being of such immense power. Just to indulge herself. "That's not a good idea."

Artem didn't seem like he was entirely awake. There was a slight slur to his words and a hazy, half-aware look in his eyes. But being on the edge of sleep didn't stop him from replying immediately. "It's a great idea. I'll rest easier if you're with me."

"You're a guest," she insisted. Paloma lifted her foot again, attempting to dissuade his tail from any more pointed tugs. "I don't usually cuddle with my guests."

Not that she had any, but he didn't need to know that.

A deep rumble filled the room. The hair on the back of her neck lifted as the ominous sound rolled up and out of Artem's chest. "I should hope so," he muttered, stroking his palm up past her knee to cup the back of her thigh. It was a proprietary touch, and dangerously close to the hem of her sleep shorts. "I'm the only one you'll be cuddling with from now on."

A warning siren blared in the back of her mind, accompanied by a remembered snippet of an extremely helpful woman's magazine listicle she skimmed only minutes before.

Listen, every woman secretly wants a dragon! No shame, ladies! We can admit we love those sexy, winged hunks. But for those of us who dare to step into the clawed embrace, be prepared for growling, possessiveness, and so! much! spoiling! If you're a woman who likes her freedom to kiss and be kissed by the flavor of the night (go, girl!) you're going to want to steer clear of a dragon. Once they've decided on you, the only lips you'll be smooching are the kind that can breathe fire. Hot, right?!

Paloma's lips parted around a broken, entirely unintelligible sound. No, that couldn't be right. He'd only just met her. He was a *dragon,* for godssakes. She wasn't anything to him. There was no way he—

Artem's fingers skimmed back down to rest against the soft skin behind her knee. It tickled, but only for a moment. Without warning, he pressed two knuckles into the tendons, buckling her leg.

Arms flailing, Paloma landed on her hands and knees beside him. Before she could catch her breath or attempt to untangle herself from the mound of pillows and blankets he surrounded himself with, Artem had one arm wrapped around her waist. He dragged her down into the nest until she was nestled against the smooth planes of his rumbling chest.

Paloma gaped at the ceiling. The light of the moon made strange shapes on the warped plaster. It was something she hadn't thought about since she was little and slept in the living room with her friends. It was also something she didn't get time to admire.

Artem's wing stretched out and over her, blocking out the light and ensconcing her in a cocoon of warmth and deliciously scented skin.

"There," he sighed into her hair. "Now I can *really* sleep."

"You've been asleep for twelve hours!" It was a weird thing to quibble over, considering her position, but Paloma still struggled to wrap her head around the fact that she was cuddling with a naked dragon, let alone form a coherent sentence about it.

She felt his nose brush her forehead as he moved his head back and forth, nuzzling into her hair. His arm was a hard band around her back. It held her tightly against his chest, which had ceased its rumbling in favor of a long, soft whistle that did strange things to the butterflies taking flight in her stomach. "Got to sleep more." His voice was barely a whisper, but he was so close that she had no problem making out the words. "Better with you. Keep you safe."

"This is *my* house. I'm perfectly safe—"

"Shh," he hushed, palming the back of her head. His claws stroked through her hair in a soothing caress. "Rest, treat."

Paloma flushed. How exactly was she supposed to rest? She was plastered against a *naked dragon*. He might be on the brink of passing out again, but she was alight with several different flavors of anxiety, nervousness, and reluctant arousal. There was no way she would be able to relax enough to sleep.

"I don't have any blankets," she complained, inanely, like *that* was the reason she couldn't cuddle with him.

Artem grunted softly before removing his arm just long enough to drag a blanket over them both. She'd only just started to wriggle out from under his wing when he clamped it around her again. "Naughty treat," he murmured, sliding his palm under her sweatshirt. "No escaping a dragon."

Paloma tried to get her breathing under control. "Is this... is this a cultural thing? Like, needing to sleep with someone?"

She thought she felt a laugh rattle through his chest. "Will you stop squirming if I say yes?"

"Maybe."

For lack of anything better to do with them, Paloma curled her arms against her chest and closed her eyes. His scent and warmth was a heady swirl around her, enhanced by the feeling of being cocooned by his wing. Artem smelled like something crisp and unidentifiable. Not quite pine. Not quite mint, but something close enough to tantalize.

"Then yes." Artem's breath ghosted through her hair. "I *need* you to sleep here or I'll be insulted and... burn your weird little dwelling down. There you go. Perfect excuse to stay."

The hand pressed against her naked spine was warm, and so was the chest she could feel rising and falling. Paloma was surprised. She'd thought that, what with their breathing cold fire and all, that dragons would be chilly bed companions. That wasn't the case at all.

The longer she lay there, listening to Artem's breath even out and his heart beat a strong rhythm in his chest, the more his body heat built under the shelter of his wing. It was the coziest she'd been in... *years.*

As the stress of the day and the comfort of her position slowly began to drag her down into sleep, Paloma gave into temptation and very carefully pressed her fingertips against the skin just above Artem's belly button. Staring at the shape her hand made against his dark skin, she marveled at the texture of it.

Smooth, but hard. Soft, but sort of... textured. Red, then dark blue. Amazing.

For a brief moment, she let herself sink into the fantasy that his embrace offered.

A small, hidden part of her thrilled at the idea of such an incredible being looking at her and thinking *she* was the one worth keeping. What would it be like to be the subject of a dragon's devotion? Would it be endless nights like this, full of warmth and a sense of safety? Would his easy smile fill up all the lonely corners of her heart?

Paloma felt the muscles of her throat tighten. It was dangerous to think about. If she let herself revel in the feeling of being *with* someone, it would only hurt her that much more when she was alone again.

What was she compared to him? A frail, soft-skinned human

with no magic. Not a fierce dragon or a powerful witch. She was just Paloma, and that meant she was a sensible, reasonable arrant who knew her place in their complex world.

Artem wouldn't stay. Her life would go on. End of story.

And if that thought made something inside her shrivel up, then that was her problem to deal with later, on her own, just like everything else.

CHAPTER FIVE

ARTEM WOKE UP WITH A START. THE FOG OF SLEEP made tracing the source of his unease difficult. The feeling of something undone, of itchy exposure, made him open his tired eyes to peer suspiciously around Paloma's living room.

He clutched his Chosen to his chest. His right wing stretched out to its full length, nearly brushing the opposite wall, before he curled it back in around her. The membrane between his bones was too thin to be of any real protection from danger, but the hypersensitive nerves in his wings were a perfect early warning system. If there was a threat, he would feel it before it came close to touching her.

The spot under a dragon's wing was a place reserved for Chosen mates and offspring only. It was where a dragon could keep them safe, but was also a show of trust. The membrane of a wing was thin. If the person being shielded wished, they could tear through it with a knife or claws easily, effectively crippling the dragon.

He didn't need to know Paloma long to trust she would never, ever do something so cruel. His Chosen had a soft heart. Maybe *too* soft, if her inviting a rogue dragon onto her roost was any indication. It would be the work of a lifetime to keep the gentle creature under his wing protected from the world.

Artem filled his lungs with the scent of her and tried to calm his racing heart. It was early, and he could smell snow on the air. By his count, he'd slept nearly twenty-four hours. It wasn't enough, but it was a start.

So why did he feel so anxious?

Because my roost is unfinished, he realized, rumbling a low, displeased note. Instinct grated against the immovable wall of his exhaustion.

If he'd been fit, Artem would have stayed up all night securing the safety of their roost. He would have laid down his ash to mark his borders. He would have flown over the surrounding area to assess any danger. He would have spent hours and hours rubbing his skin against hers, mingling their scents.

But he hadn't done any of that. Instead, he *slept.*

Artem was an easy-going sort of man. Slow to anger and quick to read social cues, he didn't feel the hard bite of his instincts too often. *Before.*

Things had changed. He knew it happened when a dragon Chose, but he was still surprised by the intensity of the shift. The compulsion to roost had left him — only to be replaced by the driving desire to makesafe and nest.

He swept his gaze around the haphazard pile of pillows and blankets Paloma supplied him with. It was fine for a night, but he couldn't stomach it for much more than that. His mate deserved all the softest things. All the silks and luxurious cottons. All the down pillows and memory foam mats. While he enjoyed the way her scent saturated everything, his lip curled at the scratchiness of the flannel blanket covering them both, as well as the flatness of the pillows that came with obvious age.

His father would balk at the sight. No self-respecting dragon would let his Chosen lay their head on couch cushions and scratchy throw blankets unless there was absolutely no other alternative.

The nest was the heart of the home. The nest was a dragon's pride and where he kept his most precious treasure. A poor nest meant he didn't care for his Chosen or his offspring, that he had no respect for either. That was absolutely unacceptable.

Artem nuzzled his nose into the crown of Paloma's head, his mind whirring with plans and tasks and visions of the future. The nest was an easy fix. He could have a new mattress and dragon-grade nesting blankets delivered in a day. He'd do that first, then try to summon the energy to set a perimeter. Once he had those things done, and his strength fully returned, he would begin planning for the full renovation of their dwelling.

Until then, he would have to content himself with simply holding her.

At some point in the night, Paloma had turned over to press her back against his chest. Her long black hair tickled his skin. One of his hands snuck up under the front of her sweatshirt to cover the soft expanse of her stomach. He closed his eyes.

So this is bliss, he thought. *My mate in my arms, all soft and trusting.*

Of course, Artem had known satisfaction in his life. He'd lived and fought and fucked and soared the highest his wings would take him. He'd made his clan proud and brought more money into the 'Riik with trade negotiations than anyone besides Taevas himself. He loved his family and he loved his life. There was nothing lacking in it.

At least, he hadn't *felt* the lack.

Now that he held his Chosen in his arms and under his wing, Artem understood the feeling of deep inner expansion the elder dragons spoke of. It was not that Paloma filled a hole in his heart, but rather that her arrival made the organ bigger. He felt anchored to her. All instinct pointed to her, to this roost. It would be the greatest privilege of his life to learn all there was to know about Dr. Paloma Contreras. It would be his greatest pride to protect her, and to be known by her in return.

Reacting to the thrill he felt at the thought, Artem's tail

squeezed around the softness of Paloma's thigh. He felt her stir. One moment she was all soft and pliable in his arms, the next she was stiff as a board.

Trying to soothe her, Artem let out a long, soft whistle and rubbed the pad of his thumb under the arch of her ribs. "Shh, treat. You're safe."

Her breathing sped up. He watched, curious, as one small human hand curled into a bunched up blanket peeking out from under his wing. "I... good morning?" Her voice was husky.

Artem's cock twitched. His body was nowhere near fully recovered, but he wasn't dead. Pressed up against all her lush curves and sweet smelling skin, he didn't stand a chance.

"Good morning," he breathed into her hair. Testing her boundaries, he gently stroked his knuckles over the soft rise of her stomach. Would she push him away? He *was* a stranger, after all, and she was no dragon. Her instincts were different. There was every chance she would see his overture as a step over a line, or even an outright threat.

He would work with whatever she gave him, but first he needed to know where those lines were.

He felt her breath stutter. Paloma's thighs pressed together, keeping his lucky tail in place. "Artem..."

Gods save me. Artem closed his eyes and swallowed a groan. She had the softest voice. When she spoke to him, she usually sounded so adorably flustered, like she didn't quite know what to make of him, and it made him want to show her *exactly* what he intended to be for her: Mate. Protector. Giver.

Going by the state of her home — tidy, but showing signs of wear, with only an old, stale scent hinting at another occupant — and her apparent isolation, Artem wondered if Paloma knew what it was like to be spoiled. Did she know the pleasure of being coddled by another? Or did she live her life in this odd little dwelling, alone and without luxury?

Certainly, she didn't appear to know what inviting a dragon

into her life would mean. It was a good thing he had every intention of showing her.

Her voice was high pitched when she asked, "Shouldn't I go make breakfast? You've been asleep for ages. You must be hungry, right?"

Artem ran the tip of his nose along her temple and down her cheek. He felt her tremble against him, but she didn't move away, or tell him to stop when he brushed his lips over her cheek. When she didn't tense up, he dared to dart the tip of his tongue out — just once, to satisfy his curiosity.

Her flavor burst over his sensitive tongue; salt, oranges, vanilla, and the sweet spice of desire.

Artem really did groan then. Pressing his aching erection against the curve of her backside, he skimmed his claws over the waistband of her sleep shorts. "My sweet treat," he rumbled, "has anyone ever spoiled you before?"

Her breaths left her in tiny pants. "I... I'm not sure I know what you're talking about." She cleared her throat. "This isn't a good idea. We don't know each other. And you're a guest."

"You didn't answer my question."

He waited for several heartbeats, reading her body language to be sure he wasn't making her uncomfortable, before he slowly pressed his palm against her stomach, pushing her back into him. Her thighs clenched around his tail.

"Have I ever been spoiled?" She shook her head as much as their positions allowed. "I don't think so."

Artem wasn't sure if he should be happy or indignant on her behalf, so he settled on both. "No one's ever taken care of you?" He slid his hand up slowly, giving her time to tell him to stop, before he lovingly cradled one silky soft breast. Her skin was delicate and warm; the weight of her breast in his palm was perfect.

He held her closer. How close had he come to missing this? One wrong turn, a different choice, a missed opportunity, and he would never have known Paloma. He would never know the feeling of her in his arms, nor the sweetness of her melting under his touch. It was fate, or perhaps pure luck, that brought them together. Artem intended to make the most of the privilege.

"No one's ever lavished you with gifts or attention? Worshipped you?"

"N-no. Why would they?" He felt her hips flex when he skimmed the tip of one claw over the tight bud of her nipple.

"Why would they?" Artem gently rolled it between the pads of his forefinger and thumb even as he gave the shell of her ear a sharp nip. She gasped, body jerking, when he continued, "Wrong answer, treat."

Using the arm curled underneath her to cup her jaw, he urged her to raise her head, baring her neck to him as he gave her soft, full breasts their due. "Pretty Paloma," he breathed against the skin behind her ear. "So soft for me. So fragile and in need of coddling. Will you let me spoil you, treat?" Artem pressed the pad of his thumb against the plush skin of her bottom lip.

She parted her lips with a shaky exhale, allowing him to run the tip of his claw over the line of her lower teeth. *Tap, tap, tap.* He scraped his own much sharper teeth along the curve of her ear. "You have no idea what a dragon's capable of, do you?"

He didn't mean strength, nor the ability to harm. He meant the reputation dragons wore proudly: that they were exceptional lovers and fiercely possessive of their Chosen mates.

He wondered if she would have risked luring him to her roost if she'd known what she was signing herself up for. Not everyone wanted a committed partner, after all.

Not that it mattered. She had one now. There was no going back. Artem would not leave her. If she didn't feel the same way, he would deploy every weapon in his arsenal to win her, as was the dragon way. They didn't give up on their Chosen. They fought until the bitter end, even if that meant death — because a dragon's mate was their heart, and without a beating heart, what was the point of continuing on?

He felt her suck in a sharp breath. Her lips moved against his thumb when she answered, "I read that dragons..." She made to wet her lips with the tip of her tongue, but ended up brushing the pad of his thumb instead. He felt her thighs clench again, harder this time. "Ah. I read that dragons need a roost. That when they pick a place, they won't ever give it up."

Artem smiled against the warm skin of her throat. "That's true. Anything else?"

There was a pause before she answered, "And that if a rogue dragon loses their roost, they will get sick again." She began to squirm, pressing back against his aching cock in ways that made him hiss. Immediately, Paloma stilled. In a tight voice, she said, "If that's why you're doing this, you don't have to. I wasn't going to — I won't condemn you to death by forcing you out."

Artem froze. "You think that's why I want to touch you?"

There was nothing but genuine confusion in her voice when she replied, "Yes. Why else would you want to?"

He had to close his eyes for several long seconds. *Gods be good, this woman is going to turn me inside out.*

Doing everything in his power to keep his voice low and soothing, he said, "I am going to make you feel so fucking good, you'll never ask that question again. I'm going to wipe it from your brain, Paloma. I don't care how many orgasms it takes."

"Artem, what—"

Ignoring the way his muscles protested any movement, great or small, he rolled them both over and stretched his wings up around their heads, creating a dim, intimate space just for them. A dragon's embrace.

He dipped his head to run the tip of his nose over her cheek. "So we're clear, I am *not* doing this because I want your roost." He brushed his lips over hers, relishing the hot puffs of her exhalations and the velvet glide of skin on skin. "I'm doing this because you're my mate. You're my *Chosen* and I'm yours, remember? You Chose me first."

Even under the shadows of his wings, Artem had no trouble making out her wide-eyed expression. "You know that's not what I meant when I lured you here! I was just trying to save your life."

Artem gave in to temptation and slowly pulled her bottom lip into his mouth. It wasn't quite a kiss, but a taste of what was to come. He gently pressed his teeth into the soft flesh before running his tongue along the mark, soothing the sting. "So?" he breathed, releasing her with one last bite. "Now I owe you my life on top of just wanting you. I don't see anything wrong here."

It wasn't easy supporting his weight on one forearm, but Artem wasn't about to let this point go unmade. Easing one hand down between their bodies, he slid his fingers just below the waistband of her shorts. "This isn't an exchange, treat. This is a done thing. You are mine. I am yours. A dragon doesn't Choose twice." His clawtips brushed tight curls as he whispered against her mouth, "And *this* dragon is going to fucking spoil you rotten."

Artem swallowed her little mew of surprise. He kissed her thoroughly, with everything he had, and felt her sweetness spread through his veins like golden honey. Her mouth was soft under his, tentative in ways that made his heart ache. Her tongue darted shyly to stroke his lower lip, to skate over the edge of deadly fang. Her taste was all he'd ever wanted and more than he could have imagined.

Paloma melted under him, the tension in her spine easing away as he kissed her again and again in the semi-darkness. In between kisses, he murmured sweet things and promises. Small sounds of desire escaped her throat, spurring him on. Forcing his aching spine to lock, Artem held himself over her and gently slid his fingers down through her curls. Slick heat waited for him.

Gods.

He tore his mouth from hers to let out a long, crooning whistle. "You are going to taste so good," he breathed against the curve of her jaw. He pressed a lingering kiss there, too, just because he could. "I can't wait to brand you into my fucking soul, Paloma."

His body didn't want to move anymore, to take more weight, but Artem didn't care. He was going to do this even if it killed him.

Sliding down her body, he paused several times to kiss a particularly alluring patch of skin and to thrust up her loose sweatshirt. Full breasts with dark nipples greeted him. He lingered there for several minutes, lavishing attention on each pretty inch of her, until she was breathing hard and clutching at his hair. Only then did he move on.

Gritting his teeth against both his demanding cock and his increasingly stiff muscles, he eased her shorts down and off her legs. Glancing up at her face, Artem watched a flush spread across her chest and upward, into her cheeks.

Closing her thighs and turning her legs slightly away from him, she choked out, "I've never done... this before."

Artem's tail, still firmly wrapped around her thigh, gave it a reassuring squeeze. He forced his tone to be as neutral as possible when he asked, "Are you a virgin?"

She shook her head, but her eyes slid away from his. "No. I slept with someone in college, but it was only a couple of times. And years ago. I'll understand if maybe you don't want to—"

Giving her an easy smile, he tried not to show his relief. While a part of him might have enjoyed the idea of being her first and *only*, a much larger, more reasonable part of him understood that a virgin wasn't what he wanted. He didn't mind shyness, nor inexperience, but he didn't want to have to completely start from scratch with a partner, either.

"Oh, I *want* to," he reassured her. "I just had to check." Using one hand and his tail, Artem kept his eyes locked with hers as he slowly pulled her legs apart.

Lowering his head, he looked up at her through his lashes. "You tell me if you want me to stop. Understood?" He waited for her shaky nod before pressing a reverent kiss to her hip bone. *My brave little mate*, he thought, heart warming with pride. "That's my sweet treat."

Seeking to keep her comfortable and pliant under him, Artem started off slow. He teased her with flicks of his tongue — longer than a human's, and more useful in this task than his clawed fingers were — and listened to her soft moans, looking for cues. Gradually, her wariness faded into enthusiasm. When her fingers curled around one of his horns, holding tight as her thighs flexed around his ears, Artem's chest swelled with triumph.

Locking eyes with her, he winked once, as a warning, before sliding his tongue into the tight channel of her cunt.

Paloma gasped, nearly shooting upright with surprise as he curled the tip against the sensitive spot inside her. Not wanting her to dislodge him, Artem used his wings to carefully pin her shoulders down into the ramshackle nest. He increased the pace of his thrusting tongue, alternating between that and firm circles around her clitoris, until she arched her back and cried out for him.

And then he did it again.

And again.

Finally, when she pushed at his horns with a weak moan, Artem allowed her to rest. Hauling his aching body back up, he contented himself with more kisses — the slow, drugging kind that came from a partner well-sated.

"Artem," she breathed, dazed. It was like she meant to start a sentence, but didn't have any other words readily available. *"Artem."*

Before he could do anything more to hurt himself, he turned them back onto their sides. Keeping her back pressed against his front, he did his best to ignore the raging ache of his erection nestled against her soft curves. It was something that would have to be borne. Going any further in his state would not be an option.

Paloma lifted her head to peer at him over her shoulder. Her hair was a wild tangle and her lips were beautifully swollen when she asked, "But what about you?"

He let out a choked laugh. "I got what I wanted. Not sure my body could take anything more right now, anyway."

Her dark brows snapped together. "Are you hurting?"

Yes, but he wasn't about to ruin the moment by telling her

that. He was a 'Riik soldier and an Aždaja. He could take a little pain.

"Shh, treat." Artem smoothed his palm down her stomach and licked his lips, savoring the taste of her that lingered there. "I'm fine, you don't need to worry about me. I wanted to take care of you."

Paloma squirmed in his hold until he was forced to loosen his arm, letting her turn over so she faced him. "I'm not used to that."

His lips thinned as he took in her earnest expression. "You should be. You *will* be."

"But I like taking care of people," she insisted, frowning at him.

"Too bad. That isn't how this is going to work." He used the tip of his claw to flick a lock of hair off of her cheek. "You're my Chosen. I get to pamper you. It's my right."

Paloma arched a brow. "Your right?"

"Yes. It's what a dragon does."

"So it's all about what I want?" Her eyes narrowed. "All the time?"

Artem gave her backside a tiny pinch. "Not *all* the time. It's about what you need, too."

"And how do you know what I need?"

He opened his mouth to inform her that, as her mate, he would figure such things out with or without her help, but never managed to get the words past his throat. While he was distracted, Paloma snuck her hand between their bodies to press her fingertips against the flat expanse of muscle above his cock.

Challenge glinted in her eyes when she asked, "Am I allowed to touch you if I need to?"

He struggled to control his breathing as the heat of her palm radiated downward, tantalizing him with what could be, if only she slid her fingers down a few more inches. "I..." Artem's throat bobbed with a hard swallow. "If you want to touch me, you have my full permission. But I'm the one who gets to care for *you.*"

The air left his lungs in a wheeze as she lowered her hand to trace her thumb through the beads of pre-come sliding down his shaft. "Maybe this is what I need right now," she challenged, stroking slowly. "Maybe I *need* to care for you, too." Paloma tightened her hold and twisted upward, squeezing the flared head to emphasize her point.

Artem gasped and buried his face in her hair. *"Paloma."*

"Yes?"

He curled his arm over her back to fist the hair at the base of her skull, trying to anchor himself as she stroked him with determination that made his toes curl. Gods, his little Chosen wasn't experienced, but when she set her mind to something, she figured it out. He didn't think he'd ever seen something as arousing as her singularly focused expression as she stroked him. For a moment, it was like he was the center of her whole world.

He wanted more of that look. He wanted more of *everything*.

The muscles of his abdomen flexed as everything in him began to draw up tight. He choked out a warning, but she didn't slow down. Instead, his little mate threw a leg over his hip to draw him closer.

Guiding him to slide between her thighs, she used her hand to keep the pressure as she rocked her hips. They both groaned as his cock slid against her hot, wet skin, over her clitoris and back down again in a torturous rhythm.

Curling his tail around her midsection, Artem rocked his hips to meet her, desperately chasing the orgasm that continued to build and build and build. He quickened his pace when he felt her begin to stiffen. If she was so determined to bring him pleasure, he could be equally bullheaded.

The fact that she still came first made everything in his dragon soul glow with pride. She came first in all things. Any dragon would approve of that.

When he followed her over the edge a moment later, Artem saw stars. He clutched her as close as he dared, mindful even then of her fragile human bones, and let the waves of his orgasm crash over his tired body until there was nothing left of him.

"Oh, Artem," he heard her breathe from far away. At some point he'd closed his eyes, but he couldn't remember when. When he tried to open them to reassure her that he was fine — better than fine! — he found that he could not.

Exhaustion was sweeping him under again, he realized, annoyed by the inconvenience. Forcing the words out from between uncooperative lips, he said, "S'okay. Sleep now. Kiss you later." He took in another lungful of her scent mingling with his before he added darkly, "Fix nest, too."

"Okay." Soft hands smoothed over his cheek and his shoulders, soothing him. "Okay. Just rest now."

I don't have much of a choice, he thought, drifting slowly from the best moment of his life.

Three days passed, and Paloma wasn't entirely sure that Artem's condition wasn't made worse by their... interlude.

She chewed her thumbnail and stared at the nearly empty refrigerator. She was hyper-aware of the sleeping dragon in the living room just behind her. He'd woken up a few times since that morning, mostly to drag her in for a few drugging kisses and to watch her work until he couldn't keep his eyes open anymore.

Still, he was getting better. Every day he seemed to stay awake longer, and she felt like every time she dared to peek at him, he was a little bit bigger, his build less rangy and more healthy; his cheeks fuller, his muscles less rigidly defined.

Paloma took stock of her dwindling food supplies and tried to squelch the nervous butterflies that filled her belly at the thought that Artem might actually be able to spend time with her soon.

Paloma really couldn't tell if she was excited or terrified by the prospect.

The little slices of time she'd managed to spend with him had been... a lot. More intense than any time she spent with any romantic partner before, certainly. The problem was that she didn't know what to make of that. Wasn't it way, way too fast for that sort of thing? And what kind of sensible woman let a man just declare that he was her mate?

One who's never been touched like that before, she thought, cheeks warming.

She tried not to feel too bad about how deeply that morning meant to her. It felt like he'd fed a part of her she didn't realize was starving. It was pleasure, but it was more than that, too. It was like he'd seen inside her lonely soul and said, *No, that space is for me now. You don't have to feel that way anymore.*

Paloma leaned against the door, her heart beating an uneven rhythm in her chest. *Foolish. No one moves that fast, Polly.*

She was well within her rights to take her pleasure when and where she could. There was no need to feel any sort of awkwardness or guilt or like it was much bigger than it was. For all she knew, he got off on spoiling every person he slept with. She was practical enough to realize that just because a man said something in the heat of the moment, it didn't mean he *meant* it. It wasn't like he'd licked the good sense out of her.

Not permanently, at least.

Quietly closing the refrigerator door, Paloma slipped her phone out of her pocket to check her notifications. An alert pinged, but it was nothing urgent. The cluster was on a direct route through the Sierras. With any luck, it wouldn't join with another cluster until it was well into the unpopulated stretches of the Nevada desert. She kept her eye on it, though. Until it moved away from any major population centers, she'd keep it flagged.

After a glance at the time, Paloma slid her phone into her back pocket. She peeked over her shoulder again.

Artem lay sprawled in his nest, his head buried in one of her well worn t-shirts. He'd requested it after waking up groggy and anxious the previous day. He stumbled into her lab to grumble about her leaving "their" nest, and could only be appeased with an offering of several things saturated in her scent. Since she couldn't very well lay in a pillow nest all day, every day for an indeterminate amount of time, Paloma gave up the clothing without a fuss.

Besides the clothing, the nest had changed in other ways. The afternoon of the second day, he'd made several calls to his family, who had apparently already sent out a squad of rogue hunters — something that sounded terribly ominous to her — and were deeply relieved to hear he was well. Wanting to give him privacy, she didn't stick around to hear the rest of his phone call. In hindsight, she probably should have.

Not four hours later, a brave and probably very well-paid delivery person pulled into her driveway. To her bemusement and mild horror, he delivered one sealed package after another until, finally, he got to the massive, "dragon-grade" mattress. Even vacuum sealed and compressed into a box, it was huge. Once it was unsealed, it took up her entire living room.

The many packages were much the same, except they contained more blankets and cushions than she could count. Watching Artem unpackage them and then lovingly place them around the mattress, as if every inch mattered, made her stomach do uncomfortable little twists. It sure *felt* like he was making a home for himself in her life, but she couldn't help but feel it was ridiculous to even entertain the thought.

So far, she'd managed to fight the temptation to crawl back into his arms at night, too, but only just. Although she was fairly certain he wouldn't mind, Paloma felt weird about invading his space when he was passed out cold. For all that big talk about being her mate, he hadn't actually made any moves in that direction since. Beyond kissing her into dreamy silence and trying to get her to feel his admittedly *extremely* soft blankets, he didn't seem terribly interested in taking things further.

She did her best to ruthlessly squash the hurt that thought inspired. So what if he didn't actually mean any of it? She would be fine. She always was.

Hastily scribbling out a note about where she'd gone, Paloma pinned it to the old fashioned refrigerator door with a gaudy crab magnet from Fisherman's Wharf before creeping out of the kitchen to don her jacket and boots.

Besides the fact that Artem had come into her kitchen like a wrecking ball, it would be nice to get out of the house. She needed to think. She needed space to assess what in the gods' names she was doing. She needed to stop looking at Artem and remembering what his kiss felt like, what his tongue could do, how he made her feel like she was beautiful and special and worth so much more than what her brain could do and—

Paloma stepped out into the cold and slowly, slowly closed the door behind her. Artem had become more sensitive to noise lately, and she didn't want to wake him up. Or rather, she didn't want to have to explain why she was sneaking out.

Taking in a deep breath of the frigid, pine-scented air, Paloma briskly crossed the gravel driveway and climbed into her truck. A light dusting of snow covered the ground and the boughs of the pines around her property. A storm system was moving in, so she needed to get ahead of it if she wanted to restock her kitchen with the necessities as well as the treats she saved for the upcoming holidays. Burden's Moon was fast approaching. She hadn't had cause to celebrate since her father's passing, but if Artem stayed...

Paloma shook her head, dislodging the thought. She found herself staring at the house and chewing her lip. She sat there idling for several moments, strangely reluctant to leave, her stomach bunched up in knots.

Would he wake up and wonder where she'd gone? Would he care? What if he needed something? What if something happened to him?

She swallowed hard. Paloma knew he was a grown man who could clearly take care of himself, but old habits died hard. Besides, she might want space, but she wasn't sure she actually wanted him to *go*. The four days she spent with Artem had been the most she'd felt alive in... maybe ever.

Even sleeping ninety percent of the time, he took up space in her home. He brought color and smiles and humor when he dragged her away from her work to ask her about her life, to make sure she'd eaten, to show her just how superior his new pillows were to her ratty old ones. When he cracked an eye open to peer at her from the mound of softness in the nest, it was always followed by a sleepy grin and a soft, *"Sweet treat, I miss you even in my dreams."*

Which was *why* she needed some space. It wasn't normal to be so enamored with someone she didn't know and who could so easily sweep her off her feet.

Paloma didn't think that Artem would mean anything by it, of course, but men like him just didn't go for women like her: practical, lonely, and inexperienced. When they touched, she'd briefly felt bold and empowered, but that rosy glow faded fast. He'd eat up her heart and spit it out without ever realizing he'd done it — and it wouldn't be his fault. It would be hers for letting herself get too attached to someone who couldn't stay.

For godssakes, he's an Aždaja! What in the world could he want with you? Listening to him speak to *Taevas fucking Aždaja,* Isand of the Draakonriik, was a cold splash of reality.

Besides her land, she had nothing to offer him that he wouldn't already have. He was a member of the most powerful dragon clan in the UTA, while she was a lowly arrant scientist with no family, few friends, and a house he hated. She didn't resent her place in the world. She understood and adapted to it, to its limitations and advantages. Being an arrant meant she was unburdened by crushing instinct or a power beyond her control. It meant she was free to use her mind in creative ways, to advance her field without distraction or limit.

It also meant that she and Artem were terribly mismatched.

When he finally got over the fog of his exhaustion, he would probably regret what they'd done — or at least realize he didn't mean it when he said he wanted her to be his mate.

Swallowing around the hard lump in her throat, Paloma shifted the truck into reverse and backed down her driveway until she hit the road.

She would go grocery shopping. She would get something to eat at The Shack. She would stop by the library to talk to her friends. She would get Artem out of her system with a cold, hard slap of her small-town reality.

Even if it was the last thing on Burden's Earth she wanted to do.

CHAPTER SIX

By the time Paloma walked out of the small general store attached to The Shack, tote bags full to bursting, the weather had taken a turn. She gave the sky a withering look. The snow was no longer falling in gentle flurries, but had turned into a worryingly dense wall of white. Adjusting her bags over her shoulders, she sighed and fished her phone out of her pocket with the tips of her fingers.

The weather wasn't supposed to change so fast. Her reports showed that the snowstorm was several hours away. But when she checked the updated data on her phone, Paloma could only let out another long sigh. Even with her advanced technology, predicting the weather was like trying to guess where a handful of jacks would fall. One slight change in air pressure or sudden temperature shift from a breeze off of the ocean a hundred miles away and all her carefully examined data went out the window.

"You stopping at the library, Polly?" The familiar voice made her spine lock.

Shoving her phone into one of her bags, Paloma eyed Jack Jr. with barely disguised distaste. Her one-time high school boyfriend turned thorn in her side, Jack Jr. thought he was something special because he'd made it to the Shifter Games in his junior year of college. It didn't matter that he'd gotten his ass handed to him in the ring by a bear from Toronto. He still thought he was the big, bad alpha of Pineridge. She would have avoided him on an average day, but after his disgustingly vocal support for "putting down" her dragon, Paloma could barely look at him without wanting to swing one of her totes at his head.

Sucking in a bracing lungful of icy air, she cast her ex a dismissive look. "No. I planned to, but the storm moved in faster than I thought. I have to head back up the mountain before the road gets too icy for my tires." At a certain point, even m-enhanced autogrip tires wouldn't keep her safely on the narrow road.

Jack Jr. stepped out of the doorway of his father's store to lean against one of the awning's old wooden pillars. Generations of staples from thousands of fliers for fundraisers and babysitting services and town notices littered the pillars — layers and layers of rusted metal flakes that winked in the snowy afternoon.

Her unwanted companion shoved his hands in the back pockets of his fitted jeans and squinted at the sky. A mountain lion shifter, Jack Jr. was built lean but strong. For many years of her life, she sighed over his sandy blond hair, pretty hazel eyes, and the easy way he carried himself. Paloma had even burned with envy as she watched him go through girl after girl in their small school, waiting for her chance to show him *she* was the one he really wanted — only to have that chance come her senior year of high school and turn out monumentally disappointing.

Too bad Jack Jr. never quite got the message. He'd never shaken the fact that *she* broke up with him after a paltry two months of dating, and he'd made it her problem ever since.

"You sure you should drive in this?" He cast her a look she knew well. "My place is closer. You could stay the night and wait out the storm."

Ugh. Paloma shifted her weight and pretended to adjust the tote bags over her shoulders to hide her grimace. "Thanks for the offer, but I should be okay." She made to step out from under the awning, but Jack Jr.'s hand on her elbow held her back.

"Look, Polly, I know you're still mad about the vote last week, but you don't need to take it out on me." His voice dropped into the distinctive shifter purr so many people found irresistible. "I'm just trying to make sure you're safe. You know that it bothers me thinking about you all alone up there on your property. You'd be better off down here, with a pack looking out for you."

Paloma rolled her eyes. "You know I can't do my job from down here, JJ."

She felt his hand ghost up the back of her arm through the layers of her flannel shirt and heavy jacket. There was no response to his blatant overture, no familiar tickle or surge of butterflies. All she felt was familiar exasperation.

"The Weather Service can put someone else up there," he insisted, hazel eyes flickering to the gold of his lion as his irritation grew. "You shouldn't be alone, Polly. And you shouldn't have to work. A good mate would take care of that sort of thing for you."

And there it was, the reason she'd so quickly fallen out of her infatuation with him: Jack Jr. didn't want a mate who was equal. He wanted someone who would worship his every move, give him all the little cubs he asked for, and be happy to give up her own life to do both.

Paloma was not that kind of woman and never had been. Too bad her resistance only made Jack Jr. that much more determined to have her.

Damn single-minded shifters. It was like the longer she remained single, the more convinced he became that she was holding out on him as some sort of test.

Jack Jr. wasn't malicious. He was bullheaded and full of himself, but not a monster. They'd known one another since they were babies. If push came to shove, she knew she could trust him with her life. She just didn't always like him. Especially when he refused to actually *listen* to her.

And she certainly had no plans to let him sink his teeth into her.

Using the need to shift her heavy bags as an excuse to step out of his hold, Paloma tartly replied, "I *like* my job, JJ. You know that."

"How do you know you wouldn't like being my mate more?"

"Because I have a—" She caught herself at the last second. Blanching, she realized that she'd been about to say she already *had* a mate. The memory of Artem's easy smile flashing in the cocoon-like darkness of his wing rushed to the forefront of her mind.

Good grief, woman. You need to get a grip.

Paloma cleared her throat. "Because I *have* a brain, JJ, and I don't need you to tell me what it's good for."

Jack Jr. scowled. "Damn it, Polly, I know you've been struggling since Emile died. It bothers the fuck out of me that you won't just ask me for help. If you'd stop being so proud and just let me take care of you—" His eyes dropped to the bags slung over her shoulders. Brow furrowing, he asked, "Why do you have so much food? Are you planning on barricading yourself up there or something?"

Paloma felt her cheeks heat with equal parts outrage and humiliation. It was a low blow to bring up her father's death. It was worse knowing that he was right. If Artem's stay in her home showed her anything, it was that she *was* struggling. She had no idea just how lonely she was, nor just how tired of the emptiness in her life she was, until he showed up with his sunshine and smiles and reverent kisses.

The truth was that she had been more or less willfully ignoring it. Now that thin protection was stripped away. As soon as Artem left, she would be worse off than before his arrival.

That didn't mean she would ever, *ever* take Jack Jr. up on his offer, though.

She didn't mind that he was an alpha to his bones — the need to protect and lead built into his damn DNA — but she would never be the woman he wanted. Striving to *be* that woman would only break her into something smaller, more fragile than she already was.

If she could be with someone, it would be a person who wanted to see her flourish, not wither in his shadow.

The fact that Artem watched her work with undisguised fascination and spent a considerable portion of his waking hours asking her questions about it, as well as how she got to her position, was not lost on her. The fact that he was perhaps the *only* person who had ever looked at her with that sort of awe wasn't lost on her either.

Feeling suddenly, terribly brittle, Paloma bit out, "I need to get home." Stepping around him, she hopped off the low ramp to hustle her way across the gravel parking lot. Snow stuck to her hair and eyelashes as the wind blew it hard against her.

Of course, Jack Jr. followed. "Polly, come on! If you'd just come home with me, we could talk about things and you'd see that being my mate isn't the damn death sentence you seem to think—"

An ear-splitting roar shook the snow dusted trees.

Paloma nearly dropped her bags when Jack Jr. pinned her against the side of her truck. She pushed at his shoulders instinctively, but he didn't even look at her. The hair on the back of her neck stood on end. That roar was huge and deep. It was the kind of sound only a massive being could make. *Oh no.*

Jack Jr.'s hands shifted into razor-sharp claws and his head lifted to scent the air. "What the fuck was that?"

She lifted her eyes to the stormy sky and felt all the blood drain from her face. Even through the swirling eddies of a growing blizzard, she could make out the flash of ruby wings overhead.

Too bad she wasn't the only one. Jack Jr. let out a vicious snarl. "Fuck me, I thought the dragon turned around!" Using one clawed hand, he jerked the driver's side door open and herded her into her truck. She fell back into her seat with a wheeze. Jack Jr. kept his eyes on the sky even as he leaned into the cab to growl,

"Get your ass home, Polly. I've got to get my phone from inside and call Patrol before that dragon decides to burn down the whole godsdamned town."

Lifting her calves with one hand, he swung her legs up and into the truck before he slammed the door shut. Paloma didn't even have time to tell him not to call anyone, that Artem wouldn't hurt a damn fly, before he slapped the hood and dashed off, back into the store.

"Shit, shit, shit!" Artem's shadow passed over the parking lot as she attempted to untangle herself from her many tote bags and swing them haphazardly into the back seat. Freeing herself from the last bag, she turned back around just in time to see her huge, ruby-red dragon land in the street, tilt his massive head back, and *roar.*

The sound reverberated through the body of her truck to rattle her bones. This was no beguiling whistle. It was an outraged sound that would make any creature with a brain run and hide.

Paloma sat back in her seat for a long, breathless second. Snowflakes began to melt in her hair and on her cheeks as she took in the sight of Artem's huge body, whipped by swirling snow, advancing on her truck from across the street. She knew it was him not only because he was the only dragon around, but because she'd know the shape of his horns and the circular tattoo on his right foreleg anywhere.

Even through the storm, she could see the very aware, very pissed-off look in his eyes.

Gripping the steering wheel, she ran through her options at lightning speed.

Option one: Get out of the truck and try to talk to him. I could calm him down, but Patrol could already be setting up an m-gate. If we don't get out of here fast, he could be killed.

Option two: I get the fuck out of here and hope he follows.

Sweat beaded under the collar of her shirt. Paloma didn't feel threatened by Artem, but she always had a healthy respect for predatory instincts. Did she think he would intentionally hurt her? No, but if she pricked at the instinct to chase down prey, she wasn't sure what would happen.

But when the alternative was sitting there and watching as Jack Jr. called a Patrol squadron to take down what they thought was a rogue, Paloma knew she didn't have a choice. Artem's life was worth the risk.

Keeping her eyes locked on his advancing form, she pressed her thumb into the ignition switch. "Okay," she breathed, blindly shifting into drive. "Let's play a little game of chase the scientist, dragon man."

Artem knew terror. In his youth, he'd flown higher than he should, soaring into the shimmering layer between life and death, and he'd fought smugglers and invaders on behalf of the 'Riik for the better part of his adult life. Not even the agonizing suffocation of too little oxygen in the highest atmosphere compared to what he felt when he woke up to find his mate *gone*.

And nothing in all of his days compared to the fury he felt when his acute dragon hearing picked up the sound of another man trying to steal his mate out from under his wing.

The scent of cat shifter burned his nose even as he hauled himself up and over a small bridge connecting two low mountains. Paloma's truck had a head start, since he couldn't lift off from the ground in his larger form, but once he leapt off of the bridge, there was no way she could outrun him.

The chase thrilled his base instincts. The part of him that was more animal than man relished the flight over the treetops. Even in the driving snow and wind, he wouldn't lose sight of his mate's truck as she traversed the narrow road back to their roost. Knowing that she was headed home didn't stop the exhilaration of the chase, nor cool his anger.

She *left* him.

It didn't matter that her excuse of needing to go to the store was a valid one, since he'd damn near eaten her out of house and home since his arrival. She should have woken him. He would have hauled himself out of their nest on hands and knees if that's what it took. She wasn't allowed to go out into the world alone, unprotected, and in a fucking *blizzard.*

Worse yet, when he finally tracked her down, he found her with a shifter.

If you'd just come home with me, we could talk about things and you'd see that being my mate isn't the damn death sentence you seem to think it is.

The words rang in his ears like the call of another dragon, a hard, screeching challenge that resonated in the basest parts of his soul. Another being wanted his mate. Another being thought he could lay a hand on her, that he could be the one to protect her and shower her with affection and build a nest with her. Paloma. *His* Chosen.

The knowledge was like claws raking the back of his mind. He *would not* lose his Chosen to another. He would cut off his own damn tail before he let Paloma slip into the hands of a tiny little cat shifter, with his weak claws and thin skin and blond hair.

If he had to chase her down and kiss her until she forgot the faces and names of every other person in the world, he'd do it. If he had to keep her in their nest, naked and sated, for weeks on end to convince her there was no alternative to *them,* he would damn well do that, too.

And then he'd track down the cat and make sure he knew, without any shadow of a doubt, that Paloma was *taken.*

Artem followed her truck closely, despite the way flying so near to the ground made his still not wholly recovered body ache. It took much more effort to glide and keep himself off the ground, but it wasn't a long trip back to her home, so he gritted his teeth and endured it.

For one thing, he wasn't about to let her out of his sight. For another, he wanted to be close just in case something happened to her truck. Even knowing that standard vehicles came with weather adaptive tires that could handle snow and ice, he worried about her taking the jackknife turns that littered the way up to their roost.

By the time she pulled into the driveway, the heavy snowfall had become a screaming blizzard — and he was even angrier for it.

He touched down onto the snow covered gravel with a ground rattling *whumf,* his wings stretched up and away from his body in a display of pure, dragonish irritation. Keeping his eyes on his wayward Chosen, Artem blew out a hard breath and stalked toward the idling truck. He smacked the ground with one foreclaw. It was a clear command.

Get out of the car.

He watched Paloma's wary expression through the windshield. There was a quiet whirring sound as she lowered the driver's side window a crack. "I'm not getting out until you shift back and tell me you're not mad at me."

Artem lifted his lip with a low growl, showing her exactly what he thought of that command, as he stalked closer. When he lowered his head to glare into her window, Paloma squeaked with alarm and rolled it back up.

He let out a low rumble of disapproval. She couldn't stay in the truck forever, but he didn't care to outlast her. The weather was getting worse by the second. She needed to be back in their dwelling, preferably safely swaddled in their nest, before the weather got any worse. It was a damn shame he couldn't extract her from the truck in this form without hopelessly mangling the vehicle in the process. Maybe reminding her that he was one of the most powerful beings on Burden's Earth would help reinforce the lesson that he existed to protect her — and that came with certain rules.

Like not driving in a fucking blizzard!

It took only a thought to bend his body back into his bipedal form. Reality fractured around him as magic burned through the air, forcing his bones and muscles to realign into the shape he desired. In a blink, he stood beside her door on two legs, one hand already outstretched to yank open her door.

Paloma made another alarmed sound and threw her hands up in surrender. "Artem, wait—"

Reaching over the wheel to hit the ignition switch, he snapped, "A *blizzard,* Paloma!" She yelped when he unlatched her seatbelt and wrapped an arm around her waist, hauling her out of the truck with no trouble.

She flailed in his arms, legs kicking as he threw her over his shoulder. "Wait, wait! The groceries!"

"I'll get them after you're safely inside and not standing out in the middle of a fucking blizzard!"

Sheltering her from the worst of the snow and wind with his wings, Artem hurried her back into the dwelling. He considered carrying her all the way back to their nest, but when she continued to wiggle and kick, he worried that she would end up smacking herself on something and begrudgingly decided to put her down.

Standing in the dark entryway, she rounded on him with small fists on her hips and an expression of pure exasperation. "Are you kidding me? You exposed yourself to the town because I went to get some godsdamned *groceries?!*"

He didn't bother shaking off the snow from his naked body, nor did he care about the fact that she was puffed up with anger. Artem threaded his claws into her hair, walked her back against the door, and kissed her.

She gasped, stiffening for the span of a heartbeat before she softened under him. Paloma's icy fingers clutched at his shoulders. He slicked his tongue along her bottom lip, coaxing her to open for him. Her lips parted on a soft sound of surprise that nearly made him forget why he was mad at her.

Holding her head between his hands, Artem pressed one hard, demanding kiss to her lips after another. His worry and his anger and his driving need to show her that *he* was the most fit, that *he* was the best match, that *he* would be the one to drape her in silk and love her until the end of their days sent him into a frenzy. He couldn't decide if he wanted to lick the foolishness out of her or bite all that sweet skin until she said she was sorry for scaring fifty years off his life.

When she was panting, the scent of her desire rich and heady in the air, he managed to reel himself in enough to rasp, "What were you *thinking?*"

It took her a second to respond. *"Me?* What were *you* thinking?!" Even well-kissed and flustered, Paloma managed to give his shoulder a light, indignant slap. "I was just getting us some food! You're the one who announced your presence to the whole damn town! You're lucky it's snowing too hard for anyone to track you, or we'd probably have Patrol here already!"

"And getting us food *had* to be done when I was sleeping? You couldn't have told me you planned to leave at any point when I was up?" Artem clenched his jaw. Truthfully, he didn't mind her coming and going. She was her own person. What he couldn't abide by was the *reason* she left without a word, and the fact that she hadn't spared a thought for her safety. He didn't care that she'd probably driven the road up and down the mountain hundreds of times. One wrong move in a blizzard like the one whipping outside the door and she could have been lost to him forever.

She had to know that, which meant that she left not for some frivolous reason. Paloma wanted to get away from him. He was determined to find out why.

Keeping his claws in her hair so she had no choice but to hold his gaze, he ground out, "Tell me the real reason you didn't let me know you were going to leave, Paloma."

He watched her blink twice, slowly. Each brush of her eyelashes against the tops of her cheeks drew his eyes, trying to mesmerize him into forgetting why he was upset with her.

"I just… needed some space," she finally admitted.

Artem's chest clenched hard in response to the invisible blow.

"Because I've been crowding you?" He tried to keep the strain out of his voice, but he wasn't sure he succeeded.

It was hard to hear the words, to see the way her expression crumbled, when he'd tried *so hard* to not overwhelm her. Even though everything in him demanded he keep her by his side, he hadn't forced the issue of her sleeping in the nest. He knew the reputation for dragon possessiveness could scare a partner away, just as he easily picked up the fact that his Chosen had been alone for a long time and would need extra care. He tip-toed around her, keeping a tight leash on the instinct to press and press until she yielded. Artem made the choice to coax her into his arms slowly. In the moments when he was awake, he tried to be as casual and charming as possible, to ease her into living with a dragon in the only way he was currently capable of.

Had he failed that endeavor, or was there something else he was missing?

If it's because of that damn shifter, I'm going to hunt him down and turn him into a rug.

Paloma stared at his chin, her expression tense. "No," she whispered, "I just..."

"What, treat?" He rubbed the pads of his thumbs into her temples, aching to soothe. "Tell me."

"I just started to get a little freaked out about how nice it is to have you here." He watched her lower lip tremble when she paused. "I've been alone a really long time, and it just— it's been nice, but I started to think about what it'll be like when you are back to normal and how you'll either want to go or won't want me like this anymore and I..."

She sucked in a shuddering breath. "And I know it's crazy to *want* you to stay with me, like this, when I have nothing to offer you but a nice cliff. I shouldn't even consider it, since we've only known each other for less than a week, but I have been." He felt the bite of her nails in his thick skin when she curled her fingers into his shoulders. "I also know that this is going to end, and it'll hurt."

Artem dropped his hands to curl his arms around her back, dragging her close. He buried his face in her damp, windswept hair and cursed himself up and down. "Oh, treat."

This was his fault. Because he'd been nest-ridden since they met, he wasn't able to do the things a mate should. He hadn't secured their boundaries. He hadn't insisted on her sleeping in their nest. He hadn't spent more than snatches of time with her.

He hadn't made her feel like he intended to *stay*. It was no wonder she had her doubts about him.

"I'm sorry," he breathed into her hair.

She stiffened. "I don't want an apology. It's fine that we're not compatible. I shouldn't have let my daydreams get the best of—"

Artem dropped his head to scrape his teeth against the corner of her jaw, silencing her. "Stop that. We're plenty fucking compatible, treat, but I've neglected you. No wonder you ran. An overlooked mate always acts out."

She let out a gusty breath. "Artem, that's not what I meant!"

"No, but it's the truth." Leaning back so he could look into her exasperated face, he told her, "This is because I haven't had the chance to follow through on my promises, Paloma. You don't feel secure. If you felt like I wouldn't leave you, would you have disappeared on me today?"

She chewed her lip before answering, "I don't... Maybe? But it's too soon to know that sort of thing. Humans don't just jump into marriages or matings like this. We take our time to figure the other person out first."

"Have you ever been married before?" He nudged her forehead with the tip of his nose. "I see no marriage sigil there, so I assume the answer is no. And I don't think you've ever been mated before, or else that *cat* wouldn't have been trying so hard to convince you to be his."

"His name's Jack Jr. and he's not my type anyway." She wrinkled her nose at him. "What's your point?"

Ugh, Jack Jr. Even his name was atrocious. No junior *anything* belonged within ten feet of his mate.

"My point is that just because you *think* you know the proper order of things, you haven't actually experienced it." Cupping her jaw, he softened his voice and continued, "There is no reason to believe our ways are incompatible. I can Choose you and make you feel secure in this mating, while you can get to know me in the human way. These things are not mutually exclusive. We are not the first dragon/human coupling, I can assure you."

A cautious hope lit her dark eyes. "You really mean that?"

"I do."

"How can you have already decided on me? You don't know me. I'm not glamorous or powerful." She swallowed. "I'm just an arrant. Shouldn't a dragon Choose someone... *more?*"

"I don't understand why you seem to think that being arrant makes you *less.*" He pressed a firm kiss to her brow, as if he could burn his confidence in her into the skin there. "You're a genius, treat. I've watched you at your computers and with your codes. When you talk about your work, I barely understand it and *love* that. What you do is so far over my head, you might as well have wings of your own."

She flushed. "You don't mean that."

Artem shook his head, amazed. Drawing her away from the door and into the warmth of the dwelling, he promised, "I do mean it, and if I have to spend every day of our lives convincing you that I'm really fucking proud to be mated to a genius, then it's no hardship."

When they were standing by the edge of the much improved nest, Artem began the process of helping her out of her boots and her sodden jacket. Paloma let him do it, though she wore a befuddled look on her face the entire time. "What are you doing?"

Plucking the phone out of the pocket of her jeans, he answered, "I'm getting you naked. I don't have energy for much more than that. I need to make the most of it."

Paloma lifted her arms, helping him raise her long sleeved flannel shirt over her head. "What about the groceries?"

He considered the shirt for a moment before tossing it into

the nest. It smelled like her and it was soft enough to stay amongst his carefully curated selection of blankets and pillows. Her jeans, on the other hand... "The truck is cold. They can wait until we're done."

"Done with what?"

Artem paused his fiddling with the brass button of her jeans just long enough to send her a slow smile. "Mating, of course."

CHAPTER SEVEN

ARTEM LOVED WATCHING THE WAY PALOMA'S EYES widened when he laid her back in the nest. "Oh," she breathed, glancing around like she was seeing the pillows and blankets and huge, dragon-grade mattress for the first time. "It's so soft!"

He smiled crookedly down at her. "That's the point. A nest should be the most comfortable place in the dwelling, so a mate never wants to leave it. Why do you think I kept trying to get you to feel the blankets?"

Paloma flushed. Her skin was a lovely reddish gold, and when she blushed it took on a luminous quality that made him sigh with pleasure. Like the sun shining through silk. He fleetingly hoped that their offspring would take her color, but he knew it was unlikely. Dragon genes were dominant in the extreme. No doubt their babies would take on the flashy colors of his line. Adapted to impress even at a glance, dragons were notoriously colorful.

"I thought you just *really* liked blankets," she replied, wiggling a little. "I get it now."

Artem dipped his head to smile against the curve of her naked shoulder. "So you'll stay in the nest now? Always?"

A shadow passed over her expression. "Artem... As much as I want to, I'm not sure this is going to work."

Undeterred, he skated one hand up her naked leg, gently urging it to bend up and to the side as he settled into the cradle of her thighs. His wings flexed outward once, stretching aching muscles, before they curled inward again, sealing them both in a comforting semi-darkness. "Why not?"

He pressed a soft kiss to the column of her throat and listened to her answer turn into a sigh. "Because we don't even know each other."

"Then let's get to know one another." He skimmed his hand up her thigh, tracing the curve of her side and upward, until he could curl his fingers around her jaw. Lifting his head to meet her searching gaze, he said, "I am Artem Aždaja, son of Constantin Aždaja and Valerie Sundström, first cousin to the Isand of the Draakonriik. I have a little sister named Alexandra, who is ten years my junior and a huge pain in my ass."

Artem lowered his head to slide his lips over the swell of her cheekbone, the fringe of her lashes, the smooth plane of her brow. "I went to school for business and economics, but I ended up serving in the 'Riik air force immediately after school. I left fifteen years ago to help Taevas run the trade arm of the treasury." He stopped for a moment to press his lips against hers. Slowly, with all the reverence he felt for the place she now held in his life, he lavished her with one kiss after another.

Gods, but he would never get used to the taste of her: the tart bite of orange with smoky vanilla, layers of rich flavor that made him want to run his tongue over every inch of her.

When she was soft and dazed beneath him, he continued, husky-voiced, "For the past two years, Taevas has been training me to take up a diplomatic position."

He felt her take in a sharp breath. "You're important. *Really* important."

Artem shrugged as he made his way down her throat, over her collarbone, to run his tongue along the curve of her breast. He followed the sweet curve reverently, with all the adoration it deserved. "I suppose. I do what I have to for the 'Riik and for Clan Aždaja. It's our way."

"But don't you see? That's why we're not going to work." He felt her shudder when he gently, gently closed his sharp teeth over the delicate skin of her nipple. "You're— *important*. I'm just a scientist. You can't stay here with me."

Blowing a cool stream of air over her wet skin, he looked up at her through his lashes. "Who says?"

Her cheeks were flushed a dark red and her eyes were hooded, but even desire couldn't wash away the real fear he saw in every line of her expression. Her voice was whisper soft when she answered, "I live a very small life, Artem. I always have. What if it turns out you can't stand it?"

Artem laid his head on the soft skin of her chest. Her heart beat a quick rhythm under his ear, a soothing song that called to every part of him. "I don't care how small your life is, as long as there is room for me in it."

Her hand came up to brush the curls away from his cheek. She traced the crown of horns with the tips of her fingers, her eyes glittering with tears in the half-light filtering through his wings. Outside, the wind howled. "I'm scared that if I make room for you, it'll crush me when you leave."

"Why do you think I'm going to leave you, treat?" He rubbed his palm up and down the inside of one silky thigh, soothing her. "Tell me where this fear comes from so we can conquer it together."

Her eyes closed. "My mother didn't stick around. She hated the mountain, and I think she got frustrated with my dad. He wasn't... He wasn't the most attentive person." There was a wealth of old hurt in that simple statement. Artem hated hearing, knowing that there was no way to erase the hurts of the past for her. "He loved me, but he was always preoccupied. It never really felt like he was all there with me. Once I was old enough, I was basically on my own. The only time I really got to spend with him was when we worked on stuff together and when he needed me to take care of him."

Artem watched her throat convulse, his chest constricting hard with sympathetic pain. He didn't like hearing what he suspected was true: that his mate had never really known true affection, let alone what it was like to be cared for. He wanted to believe her father must have loved her, but he couldn't wrap his head around the idea that the senior Contreras would let his child become his caretaker when she was so very young.

"For my whole life, it was really only the two of us," she continued, fingers threading through his hair in an unconscious search for comfort. "Dad wasn't attentive, but I loved him. He taught me everything he knew. He raised me by himself." A tear slid out from under her lashes to dampen the wispy hair by her temples. "And then one day he dropped dead while fixing a generator. I tried to do CPR, but it didn't work. I've been alone up here ever since."

Artem turned his head to kiss the spot directly over her heart. "Is that how you want things to stay?"

She let out a shaky exhale. "No."

He could feel the truth of that single word in his bones. His mate was terribly lonely and probably had been her entire life. At some point, that need for companionship and affection warped itself into the driving desire to care for others — only to have the one person she loved in the world brutally ripped from her in a way that made her feel like it was *her* fault.

It was no wonder she didn't trust that he would stay. There was probably a large part of her that, like a wounded animal, lashed out with fear at the idea of being hurt again.

Artem took in a huge breath. The scent of her, vanilla and orange and that sweet spice of desire, comforted the aching creature in him that longed to fight an opponent that couldn't be harmed. Her hurts were his now. He couldn't fight them for her, but he could support her, love her, until they faded to dull memory.

If it was possible, he would keep her safe under his wing forever. He couldn't undo the wounds of the past, but he could make damn sure there would be none in her future.

Speaking directly against her heart, he said, "A dragon only Chooses once, Paloma. We can't help it. It's like a space opens up inside of us when we Choose, but it's a space that only fits one person." There was a scientific reason for Choosing, he knew. Something tied up in that same troublesome, essential part of their brains that held their sense of direction. But he didn't particularly care about the specifics of it.

Paloma Chose him. It was a done thing; their lives were one now.

He kissed her chest and felt her heart rate pick up. "You want to know why I Chose you? Why I'll never leave you? Why I don't care that we come from different backgrounds, or that my life will have to change so I can be with you?"

"Why?" It was barely a word, more of a soft exhale, as if she feared speaking too loudly would chase his conviction away.

Raising his head, Artem held her gaze when he answered, "Because you Chose me first, when I was at my lowest and most afraid. You drew me down from the sky and saved my life. That kind of courage is..." He stopped, unable to find the right words. "It's so rare, Paloma. A heart like yours, a *mind* like yours, deserves to be treasured."

And dragons were, by instinct and by culture, a deeply acquisitive race. They didn't pass up the chance to have something unique and beautiful and priceless.

When Paloma's expression crumpled around a watery smile, her words apparently lost, Artem resumed his slow touches, his reverent kisses. He pressed his fingertips into the spaces between her ribs. He dragged the tip of his nose along the length of her collarbone. He coiled his tail around her calf and dragged it upward, sliding slowly over slopes of muscle and delicate skin.

The cradle of her thighs was slick and hot against his skin, but he didn't rush. Artem took his time brushing his skin against hers, branding them as mates to anyone with a sensitive, predator's nose. He paid attention to each finger, every inch of her skin, and the soft fall of her long black hair.

Finally, when she was twisting and rocking beneath him, seeking some relief from the driving need for friction, Artem sat up and pulled her with him. The light streaming through the windows was muted, but it felt harsh after the velvet shadows of his wings. When her pliant form was straddling his lap, Artem made quick work of enfolding them in darkness once more.

He'd fucked other women before, of course, but never like this. *This* was reserved for his mate. His winged embrace, his complete trust, given only to the woman who was the center of his universe.

Gripping her hip with one hand and his cock with the other, Artem pressed his forehead against hers and rasped, "Are you ready, treat?"

Paloma's soft hands cupped his jaw. "Yes."

The soft gasp she made when she sank onto him for the first time would be forever seared into his soul.

Artem curled his fingers around her waist, clutching her tight as her muscles contracted around him in a rippling wave. Heat and silk. That's what Paloma was, how she felt wrapped around him. Like a brand and an embrace and a homecoming and a dive off of a cliff all wrapped up into one perfect, delicate creature.

He buried his nose in her hair and groaned when she shifted her hips, rolling upwards in a tentative rhythm. She was perfect. Her scent was perfect. Her cunt was perfect. Everything about her was perfect.

And she was *his*.

His hips snapped upward, meeting her with a hard, proprietary thrust. Her core was a vice of hot, slippery muscle, and he never wanted to leave it. Artem lowered his eyes to the space between their bodies to watch her rise and fall. Tilting her backward *just* enough, he adjusted their angle until she gasped — and provided him with the spectacular view of his cock sliding in and out of her.

Paloma's voice was a breathy moan when she asked, "What's your favorite color?"

"What?" Artem's hips stuttered as he rose to meet her.

"Your favorite color," she pressed, nails digging into his shoulders. A glance up to her face showed eyes that were glazed, half-lidded, and a lush mouth swollen from his kisses. Even so, there was a determined set to her jaw that made him grin.

He let out a huff of laughter. Of *course* his mate would maintain her focus even now, when he was as deep inside her as he could go. "Orange. It's orange."

She picked up speed, the muscles of her stomach clenching as she brought her hips up and then back down again. Every time he rose to meet her, Paloma's breath hitched. "Mine's purple."

She started to lose her rhythm and her luminous skin glistened with sweat, so Artem used his hands on her waist to help her, tilting her back just a little more so he could pull out almost all the way before burying himself to the hilt once more. When her blunt little teeth nipped at his neck, he brought her down hard. Their bodies met with a burst of electric pleasure and a dull slap of skin that made them both groan.

"Tell me what your favorite dessert is," she demanded, breath hitching, as he shifted to lay her back down into the nest.

Shoving a bunched up cushion under her hips, he let himself move like instinct demanded: hard, determined to brand as well as to love. He wanted her to feel him between her legs even when he wasn't there. He wanted her to know that they belonged to one another now and every moment to come. He wanted her to come so hard, she saw fucking stars.

Curling one arm under her back to clutch her shoulder, he braced the other over her head and snapped his hips forward and backward, again and again. "Ice cream," he bit out. "Vanilla."

Paloma's hands roamed his chest, his back, as she arched her spine and breathed those beautiful, erotic sounds in his ear. With each thrust, she made a new one, as if she was keeping time for him.

"I like— I like strawberry cake." When her hands couldn't find a place to settle, she stretched her arms up and out to skim her fingertips over the thin membrane of his wings.

Artem lost his rhythm as an electric current snapped down his spine, the nerves in his wings sizzling with her innocent touch. He choked out a moan and had to hold still for a moment to regain his composure as the pressure of his impending orgasm eased.

By the startled look on her face, he figured she didn't know how sensitive his wings were, or that touching them during sex felt pretty damn close to her skating her fingers down his cock, but his Paloma was a quick study. With a sly smile, she ran her fingers up the finely wrought bone and then back down again, her touch dancing along his skin like a trickle of water.

He shuddered and dropped his head into the crook of her neck. Stars winked across the backs of his closed eyelids as she did it again, torturing him with sensory overload.

Tangling his fist in her hair, Artem panted hard against the soft, sweat-slicked skin of her throat. He wasn't the only one who could play the game of sensual torture, though.

Unwrapping his tail from around her calf, he slid it between their bodies to stroke her heated skin. He was careful with the spiked end, of course, but he knew what he was doing. In seconds, Paloma was rocking her hips into his with abandon, a string of broken babble falling from her lips as he picked up the pace.

"My mate in *my* nest," he purred, dragging his lips up to hers. Pausing to give her plush lower lip some much-needed attention, he panted, "Do you want to come, sweet treat?"

She curled her fingers around the hard bar of his wrist above her head. It was smart to find something to hold on to. With the way he was moving, he might've had to keep pulling her back down otherwise. "Yes," she gasped. "Yes, yes, *yes.*"

"Who do you want to make you come?" He pressed an open

mouth kiss to her jaw, tasting her again. *Gods, I fucking love how she tastes.* "Who do you want inside of you when you do?"

Her cunt was hot and wet and perfect. When she clenched around him like a vice, Artem cursed under his breath before giving her ear another nip. He wasn't sure she'd done it on purpose, but he wasn't about to let her take control this time. He wanted to hear her say she was his and that everything, including her beautiful, tight cunt, belonged to him. "Tell me, sweet treat. Tell me who gets to spoil you. Tell me who gets to fuck this perfect cunt. Tell me who gets to make you come. Tell me who you belong to. Tell me who you Chose, treat."

He pulled out nearly all the way, palmed her thigh to push her open as wide as she could go, and then thrust back in. *"Tell me."*

Paloma threw her head back, her throat arching in a beautiful display of passion, and cried, *"You!* Artem! *Artem!"* Her breath stuttered before she began to take in huge, gulping breaths. "Artem, *please."*

Every instinct, every dragonish desire, howled with delight at his victory. This beautiful creature with a mind too brilliant for him to ever fully understand was *his.* He'd won her. He'd built her a nest. He'd kissed her and pleasured her and chased her.

More important than any of that, though, was the fact *she* Chose *him.*

Artem brought his wings in close, sealing them into a smaller, darker space full of heat and the scent of sex and every soft sound she made, and kissed her. His tongue tangled with hers as his tail stroked her fast and hard, matching the pace of his jagged thrusts. When she splintered apart beneath him, it was the most beautiful thing he'd ever seen.

He didn't think he would ever get tired of the way she reached for him in the moment of purest pleasure, as if she needed him to anchor her there, to keep her from flying away entirely.

Using the arm under her back, he lifted her chest up to press hard against his, bringing them heart to heart, as he chased his own orgasm. Paloma's head lulled back into the blankets as he buried himself to the hilt one last time and gave her everything he had.

Gasping for breath, he slumped until they were both buried in the pillows and cushions and wonderfully soft blankets. Artem slid down her body just enough to lay his head on her chest, greedy to hear the racing heart that meant so very much to him.

One limp hand came to rest on his tussled curls. Paloma's voice was dazed, almost slurred, when she asked, "So, what kind of entertainment feeds do you like?"

Chapter Eight

The storm raged for three days. They didn't notice.

Paloma drifted in and out of a dream state, too blissed out and content to do more than the bare minimum of work. Of course she kept her eye on her readings, but there wasn't much to be done. With the blizzard, she couldn't very well go fix her equipment or tune anything up. She was wonderfully housebound with her dragon, who turned out to be one of the chattiest people she'd ever met.

She *loved* it.

Artem had a beautiful voice. She found it soothing to listen to him go on about his life in the 'Riik, a place she'd never dreamed of going but now desperately wished to see, as she worked on her tablet or went out to check on the chickens in their specially insulated hutch. He was her shadow. Despite the lingering effects of his fatigue, he couldn't be pried from her side.

Not that she wanted to. The time they spent together was the warmest, most content she'd ever felt. They shared every meal and watched feeds together. As the snow built up in huge drifts around the windows, they played board games — he was terrible — and Paloma finally came to appreciate the joys found in a lovingly crafted nest. Her bedroom became a glorified closet, for all the time she spent in it.

She still wasn't quite on board with Artem's plan to completely overhaul the house, though.

"Treat, we can't sleep in the living room forever," he explained, claws carding through her hair. They were bundled under several blankets and lounging against a mound of pillows after a filling lunch of stew and homemade bread. It turned out that Artem was quite the cook, which was a delightful discovery, considering she really only enjoyed the steady formula of baking.

"My dad built this house," she argued. "I don't want to knock it down just because you think we need more space."

"We *do* need more space." To prove his point, he stretched his wings out as far as they would go. The clawed tips touched the far walls with a smug little scratching sound. "See? What happens when we have offspring? There will be more wings, and little ones who don't understand that flying in the house isn't advisable."

Paloma flushed to the roots of her hair. "Who says we're having kids?"

Artem tugged on a lock of her hair. "Did I imagine that pamphlet I saw in the lab?"

She shook her head and willed her blush to go away. It wasn't like there was anything to be ashamed of. Yeah, she'd looked into having a baby on her own. There was nothing embarrassing about that. It wasn't the concept of him knowing she had researched sperm donors that made her flush to the roots of her hair. It was the memory of him finding the pamphlet, setting it on fire, and then bending her over her desk to screw her senseless that did it.

He was a modern man and didn't have a problem with her contemplating single parenthood, but Artem was still a dragon. She was beginning to understand that sometimes a dragon's instinct overruled logic. More often than not, that instinct involved making absolutely, entirely sure Paloma knew who she belonged to. She didn't have to be a genius to understand that the suggestion of her having another man's offspring sent her poor dragon's territorial instinct into a tailspin.

Not that she was complaining. If it got him to have sex with her on her desk again, she'd be happy to order more pamphlets.

"Well, that was before," she replied, sniffing, as she swiped to the next page of the *San Francisco Light* article she was reading. "I don't plan on rushing into having kids right now."

Artem dropped his head down and angled his neck so she was forced to catch his eye. His brows rose. It really wasn't fair that he was so pretty even when he gave her a *look*. "Is this sudden change of heart because you still aren't sure about me? Or is it because the thought of a brood of dragon offspring makes you nervous?"

"Neither." Actually, the thought of a bunch of tiny, winged menaces filling her home with raucous laughter and movement made her chest tighten with acute longing. Artem's children would be rambunctious and lively in ways she never had the chance to be. She didn't have to think too long to come to the conclusion that being the mother to those children would be the greatest joy of her life.

Still, she wasn't in a rush.

Setting her tablet in her lap, briefly frowned at the lack of signal — the storm really had done a number on the things, including the signal relays placed around the mountains — before she turned to press a lingering kiss to Artem's cheek.

"It's not that I'm worried or that I don't want to have your babies," she assured him. "It's that I don't feel alone anymore. I want to know what it's like to be with *you* and just you for a while before we decide to do that. We have time to just enjoy each other, don't we? When it happens, I'll be happy, but right now..."

Artem's grin was huge and breathtaking. "I like that idea." He nudged her temple with the tip of his nose. The tail coiled around her waist gave her a possessive little squeeze when he said, "I like having you to myself, sweet treat."

She didn't fight her own grin. Would hearing him say how much he adored her ever get old? No, probably not. Paloma didn't think the butterflies in her stomach would ever really go away, either. Not when Artem was there to look at her like *that*.

"We still need to renovate the dwelling, though."

Paloma's smile fell. The butterflies flew away and were replaced by tiny knots of guilt. "Artem, my dad built this house. I can't just gut it."

Drawing her close, he gently argued, "Treat, your father didn't care for this dwelling. He might have built it, but he didn't *care* for it. The appliances are decades out of date. There are cracks in the walls. Your windows aren't properly sealed and I don't believe the insulation is sufficient for this altitude." He hooked a claw under her chin to tilt her head up. "Mate of mine, did you *ever* see your father work on this dwelling unless it was absolutely necessary? Or did he treat it like he treated you — as long as it was standing, it no longer needed his care?"

She flinched. Her sinuses began to sting with unshed tears as she considered the blunt but reasonable question. "I..." She glanced around and tried, for the first time, to see her home through his eyes.

He was right. Her father never really cared about making things nice. He would repair things, sure, but he never bothered to make things comfortable, or to improve their home. As long the roof kept the rain off of his lab, he didn't care if it leaked elsewhere. As much as she loved the place, she struggled to keep up with all its mounting problems that resulted from years of patchwork repairs and slapdash construction.

And if she were truly being honest, Paloma didn't think her father would give even a passing thought to the home if he were still alive. The lab was all that mattered. Artem could build a Hearst Castle-style behemoth and her father probably wouldn't have noticed.

She clung to the home because it was all she'd ever known. It was a familiar companion in her loneliest days. That didn't mean it had to stay that way, though.

Paloma blinked back tears as Artem crooned a soft note in her ear. The sound was both apology and comfort. "Okay, I see what you're saying," she whispered hoarsely.

She could feel Artem's chest puff up with pride next to her when he rasped, "Ah, my sweet—"

"*But,*" she interjected, "I want to keep my kitchen."

Paloma watched him grimace. "The kitchen is ancient, treat. Wouldn't you rather have something new and airy? I have more money than we can ever spend. Let me make it nice for you."

"I want to keep the parts of the mining shack. I like that it's part of the history of the home." She paused, thinking, before adding, "But I will allow you to replace the appliances."

Artem huffed. If he wasn't grinning from ear to ear, the sound might have come off as annoyed. "My, what a generous little mate I have."

She lifted her chin and teased, "Aren't you lucky I'm so ni—"

The squeal of an alarm cut her off. Artem stiffened, instantly on alert, as Paloma dove for her phone.

"What's that? What's happening?"

"That's my cluster alert," she explained, unlocking the screen with a touch of her finger. She stared at the reading for the span of several heartbeats, trying to process what she was seeing, before she lurched upward and out of the nest.

"Paloma!"

She didn't stop to explain as she hurtled out of the living room and down the hallway. Throwing herself into her lab, she immediately saw all of her screens lit up with an emergency alert. Huge, flashing warnings covered the monitors.

A wave of nausea rolled through her as she bent over her main monitor to triple check the readings. There was no mistaking it. There was no glitch or error from the weak signal.

A familiar hand settled on her lower back. "Paloma, tell me what's wrong."

She gripped the edge of her desk so hard her knuckles bleached white. "The cluster I was tracking," she began, voice thick with panic, "the storm must have knocked it off course. My data just got its delayed refresh and recalculated its course."

She nodded to the screen, her stomach twisting. "My signal is weak because of the snow pile-up. That's why I didn't get the alert sooner." Fear made her breath short when she continued, "It joined with a cluster over Tahoe and is on course to land in the mountains. Here."

Artem hovered close, his concern palpable. "I don't understand. What does that mean?"

"It means that we're about to have a full scale spontaneous event right here in Pineridge."

His wings flexed out in a sharp little movement as the real scope of the danger finally settled in. "A spontaneous event. Like... like in San Francisco?"

Paloma felt the blood drain from her face. "No," she answered, lips strangely stiff, like they didn't want to form the words, "San Francisco survived their event. A town the size of Pineridge will be wiped off of the map." Worse, it would not even be the first time.

There was a reason Pineridge had been settled and then abandoned so many times over the centuries; why it never really grew beyond mining shacks and distant homes and one perfectly situated research station.

His claws dug into the fabric of her shirt, pricking her skin. "Why?"

She turned her head to look at him. "Because that cluster is huge, and if it touches down in a populated area, the magical blowback of the birth will level everything within a fifty mile radius."

Artem's eyebrows snapped down over his eyes. "Birth?"

"Yes, birth." Paloma swallowed. "An event like this isn't just an m-storm, Artem. It's the creation of a new being."

He stared at her for a long moment, perhaps trying to comprehend something even she, one of the world's foremost experts on the subject, struggled to wrap her head around, before his expression smoothed out. A seasoned Draakonriik soldier stood in the place of her usually easy-going, smiley Artem. "Tell me what you need me to do."

She shook her head. "We need a Spot Unit to draw the cluster away from the town. We need to *evacuate* the town, but I don't know how. With this snow, they won't have anywhere to go besides the storm shelter. They *might* survive it in there, but depending on where the cluster touches down, the odds aren't great. The chance gets better if a Spot Unit can draw it away, even a little bit, but..." She glanced at her phone and seethed. "The fucking storm took out all but the weakest signals. I won't be able to get a hold of them in time."

Artem peered at her. "Where is the Unit stationed?"

"The closest one is in Auburn. They have m-gates on command so they can meet a cluster wherever it lands, but it won't make a difference if they don't know one's coming."

He nodded toward her screen. "Show me on the map where it is."

She frowned at him. Fear and panic were a buzz under her skin. "What? Why?"

"Because I'm going to fly there," he explained, matter-of-fact.

Paloma blanched. "Artem, it's too far. You're the one who said your wings still can't take too much flight. What if—"

"It doesn't matter," he said, cutting her off with a hard look. "This is about your safety, Paloma. That always comes first."

"Your safety matters too," she protested. She couldn't take the thought of the town being wiped out, but the idea that something terrible could happen to Artem made her feel like the floor might open up and swallow her whole. She wouldn't survive that.

Artem skimmed the backs of his claws over her cheek, but his expression didn't soften. "Show me the map. Let me protect our territory, treat."

Her breaths came out as short pants. Gods, but the fear of losing him so soon after finding him was enough to steal the breath from her lungs. "What if something happens to you? What if—"

He squeezed the side of her neck, anchoring her. "Nothing will happen to me. Do you trust that I will return for you, Paloma?"

She felt the vicious sting of tears even when she answered, "Y-yes."

"Then let me do this. Let me show you that I can be the mate you need." He bent to brush his lips against her forehead. "Trust me, Paloma."

"I do trust you." She looked back at the screen, at the snarled lines of vivid color that warned her of impending disaster and creation. "I just can't lose you, Artem."

"You won't," he promised.

And even though it tore her up inside, Paloma held onto that promise as she showed him the quickest route to the Spot Station. She held even tighter when she stood on the deck, arms wrapped tight around her middle, and watched her mate leap off of into the gorge, his great wings unfurling to catch the icy wind.

Far below him, the world was white and calm. After days of vicious wind and driving snow, the air was still. The sun reflected off of the snow in a radiant glow and Artem pushed his wings to take him higher. The wail of an alarm rang off of the granite cliffs, spurring him on.

He couldn't pretend to understand half of what Paloma specialized in, but he knew the danger m-weather could do. The Draakonriik was home to thousands of high rises and specially designed roosts, all of which were equipped with advanced warning systems for this sort of thing. It didn't happen often enough for him to experience it in his lifetime, but he'd seen the photos of San Francisco's devastation. When m-weather hit, it could wipe out whole cities in the blink of an eye.

Besides, no dragon flew for long without encountering a strange storm or two — what he realized Paloma called a *cluster*. Dragons were trained to use their ability to see fluctuations in the magnetic field to avoid them, lest they want to be caught in a patch of magic so thick, it could change your perception of time or turn you insides out.

Not that he needed the experience to convince him. If Paloma said something was a threat, he wasn't about to hesitate. It was his privilege to defend his mate and his roost. Even though circumstances prevented him from marking his territory as he should, Artem would defend it and her with everything he had.

His only regret was his lack of harness. If they had one, he would have been able to take her with him, to fly her out of danger even if they failed. But they didn't have one, forcing him to leave his mate vulnerable in their unsafe dwelling.

So he pushed himself hard, though his body protested the treatment. It meant nothing to him. Even if it killed him, he would do this.

The air began to warm as he swooped down from their mountain. It wouldn't take him nearly as long as she thought to get to the Spot Station, but he still worried about leaving Paloma. He wasn't a fool. He knew that his mate wouldn't just sit and wait for help. No doubt Paloma was already in her truck, despite the snow drifts and the ice, headed to the town.

Artem shoved that thought aside with considerable effort. He couldn't think about what would happen if her tires lost traction, or if she got stuck. He couldn't consider what might happen to him if he were to lose his heart and soul to a dangerous road and reckless courage.

So he threw himself into flying faster, into pushing himself harder. Unfortunately, there was no wind to carry him, and the air crackled with the ozone and electric scent of magic. It rippled along the toughened skin of his hide and through the membrane of his outstretched wings.

He could see the change in the magnetic field, too: The denser the magic in the atmosphere, the more warped the thin, nearly invisible fabric that guided him became. Artem could even taste it on the back of his tongue.

Magic of the wild, primordial kind had a sharp, almost bitter flavor. *Like blood,* he thought, dread pooling in his stomach.

He was barely down the mountain. With the magic pressing in from all sides, even the gathering clouds over his head began to warp, their once fluffy shapes stretching into ominous altostratus swirls.

What once was a beautiful, bright day rapidly became dark. Artem didn't need light to see, but he *did* need the magnetic field to find his way. The sudden loss of it as it distorted and tangled before his very eyes brought back the vivid memories of his rogue flight, of the madness that was roaming, of the compulsion and bone-deep despair. His stomach rolled as he soared lower, dipping into a gorge connected by a rail-thin bridge.

Fear and the need to protect were a heavy fist in the back of his mind, hitting him again and again. *Go faster! Go!*

He needed to move. He needed to keep Paloma safe. He needed to *go.*

But it was useless. There wasn't enough time, and he wasn't at full strength yet. Even if he had been, Artem didn't think he would have made it. Not that it mattered. He was distracted, so he didn't notice the opening of the m-gate until it was too late.

His head turned, eyes darting downward, just in time to see the fracturing of time and space that allowed a Patrol squadron to pour through, their bolt guns raised.

Fuck!

He wheeled upward, trying to change course so he didn't fly within range of the bridge, but he was markedly less agile in his larger form. His dragonish body was built for long distance travel and endurance, while his human form allowed him the flexibility of quick flights and agile movement. That was why most dragons soared so high. Too close to the ground meant they couldn't outmaneuver enemies.

In a desperate last ditch effort to keep them from shooting, Artem let loose a stream of cold fire over their heads, but he knew he was too close.

The Patrol unit didn't even flinch. Clad in matte black armor and smoky face shields, they held their position as he soared over them — and shot.

Artem expected the instant, searing pain of bolts through his wings, his chest and belly, but there was none. Instead, several small barbs buried themselves in the first, tough layer of his skin and, with a low click, connected with one another to form a mesh of light around his body.

Only *then* did the pain start.

A current of pure electricity coursed through him, forcing his wings to seize in mid-air. Artem let out a roar of outrage as he plummeted onto the narrow strip of bridge. The mesh tightened, drawing his wings in against his body with a snap as he rolled into the barrier *just* tall enough to keep him from falling into the yawning gorge below.

The whole bridge shook with the force of his fall. The sound of it echoed off of the walls of the gorge and the sluggish river below. Artem tried to move, his eyes swiveled upward to watch the magic-heavy clouds as they continued to bear down on them, but he couldn't even twitch. His muscles were locked, each one drawn tight as the mesh convulsed around him, conforming to his shape.

It was all he could do to let out a deep, desperate rumble as the squad moved silently toward him, their clawed fingers on the triggers of their guns.

They were like fucking wraiths, fitted in black and faceless, their tall, elvish bodies moving without even the rustle of cloth. Artem knew an elite unit when he saw one. He was a soldier himself. He knew how a creature willing to kill moved.

Every last one of the squadron moved with a catlike lethality. Even the snow under their boots didn't crunch, as if it too feared what would happen if an elf turned its attention on it.

Artem didn't fear them, though. His fear lived outside of him, in the heart and flesh and blood of another. Whatever happened to him didn't matter, so long as Paloma survived.

But she wouldn't if he didn't *move.*

The mesh was unlike anything he'd seen before. Nothing, as far as he knew, existed that could restrain a dragon. They were too damn strong. Only the vilest, most complex curses could manage it — until now, apparently.

The harder he struggled against the glowing mesh, the tighter it constricted around him. He could feel it biting into his skin with a strange sizzling sound every time he dared to flex.

Terror for his mate and burbling outrage made him roar, but the sound remained locked in his throat as the ribbons of light closed around his snout.

Head forced down onto the snowy asphalt, Artem panted and watched a pair of black, steel-toed boots step into the snowflakes his panting breaths swirled in the air.

He couldn't see the Patrol soldier's face from his angle, but it wouldn't have mattered anyway. The helmet he wore had a smoked glass front piece that covered him from chin to forehead. It was an imitation of the expensive glamours the Sovereign's Guard famously used. A fine intimidation tactic.

Behind that glass, there could be anything and nothing. The highest level Patrol soldiers were little more than elf-shaped voids radiating cold, swift violence.

"Rogue, you have been caught trespassing in elvish territory." The voice was deep, but heavily modulated. If there was any emotion in it, the helmet's mic saw it scrubbed clean.

The soldier crouched slowly, oblivious to the urgency pounding in Artem's veins and the danger brewing over their heads, until he was balanced on the balls of his feet. Like most elves, he was built of powerful muscle and dense, almost unbreakable bone. Artem flicked his gaze over the soldier's chest and helmet. A rumble built in the back of his throat.

Captain, the Solbourne crest on the left side of his chestplate declared. Second only to the General of Patrol, Valen Yadav, the captains of Patrol were some of the fiercest beings in the EVP. The rumor was that climbing the ladder in Patrol meant slitting the throats of those above you. To climb as high as captain, this man had probably done much, much worse.

"Hmm..." The captain holstered his weapon before he balanced his wrists on his knees. Matte black clawtips stretched out from gloved fingers and drummed against his padded kneecap. "You didn't move like I expected you to, dragon."

Artem tried to thrash, to shift, to do *anything*, but all he managed was a wild-eyed look and a sound that, if he were human, might have been a muffled scream.

In the distance, a crack of unnatural lightning lit the dark clouds.

Paloma! Artem imagined her careening into town, desperate to help evacuate the people she knew and loved, as he lay there on the snowy bridge, seconds away from having a bolt put between his eyes.

He thought of her alone in that run-down dwelling, and how her heart would break if he let her down. He thought of the innocent lives at stake, and how his pride, his heart, his very being was tied to this place and the love his mate had for the people who lived there.

He couldn't fail them. He couldn't fail *her*. Artem refused to lose the home he'd only just found.

The mesh was like a thousands of tiny brands cutting into his flesh, and his muscles jumped with the unnatural current being forced through them, but Artem didn't let the pain stop him. Straining so hard spots floated in front of his eyes, he forced his body into its bipedal shape.

Immediately, tension rippled through the assembled squadron. A line of boots appeared in front of him, the barrels of their guns aimed straight for his head as Artem forced his body to do exactly what the mesh *didn't* want.

Panting hard, Artem ignored the pain of the mesh reforming

to his new shape and shook head, forcing one of the barbs out of his cheek by scraping it against the road. He ignored the way the asphalt bit into his naked skin. He even ignored the guns. Nothing but Paloma mattered.

"You," he growled through the gap in the mesh around his mouth and nose. "Fucking *listen* to me!"

A gloved hand grasped his jaw, pinching until the insides of his cheeks bit into his teeth. Black claws dug into the skin as the captain turned Artem's head more fully toward him. "Never known a rogue to shift and start making demands before." The modulated voice might have been amused, if only it didn't sound so infuriatingly robotic.

Speaking through the discomfort, Artem spat out, "There's an m-storm brewing right over your head. I'm not a rogue. Not anymore. I'm just trying to save my mate! You need to call a Spot Unit!"

The helmeted elf tilted his head to one side. Another flash of lighting reflected on the smoky glass hiding his face. "There are no registered dragon residents in this area, but there is a m-weather research station. We haven't received any word of a spontaneous ev—"

"Paloma's relays lost signal during the blizzard!" Artem jerked against his bonds, too frenzied to do more than attempt brute force. "There's a cluster right over your fucking heads and if I don't get help or get her out, she and everyone in town are going to *die!*"

The captain turned his head to the soldier standing next to him, bolt gun raised. Artem got the feeling that they were communicating, but their helmets were probably programmed to keep inter-unit conversation muted.

After an infuriatingly long few seconds, the captain turned back to Artem. "You know Doctor Paloma Contreras, the arrant assigned to the Pineridge research station?"

Artem lifted his lip to snarl at the elf. "That's my *mate.* My mate, who is going to die if you don't let me go!"

The captain sat back on his heels once more. Withdrawing his hand from biting range, he lifted it to touch the underside of his helmet, just below his chin. There was a low, hydraulic hiss as a latch released. Using a clawed thumb, the captain lifted the helmet up and off of his head.

A deep cobalt face stared down at him. Shiny locks of the darkest blue, shaved close on the sides and mussed from his helmet, sprang from the top of his head. A silvery scar bisected his forehead, left eyebrow, and the top of his cheek. Artem knew the tremendous force it would take to scar an elf like that — and what it meant that the captain didn't bother having a healer see to its removal.

The captain's eyes were a flinty, vivid blue that gave nothing away. Artem's instant impression was that this man was a seasoned soldier who wouldn't think twice about putting him down if he deemed it necessary.

"Now, we can't have that," the elf drawled. Artem blinked, momentarily surprised by the twang he detected in the elf's unmodulated voice. "You're trespassing in elvish territory, dragon, but I'll give you a temporary pass if you explain what in Glory's name is going on here."

"Let me go," he grunted. "Let me go and I'll explain."

The elf raised his scarred eyebrow. "No."

Artem slammed his shoulder against the asphalt and bellowed, "Look! Look at the sky! Can't you *see* it? Smell it? Fucking *anything?*"

The captain glanced up, but if he saw anything unusual, he didn't show it in his expression. "Weird weather, but not unusual for this area."

"Godsdamned weak-eyed elves." Artem glared through a hole in the mesh. "There's a cluster *right here,* right now, captain. If we don't move, you and everyone in that town are going to be blown to pieces."

And he'd die before he just let that happen.

As Artem struggled against the mesh, the captain stood up

and walked a few paces away to speak to another soldier. One of the squadron nudged his shoulder with the tip of a boot. "Stop squirming, dragon," a new modulated voice commanded. "You'll only cause yourself discomfort."

Artem shifted until he lay partially on his side and glared up at the soldier. Lean and tall, they stared back at him from over the barrel of their gun. "I'm not going to stop. Not until you let me get my mate. Don't you elves understand matehood? Don't you *know?*"

Truthfully, Artem didn't have the faintest clue if the elf could possibly understand what it felt like to have a mate, to know that they were in mortal danger while he remained helpless. Rumors were that elves had a compulsion just like many of the races that lived and ruled the UTA, but the damn tight-lipped bastards never would confirm or deny it.

But going by the way the elf standing in front of him stiffened, he thought the rumors weren't far off.

"Once we assess the threat, we will investigate—"

"Investigate? *Investigate?*" Artem let loose a rattling hiss of pure blue fire. If his tail was free, it would have lashed back and forth with barely subdued violence. "My mate will be dead by the time you finish your investigation! And so will you!"

"Doubtful. It takes a lot more than bad weather to kill an elf."

Gods save me from the arrogance of elves! Artem glared, hissing, "Wanna test that theory?"

He watched a gloved hand tighten on the butt of the gun. "Dragon, do not—"

A sharp whistle cut the elf off. Instantly on alert, the soldier took one precise step back as the captain came striding back. Casting the soldier a sharp, reproachful look, he said, "We can't reach Dr. Contreras by phone or by relay to confirm your information, dragon."

Artem felt like he couldn't breathe for the panic that was quickly overtaking him. Every second he spent on the ground, every minute he argued with these elvish soldiers instead of getting help or just flying off with his mate in his claws, was another moment lost. A dragon was supposed to protect his mate above all things. To fail so soon after Choosing her, after being Chosen *by her...*

The thought damn near choked the life out of him.

In a voice that was all broken fury, he begged, "Please, I don't care what you do to me after — just let me save my mate. Nothing else matters to me. *Please.*"

There was no flicker of compassion in the captain's eyes. There was no sympathy or understanding. He was too well-trained to show any reaction to a proud dragon's begging, save for an almost imperceptible shift in his body language.

"The safety of our citizens comes first," he crisply replied. "We can deal with you after—"

A huge crack of unnatural lightning, lit blue and green and vivid magenta, sliced through the darkened sky to strike the rocky floor of the gorge. Every soldier on the bridge turned as one to level their guns on a threat they couldn't fight. Artem gasped and turned his head as much as he was able to peer over his shoulder, his dread a solid knot in his stomach.

Behind him, the lightning bolt hovered, frozen mid-strike. All around it, dozens of other, smaller bolts sizzled in the air, casting a terrible glow over the bridge. And beyond that awful, astounding sight, a single white truck barreled down the road and onto the opposite side of the bridge — a dragon, wings pulled up high and one clawed hand dug into the metal roof, standing in the bed.

CHAPTER NINE

PALOMA KNEW THAT ARTEM PROBABLY WOULDN'T approve of her risking her safety to warn a doomed town, just as she knew he probably expected her to do it anyway. It was the most harrowing drive of her life. Even with her special tires, and even with her lifetime of experience driving the road, she nearly crashed several times before she careened into town.

Jack Jr. and his father were already hustling people to the small storm shelter by the fairgrounds, which was a small relief. The shelter was built back before the war, with reinforced concrete layered with warding sigils. It would be tough to knock down, but with an event the size of the one brewing over their heads, she doubted even it could survive.

Not that she told them that, of course.

People were already panicking, trying to get a hold of neighbors who lived in the farthest flung corners of town, hidden away behind pines at the end of spindly dirt roads. Not everyone would listen to the sirens, but for all that they were a far-flung bunch, Pineridge's residents tried to look out for one another. They would do their best to get everyone to safety.

As soon as she climbed out of the truck, the nervous sweat coating her body chilling instantly, she was swarmed by people.

Hands grasped her arms and a sea of worried and annoyed faces pressed in close, all of them talking at once.

"Polly, what's happening?"

"Did you see something on the radar?"

"What are those clouds, Polly? Do we really need to evacuate?"

"This is ridiculous! You can't just turn on alarms like that for any bad weather. I'm going to file a complaint with the Placer County Council to have you—"

"You shut your fucking mouth, Todd." Jack Jr. elbowed his way through the crowd, pushing out an overzealous were, a veteran of the the Great War, who couldn't seem to stop asking about her radar and whether it had picked up something more nefarious than a storm. The were took one look at the shifter bearing down on him and hopped backward, moving into the relative safety of the shelter and her small pack.

Jack Jr. rounded on Todd, a middle aged arrant who never particularly liked anything, but liked women telling him what do the *least*. He snarled in Todd's fleshy face, "Get in the damn shelter. If I hear you say one more thing to Polly, I'm going to make sure your wife finds out about exactly why you spend so much time chatting with Jeanine at the restaurant, got it?"

Todd paled. The old, healed marriage sigil between his brows stood out starkly against the pallor of his skin at the threat of his wife finding out about the affair nearly half the town was unfortunately privy to. "I just don't think that this is anything we needed to be dragged out of our homes for," he protested. "How do we know she isn't just panicking?"

"Because I'm actually good at my job," she answered tartly. "Unlike *some* people, who got caught watching explicit entertainment feeds instead of running the school they're in charge of."

Before a red-faced Todd could reply, Jack Jr. shook his head sharply. Grabbing Todd by the scruff of his neck, he gave him a shove in the direction of the shelter. "Get inside, idiot."

After hitching up his sagging slacks, Todd cast one last mutinous look over his shoulder before hurrying away. Jack Jr. clapped his hands to get everyone's attention and bellowed, "Everyone else, too! Inside *now!*"

Paloma was as surprised to see everyone jump to follow his orders as she was to see Jack Jr. giving them — and not in his usual arrogant way, either. He held himself with the air of a man who knew what he was doing, and people took comfort from that grim confidence.

It was like she was finally seeing him in his element, protecting people, and she wondered if that solid core of steadiness she saw was new, or she'd been blinded by his fruitless quest to win her.

It was probably a bit of both. Jack Jr. was an alpha, after all, and until his father gave up the ghost or otherwise handed him power over their small pack, he really didn't have much room to breathe, let alone do what his instincts probably pressed him to. She briefly wondered if he'd be calmer, less of a dick, if he actually had room to stretch himself.

He needs his own pack, she realized with a little stab of guilt.

The sight of him guiding families into the shelter lit a spark of hope in her belly. No, they would never be compatible, but she had hope for Jack Jr.'s development yet. *Maybe* if he actually got a little of the responsibility he craved, he wouldn't be such an asshole.

After helping a little girl and her mother, a new addition to the town Paloma hadn't met yet, into the shelter, Jack Jr. stormed back to her. Clamping a hand around the back of her neck in a purely *alpha* move, he commanded, "Now tell me what's going on, Polly."

If she wasn't so terrified, she would have rolled her eyes. *Nope, he'll probably still be an asshole.*

Wiggling out from under his hold, Paloma checked to make sure there were no listening ears around before she explained the situation. When she finished, she could see the hard lines of stress in Jack Jr.'s handsome face. She'd struggled for years to not see him as the same petulant, bratty boy he was for so long, but just then, with real fear for others burning in his blue eyes, he finally looked his age.

"You couldn't send out an emergency signal to the Spot Unit?" he asked, eyes flickering back and forth between blue and lion gold.

"No, but I sent someone out to deliver the message." She swallowed convulsively. Her fear for Artem was a jagged shard of glass in her throat. What if his wings failed? What if the cluster caught up with him? What if something happened to her? What would that do to him?

Jack Jr.'s gaze sharpened on her face. "Who?"

Lifting her chin, Paloma told him, "My mate."

His boot slid backward through snow turned muddy with countless footsteps, before he lurched forward again to lean against the side of her truck. His expression was shell shocked, but not angry like she feared he might be. *Probably because he never actually wanted me as a mate,* she thought, wishing she could give him a good punch to the gut without breaking her fool hand. *Damn stupid mountain lion.*

"What?" he barked out. "Who? When did this happen?"

A crack of lightning lit the sky over his head. Fear was a cold drip in her veins, pushing out any discomfort she might have felt. "It doesn't matter! He's flying to alert the unit right now. If he gets there in time—"

Jack Jr.'s brows snapped down in a look of pure, stubborn confusion. "Flying? What is he? A bird shifter? A—"

Sucking in a sharp breath, she told him, "He's the dragon, okay? And he's going to be the one to save our lives, so if you'd quit interrogating me, we should get into the shelter before the storm gets any worse." It might not save them if the cluster touched down too close, but she would stay with them regardless.

"The *dragon?*" Jack Jr. reeled backward, his expression a mask of incredulity. "The rogue?"

She dug her elbow into his ribs to get some space to pass him.

Heading for the open shelter door across the slushy parking lot, she bit out, "Yes, but he's not a rogue anymore, he's—"

He grabbed her elbow. Swinging her around to face him, he demanded, "Did you send a dragon to get help?"

"Yes," she answered, seething. If he said one word against her dragon, the man actively trying to save their lives, she didn't care if he had hard, shifter bones. She would haul off and hit him. "Have you got a problem with that?"

"Polly, listen to me." Jack Jr. drew her in close. His expression was stark. There was no jealousy there, no anger. He was just pale, his lips set in a grim line. A stone of dread dropped in her stomach.

"Listen," he continued, speaking fast, "I called Patrol after the dragon landed in town. They couldn't find him because of the blizzard, but they set up perimeter sensors around the mountain."

Paloma's mouth went dry. "What... what are you saying?"

She felt his fingers tighten on her arm before he answered, "I'm saying that if your dragon flew anywhere over the mountain, they probably already shot him down."

Paloma didn't think. She didn't panic. She *acted.*

When Jack Jr. tried to wrestle her into the shelter, she bit and clawed and fought him until he had to choose to either let her go or find some rope. When he stood in front of her truck, trying to reason with her, she put it in drive and nearly ran him over, forcing him to dive out of the way. He bellowed at her as she drove off, but Paloma didn't hear him.

She didn't care what he thought. She didn't care about anything other than finding her dragon.

Her mind raced as she took the slushy, icy roads, her eyes wide and her knuckles white from her death grip on the wheel. Every few seconds, she used voice commands to check for signal, hoping that the farther she went down the mountain, the higher the chance that she could contact anyone, *anyone* for help.

Lightning flashed outside her windshield as the sky darkened. A strange sound followed — distant, like tiny fireworks popping at the same time — and made the hair on the back of her neck stand on end.

That had to be Artem, didn't it? Or was it her imagination, conjuring images of him being shot down from the sky to land in a broken pile by the river?

Bile crept up the back of her throat. Tears threatened, but she blinked them away. There could be no tears when she needed to *focus.*

"Check signal," she commanded, voice breaking. "Check—"

"Weak signal uplink acquired. Would you like to make a call, Dr. Contreras?"

Relief nearly made her swerve over the line. Sucking in a ragged breath, she rasped, "Yes! Call..." Who? Who could possibly help in this situation? No one she knew personally, and a Spot Unit wouldn't save Artem.

Except...

"Oh boy," she muttered. "Am I really doing this?"

"I'm sorry, I didn't hear you. Can you repeat that?"

Clearing her throat, she tried again. Her voice cracked with nerves when she said, "Call the last outgoing number, please."

"Of course, Dr. Contreras. Calling Taevas Aždaja."

She held her breath as the dial tone rang through her truck's speakers. Once, twice, and a third time. Just when she was about to scream with frustration, her hopes shattered, a click came through the speakers.

"Is this my cousin, or his lovely new mate?"

Taevas's voice was impossibly deep and smooth, like something deliciously indulgent. It had a cultured edge to it, but the same strange cadence she recognized in Artem's voice. At any other time, she might have been intimidated by a voice like that, by the fact that she was speaking to one of the most powerful people in the UTA without invitation.

But her mate's life hung in the balance. Her people's lives, too. She didn't have time to think about the fact that she was just a lowly arrant, cold calling one of the most terrifying beings in the world.

"This is Artem's mate." She tried to keep her voice from breaking, but she didn't succeed. Worry for her mate was a blade against her throat. "I'm sorry to call you, but I don't know what to do."

Instantly, the playful drawl vanished from Taevas's voice. *"Tell me what's wrong, Paloma."*

She was surprised he remembered her name, but didn't waste time saying so. Speaking as fast as she could, she relayed the situation, including the broken relays, the m-storm, and the Patrol squadron that likely had Artem in custody, if not already in a body bag. By the time she finished, she felt like a chain had been wrapped around her chest, slowly squeezing until she couldn't take anything more than shallow breaths.

"Pull over, Paloma."

"What?" She turned a corner. Soon, she'd hit the River Bridge, the tiny spit of engineering that connected her mountain to the rest of the Sierras. It was the only way off the mountain — by vehicle, of course. It would have been directly in Artem's flight path, so she headed that way as fast as she could.

"I said pull over." The whip of command was impossible to miss, and almost as impossible to fight. It was like he'd reached through the speakers to grab her by the throat, forcing her to do as he commanded with nothing but his presence, his deep, deep voice. Paloma found her foot hitting the break before she'd even realized she'd done it.

There was movement on the other side of the line. Hushed voices, too, like people were coming and going around him. *"Are you stopped?"*

Paloma panted, her whole body trembling. "Yes, I'm— Why did you—"

"*Good girl.*" It was a silky purr, but beneath the softness there was nothing but sharpened steel. "*Now you're going to tell me your exact coordinates. You have that on your phone, don't you? Send them to me now.*"

"I..." She blinked hard. Her phone was mounted on her dash and open to her satellite maps. With a trembling hand, she tapped the screen until she got confirmation that her position had been sent.

There was a dull ping from his end. "*Ah, that's a good girl. Very good. There we go. Now wait just a moment and don't move, sweet Paloma. Your clan is coming.*"

Before she could ask what was going on, the line disconnected.

Paloma stared at her phone in disbelief. *What could he possibly be planning?*

Her answer came a bare minute later when, to her shock, an m-gate broke the universe open right in front of her truck.

A massive dragon emerged first, his wings folded neatly against his broad back. Taevas was instantly recognizable. A deep, royal violet, he wore a black on black suit that was cut to emphasize his build and wings. Two tall horns arched high over his head, framing a hard, beautiful face matured by centuries. Two smaller ones, similar in size to Artem's, nestled beside the much larger pair, giving the strange, dragonish impression of a crown.

His hair was long and black, with twin braids threaded by his temples to keep it out of his eyes and, she guessed, from getting tangled in his horns. She couldn't be sure from her position, but she thought she saw hints of silver strands in those braids, too.

Two more dragons quickly followed him through the gate. Neither were as intimidating as Taevas, who carried an aura of pure, unchecked power, though they were wearing svelte body armor and clearly carrying weaponry.

While she gaped, the m-gate closed with a teeth-rattling snap.

Taevas sauntered forward to tap on her window with a single claw. She fumbled with the button, but eventually managed to roll her window down.

"My, you *do* smell delicious," he said by way of greeting, his smile all sharp teeth and sin. Taevas was perhaps one of the single most handsome beings in all the UTA, if not the entire world. Too bad he was also *terrifying*.

Paloma's brain short-circuited. "I..."

He reached through the window to brush a lock of her hair behind her ear, just like Artem loved to do. Claws traced the curve of her cheek in what she'd come to recognize as a distinctly dragonish gesture of possessiveness. Paloma's throat constricted painfully as he said, "Now, my sweet new clanmate, let's go save your wayward dragon, shall we?"

Never in her life did she think she'd go toe-to-toe with a squadron of armed to the teeth, scarier-than-anything elves in the middle of a bridge *during a spontaneous m-event,* but that didn't stop Paloma from doing just that.

As Taevas and his guards sprang from the back of the truck, wings unfurled, she threw herself out onto the bridge. One look at Artem lying prone on the ground, wrapped in some sort of sizzling, glowing net, and she bolted.

Guns swung to aim her way and a series of shouts rose up, some strangely robotic, but she didn't heed them. Panic was a raw note in her voice when she yelled, "Get away from him!" Eyes on her mate, she stormed up to the person between her and Artem, the only soldier without a helmet on, and pushed him with every bit of strength she possessed.

Well, she tried.

The elf was as big as a damn house, so he didn't move an inch, no matter how hard she tried to move him out of her way. Lightning fell in a slow-moving, unnatural waterfall around them when she demanded, "What have you done to my *mate?!*"

"*Paloma, stop!* I'm fine! Please don't—"

She sucked in a gasp and made to lunge around the elf, to get on her knees and fucking *crawl* if she had to, but a gloved hand held her bicep, restraining her. The elf peered down his nose at her.

Ignoring the way Artem howled with outrage at his handling of her, he dryly asked, "Dr. Contreras?" Luminous blue eyes with vertical pupils flicked over her shoulder. "And... Isand Taevas. I don't remember receiving word that you were planning a state visit."

"That's because I'm trespassing, Captain Aman." Taevas strolled up to the armed group with a swagger that couldn't be forced. It was like he lived for the moment when all eyes were on him and had no problem with the guns joining the party. His wings flexed behind him — huge and deadly, with those wicked clawed tips. "Let's get things settled, shall we?"

Captain Aman arched a brow. "Settled, sir?"

Taevas glanced pointed at where the elf held her arm and then to the side, where Artem was gnashing his teeth and straining against his bonds.

"Yes, this mess." Flicking a clawed hand up, he gestured toward the lightning streaked sky. "I assume you'll want help with this." Something in his charming facade darkened. His easy smile fell away when he added, "I'll need you to take your hand off of my clanmate first, though. If you want to keep it, of course."

Captain Aman held Taevas's stare for a handful of seconds before he slowly released her arm. Paloma didn't hesitate. As soon as she was free, she dove for Artem.

The captain's drawl was just a smidge tighter than before when he asked, "Clanmate?"

"Yes. Our dear doctor is the Chosen mate of my most beloved cousin, Artem Aždaja, the dragon you have ensnared at your feet."

Taevas smiled, but it wasn't pleasant. It was like the grin a seal sees just before a shark sinks its teeth into its hide.

Paloma landed on her hands and knees beside her dragon. She didn't feel the snow melting into her jeans, or the bite of asphalt under her palms. With the utmost care, she brushed Artem's curls back behind his horns and asked, "Are you okay? Tell me where you're hurt."

Artem stared up at her, his expression torn between awe and anger. "I'm fine, treat," he rasped, "but you shouldn't be here. You should be back at the roost, where you're safe." He strained to sit up, to reach her, as he added, "You shouldn't *be* here!"

"Shut up," she sniffed. "You're my mate. Of course I need to be here."

Tears made cold tracks down her cheeks as she bent to inspect the small barbs connecting the mesh that held him captive. She'd never seen anything like it before, but that didn't mean much. The EVP had some of the most advanced m-tech in the world. They *did* employ scientists like her, after all.

"I couldn't let you go without doing something," she continued, testing her fingers against the mesh. It didn't hurt when she touched it, but sent a current of buzzing energy up through her arm that made her yelp anyway.

"Careful!" Artem tried to squirm backward, but with his wings, tail, and arms strapped against his body, he couldn't go far. "Don't touch that! You don't know if it could hurt you."

In a furious whisper, she argued, "I have to get you out of here! We're in the eye of the event, Artem. If we don't move now—"

"Everyone here is going to die." Taevas's voice came from over her shoulder. She looked up just in time to see him sticking a hand into one of his pockets, his massive, violet wings stretching out as far as they could go. In the half-light, his skin flickered between violet and a deep, bloody red.

He glanced away from the sky to toss her a wicked grin. "Don't worry, pet. Your Isand is here to save you." She caught

Artem's hiss of displeasure as Taevas reached down to pat the top of her head.

"You can't stop it," she insisted, shifting on her knees to nearly drape herself over her mate, like she could protect him from the world with her weak body. Her heart was a hard lump in her throat. "Not even a Spot Unit could draw it away now."

She looked up at the sky. It was a breathtaking sight. Huge, swirling clouds hovered overhead, and lightning bolts hung in the air like suspended rain. Magic was thick in the atmosphere; so thick she could taste it like metal on her tongue. A part of her was thrilled to *finally* see an m-event in person, but the rest of her knew that escaping alive was not going to happen.

Stricken by the thought, Paloma dropped her forehead to Artem's and closed her eyes. Breathing him in with great gulps, she whispered, "Thank you for Choosing me. Being with you has been the best time of my life."

Her dragon managed to nudge her nose with his. "My heart," he rumbled, voice thick, "I'll never forget that you Chose me first."

"Captain," Taevas called out. Through her hair and tears, Paloma watched him stroll up to the tall barrier and leap, with the utmost confidence, directly onto the top. Captain Aman followed him, as did the two other dragons, who didn't appear the least bit alarmed by their leader's proximity to an m-event *or* the edge of the bridge.

"Yes?" The captain watched Taevas with an expression of dry interest, as if this sort of thing happened every day. For all she knew, it did. What the highest levels of the elvish government did on a daily basis was beyond her.

Taevas shook out his wings and, pulling a small silver sphere from his pocket, turned his head to pin the elf with a hard look. It was no bigger than a tennis ball, but something about it made the hair on the back of her neck prickle with unease. "Release my cousin and I'll let you live through this."

The elf blinked slowly. "You think you could kill me, Isand?"

"I know I could." He smiled and tossed the little sphere into the air. Catching it in the palm of his hand, he added, "But with *this,* I could save all of you. You just need to let my cousin go. *Now.*"

The captain weighed the offer for several long seconds before he glanced at the sky one last time. Lips thinning, he moved to tap a button on his gun, but Taevas stopped him.

"Oh, and one more condition."

The captain narrowed his eyes. Clearly unenthused, he drawled, "Yes?"

Taevas tilted his head to one side, his silky hair flowing over one shoulder to blow in the icy breeze. His expression went from smug to shrewd in the blink of an eye. "I want that tech."

The captain's expression hardened. "That's not possible."

"It is if you want to live." Taevas threw the sphere and caught it again, just as a massive lightning strike rattled the bridge. Paloma yelped and covered Artem as best she could. The bloom of magic, an umbrella of frozen electricity, hovered over them, terrifyingly close.

Captain Aman didn't need another sign. "Fine. You get *a* gun." Flicking the switch, he added, "You won't be able to recreate it anyway."

The mesh flickered once before it winked out of existence. Artem was lurching up from the ground to wrap her in his wings and his arms in seconds. Paloma could feel his heart pounding under her cheek as she clung to him.

Taevas grinned. "Delightful!" Turning to look at Paloma, who managed to peek over her mate's shoulder, he held up the sphere and explained, "We've been working on this for a while. This will act like a reverse m-siphon. Instead of conducting power, it will bounce it back and disperse it evenly. Never tried it in the field before, but now's as good a time as any."

Saluting her with two clawed fingers, Taevas leapt off of the bridge, the sphere in his hand humming a high, droning note. When he was far enough away from the bridge as he dared to be, he launched the sphere into the air and dove down, wings tucked against his back as the world exploded into light and heat.

She held onto Artem with everything she had as light and time and reality bent, broke, and refused around them. All the lightning bolts fell from the sky at once, arrowing down, down toward the river below, as a high pitched whine bounced off of the gorge's walls. A massive wave of energy crested over them all — so thick and heavy it sucked the air out of her lungs before it began, almost miraculously, to retreat once more.

Paloma buried her face in Artem's shoulder, her body safely curled under his wings, but couldn't resist a peek through her hair as a brand new being came to life before her stinging eyes.

In the frothing energy and light of the warped sky, a silhouette coalesced. It began to fall, limbs limp and long, long hair streaming like a banner through the sky, but was saved from a terrible start in life by a quick, armor plated dragon. One of Taevas's guards snatched the new being from the sky to land with them ever-so-gently on the bridge.

Paloma only caught a glimpse of pale silvery skin and an angular, feminine face before the guard curled his wings around her with a snap, hiding her from view. One dainty foot peeked out, but that too was quickly covered by a possessive, coiling tail.

Almost as soon as it began, the event was over.

The magic melted away, buffeted back into the atmosphere by that strange little device Taevas caught once more as he glided, unhurried, in his bipedal form around the gorge. There was a collective murmur as elves and dragons alike began to shake off the awe and terror of the moment.

Paloma felt the moment Artem realized the danger had passed. Without wasting a second, he turned them over and clutched her to his chest, his wings tightening around her and his face pressed into her hair. Huge breaths puffed against her cheek, as if he needed to take her into his lungs to reassure himself that she was alive and well.

"My courageous Paloma," he murmured, kissing her neck again and again. "Don't you *ever* do something like that again."

She laughed, but it quickly turned into a sob of relief as she held on tight. *Gods, I almost lost him.* It didn't matter that they'd only known each other for a handful of days. He was her mate. She felt it in her bones, in her soul.

Burrowing her face against his throat, she gasped out, "Deal. No more life threatening situations."

There was a rush of wind, then a *thump* to her right. A hand touched her hair briefly before Taevas's voice cut through the murmuring on the bridge. "Well, I think that's a job well done. Vael, you wrap up that poor new girl so she doesn't catch a cold." He paused, perhaps noting the way his guard had already curled his wings around her as tightly as they could go, before he added, laughing, "Ah, I see. She'll be coming with us back to the 'Riik. And *you*, Captain Aman — I think you and I should take a little trip to San Francisco. I'd like to have word with your fresh-faced sovereign."

Paloma didn't bother looking up. Whatever happened now, she only cared about one thing: going home with her mate. Sure, she wanted to help the new elemental currently wrapped up in her own dragon, but Artem came first.

"Isand," the captain began, finally sounding exasperated, "you can't take the elemental, she was born in the EVP and that makes her a citizen. And you can't just drop in on the sovereign. He's very bus—"

"I can and I will on both counts. My man caught the girl, so she belongs to the dragons now. Isn't that what elves believe? Whoever catches the newborn has familial rights?" He paused to make a small sound of amusement. "We're claiming her for clan Aždaja, and if you're so worried about it, dear Teddy will *make* time for me, I promise you."

Taevas's voice was closer when he asked, laughter in his deep voice, "You two. What would you like to do now that you're not in immediate peril?"

Artem's arms squeezed her hard. His claws pricked through her jacket and shirt to poke her delicate skin. His tail curled around her waist like a vice. Even his teeth closed over the side of her throat, briefly holding her between powerful jaws like he wanted to prove to her and to everyone else that she belonged to him. She *loved* it.

Holding each other as tightly as they could, they whispered as one, "We're going *home.*"

Epilogue

"Go ahead. You can admit you were wrong," he teased. Artem leaned against the wide doorway to their new nesting wing, a smug smile curling his mouth. He watched his mate tiptoe into the huge, circular room, her head tipped back to take in the sprawling skylights he had built into the ceiling as a surprise for her.

Typically, a dragon's nest was enclosed, with no windows save for whatever was necessary to access a perch from which to lift off, but he knew how much his mate loved the sky, so he squashed his instinct to give her a view she would never get tired of.

It took nearly six months to finish planning their new dwelling, knocking down *most* of the old structure, and building a new, sturdier one in its place. It was the blink of an eye, but to him it felt like a lifetime. Artem didn't like not having a dwelling in which his mate could feel secure, nor the fact that they were forced to stay in a temporary dwelling on the property during the construction, but it was necessary.

He pored over every inch of their new dwelling, making it as perfect as he could for her. A new lab was built to her exact specifications and supplemented by a generous grant provided by the Weather Service at the sovereign's personal request. Taevas had gone ahead and declared Artem a member of the diplomatic service anyway, despite his remote location, so the sovereign had taken an extra interest in seeing to his mate's needs.

Not that Artem *needed* them to look after Paloma, of course, but it was the principle of the thing.

He built their dwelling to withstand anything the world threw at them. The walls were sturdy, sigil-reinforced stone. The deck was replaced with a dragon-grade perch, designed to take the weight of his and their offspring's bodies taking off and landing. The dwelling was three times as large as the old one, too, though he bowed to his mate's wishes and kept some of the bones of the old structure.

The brick in the kitchen, a holdover from the ancient mining shack, remained. As did the chicken coop, though it underwent a considerable upgrade. Artem had more or less taken over the flock, since they listened to him more than they did Paloma, and he liked to pamper his girls.

But the thing he was *most* proud of was the nest.

Artem watched his mate turn in a slow circle, her expression one of slack-jawed awe. Paloma hadn't seen it since it was little more than beams and stone. He made sure she didn't, because he wanted this to be a surprise.

The nest was the heart of the home. As the dragon of the relationship, it was his duty to provide a nest his mate could feel safe and comfortable in at all times. If she were a dragon, it would have been a more collaborative effort, but Artem enjoyed doing it on his own.

This was his gift to her.

Paloma honored him with her choice and by saving his life. *Twice.* Giving her the most luxurious nest he could imagine wasn't a hardship.

"Artem, this is..." Her voice was a whisper, as if she worried that speaking too loud would make the nest disappear.

Easing away from the doorway, Artem walked across the room to press his front against her back. His tail clasped her ankle as he wrapped his arms around her shoulders. "This is a *real* nest," he finished for her, all smug satisfaction.

He was damn proud of it. Their nest was a sight to behold — not that anyone besides their offspring would ever see it, of course.

A massive, circular space, it was the crown jewel of their dwelling. The ceiling was domed and high enough that, should he wish to, he could transform into his larger shape and still comfortably move around.

Sunlight streamed in through the skylights during the day, and at night, soft, nearly invisible strips of lights glowed around the perimeter of the ceiling and floor. They could be dimmed on command, giving the nest an intimate feeling despite the soaring ceiling.

The walls were a soft white and covered with colorful tapestries his clan gave to them as mating gifts. Silken threads wove together to depict the 'Riik, their clan's history of rise and fall and rise again, and, the most treasured of all, their mountain — a gift from Taevas himself. The last was particularly huge and had pride of place over the *true* nest, a sprawling sea of pillows and luxurious blankets spread over a mattress that took up nearly the entire floor.

There was an ensuite bathroom, of course, as well as two closets for the clothing he'd finally had shipped over from his apartment in the 'Riik and all the things he'd bought for his mate since they met. It was smack in the middle of the dwelling, too, so Paloma could get to her lab quickly in an emergency and he could protect their offspring, whose wing connected immediately to theirs, in less than a handful of seconds.

Not that they had offspring yet, of course, but he was thinking ahead.

Paloma leaned her head back against his shoulder to gaze up at the ceiling once more. "You've built us a cathedral! I can't believe you actually put in a domed ceiling!"

He laughed. "A nest *should* be a place of worship, don't you think?" Artem dropped his hands to her hips and gave them an appreciative squeeze. Dropping his head to rub his lips against the column of her throat, he added, "Should we get started, treat?"

He felt her shiver of delight even as she shook her head. "Taevas wanted me to look at the readings on the r-siphon, remember?"

Artem began to slowly walk them toward the nest, one hand dipping to the waistband of her shorts. "You don't work for my cousin." He gave her tender throat a delicate scrape with his fangs. "Come on, treat. We have a nest to break in. Don't you want to appreciate all my hard work?"

Paloma let out a long, familiar sound. Desire was a warm, heady scent in the air as he slid his claws under her clothing to tease her. "Well, no, I don't work for him, but he asked for my help with the—"

"To the underworld with my cousin," he growled, stroking her hot, slick skin with the pads of his fingers. "I'm going to be between these thighs for the next several hours, so he's just going to have to wait."

Paloma giggled, but only for a moment. As soon as he stroked his fingers over the tight bundle of nerves he'd come to know so well, she gasped, her hips rocking forward with undisguised need. "Okay, yes, I can clear my schedule."

He huffed against her throat before he spun her around. "Trust me," he muttered, easing her down into the fortress of softness he built for her, "when Taevas has a mate, he'll understand the delay."

Paloma welcomed him into the nest with open arms, her legs falling wide to cradle him as he enfolded her in the semi-darkness of his wings. Looking up at him through the fringe of her lashes, she smiled crookedly. "Gods help the poor creature who ends up with your cousin."

Artem snorted. Sliding one hand under her t-shirt, he replied, "Count your blessings that I saw you first."

"Oh, I don't think Taevas and I would have made good mates," she teased.

"Of course not." He gave her collarbone a sharp nip as punishment for the suggestion. "You were always meant to be *my* mate, not his."

Not that it stopped his damned, trouble-loving cousin from showering Paloma with gifts and attention anyway. Taevas had welcomed her into the clan with enthusiasm, paving the way for her to be accepted by the rest of his family, but he took it a step farther than was strictly necessary because he *liked* Paloma. He claimed to find her intelligence and guilelessness deeply charming.

He also really, *really* liked fucking with his cousin.

Paloma smoothed her hands up his sides. Arching her back, she reached out to skim her fingertips over the membrane of his wings, sending delicious little shocks of pleasure down his spine. "Oh?" Her voice was husky. "And why is that?"

"Because you Chose *me,*" he informed her. Raising his head, Artem ran the tip of his tongue along the seam of her lips, tasting the sweetness that was branded in his soul. "Because you're *mine,* treat. Always."

He felt her smile against his lips. "Always?"

Artem breathed in the scent of her, all oranges and vanilla and desire. He felt the softness of her mouth under his. He heard the thundering of her heart pressed so close to his own. He knew, deep in the part of him that was nothing but instinct and raw power, that this place, this woman's arms, was where he belonged.

Never again would he be lost. Never again would she be alone. They Chose one another. They were one.

"Always," he answered. *"Always."*

THE END

Weathering

DESIRE FOGS THE MIND

CHAPTER ONE

*FEBRUARY 2045 - SAN FRANCISCO, THE ELVISH
PROTECTORATE*

FROM THE DESK OF ELISE SASINI, FREELANCE
JOURNALIST FOR *THE SAN FRANCISCO LIGHT* &
INTERNATIONAL BESTSELLING AUTHOR OF *A
GOLDEN LAND: THE UNVARNISHED HISTORY OF
SAN FRANCISCO'S ELVISH TAKEOVER*:

> *Dear Ms. Sasini,*
>
> *We are so excited about your proposal! You're right — it is
> well past time someone tracked down the story behind all those
> social feed pics and urban legends. I can't wait to see what you do
> with the story! If you need any resources from our research team,
> let me know. Good luck!*
>
> *Best wishes,*
>
> *Dorothy Fan*
>
> *Non-Fiction Editor at West & Cape Publishing*
>
> *Penguin Random House LLC*
>
> *P.S. Say hi to your dad for me! He owes me a damn
> manuscript!!*

Elise was an extremely lucky woman.

Only incredible good fortune could explain how she'd managed to secure the best view of San Francisco for nothing more than a signed copy of her father's latest book and a tiny bump in her rent.

Normally, an apartment with a view like hers would be snatched up before she could slide her application into the building manager's inbox, but through a series of unremarkable miracles, she'd learned that the previous tenant was moving out and that the landlord happened to be a huge fan of her father's work.

Elise didn't feel a lick of guilt over bribing her new landlord, either. In San Francisco, you did what you had to do to get a good apartment. She'd lived in the city her entire life, just as her father, Bob Sasini, had. She knew when to move and when to grease the wheels a little to get what she wanted.

Tucking her legs underneath her, Elise sighed with unrestrained pleasure at the sight of the glittering mass of urban life sprawled far below her. The bedroom window she gazed out of overlooked the entirety of downtown San Francisco and beyond, to the black stretch of dangerous water of the Bay and the glowing beacon of Solbourne Tower perched on Treasure Island.

There were only a handful of small apartment buildings scattered this high on the hills, so the streets below her were quiet and lined with scrubby greenery — the only kind that could survive the skin-stripping wind that raked through the area on a regular basis.

But the thing she loved most was the fog.

Sitting on the padded window seat by her bed, Elise held her breath as she watched a curtain of pillowy mist creep in from the Bay. Tonight, it held the shape of downy waves.

San Francisco was famous for its fog, but only locals understood that it was not just a veil of mist that blew in from the sea at a moment's notice. It had wildly different shapes and moved unpredictably.

One day, it might roar in from the water in a single mass, a wall of wet white so thick you couldn't see your hand in front of your face. The next day, it could sweep in gently, unspooling around buildings and through streets like tendrils of smoke from a cold fire. It bounced in like a giant's handful of cotton balls, carelessly tossed, or appeared as a wraith in the time between footsteps.

It was part of the spirit of San Francisco — changing constantly, never settling into dull routine. It was beautiful.

It was *alive.*

Elise's pulse quickened. Everyone knew that the fog had a mind of its own, but no one had been able to catch more than a glimpse of the mysterious, ethereal being who lived in the heart of it.

Even her father couldn't tell her what he looked like or what his name was. The elemental was as hard to catch and mercurial as the fog he was born in.

But Elise wasn't a woman to back down from a challenge.

Born to one of the most legendary crime reporters in the UTA and a weather witch mother, she didn't let her curiosity lie flat and lifeless. She followed the threads of her interests until there was nothing and no one left to question.

The fog had been her longest running obsession. Always simmering in the back of her mind, her fascination with the elemental who guarded the city looked for any excuse, any chance to find a foothold in her life.

Now, at long last, she had a reason to follow the fog.

The ferry responsible for getting Elise to Alcatraz was, to put it mildly, *fucking ancient.*

She clutched the metal railing of the deck as the ferry rocked over another set of white-crested waves. She'd only done the trip once before, but it looked like even twenty years didn't fix her motion sickness.

Elise focused on the gleaming white walls of the Alcatraz Aerie in the distance, hoping it would help her equilibrium. Waves lashed at the jagged rock of the island. Hardy coastal plants and low-lying shrubs clung to the earth around the Aerie, holding on with determined roots to thin soil and brittle stone.

Salty spray coated Elise's cheeks as she stared up at the island and its only structure. White walls and tall towers pockmarked with narrow doors and rickety stairways stretched up from the craggy surface. It was the only place of worship Loft's acolytes claimed in the Bay Area, and it was beautiful in the brutal, unadorned way the god's worshippers were famous for.

The last time she'd been there, a pilgrim had been found dead in the boat house. Her father was sent by *The San Francisco Light* to write about what quickly turned into a snarled case full of jurisdictional squabbling and she'd begged to come along.

She wasn't sure if she felt pride or queasiness when she stepped off of the ferry and onto the dock. Was it a mark of coming full circle, of stepping out of her father's shadow, to chase her own story across the water?

Maybe, but Elise wasn't the overly sentimental type. It was hard to be when you spent your life in the passenger's seat of a crime reporter's car or getting eviscerated by your editor every time you pushed so much as a sticky note past him.

She was a dogged sort of witch with a goal. Seasickness certainly wouldn't deter her from getting what she was after.

Hitching her overnight bag over her shoulder, Elise adjusted the old, faded baseball cap over her eyes to block out some of the glare bouncing off of the water. She and her handful of fellow passengers, mostly gaunt-faced pilgrims, hurried off of the dock and onto the wide concrete platform below the haunting structure of the Aerie. A dizzying set of stairs linked the platform with the structure, but she knew many of the pilgrims didn't bother with them.

Most who sought succor in the cold arms of Loft were those

people who lived and died in their domain — the sky. Harpies, winged shifters, even the rare dragon or two came as pilgrims to the Aerie. They didn't need the stairs, nor the ferry, for that matter.

She tried not to feel too bitter about that as she began the slow trek up the old, weathered stairs. Her fellow wingless travelers were a quiet bunch behind her. Only the sound of the waves and the whistling breeze of a clear San Francisco day joined the steady beat of their footsteps on the creaky wood.

Salt was heavy in the air. Elise took in deep breaths and savored the scent. Living in the city, it was easy to forget that she spent her whole life no more than a few miles from the cold, hungry ocean. The smell of salt and water didn't travel far beyond the immediate shore, and unless you were in a high rise or at the top of a steep hill, you lost sight of the water almost as soon as you stepped off of the beach.

It was impossible to forget on Alcatraz, though.

The sea sprawled around the rocky island, full of sharks and rip currents and schools of sharp-toothed mermaids. Even when she had her back to the waves, Elise felt the lash of them against the sheer rock and felt the salt on her skin, smelled it in her nose.

It was heady and terrifying, just as Loft and their twin brother, Tempest, was.

Elise wasn't particularly religious, but she wasn't immune to the shiver of awe that ran through her as she stepped under the white washed archway of the Alcatraz Aerie. A single compound, it housed devoted acolytes and pilgrims alike. The feeling of so many souls worshipping in one starkly beautiful, isolated place gave the air a heaviness that settled deep into her marrow.

She wasn't there to worship a capricious god, though.

Following the plain, no-nonsense signs, Elise and her fellow sweaty pilgrims made their way across the courtyard in the center of the compound to the visitor's office.

Inside, the decor was just as stark as the outside. A simple wooden desk sat in the middle of the room. Behind it, a harpy dressed in simple off-white robes sat typing on a projected keyboard, her claws clacking against the unpolished surface of the desk.

Her wings were mottled gray flecked with black, matching the hair she kept in a tight bun at the nape of her neck. When the last of the pilgrims piled in, her black claws stilled just long enough for her to flick gold eyes in their direction.

"Welcome, pilgrims," she trilled. Her tone was dry and professional, but even so, it rang with the beautiful notes of a full-blooded harpy. Scanning the clear, razor-thin screen in front of her, she explained, "The ten AM arrivals have been assigned nests twelve through sixteen of the eastern tower. They are all the same, so do not disrespect this sacred place by squabbling over who gets what."

The harpy reached for something behind her desk before she placed four pamphlets down. "Those are maps. Take them or don't. Meals are at eight, noon, and six. Eat them or don't. Communal showers are available in all towers. Water is strictly regulated on the Aerie, so you will get exactly four minutes of showering time. Use it wisely."

Elise swiped one of the pamphlets off the desk and, giving the harpy a nod, moved behind the small group to head towards the door. Someone piped up to ask about what happened if they were to miss a meal, but she didn't need to stay to hear the rest of the harpy's lecture.

She wasn't staying for days of mediation or religious contemplation in the high rookeries, nor terse discussion with the acolytes.

Elise was there to catch a glimpse of a rumored visitor.

Following her map, which was printed on cheap recycled paper in black and white — the acolytes of Loft were a *no frills* bunch even when it came to paper — she found the nests assigned to her group. They were little more than featureless alcoves built into the sides of the spiraling towers connected by staircases and landings that jutted out from the building.

Each level had its own bathroom, but that was the extent of the amenities. The walkways and stairs were exposed to the elements. Only a thin metal railing separated pilgrims from an ugly fall onto the rocks and waves below. The nests themselves were only slightly better off, as they had narrow wooden doors to keep the elements at bay.

Choosing the nest farthest away from the bathroom so she wouldn't hear people coming and going at all hours, Elise ignored her protesting leg muscles and stepped inside.

They really take the "no luxury, only contemplation" bit seriously, she thought, examining the cot on the far side of the room and the bare plaster walls. A single light fixture built into the far wall above the cot illuminated the tiny, windowless space. The sound of gulls calling filtered through the thin wooden door behind her.

Seeing as there was no other choice, Elise shrugged off her bag and took a seat on the cot. She used her forefinger to flick off her baseball cap and stretched out her aching legs.

As someone who spent her entire life wearing down the soles of her shoes on the San Francisco hills, she counted herself as pretty fit. But the stairs of the Aerie were built by people who didn't care about comfort or ease of use. If anything, they went out of their way to do the exact opposite of those things.

Running the fingers of one hand over the bumps of her hasty braid, Elise slid her tablet out of her bag and pulled up her notes. Her stomach felt light, full of fluttering wings. The thrill of the hunt combined with all the exertion made her heart race.

Finally, she could begin.

As far as Elise could uncover, no one knew the fog's name. Everyone knew his birthday, though.

April sixteenth, 1906. Five o'clock in the morning.

It was the deadliest m-event in the twentieth century, and

coming at the tail-end of the Great War, it nearly shattered the very heart of the Elvish Protectorate. There was speculation that all the magic use during combat helped make the m-event, but there was only circumstantial evidence to support the claim.

What they did know for certain was that eyewitnesses claimed the elemental appeared in the rubble of the original Aerie approximately ten minutes after the event. As buildings crumbled from the force of the magical wave and fires raged through San Francisco, he was said to have climbed out of the frigid water and onto the rocks of Alcatraz's bony shore.

After that, information was spotty. Some people claimed they saw him wreaking havoc along the Embarcadero as people scrambled to put out fires and save lives. Some people reported to have seen multiple beings form in the storm of energy that was an m-event. More claimed the whole thing was a new, chaotic weapon developed and deployed by the Iron Chain in a last ditch effort to wipe out the capital of the EVP.

In all Elise's considerable research, she never found a single piece of evidence to corroborate those claims. Going by what they knew today about spontaneous sapient events, the 1906 disaster was just that — a *natural* disaster. Perhaps the war contributed to its severity, but it was almost certainly not something developed or seeded by another territory. It just was.

The only rumors she could even partially substantiate were the ones that claimed Patrol took custody of the elemental for a time, but there was no way to check whether it was true or not. When it came to EVP security, Patrol was under no obligation to disclose its records to the public — particularly during the long, terrible years of the war.

Whatever the case, she knew he began appearing again two years after the disaster. Photographs were rare and almost impossible to authenticate, but Elise had them all, as well as every eyewitness account of a man bleeding out of the fog to rescue a drowning child or to put out a fire or to stop a murder. Once a bad omen, a sighting of the elemental had come to mean safety, *help*.

Part vigilante, part cryptid, all mystery.

One hundred and thirty-nine years, and still, no one knows his name. If the mystery wasn't so very, very tantalizing, Elise would have found it heartbreaking.

No one knew *anything* about the elemental — or, perhaps more likely, those who knew him simply kept his secrets close.

But why?

She contemplated the question all throughout the day as she wandered the Aerie, peeking into meditation rooms and avoiding eye contact with any acolytes that looked a tiny bit too enthusiastic. She was biding her time until nightfall, when the fog typically rolled in off the water. There was the slimmest possible chance she would see the elemental, but being on the island where he was born and rumored to haunt, Elise had far better odds than in the city proper.

Keeping her head down throughout the simple dinner of barley and mushroom soup and a single fluffy bread roll, she tried to keep her expression properly solemn around her fellow diners in the long, drafty hall.

It wasn't easy, considering she wanted to do nothing more than pace the length of the island until sundown. Elise didn't fear getting in trouble, exactly, but she also didn't care to broadcast her reasons for her own special pilgrimage to the people around her. She suspected they might disapprove of her motives, considering just how little they had to do with their boundless god.

So she waited, and she made polite discussion when absolutely necessary, and she watched the clear February sky bleed into vivid streaks of tangerine and maroon and electric yellow.

As pilgrims and acolytes swooped from perch to perch, heading in for an evening of what Elise could only assume was quiet contemplation of the vastness of Loft's gaze, she sat on a crumbling bit of stonework behind the shrine and watched the fog roll in.

Was he religious? Was that why he was rumored to return to the Aerie?

Elise held her breath as she tracked the creeping mist, her eyes tracing the familiar contours of something always changing, never quite the same as the last time she saw it, but as familiar to her as the lines on her palms. The hunger to know what lay within that beguiling force of nature was a hot, constant burn in her gut.

Maybe it was the weather witch in her that keened for the wildness of discovery, or perhaps it was a lifetime of conditioning from her father to chase down anything and everything that caught her interest. Elise didn't know. At any rate, she wasn't inclined toward introspection.

As soon as the fog reached the farthest edge of the island, Elise hopped off her crumbling seat and made her way back through the archway and down the steps. The light was fading fast and there were no safety lights fixed to a railing — which also didn't exist — to help guide her way down the steep slope, but she didn't think to worry. Her eyes were locked on the jutting dock below, naked without a single boat or the bloated ferry moored to its sides, and where she needed to be when the fog swept in.

Gulls called, and she could hear the sounds of distant horns blaring over the water. Cold wind, so much sharper with its accompanying sting of salt, snapped up to lash her cheeks and the exposed skin of her throat as she half-ran, half-climbed down the steps. She felt no fear as she skidded and nearly stumbled over onto the concrete platform far below her.

The odds that she would encounter the elemental tonight were vanishingly slim, but they carried away all her worries, her mortal fears, and even her common sense with the efficiency of the riptides that coiled like hidden snakes in the water. Her nails were crusted with dirt from gripping the sheer face of the cliff for balance and her breath wheezed in and out of her lungs with the hard scrape of cold air, but Elise didn't notice either discomfort.

The soles of her boots barely made contact with the concrete of the platform before she was launching herself toward the dock. The boathouse was still and dark. Only a single safety light mounted on the lip of its pitiful little awning illuminated the lonely stretch of the dock as darkness dropped like a velvet curtain over the sky.

That happened in San Francisco sometimes: a gorgeous sunset followed by a swift, shockingly dark night. No fuzzy fade, no lavender blush melting into deepest blue. One moment it was all vivid color, and in the next, Darkness had her hands over your eyes.

Elise hadn't spent a whole lot of time outside of the city, so she wondered if it was another peculiarity of her hometown or something that happened everywhere. Not that the darkness scared her. It meant about as much to her as the memory of the murder in the boathouse she jogged by without a glance. It was all just context — set dressing for the stage of her endless curiosity.

The world seemed to quiet as the fog closed in. It muffled the sound of the small, choppy waves and the distant bellowing of horns on massive container ships. Even with all their advanced m-tech, a ship never outgrew its need for horn.

Stopping at the edge of the dock, where old rope coiled around soggy pillars and the smell of brine and oceanic decay clung onto the wet air, Elise unzipped her windbreaker and shrugged it off. She tied it around her waist with a quick knot. Her exertion made her sweat, and that thin sheen of moisture immediately cooled to an uncomfortable layer of tacky coldness on her limbs and throat.

She was dressed unseasonably in an athletic tank top and form fitting black pants, but the cold didn't bother her. She was, after all, a weather witch.

As far as she knew, no one who had ever publicly attempted

contact with the elemental had her set of skills. With no other way of tracking him down besides being everywhere in the city at once, Elise planned to try something enormously, deeply stupid.

I'm just going to keep hoping this won't offend him or end up with me smeared on the dock and left for the seagulls, she thought, shaking out her arms and legs with a quick little jiggle.

Truly, what harm could it do? Her chances that he was actually close enough to notice her minor meddling were greater on Alcatraz, but not exactly *stellar.* In all likelihood, she would do little more than waste her evening in the cold and wet, never having seen a glimpse of the being who haunted her dreams.

It was unlikely, but not *impossible,* that the elemental might take offense to her overture. The fog was his home. It was, for all intents and purposes, *his* territory. By interfering with it, would she be trespassing? Possibly. Probably. But there was nothing gained in nothing risked, was there?

It didn't matter that trespassing on a predator's territory was considered a capital punishment in most of the UTA. Nor did it matter that it was not a crime that would go before jury or judge. If it came down to it, the elemental would be well within his rights to kill her without so much as a warning.

She might just end up like the scum feyrunner: left for dead on the dock because they crossed the wrong person.

"Buck up, buttercup," she muttered, raising her hands to be level with her shoulders. "You die here, at least you died chasing a story, right?"

Magic rippled out from the place all witches kept sacred, a core of solid energy that pulsed bright and hot with Glory's gifts. It lapped at her insides in a gentle hello before it surged outward, pouring through pathways that branched ever smaller and closer to the surface of her skin.

Elise breathed out, once, in a long, cleansing exhale, before she let the magic erupt from her skin in a flash.

Ordinarily, she never would have stood a chance of influencing the fog, but this close to the source, her keen inner senses snapped like a steel trap around the currents, the low hum of wild magic. Every fine hair on her body stood on end as she made contact with the behemoth swirling closer.

Magic had so many variations. It came in every color, every texture, every mood and flavor and scent and temperature and speed. It was at once all the same and so different between one pair of hands to the next that it seemed almost unrecognizable.

Elise's stomach swooped low. Like a gull diving to skim the waves just beyond her feet, it dropped into an exhilarating dive before rising, with a swift turn, to fly upward once more.

The elemental's magic — the *fog's* magic — was like clean, cold rain on her tongue. It slid against her senses with an exploratory caress. It did not buck her off like a stiff wind might, or tease her with what she could not influence like the golden rays of the sun. When she reached a hand out to it, Elise was shocked to feel it *reach back*.

"Come this way," she gently coaxed, using her affinity for manipulating water droplets in the air to slowly reel the smallest edge of the fog closer. "Come on. Just turn a little."

She didn't try to reel in the whole fog bank. Only a gloriana might be able to accomplish something like that. But even if she could have done it, Elise didn't need to. All she needed was his attention.

Which... I think I have.

It didn't take much to coax the fog, it seemed. Within a minute of contact, Elise was amazed to see the rolling, heaving clouds of the bank turn from their natural course toward the island. Normally, on a night like this the fog would have merely skimmed the jagged edges of Alcatraz.

Not tonight.

Elise dropped her arms and watched, wide-eyed, as the fog drifted over the waves to enclose the island in a white veil.

Cold licked up her arms and the exposed skin of her chest and throat. Tendrils of fog snaked around her shoes and through the wisps of hair that escaped her braid. If she thought it was quiet before, it was nothing compared to the muffled silence that pressed close to her now that she could no longer see an inch in front of her face.

Her breaths were too loud, so Elise sucked in a lungful of damp air and held it. Her muscles tensed. Her eyes flickered around her, as if she might be able to make out a shape in the impenetrable fog cocooning her.

Was he here? His fog was, but that didn't mean *he* would show his face. The fog had a magic of its own. She'd felt it and its will clearly, separate from a being of higher intelligence. Perhaps he wouldn't even notice—

A slight tug on the end of her braid made her jump.

Elise whirled around, her heart lodged in her throat somewhere. The tug felt distinctly *human*. Except there was no one there. Even the old boat house had disappeared under the blanket of fog. There was no chance she could make out a figure who stood even six inches away from her.

Trepidation tickled the back of her mind, souring the thrill of the hunt, the discovery. She really *couldn't* see anything. Even when she stretched out her senses, Elise couldn't pick up anything beyond the background roar of magic that filled the air around her.

"Hello?" she called, inanely. Was he there with her? Had her audaciously simple plan actually worked? Elise swept her gaze left and right as she tried to come up with something more to say than *hello*. "My name is Elise. I'm—"

Another tug, just on the very tip of her braid, had her whirling around. That *definitely* wasn't the fog.

Despite the way her heart pounded with excitement, Elise frowned. She liked teasing, but she didn't want to start off on the wrong foot. If he thought he could get away with playing tricks on her, she would never get what she came for.

"I don't scare easily, so you can stop trying," she calmly informed him. Swiping a lock of damp hair out of her eyes, she added, "You can't threaten me, either."

"Can't I?"

The voice was deep and smooth, with an unusual lilt that implied neither amusement nor annoyance, nor much of anything at all. It was soft, almost. As if he was used to speaking in the cotton wool quiet of the fog's embrace, or whispering against the shell of an unsuspecting woman's ear. Elise gasped as a prickle of more than just awareness danced across her skin.

Turning sharply on her heel, she intended to lay eyes on the source of the voice that could only be inches from her, but she didn't get that far.

The heel of her cute but mostly practical black boot slid against the mist-soaked boards of the dock. In the confusion of the fog, she'd misjudged how close she'd come to the edge. Like everything else on Alcatraz, there was no railing to keep her from falling.

Elise swore as she tipped sideways, fear clamping hard around her throat. Everyone knew not to enter the water after sundown. *Everyone.*

What goes in doesn't come out.

She couldn't see the water, nor the edge of the dock, but she fell all the same. There wasn't even time to panic, nor to consider what it would be like to be torn to shreds and turned into picked over bone as her other foot also lost its grip on the edge of the boards.

A hand clamped around her forearm. For a breathless second, Elise hung there, the toes of her boots pressed against the thinnest edge of the dock as a faceless being held her weight, suspending her between life and certain death in the inky water.

Elise blinked hard as a man materialized before her — not quite all the way, but enough. *Enough.*

The cool, dry palm and fingers wrapped securely around the bar of her forearm led her eye upward, over ropes of lean muscle and smooth, alabaster skin. A shoulder led to a neck, half concealed by a waterfall of white — silver? gray? — hair, and even further, up and up, to a face of smooth lines and eyes of deep, unbroken black. No whites. No irises. Just black.

His expression was placid when he murmured, "I suppose I don't need to threaten you, witch, when you're doing it perfectly well on your own."

Chapter Two

Cal held the woman over the water but didn't pull her back to safety.

She was smaller than him, but he guessed she was slightly above average height for a human. Her hair was blonde — a deep, dark gold that curled when water touched it. She had a strong, athletic frame and sharp features liberally sprinkled with freckles. Big eyes, perhaps dark green or brown or hazel, stared up at him from underneath a fringe of blonde-tipped lashes.

She was pretty, but if he wanted to, he could let her die.

It wouldn't take any effort to simply slacken his grip. She would plunge into the cold water of the Bay and be gone in an instant. The temperature would shock her system, keeping her immobile and triggering her reflex to suck in a lungful of salt water. As she fought off the paralysis of cold, the current would already be working to take her out to sea, where predators wouldn't hesitate to strip flesh from bone.

He'd seen it happen more times than he cared to remember. Luckily for this mad witch, he had no desire to see it happen to her, either.

Carefully, Cal used his much greater strength to pull her back onto the deck. The skin of her forearm was warm under his palm, just as her magic was. Even now, when she was no longer daring to influence *his* fog, it hummed between them like the aftershock of a lightning strike.

He ran the tip of his tongue along the backs of his teeth, tasting the ozone and power of her scent. It had a bite to it that tantalized as much as it aggravated.

When she was firmly on her feet, Cal released her to ease back into the comfort of his domain. He didn't retreat entirely, but he was sorely tempted to. No matter how many people he interacted with over the centuries, he never could get used to the prickly, exposed feeling that came with being observed. Best he get whatever this *Elise* wanted out of the way, then.

"Why did you summon me?"

Elise hurried to step away from the edge of the dock. He watched the exposed skin of her throat bob as she swallowed. A bead of moisture — mist condensed on her warm skin or sweat, he couldn't tell — traced the contour of her cheek and jaw.

"I didn't *summon* you," she argued, drawing her narrow shoulders back. She peered at him with open curiosity. He'd seen the look before and he didn't care for it.

Cal had no desire to be gawked at, least of all by a madwoman who thought she could tell *his* fog what to do.

Curling his fog in close, he lunged toward her suddenly, bringing them nearly nose to nose. He knew from past experience that humans tended to feel unsettled when he moved unexpectedly or in ways they couldn't, and he liked the idea of this composed, foolhardy woman feeling a little unsettled by him. Perhaps it would teach her a valuable lesson in caution.

Unfortunately, it didn't work. Elise stood straight and tall, her eyes locked on his. She didn't even blink when he accused, "You touched my fog. *No one* touches my fog. I can only imagine you wished to summon me, or else you wouldn't have dared. It's either that or you don't have any sense in that head of yours."

"I'm a weather witch," she calmly replied, unruffled, "and fog is weather, isn't it? There's no law that says I can't make contact with it. Besides, it's not like you *own* it."

No, there wasn't. Not that he gave a single thought to laws on the whole, of course. What did he care for laws? For social contracts? For politeness or imaginary authority? He was *weather*.

While she was right that he didn't *own* the fog, it was an extension of himself as well as his steady companion. It was the only home he had. No one got to influence it except him. Full stop.

He scowled. Circling her slowly, just to put her on edge, he said, "So you deny that you were trying to summon me? In this place?"

This place. Cal felt a familiar twinge of bitterness when he thought of the Aerie and its rookeries, its featureless rooms and its stern-faced acolytes. It was the closest thing he had to a real home, surely, but it brought him paltry comfort.

The acolytes might have taught him his letters and guided him through his first clumsy year of physical life, but they'd also feared and admonished him. They took him in not because they loved him, but because they felt it was their religious duty. He was a hard lesson dropped in their laps by Loft — punishment and teaching wrapped up into one confused, shaken man.

Cal swept his gaze over the witch, taking in her form fitting clothes and her flushed cheeks. He would bet anything that *she* had a real home. She looked like someone who came from a family, who knew love and bonds and what it was like to live. It was in the air around her as surely as her magic.

Unlike me.

He and this willful creature were separated by more than the fact that he was an elemental, born of sky and power and chaos. A vast gulf of understanding existed between them.

He hated it.

"Well, I'm not going to start off by lying. I did want to meet you. I just have a problem with the word *summon*. I wasn't trying to conjure you for some nefarious purpose." A smile quirked the corners of her lips upward. Cal dropped his gaze to examine that little smile. The witch had lovely, full lips but a sardonic expression that turned what might have been a sweet face into something... more. Something clever and arresting.

When he lifted his eyes back to hers, he found her watching him with a peculiar expression, as if she didn't quite know what to make of him.

He knew exactly what to make of her, though. He knew what she was and what she was after. Not even that compelling little smile could blind him enough to miss it.

Anger simmered under his skin. The fog, always attuned his emotions, rolled in agitated waves over the water.

"I see," he murmured, pushing his half-corporeal form into her space once more. Up close, he could make out every individual eyelash and sun-made freckle. He could even smell her. Below the familiar scent of brine and water, she smelled clean and fresh, like soap and flowers — exactly how he imagined a loving home would smell.

Elise blinked, but otherwise didn't react as he hovered nearer still, drawn in by the desire to unsettle her and something else he couldn't name. Perhaps it was the way her magic radiated through him, familiar and yet pleasantly foreign. Perhaps it was the warmth of her skin he could feel filling the spare inches separating them. Perhaps it was the way her tiny, nearly imperceptible gasp made the muscles of his abdomen clench.

Cal didn't know what it was that pulled him closer. He didn't care.

"You are just like the others, then," he snapped. Or rather, as close as he ever came to snapping. He spoke so infrequently that his default tone was mild, almost whispery. Even so, his displeasure came through loud and clear.

Elise blinked twice. "What?"

"You say you don't have a purpose, but you do." Cal lifted a hand to flick a damp lock of hair away from her eyes just to show her he could and would do whatever he liked. She gasped again. This time her cheeks flushed a deep, dark red. It pleased him to see it, though he didn't understand why. "See?" he accused, suddenly unreasonably angry with her. "It's in your eyes. The way you look at me. You want something."

He so rarely got truly angry, but this witch made everything in him bristle. He didn't want her to be like the others, he realized. He didn't want her to only speak to him because she wanted him to spy on someone, or kill someone, or trade something for the knowledge only he had.

Elise was pretty and he liked her smile. She smelled like comfort and her magic sang a song that made his entire being sit up and take notice.

All of that made her clear desire to use him more galling than usual.

He never hurt another being, no matter what the public thought he did. When he encountered the scum of Burden's Earth, he preferred to drop them on Patrol's stoop rather than let another stain bleed onto his soul.

But Elise didn't know that.

Surging almost out of the fog, until all but his lower legs were visible to her, Cal closed his fingers around her throat and pulled her closer, closer, until their noses brushed.

"What is it you want from me?" he rasped, staring into her wide eyes. The witch was not so composed when he had his fingers curled around her neck. He could feel the warmth of her breath ghosting over his lips, sending a bolt of some hot, hungry feeling through the brewing rage in his gut. "Are you looking for an assassin? An informant? Perhaps a spy?"

Her pulse was a thundering beat under his palm, but he had to give her credit. Elise the weather witch didn't panic. She didn't fight him. Her hands came up to stop her fall into his chest, her palms two hot brands on his naked skin, but she didn't claw or kick or shout for help.

She met his gaze squarely, without fear, when she answered, "None of the above."

Cal felt a jolt move through every fiber of his being when her fingers spread ever-so-slightly over his ribs. It was a twitch, barely anything at all, and yet he could have sworn he felt the whorls of her fingerprints moving over his skin.

His breath quickened. The pad of his thumb moved before he thought it through, pressing just under the corner of her jaw, where he was treated to the rhythmic pounding of her pulse. Each beat reverberated through him, bigger and louder than the last.

Like the familiar cadence of lapping waves, her heartbeat made a home for itself where it didn't belong: under *his* skin.

Cal's hand was much larger than her throat. Everything about him was much larger than her, despite her athletic build and long legs. When he held her this close, his hand engulfing her vulnerable neck and her face turned up to peer at him through thick lashes, she looked very fragile.

He was surprised by the way the sight, the feeling of her relaxing into what *should* have been a threatening hold, made his blood run hot in his veins. Cal wanted to shy away from the foreign feeling at the same time that he yearned to clasp it in his hands and crush it close, to keep it with him always. It was terribly heady.

A rush, he thought. Just like that time Kaz convinced him to drink one of his dark liquors, Cal felt the foreign thrill bleed into his bloodstream and cloud his thoughts, the righteous anger siphoned away to make room for something else.

"Then what are you?" he breathed, only succeeding in hiding the tremor in his voice at the last possible moment.

He saw the thoughts flashing in her eyes — what *color* were they? Why did it matter so much that he know? — seconds before he felt her fingers drag slowly down his stomach to fall away. He felt the touch all the way down to his incorporeal toes.

Her shoulders relaxed as she leaned into his hold: a sign of surrender or complete confidence?

"My name is Elise Sasini," she told him. She paused briefly, eyes flicking back and forth as if she expected some recognition he couldn't offer. Her posture was easy, submissive even, but her expression wasn't cowed. She looked at him with a confidence that raised his hackles — like *she* was the one in control. "I am a writer. I came here to talk to you. That's it."

Cal narrowed his eyes. "You're a reporter?"

She tried to shake her head, but when he tightened his grip just enough to send a message to hold still, she stopped. "No. I used to be a journalist, but now I mostly write books. Histories. Non-fiction."

Suspicion niggled at him. "What story do I have that a writer might want?"

He watched, transfixed, as Elise's expression transformed. Gone was the easy confidence. In its place, she *glowed.* Her eyes gleamed with unconcealed pleasure and that ever-present smile widened until he could see a hint of white teeth. "You have *all* of them," she explained, leaning forward unconsciously.

Cal found himself easing backward. Now *he* was the unsettled one, and yet he still had his hand wrapped around her throat. He still had the power. Didn't he?

How in the world did she manage to make him feel like she was the dangerous one?

"So you are looking for information." He tried to infuse the right amount of disgust in his voice, but he fell woefully short of his goal.

"Not like you're thinking, no." Elise lifted her arms, palms up and fingers spread, in a movement that encompassed the cocoon of fog that concealed them from the world. "I want to write about *you.* This!"

He felt her heartbeat speed up under his thumb, his own quickening to match hers, before he released her abruptly. Shock crumpled what little remained of his composure.

It was not fear that made her heart race. It was *excitement.*

Just what kind of woman was he dealing with? Realizing that

he had dreadfully miscalculated, Cal took a hasty step backward. Luckily for him, his natural grace and only partially corporeal form made the movement seem like an easy glide into the mist rather than the clumsy retreat it really was.

"Why would you want to write about me?" He shook his head. His long hair, bone white and with a will of its own, slid over his naked shoulder to wave like a flag between them. "I'm no one."

Some of Elise's radiant enthusiasm dimmed. Her brows snapped down into a harsh angle. "What? No one? You're... you're *him*. The fog! That's hardly *no one.*"

She stepped forward, completely heedless of the fact that they were invisible to the outside world, that she stood on a rickety old dock over deadly water, and that her only company was a man of untold power she didn't know.

In the years since his birth, Cal had seen every manner of depravity and form of violence. Watching over the city he once destroyed, the descendants of all those he so ruthlessly slaughtered, was his penance. It was his vigil.

He knew what could happen to a woman who stepped into a shadowed corner with a man she didn't know. He knew what happened when someone fell into the water. He knew the danger that writhed in every shadow and under every stone. He knew it all and more than he ever wished to.

Cal was suddenly vexed by her lack of caution. He was also infuriatingly charmed by it.

"You dared to touch *my* fog for this?" He gestured sharply at nothing, too agitated to much else. "What if I'd been territorial? What if I'd seen you as a threat? What if you'd slipped and *actually* fell into the water? My story can't possibly be worth what would have happened to you if I wasn't what I am."

"And what are you?"

That drew him up short. It was on the tip of his tongue to say he was a good man, one who would never actually hurt her or anyone else if he could help it, but that wasn't true. He wasn't good. He'd never had the chance to be. No one born into so much misery and bloodshed could be good.

Instead of saying any of that, Cal huffed and answered, "Someone who doesn't hurt foolish witches."

Elise's smile widened into a full grin. The power of that smile was beyond reckoning. Cal held his breath, afraid that if he moved a single muscle, that pressure building inside of him would burst, leaving him nothing but shards around her feet.

No one, not even those lucky people he rescued in all his long, long years, had looked at him like that.

"See? There was no harm in it." Her eyes twinkled with humor, like she knew how foolish she'd been and actually found it *funny.*

Cal blinked, dazed. Had he thought her pretty? Maybe he was the foolish one.

When Elise Sasini smiled at him like she kept all the secrets of the universe in her hands and found them all dreadfully silly, it made him feel the same way he did when he drifted with the fog bank over the water — weightless, exhilarated, *free.*

Like I'm home.

"No harm," he repeated numbly. "I think... there could be a great deal of harm, witch."

Not to her. She wore her confidence like armor. Maybe it really did protect her from the evils of the world. But *him...*

Cal got the uneasy feeling that if he followed the path she laid before him, he would not come out the other side the same. This woman was a force of nature all her own. Whether that was a good thing or not, he had no way of knowing. Would he like the man found on the end of the journey she promised?

Well, I can't really dislike the one I am now more, *can I?*

"What is your proposal?" he found himself asking, against his better judgment.

Elise lost her smile, but he didn't mourn it. Instead, he found himself admiring the way she pressed her lips together tightly, as if she was forcefully reining in her enthusiasm. He felt the unsettling impulse to press his fingertips against her lips, just to feel the grin they so valiantly tried to contain.

Joy burst across her expression anyway. It was uncontainable. It was in her eyes and in her flushed cheeks and in the way she propped her hands on her hips — it bled into every line of her body, like this moment in time was the most wonderful thing she'd ever experienced. It was a separate sort of magic from the one that fizzed in the air between them, but Cal was convinced it was magic all the same.

"I want to write a book about your life. All of it. From the beginning to now. How you got to be what you are, *who* you are, and everything that you've done for this city."

Cal's stomach churned. She wanted to know all of it? Why? Surely she already knew of his savage beginning. What more was there to know? His story began and ended that day. Any chance of being more was buried with his victims.

Still, he asked, "And what would I get out of this?"

Elise let out a huge breath and rubbed her hands up and down her arms. "Well, you'd get money from the book, of course. Part of the advance and royalties."

He frowned, watching closely as she unwound the knot she'd made of her windbreaker's sleeves, which were slung around her waist. She slid the jacket up and over her bare arms. When she zipped it up, he slowly replied, "I don't need money."

She cocked her head to one side. Her braid, only long enough to reach the tops of her shoulder blades and barely contained by the elastic band at the end, rustled against the reflective fabric of her windbreaker. "Everyone needs at least a little money. Surely—"

Cal waved her comment away, his skin prickling with a pleasant sort of impatience. His mind raced.

If he said no to the money, what *could* she offer him? The possibilities were at once beyond his comprehension and deeply tantalizing. "I have plenty of money I never use," he answered, thinking of the citizen's stipend he hadn't put a dent in for over a hundred years. "What else can you tempt me with?"

Elise peered at him, her brows furrowed. He kept his focus on her face, afraid to breathe, but he didn't need to look down to know her fingers moved absently through the fog caressing her hip. He *felt* it.

A shot of pure heat coursed through that simple connection. Her magic, unconscious and benign, meshed with his in an intoxicating blend. Electricity like he'd never felt leapt from her to him in a playful, erotic introduction.

It was with great surprise that Cal realized he was actually *aroused*. That had never happened before.

"What do you want?" she asked, completely unaware that her mere presence, the barest brush of her fingers, knocked his world off its axis.

Cal swallowed. It was as easy as a thought to bring the fog in thicker around him, hiding any evidence of his desire from her. He spent more than half his life in his skin, so it wasn't that he was ashamed of his nudity. Rather, he wanted to sit with this eye-opening revelation for a while before he—

What? What will I do? Tell her about how she makes my cock hard?

Maybe. He wasn't sure how something like this — his visceral attraction — was handled. Cal had never experienced its like before. His time in the Aerie and his subsequent imprisonment hadn't exactly encouraged sexual exploration, and since he'd never felt desire before this surreal moment, he had always just assumed it was part of his nature to feel no procreative impulse.

But *now*...

Now he looked at Elise and felt like a whole world had opened up to him. A gnawing hunger grew in the pit of his stomach. He wanted her to smile at him again. He wanted to feel the rush of it, the weightlessness of it. He wanted to know what it felt like to feel more than the fleeting touch of her fingers on his skin. He wanted to ease the ache in his cock and know what her kiss felt like and breathe her in with every inhale.

He simply *wanted.*

That wanting disturbed him. More than the idea that she wanted to *know* him as no other being in the world did. More than her audacity. More than the thought of her digging up all the graves he carried in his pockmarked soul.

Cal wasn't used to wanting. He didn't care for it. Certainly, wanting and yearning had never helped him before. It only caused more pain. Better to accept the ache of loneliness than to make it worse with the never-ending hunger of *hope.*

And yet, he was a curious being by nature. If there was one benefit to his vigil, it was that he got to observe and satisfy his inquisitiveness whenever it suited him. Here, now, Elise was giving him a chance to chase this new interest in an unprecedented way. Would he ever get this chance again? Would he even want it if it came?

He didn't know, and because he didn't know, Cal chose not to answer her. Not yet, anyway. "I will think on what I want," he promised her, "and give you my answer tomorrow."

"Good! Fine. That's— that's great!" Elise balled her hands into fists by her thighs, her grin surging back onto her face like an electric bolt of pure joy. "I'll be here."

Cal tried not to look at her smile, fearing what he might say and do if he let it blind him. Nodding once, he began to make his escape by way of fading into the fog, but was stopped when she made a sound of distress.

"Wait, wait!"

He paused, eyeing her suspiciously. "Yes?"

"I..." She stepped closer, her movement sending eddies through the fog clinging like a lover to her legs, hips, and sides. He shuddered at the feeling. Did she know that he and the fog had a symbiotic link? That he could feel, in a secondhand sort of way, the shape of her? No, he didn't think so, and he wasn't about to tell her. For all that it unsettled him and made the ache in his cock worse, he liked feeling her.

Her eyes were soft, almost shy, when she said, "I didn't get your name."

His stomach knotted. There was a reason he didn't give out his name. Even when the people he rescued begged, just so they knew who to thank, he refused. Only Kaz knew it, though it took a decade for the orc to earn the privilege. But for reasons he could not understand, he looked into those soft, keen eyes and felt compelled to be known.

He swallowed the lump in his throat to whisper, "Cal."

Elise made the smallest gesture — barely a gasp, almost a jolt, all pleasure — and he felt something deep inside him give way. A staggering release of internal pressure nearly sent him reeling backward. *Gods,* he thought, *I'd do anything to hear that noise again.*

"Cal," she breathed. Her eyes gleamed in the darkness, catching the glow of the boat house's light through the fog. "Is that short for something? Calvin, maybe? Callum?"

Cal's chest seized as the crack inside him expanded and filled with a desire he'd never known. Panic mingled with the overwhelming urge to step out of the fog and just *touch* her. Gods, but he wanted to know what it was like to feel the silk of her cheek or the ticklish brush of her lashes with his own tarnished hands.

He didn't know how to handle all the *wanting* that threatened to drown him in a deluge, so he needed to make his escape. Cal wasn't certain he'd survive another moment in her presence.

"No," he answered, fading into the familiar obscurity of the fog at last, "it's Calamity."

∾

FROM THE DESK OF ELISE SASINI, AN EXCERPT FROM THE MANUSCRIPT *THE SHROUDED CITY:*
No one knows weather like a weather witch. That's what my

mom told me, and what her mother told her. I come from a long line of weather witches — an unbroken chain that stretches back into the fuzzy obscurity of witch hunts and elvish rule, the wild thicket of generations past. I'm no gloriana, but I'm no slouch, either. Weathercraft is in my bones. I respect the craft as much as I respect those witches who came before me.

That doesn't make my forebears right, though.

A weather witch is an interpreter. We are translators of a language in which we can never truly claim fluency. We understand and often influence, but we don't truly know the weather. That claim can only be held by those born into the currents and storms, those rare beings who are hammered magic and earthly power.

Elementals.

The next day was miserable and incredible in equal measure. Despite the precipitous adrenaline drop, Elise hardly slept. The thin cot and frigid room weren't the issue. Nor was the sound of people moving across the platform outside her door, presumably night dwellers and bleary-eyed pilgrims going about their business.

It was *Cal.*

Elise felt breathless and windswept for many hours after he slipped back into vapor. Her mind raced in ever-tightening circles around one subject: *him.*

He was both everything and nothing like she imagined. He was beautiful in an ethereal way that she never could have pictured. Miles and miles of smooth alabaster skin stretched over a body of lean muscle. Long, long hair flowed in currents around his aquiline face. His eyes were nothing but spilled ink, reflecting all that they saw.

Even in the dark, the sight of him made her stomach muscles tighten with ripples of awareness. Never, in all her life, had she been so potently *aware* of another being's physicality. It was as if she was hyper aware of every movement, every twitch of his beautiful fingers and flick of his hair.

Worse than all that, Elise couldn't get the sound of his voice out of her head.

Cal was soft spoken. Even when he was furious, he didn't truly raise his voice. He spoke in a murmur — a low baritone of the softest velvet. When a man spoke as if every word was a secret to be shared between them, he held untold power over the senses.

And he told me his name, she thought, staring at her half-eaten oatmeal the next morning. Her smile refused to fade even in the face of bland, overcooked oats.

Cal. Calamity.

Instead of satisfying her curiosity, he'd only thrown fuel on the fire.

Why was he named that? Did he pick it himself, or did someone else? Why? Elise couldn't imagine a person less suited to being called *Calamity* than the hauntingly beautiful elemental.

And then there was the question of his accusations. He expected her to seek him out for *assassination?* That meant that someone had done that in the past, and Elise was terribly curious about who and when.

All day she paced the Aerie, her thoughts spinning in circles of disbelief and dizzying joy. She still couldn't wrap her head around her success, nor that he was actually considering her offer.

Well, sort of.

He did intend to ask her for something. It might have made her nervous, but Elise was aware enough of her own flaws to realize that, no matter what he asked for, she would almost certainly agree. Short of murder, there was very little she wouldn't do to satisfy her curiosity.

But if there was something else there, layered under the curiosity and the driving need to break into the marrow of a story, Elise didn't care to examine it. She understood that she was attracted to Cal, of course, but she didn't spare it much thought.

The smooth skin of his palm cupping her throat might have been the single most erotic moment of her life, but she doubted he felt the same.

Could an elemental even feel lust? Elise didn't know. Not every race did.

Not that it matters, she thought, standing in the glow of the single light of the boat house. She stared out at the choppy water and hugged her arms tightly around her middle. Anticipation was a current under her skin. Would he show? Would he demand something impossible? Would he touch her like he did before?

No, stop that. Elise shifted from foot to foot. *Even if he did feel lust, you can't just assume he would be attracted to you. He's a fucking elemental. He could be into, like, clouds or something.*

But even that thought didn't stop the swooping butterflies that filled her stomach when she watched the fog move in. When it crept over the edge of the dock, she held her breath.

Cal emerged with a rolling, floating step forward. The moon was full and the sky clear. The moonlight bleached him of what little color he had, leaving him in varying shades of silvery white. Just like the previous night, he was completely naked. Not that it mattered. The fog swirled around him such that he might have worn clown pants and she would have been none the wiser. Not that she was looking, of course.

Elise swallowed, hoping her cheeks weren't flushed with her signature cherry red blush. She wanted to make a good impression, not *ogle* him. It wasn't easy, though.

Cal's expression was pensive, but there was a determined tilt to his brows that made her heart race. "Hello," she called out, trying to rein in her instinct to grin at the sight of him. *Keep it cool, Elise.* "I'm glad you came back."

He gave her a quizzical look. Gliding closer, he replied, "I said I would return."

"Well, yes, but you might have changed your mind."

Cal's lips quirked. It wasn't a smile, but more of an endearing little tick, as if he couldn't decide whether he wanted to grin or grimace. "I don't change my mind. Once I decide to do something, I keep my word."

Elise held very still, her eyes fixed on his expression. He came to a stop close to her. Only about a foot separated them. It felt like no space at all and also like a hundred miles too far.

"Oh?" she breathed, heart leaping. "Have you made a decision about my proposal?"

"I have."

Elise waited, but when he simply stared at her rather than tell her what he wanted in exchange for his story, she licked her lips and asked, "So... what are your terms, Cal?"

He lifted one long-fingered hand to touch her lips. Barely a brush, it still sent a shock of pure heat through every single one of her nerves. "I'll tell you my story," he murmured, a look of intense concentration on his aquiline face, "if I get to be with you."

Elise's mind blanked. Surely, she'd heard him incorrectly. "I... what?"

Cal's fingers slid into the hair behind her ear. Cupping the side of her head, he bent slightly to hover his mouth over hers. She felt the brush of his lips when he said, "I spent all night and all day considering what I want. I don't want money. I don't want fame or recognition. I want to know what it's like to be like everyone else for a while. I want to know what it's like to kiss you, to live like you, to touch you."

She gasped, surprised and aroused and completely baffled. This force of nature wanted *her*? Surely not in the way he implied. "For how long?" she found herself asking, as if this was something she could possibly agree to.

She couldn't. Of course not. You didn't trade that sort of thing for a story. That was at least the tenth or twelfth rule of journalism, right?

Cal's lips ghosted over her own. Cool and smooth as polished stone, they tantalized and terrified all at once. He was quiet for a moment, thinking perhaps, before he answered, "Until you finish the book."

"And you... want *what,* exactly?" On this she needed absolute clarity.

"Everything," he murmured, a strange note of pain in his voice. "I want everything you have to give me, witch. I want to try it all. But for now, I'll settle for a kiss."

Cal's kiss, when he finally committed to it, was a chaste press of his lips against hers. There was no tongue, no teeth, no groans of pleasure. It was stark and intense in its simplicity.

It wasn't like any kiss she'd had before. It tore Elise's soul out by the root and replaced it with something new. Something bigger and fuller than anything she knew before.

It was like kissing pure, intoxicating magic.

The possibility that she might say no fled under the onslaught of the desire that roared through her. When Cal gently, so very gently, sucked her bottom lip into his mouth and let out a sound of pure, unfiltered surprise — as if he'd never kissed before, gods help her — Elise knew she was lost.

Magic sang in her veins, crowing a possessive, age old song she'd never heard before: *He's mine.*

CHAPTER THREE

FROM THE DESK OF ELISE SASINI, A NOTE SCRIB-
BLED ON THE BACK OF A BODEGA RECEIPT FOR
ONE MNT DEW, A THREE PACK OF MEGA FREEZE
MINT GUM, AND A BAG OF JALAPENO CHEDDAR
CHIPS:

*Where does he go? Someone has to know. SF is the biggest
small town in the country. Everyone knows everyone. How can he
have lived here for over a century and no one knows who he
is/where he goes? Must live outside of the city. Why come
back, tho?*

HE'D NEVER KISSED ANYONE BEFORE. HE WONDERED IF
it was always so...

Much.

Was it normal to feel like he couldn't be close enough to her?
Did a human man kiss someone and want more with every
passing second? Cal floundered under the onslaught of
conflicting desires — to be closer, to tear himself away, to search
for that mysterious *more* he couldn't quite grasp.

When Elise's hands slid up his chest to curl over his bare
shoulders, he shuddered. Her skin was so warm against his. So

different, but tantalizing. He'd never felt more comfortable in his flesh than he did when she grounded him there, her nails scraping gently at the slopes of his muscle and bones. She stepped closer, her head tipping back to a more comfortable angle, and made a soft sound of encouragement in the back of her throat.

He let out a low *whuff* of air against her lips, astonished by the headiness of touching her.

Yes, this was a good idea, he thought, the agony of his indecision firmly cast out. *Yes. Yes.*

Cal wrestled with himself over what he wanted from her, what he was willing to give her. He wanted to turn her down. His secrets were his own. He'd given his entire life to the city as penance for his crimes. He didn't owe anyone anything more.

And yet, when he thought of her sunny smile and the pulse of her magic over his skin, he could not shake the hollow ache that settled into his soul, that great fissure she had opened up in him. Cal was not experienced, but he understood that *connection* was a rare and coveted thing. Perhaps being so alone meant he understood it all the better.

Was he willing to toss away his first chance at exploring that connection with another being just to stay exactly as he was?

No.

There was no telling how this might damage him, and he wasn't even certain she would agree to his terms, but Cal wasn't a fool. He wanted to grasp this chance at that mysterious, tantalizing *something* with both hands.

And now that he held her in his arms, pressed his lips to hers, he knew there was no way he would regret this. Even if this woman somehow managed to break him into pieces, even if she betrayed him at the first opportunity, he would not regret this experiment in intimacy.

Elise's hands drifted down to trace the contours of his arms. He felt every drag of her fingertips and every soft, rapid exhale of her breath as she pulled back enough to speak.

"I... I think you need to tell me exactly what you want out of this deal," she said, voice husky.

Cal opened his eyes to find her staring up at him. Her eyes were wide and her cheeks were a deep pink. The light of the moon glinted off of the tips of her lashes. Elise was beautiful, but Cal had seen plenty of beauty in his lifetime. What was it about her that *captivated* him?

The source of his attraction was exactly what he intended to find out. *Amongst other things.*

"I want to know what it's like to be..." Cal struggled to find the right word. Didn't the races all use different words for the same thing? All he could come up with was the word his only friend used. "Mated," he finished, nodding. "I want to know what it's like to be mated."

Elise blinked. The hot pink of her blush began to cool. "That... uh, that's a big ask, Cal."

"Why?" He frowned. Smoothing his fingers through the loose strands of her hair just because he liked the texture of it, he asked, "Why is it a big deal? Don't couples do that sort of thing all the time? Explain."

"Well, yes, but not typically as an exchange for something." Her eyes darted to the side as he skimmed his fingertips through her hair. Was she shy? Or did he make her nervous?

Elise's cheeks were flushed when she continued, "What you're saying could mean anything from *we hold hands and eat dinner together* to *you want to have sex with me whenever you want.* The first one I can do, but the second one..."

Cal shook his head, suddenly aware of the vast hole in his vocabulary. What *did* he mean? Certainly not that she should feel coerced into having sex with him. He could theoretically get that anywhere and from anyone. That wasn't what he meant. Unfortunately, he lacked the experience to really articulate what he *did* mean.

Frustrated, he tried to explain, "No, I don't want that. I want... I want to know what it's like to have *everything.*"

Elise's brow wrinkled. "You said that before. *Everything.* What does that mean?"

"I don't know," he admitted. Cal blew out a breath and forced himself a few steps away from her. Being too close made an already confusing series of impulses that much worse. "I want to know what it's like to not just be *this.* I want to have a life like yours. Like everyone else. I want to know how it feels to live like you do, to have a person to *be* with. Just to see what it's like."

"You want to experience a *relationship,*" she replied, expression clearing. Elise propped her hands on her hips. "Okay. I think I know what you're asking for."

"Do you?" He narrowed his eyes at her. Cal barely understood what he struggled to put into words. How could she figure it out so quickly?

"Yes, I think I do." Elise peered at him, her expression thoughtful. "How about this: For however long it takes to write the book, you and I can be... we can explore what people in a relationship do. We can have dinner. Spend time together. If you want to know what it's like to be in a couple, we can do couple things. How does that sound?"

Cal considered her proposal for several long moments before he shook his head. "No."

"No?"

"No, I don't just want to see you occasionally," he confirmed, suddenly certain he didn't want to let Elise out of his sight. Who knew what would happen? She could decide he wasn't worth the trouble, or slip away as soon as she had what she wanted. He couldn't allow that. He *wouldn't.* "I want to know what it's like to be with someone all the time," he insisted. "I've never had that."

"You've never lived with someone else?" A curious look of sympathy settled on her features. "Do you have a home, Cal?"

It was his turn to be confused. "Yes, the fog." He gestured over his shoulder, to the rolling waves and distant, twinkling skyline. "I drift."

The closest he'd ever come to having a *physical* home was the

Aerie, but even he knew it barely counted. The acolytes kept him in isolation for the first year after his creation, only allowing him companionship when it was intended to indoctrinate him into their cult. In the second year, the elves discovered his presence in their city and took custody of him. He wouldn't say the cell block beneath the Tower was his home either. Considering he escaped their dungeon and spent the next one hundred and thirty-seven years dodging Thaddeus II's increasingly aggressive attempts to recapture him, he doubted she would count it, either.

Looking at Elise's tightening expression, Cal decided to withhold those stories for now. He didn't want her pity, after all. He wanted *more* from her. Much more.

"Right, okay." She cleared her throat. Elise was quiet for a moment, her eyes pinned to some spot in the middle distance, before she appeared to come to some decision. Chin lifting, she asked, "So... why don't you come home with me, then?"

Cal was moving before he'd made the conscious decision to do so. In a moment, he was before her again, his fingers seeking out the wispy ends of her hair. He couldn't seem to keep his hands off of it. Did it only curl in the moist air, or did she wake up with a head full of curls each morning? Cal wasn't sure why it mattered to him — why all the little details that made up Elise *mattered* — but it did.

"You would take me into your home?" he pressed, incredulous, as he scanned her face for any hint of unease or guile. Surely he couldn't be that lucky. "I've never been in a real home before."

He didn't think to censor himself, but watching her expression pinch with sympathy reminded him that he probably should. Cal would give her his grim story, but he didn't want her to look at him like he was some broken thing. He wanted her to look at him like...

Well, he didn't know what he wanted, but he knew he *didn't* want that.

"I don't need a home," he felt compelled to add, for his pride's sake. "I live in the fog. I usually have everything I need, but when I don't, I come here and get whatever it is from the acolytes. What they can't give me, I seek elsewhere."

And if something was truly beyond his reach, he wasn't above trading favors with Kaz, who seemed to have his green fingers in every shady part of the city. That was how Cal ended up with so many caches, hidden behind rocks or high on unscalable cliffs or in alcoves between massive bridge supports.

Kaz was happy to provide him with whatever he asked for, but that didn't surprise Cal. The orcish spymaster belonged to the Solbournes after all, and even though he liked Kaz, he also knew that getting on his good side was all a part of the long game he and the Solbournes had been playing for over a century.

They would never get his loyalty, but he could give them a favor or two when it benefitted him to do so.

Elise bit her lip hard enough to make the rosy flesh turn white before she released it again. "But you've never had a *home,* Cal. A place where you feel safe and warm and loved."

It wasn't a question, so Cal didn't feel obligated to answer it. Instead, he soothed some of his agitation by playing with the ends of her hair. The texture was different from his. While his hair always felt thin and silky enough to be difficult to hold onto, hers was thicker, with a slight curl that continued to fascinate him.

"If I go home with you, will I feel those things?" He looked up from where he'd curled a lock of her hair around his fingertip to fixate on her lips again. They were a lovely peach color and ever-so-slightly glossy. Would she let him kiss her a second time? He felt like he'd missed something the first time and he desperately wanted to find out what it was.

Elise touched his arm. It was the lightest brush of her fingers, but it ran through him like a lightning bolt. "I don't know that I can promise that, but there's no harm in trying, right?"

Cal sucked in a sharp breath. He didn't know much about *relationships* or what it was like to have a home, but he knew there could be a great deal of harm in what they planned to do. Not to her — never to her, if he could help it — but definitely to him.

Too bad he didn't care.

Cal was hungry for the warmth she spoke of so reverently. He wanted to taste the life she lived, to bask in her smile and eat at her table and get even the briefest glimpse of what Kaz called *mate-hood*. He wanted all of it with a desperation that had transformed into an endless, cavernous ache, and he damn well intended to get it.

Bringing a lock of her hair to his lips, Cal murmured against the strands, "Deal."

～

FROM THE DESK OF ELISE SASINI, TEXT MESSAGES RECEIVED ON FEBRUARY 3rd 2045:
    DAD - 10:08 AM: Tell Dorothy to kiss my ass
    DAD - 10:09 AM: Proud of you, kid. Keep making trouble
    DAD - 10:10 AM: You should stop writing books, though. I don't need this kind of competition ;D

～

When she dared to imagine what it would be like to sit down with the elemental, Elise always pictured it would be in a public place. A secluded corner of Golden Gate Park, perhaps, or on the jagged rip-rap that edged the Bay, where selkies basked and foam bubbled against the shore. Their meetings would be clandestine, but in the neutral territory of a public space.

Never, in all her planning and daydreaming, did she imagine he would follow her home.

When Cal told her he would meet her on the mainland early the next morning, she didn't know what to expect. Not that she knew what to expect from *any* of this, of course. After all, who could have imagined the bargain he'd strike?

And what a bargain it was: Cal wanted to know what life was

like for regular people, so for the time it took her to write his story, he would live with her, eat with her, and...

Be with her. Whatever that meant.

By the time she stepped off of the ferry and onto the early morning bustle of Fisherman's Wharf, Elise had a kink in her neck from two nights spent in the sparse conditions of the Aerie and a stomach full of butterflies.

Why exactly had she agreed to his terms? Why did she feel this gnawing, possessive feeling in her gut? What if it turned out he couldn't stand her and abandoned the deal after a night? Would he appear out of thin air? Would the fog roll in despite the bright, clear February morning, heralding his arrival?

The answer, at least to the last question, was no.

Elise adjusted her baseball cap to fight the glare of the sun bouncing off of the slate gray water. Maneuvering her way around throngs of tourists *oo*-ing and *ah*-ing over the old decommissioned warship the *EVP Shadowbreaker* docked by an overpriced seafood shack selling lobster rolls, she peeked over her shoulder at the lapping waves. He said he would meet her on the dock, but—

A hand closed over hers. The fingers were cool and smooth, the grip firm but not aggressive. Elise jumped, her head swiveling to her right.

It took her a moment to recognize him. Cal stood in the shadow between two salt crusted buildings. His face was unmistakable, but dressed in dark jeans and long-sleeved black shirt, he could have blended in with any crowd in the city. Only his long silvery hair and black eyes might have drawn scrutiny.

"Oh," she breathed, letting him slowly reel her into his shadowed alcove. Her legs felt curiously unsteady. That possessive feeling grew with a lurch, digging into her with a ruthlessness that took her breath away. Her magic fizzed in her veins. *This one is mine,* it seemed to whisper. *Don't let him go.*

Swallowing hard, she choked out, "You look..."

Cal quirked a brow and waited for her to finish her sentence, but Elise didn't have the right words to do so. Not any ones that were appropriate, at least. He looked *good.* Not in the devastating, force of nature way he looked when he melted, buck naked, out of the fog, but in the *'I could be in entertainment feeds or the face of a perfume house if I wanted'* kind of way.

Elise cleared her throat and tried again. She could feel her signature vivid blush already rising to her cheeks. "I'm sorry, I just didn't expect you to wear clothes."

Embarrassment made her cheeks flush an even deeper, darker red almost as soon as the words were out of her mouth. *Gods,* why *did I just say that?*

"Nudity draws attention." Cal's lips thinned as he glanced at the tourists shuffling across the dock. If he noticed her embarrassment, he didn't seem to care. "I don't like attention, so I've learned to stash clothing in places I can easily access."

"Right. Makes sense," she replied, vividly recalling all the beautiful, almost opalescent skin she'd been lucky enough to see. Of course it would draw attention. Any person with a functioning brain stem would notice Cal, naked or not. Close behind the memory of all that beautiful, naked skin came their kiss, which she still felt all the way to her toes.

Seeing him there in the shadow of the alley, feeling his hand holding hers, she got a dizzying sense of vertigo. Was she really doing this? Trading her companionship for a story? Was she really taking *the* fog home with her? What would her father say if he knew?

As a father, he wouldn't like it. As a journalist... Well, Bob Sasini had done a number of unscrupulous things in his lifetime to get the scoop. Surely playing house with a man for a few months wasn't worse than going undercover as a feyrunner, or becoming a temporary anchor for a crooked vampire clan.

Right?

At any rate, she knew what she was doing. And even if she didn't, Elise wasn't certain she could just let Cal waltz back out of her life and into the fog, never to be seen again. Their meeting had altered something fundamental in her, though she still couldn't — or wouldn't — figure out what it was.

Cal's gaze slid over her flustered expression. Brow crinkling, he asked, "Is the clothing wrong? My friend chose them for me. I assumed he knew what he was doing." He frowned down at his shirt. "I did not consider the fact that he might have played a prank on me. He does that sometimes."

"No, no, you look great!" Elise waved a hand in front of her face. "I was just surprised, that's all. Your friend did a good job." Hoping to steer the conversation in a less embarrassing direction, she asked, "Do you have a lot of friends?"

Cal's expression gave nothing away. "No. Just one."

Elise didn't do what she did for a living and *not* know when someone didn't want to talk, so she let the subject drop. She made a mental note to follow up on the conversation later. "Right, well, if we want to beat the early lunch rush downtown, we should probably head to my place."

He cocked his head to one side. She watched, fascinated, as his hair flowed in the opposite direction — as if it moved with a will of its own. Was it an elemental thing, or something particular to him? "How will we get there?"

"I was going to take the m-lev. Why? How do you get around the city?"

Cal lifted a hand and flicked a finger in a dismissive gesture that was not quite wave and not quite wiggle, but some strange combination of both. "I don't need transportation."

Elise leaned forward, her interest piqued. The sounds of chatter and a busker playing kettle drums faded into nothing as she pinned her entire focus on the elemental. "How do you travel? Do you have some sort of m-gate ability?"

"M-gate?" He looked vaguely disgusted. "No, I dematerialize and ride the air currents to my destination."

Fascinating. He didn't have to travel *with* the fog to move unseen. It explained a lot of the sightings, and how he was sometimes said to appear out of thin air. She'd have to remember to put that in her notes.

"Can you take passengers?"

He shook his head. "No. Unless you can become incorporeal, you would just fall through my arms."

Elise colored as she pictured herself cradled in his arms, sweeping through the fog banks over the water at night. Butterflies fluttered low in her stomach. Of course, that sort of thing only happened in feeds, but even practical, driven Elise could indulge in a fantasy every now and again.

Shaking herself, she replied, "Well, since you can't take me with you and you don't know where I live, you'll just have to take the train with me."

She gave him her usual sunny smile to cover her nerves. Taking a step out of the shadows, she was surprised to find he still held her hand. Looking pointedly at where they were connected, she said, "Ah, you can let go. I promise I won't lose you in the crowd."

"Why?" He stepped close behind her. Cal's expression was aloof, but she didn't miss the way he scanned the crowd, nor how tense his shoulders became when a family with several young children in *Ripley's Believe It or Not!* museum t-shirts squeezed past them. One little boy clutched a colorful sparrow-shaped kite in a chubby, clawed hand.

"Oh, it's just—"

Cal nudged her forward, toward the entrance of the wharf and the m-lev station across the street. His fingers tightened around hers as his aquiline features hardened into a mulish expression. "I watch people holding hands all the time. I want to do it." He lifted his chin, adding, "It's part of my terms."

Elise swallowed. He hadn't told her much the previous night, but she didn't have to be a reporter to see the context hovering around his bargain. No one who wanted to *try* living a normal life had ever truly *had* one. Until that moment, she hadn't quite grasped what that meant.

Has no one ever held his hand before?

"Okay," she replied, smoothing out her expression so he wouldn't see her dismay. "We need to go to the other side of the street and take the outbound train."

Cal eyed the stop across the street, his brow furrowed. She wondered if he'd ever been on an m-lev before, but that question was quickly answered when she had to help him board. Elise didn't blame him for his trepidation. Although San Francisco's public transportation was top of the line, running on a combination of super charged magnets and a constantly monitored m-grid, the speed at which they traversed the hilly terrain and packed streets unsettled even seasoned riders.

However, like most public services in the EVP, it was blessedly free, so no one complained too much.

The ride took thirty minutes and was mostly fine. Cal sat beside her silently, his black eyes sweeping over the other passengers every few seconds like he thought they might whip out weapons when he wasn't looking. He never let go of her hand.

The only part that truly seemed to unsettle him was the ride through the inky darkness beneath Twin Peaks. The tunnel was only a little over two miles long and notorious for the secret alcoves and underground passageways that fed directly into the Markets up above, though the EVP government routinely sent Patrol out on sweeps to close off the illegal tunnels.

Elise was used to the stretch of pure blackness at the end of her rides home, but Cal wasn't. As soon as their car dipped smoothly underground, his fingers clenched around hers, his entire body vibrating with tension.

"It's okay. It's just a tunnel," she whispered, taking in his suddenly rigid profile. His hair, which had previously only swirled with a gentle current against his back, began to whip around them, drawing the curious eyes of their fellow passengers.

Cal turned his head to stare down at her. His expression was as aloof as it always was, except for the marked tightness around his eyes and mouth. "I don't like being underground," he explained, barely audible over the low rumble of the m-lev.

Elise wanted to pinch herself. Of course an elemental wouldn't enjoy being underground. She couldn't imagine how unnatural that would feel to someone literally made from the *sky*.

Squeezing his hand, she soothed, "It's almost over. We get off at the next stop, and then we walk up a hill. No more tunnels."

Cal nodded, but his grip on her hand didn't loosen until they were exiting the brick-lined station and stepping into the sunlight. It wasn't a quick walk back to her place, but Elise didn't mind. The trek up the steep hill to her new apartment gave her time to think.

Bringing Cal home with her was a risk. There was no telling what he was capable of. Being a weather witch meant she had some small ability to protect herself, but against a force of nature like Cal? Elise wouldn't stand a chance.

But what was the worth in uncovering a story without an element of risk? She'd made a deal, and she intended to keep it. Getting the truth about what exactly Cal did for the city and *why* would be worth it.

At the very least, it was a good excuse to keep him close.

By the time they got to her floor, Elise was flushed with exertion and giddy with nerves. Would he like her home? Did it matter? What was she going to do with him once he was settled? She'd promised him something totally amorphous. Just how far was she willing to go to give him the experience he wanted?

If she could stop thinking about his eager but infuriatingly chaste, world-shattering kiss, she might actually be able to dig up an answer or two.

Unlocking her door with an old fashioned key and a slightly out of date thumbprint scanner, she sucked in a deep breath and stepped inside.

As soon as she crossed the threshold, a pleasant, androgynous voice called out, *"Welcome home, Elise. Would you like me to turn the lights on?"*

Cal's hands closed over her hips and drew her backward into his chest. Elise let out a squeak on impact. His voice was a low bark when he demanded, "What was that? Who's in your home?"

"No one!" She wiggled to get out of his grasp, but it was no use. Cal's grip was immovable as he carefully leaned around her, his head angled to see past her entryway and into the kitchen and small living room beyond. She felt the cool brush of his magic ghosting up her spine, its tenor more aggressive than she'd felt so far.

"It's just my Met," she explained, embarrassingly breathless. "I keep weird hours, so it helps me keep track of everything. I can turn the voice activation off if it'll make you more comfortable."

"There's no one in there?"

"No, just a little rubber ball thing that knows too much about me."

Cal made a soft rumbling sound in his chest. It vibrated up her spine as he slowly eased them inside. Elise was hyper-aware of every bit of him that pressed against her back, as well as the hands that were curled over the bows of her hip bones like they were made to fit there. Magic licked over her nerves, raw and deliciously cool.

When he marched them into the space between the kitchen and the living room, she cleared her throat and pointed to the feed screen mounted on her wall. Just below it, on a small wooden cabinet, her Met sat waiting for instructions. A dull glow pulsed in its center.

"See that? It's my Met."

Cal's fingers flexed on her hips. "I don't know what that is."

Gods, just how feral is this man?

It boggled her mind to think that someone born in 1906 didn't know what a *Met* was. Surely, even if he'd never lived in a home, he'd been *inside* places before? He had to know at least some modern technology. He had to understand things like lights and showers and microwaves. If he could put on a pair of jeans, he had to know how to use a toilet, right?

Giving his hands a brisk pat as a signal to let her go, Elise explained, "It's just an extension of the internet. It's a fun bit of m-tech that can do things like manage my schedule, do basic cleaning, and set perimeter wards. Tons of people have them in their homes, Cal."

Cal slowly released her and took a step back. Turning, she watched him scan her half-unpacked apartment with narrowed eyes. "You're a witch. Why don't you set your own perimeter wards?"

Setting her bag down by the couch, she answered, "I do, but it's a convenience thing. Not all of us have the time to refresh wards every week. When I get busy, the Met does it for me."

When Cal only made that same low rumbling sound in response, Elise shrugged. "Right, well, this is my place." She waved a hand at the stacks of half unpacked boxes littering the floor. "Please excuse the boxes. I moved in last week, so I haven't had much of a chance to unpack yet. I didn't think I'd have a guest coming home with me when I left for the Aerie, or else I probably would have done more."

Or not. Elise wasn't the neatest of people. She didn't have time for all that fussing when she had words to write, stories to unspool, hidden worlds to examine. In fact, she was pretty sure some of the boxes hadn't even been unpacked in her *old* place.

Cal prowled past her, his hair moving in slow eddies around his shoulders and back. He didn't move like a man his size should. He glided across the floor and around the boxes in his way almost like he was *floating* past them. Not one of his steps made a sound.

She watched him move to the wide window that took up most of the wall opposite her feed screen. The view wasn't perfect, since the sunshine had a tendency to dredge up smog that obscured a bit of the city, but it was still gorgeous.

"You're new to the city?" Cal glanced at her over his shoulder. He looked just as intimidating silhouetted against the window as he did on the dock, though it was in a different way. Then, he hit her like a wild force of nature. Now, dressed in his black clothing and with the hard plains of his body standing out starkly against the view, he looked *dangerous.*

Elise's stomach swooped. Gods, but she wanted to unravel all of this mysterious man's secrets. Like the very first time she basked in a storm, Elise wanted nothing more than to get closer to that magnetic force, the danger he represented, and take him into the hot, burning core of magic inside her.

It was a raw sort of feeling that welled up in her from the same part of her that chased stories and scaled dangerous heights and turned her face up to feel the howling storm lash her cheeks. It was a *craving.*

"Elise?"

"Sorry!" She turned on her heel, hoping to cover up the way her blush had spread to her chest and how quick her breathing had become. Their arrangement was complicated enough. They didn't need to add her lust for thrills into things.

Swallowing her embarrassment, she waved over her shoulder, asking him to follow her as she escorted him to her office-and-guest-room. "To answer your question, no, I'm not new. I was born and raised here. I just moved into this place because it was better than my old apartment."

She couldn't hear his whispering steps moving across the floorboards as he followed her down the hall, but she could feel his nearness. "Why is it better?"

Casting him a smile over her shoulder, she answered honestly, "Because it has a better view of the fog, of course."

CHAPTER FOUR

HOMES WERE STRANGE PLACES. CAL KNEW THAT LONG before Elise invited him into hers, but he experienced a whole new appreciation for the concept after he stepped inside.

It had all the basics he was familiar with from his time in the Aerie and his confinement under the Tower: walls, doors, a mattress he presumed was for sleeping, and a washroom. He'd peered through enough windows in his lifetime to know that Elise had much of what everyone else seemed to have, too, such as comfortable furniture and a vast collection of baubles he couldn't quite wrap his head around.

However, there were several key differences between what he expected and what he experienced.

First, Elise's home *smelled* nice. As soon as he walked through the door — an oddity on its own, considering he had never been invited into a home before — Cal was hit by a pleasant, unnameable fragrance. A blend of her natural, crisp scent and something warmer, it made his stomach tighten with a tension he couldn't decipher. A far cry from the cold, musty smells of the Aerie and much better than the dank, chemical scent of the Solbourne dungeon.

Second, she didn't lock the doors or set wards. Elise barely even glanced at her perimeter wards. When he reluctantly stepped into the guest room she provided for him, he half expected her to slam the door and immediately throw up a ward to try and imprison him inside. Despite his eagerness, he was morbidly curious: Would she reveal a true, darker motive behind her story?

It turned out the answer was no.

Elise was sunny and cheerful as she arranged a bed for him, chattering about how she'd been lucky enough to "snag" the apartment, and how her father's book somehow played into it. He could barely follow the story, since he was too caught up in watching her move and listening to her chipper, fast-paced voice. When she was done, she didn't even close the door.

She walked out of the guest room, hips swaying in her tight black leggings, and Cal stared after her. He listened to the sounds of her moving about the half-unpacked apartment with growing perplexity.

Yes, he made the deal and intended to follow through with it, but there was a large part of him that still believed she was somehow looking to use him. Even when he stood on that crowded dock and held her hand, he wondered how long it would take for her to show her true intentions.

But Elise hadn't shown him anything other than genuine kindness. She wanted something from him, but it was nothing he couldn't afford to lose. What he stood to gain from their deal was worth far, far more than his story.

Cal sat on the edge of the fold out bed. It creaked under his weight, but he barely noticed it as he glanced around the room. The guest room held a few scattered boxes with hasty scrawl across their faces. Spiky handwriting labeled them as '*office I guess*', or '*fragile - DO NOT DROP!!*', and even the amusing '*????*'. He didn't know why that made him smile, nor why seeing it made him feel like he knew Elise a little better.

Cal's gaze wandered over the haphazard stacks of cardboard to land on her desk. A bulletin board loomed over it, so laden with pinned notes and photos that none of the cork board could be seen. The desk itself was nearly swallowed up by stacks of recycled books and scattered sticky notes. What did it say about her that she seemed to prefer old fashioned pen and paper? Cal didn't know, but he found it endearing anyway.

Eyes lingering on what looked like a photo of the fog sweeping over the ruins of the Sutro Baths, Cal focused on the sounds of Elise moving around in the kitchen. A door opened with a strange sucking sound, and then there was a smaller clatter of glass knocking against itself.

He could picture the scene perfectly in his mind. How many times had he glimpsed people in their kitchens, moving with a rhythm he didn't understand? He could imagine Elise standing over a cutting board, knife in hand, as a man slid up behind her to kiss the long line of her throat, fingertips sliding under the hem of her shirt to tickle her skin.

Cal scowled. He didn't like that image.

Fisting a handful of the blankets she'd so painstakingly laid out for him, he considered the complex question of what he wanted out of this deal and how he planned to get it. She was right that he wanted a home, but he felt in his bones that he wanted something more than that, too. Unfortunately, he didn't have the vocabulary or experience necessary to define it. A mate was the closest thing he could manage, but even that didn't feel right.

Kaz explained to him that a mate was something special. Something like a home and a lover and a best friend and a fascinating stranger all wrapped up in one being. Cal hungered for that. He just wasn't sure he was going about getting it in the right way.

Would Kaz approve of his bargain with Elise? Not that Cal *needed* the orc's approval, of course, but he was the only person he could even passingly count as a friend. He was also the only person Cal knew who understood matehood, even if he wasn't personally mated yet. Orcs held matehood sacred. Though he never understood the appeal in the past, he was beginning to get an inkling as to why so many revered the bond between mates.

What would it be like to be allowed into every corner of someone's life? Would he see himself in the home as much as he saw Elise in every note, in every breath he took? What kind of privilege was it to be let that close to another being? Cal could barely comprehend the enormity of the questions that circled his mind in agitated gusts. He'd never given himself the luxury of imagining himself in the position he now found himself in.

If he had learned anything since his disastrous birth, it was to follow his instincts. They had yet to guide him wrong, and they were currently telling him that whatever it was he *needed,* Elise had it. That impulse was clear enough, at least.

Feeling confined, as he usually did when he spent too long in his physical form, Cal stood up from the bed he probably wouldn't use and followed the sounds and smells coming from the small kitchen.

"I don't sleep," he announced, agitated and craving her attention.

Elise froze, a silver spatula poised over two identical sandwiches in a pan. A heartbeat later, the tension unwound from her shoulders. She turned her head to look at him with a baffled smile. "Oh, I didn't know that. Sorry. Don't worry about the bed, then."

Cal prowled closer. The smell of something savory drew him in, as well as the unwavering impulse to be close to her. "I rest, but I don't sleep like you do. When I dematerialize, I can do something *like* sleeping, but it's not the same."

He wasn't sure why he felt compelled to tell her this, but he did. Perhaps it was because he felt like he'd learned so much about her since he stepped into her home, or maybe it was that hungry thing in him, desperate to be known by someone, anyone. Whatever it was, the words came spilling out without his permission.

She blinked, her smile dimmed only slightly, but otherwise appeared unfazed. Did nothing ruffle her? Surely she didn't spend enough time with other elementals to take *everything* he did in stride. There weren't exactly scores of them dropping out of the sky — as far as he knew, anyway.

He didn't like how that thought made him feel, either. He wanted to be the only elemental she spent her time with. She was his mate for the time being, wasn't she? That meant he was hers. He didn't want to share her even in his imagination.

Feeling vexed and more confused than ever, Cal did the only thing that actually seemed to help his mood. He stepped up behind her and wrapped his hands around her trim, athletic waist. Coils of mist unfurled from the edges of his form to curl around her shoulders and lithe legs, anchoring them together.

That's better, he thought, releasing a harsh breath. The feeling of constriction vanished when he slid his dematerialized form over her. Magic sparked between them — her innate, stormy nature calling to his own wild energy. Together, they hummed in perfect sync.

We fit, he thought, fingers tightening around her waist.

Finally, Elise looked surprised. The spatula made a soft *ting* when she lowered it to the rim of the pan. "Cal? Are you okay?"

"I'm not used to being in this form for so long," he admitted. It was true, if not the whole reason for his agitation. "It is restricting."

"I can imagine it would be." She flipped one of the sandwiches, revealing a perfectly browned slice of bread. Cal watched her movements greedily, never having been afforded such an intimate view of a domestic task. "Does touch help?"

He eyed the way her long fingers curled around the handle of the spatula and was surprised by the vivid, erotic image that rushed to the forefront of his brain. His cock chose that moment to remind him of its crucial role in this deal of theirs. The sensation still unsettled him. Would it react like this to everyone now, or just her? Did he even *want* to feel this way for anyone else?

"I'm not sure," he answered, for more reasons than she could properly guess. "But I like touching you. I've never gotten to touch anyone before."

Elise turned her head so fast, she came very close to slamming her cheek into his shoulder. He frowned and leaned back as she said, "You've— I'm sorry, what?"

He eyed the sandwiches in the pan. They were beginning to smoke. "Are they supposed to do that?"

"Shit." She waved her hand over the induction stove's keypad. A friendly chime sounded, apparently to let everyone know that the burner had been deactivated. Carefully scooping the slightly charred sandwiches onto two waiting plates, she asked, "What do you mean you've never gotten to touch anyone before, Cal? Everyone touches people."

"I don't." He found himself giving her waist a small, possessive squeeze. "Not until now, anyway."

And what a luxury it was to touch her. Elise was warm and soft, but with a strength to her that spoke of activity, vitality. She was the kind of woman he might see jogging across the black sand beaches at sunrise, or hiking the Twin Peaks trail on a hot day, sweat glistening on her golden skin. He felt like he was holding something more tangible, more preciously human, than he had any right to be.

Guilt and shame gnawed at him, demanded he wash himself of such small, essential pleasures as touching and being touched, but Cal selfishly pushed them aside. For once, he didn't want to listen to the damning voice the acolytes had given him. He wanted to know what it was like to have a mate, and he intended to do so.

With the sandwiches settled and the stove turned off, Elise turned slowly in his arms. With her arms extended backwards, she curled her fingers around the oven door's handle, as if she needed to brace herself for what she said next. "Cal... Have you really never had any human contact before? *None?*"

Cal indulged his selfishness by skimming the pads of his fingers down the length of her arms. She was wearing a little blue t-shirt with the words *RUTH ASAWA HIGH* printed on the front. It was faded and thin, with short sleeves that revealed all the strong lines and smooth skin of her freckled arms.

"Loft's acolytes aren't exactly known for being touchy," he dryly answered. "The year I spent with them did not include hugs and kisses. The year I spent in the Solbourne dungeon didn't either."

Oh, he'd certainly had physical contact, but only the kind that came at the end of a fist, so he didn't bother counting it.

And after an introduction to the world such as that, why would he seek out companionship? The only kind he was ever offered came with deadly strings attached. Kaz didn't count. Their friendship was based mostly on a mutual exchange of information and the respect two predators had for one another. It was the closest thing to companionship he ever had, but even he knew it wasn't what he really wanted.

After a while, he stopped wondering what it would be like to be held the way he saw others hold their loved ones. To kiss. To have his hair stroked. To fuck.

Until Elise, of course.

Their arrangement had strings, but they were the kind he could tolerate. She didn't want him to commit more sins, but simply to tell his story. In exchange, he would finally know all the delights he assumed were out of his reach.

She stared up at him with wide eyes, her lips parted with surprise or horror or something else he couldn't fathom. Her fingers went white around the silver handle of the oven door. "So you've never hugged anyone? Kissed? Nothing at all?"

Cal's eyes darted back up from where they had been contemplating the delicate curve of her clavicle. At some point, she'd cut a slit in the collar of the old shirt. It sagged, just a little, and revealed her winged collar bones to his hungry gaze.

"I've kissed *you*," he reminded her. *And I will do it again.*

Cal chose not to say the second part aloud, but the flush in her cheeks told him she picked up on it anyway.

He watched, fascinated, as Elise took in a large breath and

then slowly let it out. Her fingers uncurled from around the handle one by one. Turning slightly to the side, she picked up the plates. When her eyes met his again, they were glowing with a sort of determination he'd never seen directed his way before. It was at once breathtaking and terrifying.

Her voice was low with restrained emotion when she said, "Let's have lunch, and then... *Then* you need to start telling me your story, Cal, because I have so very many questions."

FROM THE DESK OF ELISE SASINI, A TRANSCRIPT OF A VOICE RECORDING DATED FEBRUARY 4th 2045:

CALAMITY: What do you want to know? Everyone knows my story already.

ELISE: I don't think that's true. People know the story of the disaster, and they know the legends about you, but they don't know the truth about who you are and what you do.

CALAMITY: And what makes you think those things aren't the truth?

ELISE: Maybe truth isn't the right word. I'm talking about... [PAUSE] everything else. You're more than just what happened in 1906, Cal.

CALAMITY: [LENGTHY PAUSE] That's where you're wrong.

Elise had interviewed many people in her career. She had, after all, started working as a journalist when she was ten — for her own newspaper, of course. *The St. Francis Chronicle* wasn't the most prestigious paper of record, but it kept the neighborhood abreast of all the latest developments, like when Mrs. Manfredi put an illegal pool in her backyard or that time the neighborhood association tried to exterminate the pixies in the park's shed, despite it being against the city's environmental bylaws to do so. It's reputation was helped by a ringing endorsement from San Francisco's most celebrated crime writer, Bob Sasini, who lived on 113 Santa Clara Avenue, and happened to be the publisher's amused father.

Hopping from her little paper to school journalism, then to *The Light* and her own books, Elise had more experience with interviewing than most journalists her age. She learned all the best tricks at her father's knee, and she'd honed her skills on the rolling, bouncing San Francisco streets.

None of that helped her with Cal.

No matter how hard she tried to keep things straight, to stay in the cool, professional headspace that allowed for an objective interview, she just... couldn't manage it.

Perhaps it was the memory of his kiss and the greedy, possessive hands that reached for her at every opportunity. Maybe it was the way he sat across her small kitchen table, his black on black eyes fixed to her face like he was the one trying to figure *her* out. Elise suspected it was a mix of both, as well as the fact that she struggled to stomach some of the things he told her.

Cal was stark in his honesty. He didn't sugarcoat things, and he didn't seem to understand social niceties. He was reluctant to talk about some things, but she didn't think it was because he was trying to hide anything. Elise quickly realized that, like his heartbreaking inexperience with physical contact, Cal was similarly unfamiliar with *talking* to people.

And no wonder. The more she learned about his story, the more she tried to understand why he talked to anyone at all.

"Cal..." Elise's voice trailed off into nothing, her words evaporating into so much dry air in her throat. She sat across from him, both of their grilled cheese sandwiches sitting cold and untouched on their plates, and tried to quell the urge to reach across the table to hold his hand.

That wasn't what interviewers did. They let their subject say what they needed to with a patient detachment, guiding only when absolutely necessary. She wasn't supposed to feel the prick of tears behind her eyelids when he explained, expressionless and without inflection, the circumstances of his birth to her.

"It was my fault," he continued in his soft, deadpan voice. "Every one of those deaths is on my soul. All three thousand of them."

Elise had to swallow twice before the lump in her throat shrank enough to allow her to speak. She shifted her weight in her chair. Fighting the urge to comfort him somehow, she tucked one leg under her and fisted her hands in her lap.

"Is that what the acolytes told you?" she asked, her tone brittle with outrage.

Cal inclined his head. His hair, starkly white against his black shirt and the glorious sunset streaming through the windows behind him, flowed in slow currents around his shoulders. "They took me in," he explained, "and they taught me how to be with people. I didn't understand what had happened to me for weeks afterward. I couldn't understand them, the things they said, or why my form was different than it used to be. When I finally learned their language, all they ever talked about was my sin, and how Loft had given me to them so that they could teach me how to atone for it. They thought I was a test of their devotion."

Elise knew it wasn't helpful, but words spilled out of her anyway. "But.. But Cal, it *wasn't* your fault. You didn't have any control over it. No one gets to control how or where they're born."

Cal's fingers moved restlessly over the tabletop. Although his expression didn't change, she could tell he was getting restless. His long hair had begun to dematerialize into wisps of fog, and she could feel the cool kiss of it along the skin of her arms and bare feet.

Remembering what he said about feeling confined, Elise eschewed the last of her tenuous control over her professionalism and reached across the table.

Cal's eyes widened when her fingers curled around his. For a moment, he felt strange, almost not-quite-there, and Elise realized that he had barely managed to keep his physical form as he told his story.

As soon as their skin touched, he solidified. That hungry look gleamed in his eyes as he snatched at her hand, holding it like he thought she might try to rip it away from him.

Tracing the contours of her knuckles and short, clear-coated nails with his fingertips, he said, "It doesn't matter. It's my fault, and I'll spend the rest of my life trying to make up for all the death I caused."

Elise's fingers spasmed. His naked honesty hit her like a bolt to the chest. She expected him to be mysterious, not *tortured*. "Is that why you watch over the city? Because you feel like you have to atone for 1906?"

"Yes."

Trying to make sense of the tangle he presented her with, she shifted subjects. It was much for his sake as hers. She wasn't sure how much more sorrow she could withstand before she leaned over the table to take him into her arms. "You mentioned that you were imprisoned. How does that fit in with the Aerie?"

"Much of the Aerie was destroyed in the disaster. They needed to rebuild. I wasn't locked away so much by the end of my first year, mostly because I didn't know where to go or what to do with myself. I used to stay around the dock to be closer to the fog. One day, a builder caught me rematerializing and contacted Patrol." He shrugged, but she could feel the tension in the hand that held hers. "The acolytes fought for custody of me, claiming it was their religious right, but the sovereign wanted me under his control."

Elise paled. Although it was before her time, she knew there was no arguing with Thaddeus II. Even before he lost his mind, the man was legendarily autocratic. His word was law, and if he wanted something, he used any means to get it.

"How long were you imprisoned?" she dared to ask, her dread solidifying into a sickly weight in her stomach.

Cal lifted her hand up to his mouth almost experimentally. Slowly, he pressed his lips to the center of her palm. A *zing* of magic shocked her nerve endings and sent a wave of heat through her, adding to that possessive fire in her belly. She watched his eyelids flutter, white lashes brushing the tops of high, blade-like cheekbones with a breathless sort of hunger.

His whisper tickled the sensitive skin of her palm. "Four hundred and three days."

Horror wiped away the tantalizing rush of desire in her veins.

Four hundred and three days. On top of what was a sort of de facto year of isolation in the Aerie. Over two years of confinement and indoctrination of a being meant to run as wild and powerful as the rolling fog.

The isolation and confinement alone would be enough to scar anyone, but an *elemental...* Elise shuddered to think about what that must have been like for him. And that was before she dared probe into what exactly Thaddeus II did to him during that time.

Even before he became Mad Thad, the sovereign wasn't known for his mercy. No elves were.

Elise angled her hand to cup his jaw. Cal's skin was perfectly smooth, no hint of stubble. The deep black of his eyes glittered in the orange light of the sunset as she smoothed her thumb over one beautifully cut cheekbone.

"I'm sorry," she whispered, blinking back tears. "I'm so sorry, Cal."

Gods, when she made her proposal to Dorothy, when she thought up the idea to write *The Shrouded City,* she never once considered it would end up with her sitting across her kitchen table from a man carrying so much hurt.

Cal was an almost mythic figure. He was a legend she grew up with, an all-powerful child's daydream and seductively dangerous adult fantasy.

He wasn't supposed to be... broken.

And he was broken. She could see it in the suspicious way he watched her, as if he expected her to do something to hurt him every time she opened her mouth. It was written in every gesture, every flat word and in the almost defiant way he reached for her, as if daring her to deny him this comfort he so obviously craved.

Glory save me, she thought, wracked with a sudden wave of bitter guilt. Bile crawled up the back of her throat. *I can't write this book.*

Elise withdrew her hand abruptly and stood up from her chair. She turned her back on him and tried to get her composure. Of course she'd heard tragic stories before. Of course she'd done hard, gut-wrenching interviews. This was different. Something about Cal twisted her up inside until the tension was too much too take.

There was no thrill of discovery in his story anymore. There was only a deep, painful ache in her heart.

Pressing her palm over her racing heart — the same one he kissed — Elise choked out, "I... Cal, I don't know if this is such a good idea."

His gaze sharpened. "What?"

They hadn't even gotten to the part about people always wanting to use him for something, but now she could imagine it all too clearly. Mad Thad wanted to use him, probably as security for the city, if not as part of his secret shadow arm of Patrol. No doubt others had the same idea. A person who could be anywhere he wished without being noticed, who could see and hear anything in the city, was someone to have on your side whether they actually wanted to be there or not.

Of course people would want to use him.

Just like I am.

It didn't matter that he'd agreed to it. It didn't matter that he was getting something out of it. It didn't even matter that she felt like his story still ought to be told, so he could finally see that he was more than the crushing guilt he carried. She talked a big game on that dock about not wanting to take advantage of him like he thought, but was she really so different from those who came before her?

No. She felt a deep kinship with this exquisite, broken being, and now she couldn't bear the idea of exploiting him for something as shallow as a *book*.

No contracts had been signed yet. Things were still in negotiation. There was time to back out, to say she didn't feel comfortable with the story. It wouldn't look good, but a hit to her reputation was better than this ugly feeling of guilt that ate at her insides like corrosive acid.

Turning around, Elise found Cal standing up from his seat, his brows lowered over his eyes and his mouth pressed into a hard line. One hand was flattened on the table top, while the other was a tight fist by his thigh. He looked furious. Of course he did. He probably realized just how awful she was.

Elise lifted a shaking hand to push a lock of hair out of her eyes. "Look, Cal, I'm sorry. I didn't know. If I had, I wouldn't have— I wouldn't have done any of this. I would have just left you alone. I'm sorry. I'm going to call my editor and tell her that I can't write the—"

Magic slid over her skin. In the blink of an eye, her apartment filled with a haze of cool fog. Elise gasped. The air was wet and sweet on her tongue, but she didn't have time to appreciate it.

Cal rose to his full height, his expression thunderous. His hair whipped behind him, almost entirely dematerialized into his summoned fog, and his black eyes were hardened into pitiless obsidian.

"You're going back on our deal?" he demanded, swooping toward her in one long, very *unhuman* stride. Elise backed up until her spine hit the edge of the kitchen counter, but he didn't stop his advance until he was pressed up against her. Cal's fingers gripped the edge of the granite slab, trapping her there.

Elise felt the hard press of his body along the length of hers more than she felt the edge of the counter biting into the small of her back. Magic was thick in the air between them, bright like ozone but with a sharp metallic tang like blood.

"Cal, you've been used *enough*," she explained, voice hoarse. "I don't think I can go through with this knowing that I would just be another in a long line of people trying to exploit you."

His eyes narrowed until they were little more than glittering shards of black stone in his silvery face. "I don't care if you exploit me. I want what you promised."

Gods, and what a cruel promise it was. More guilt curdled her stomach. Thank Glory she hadn't actually touched her grilled cheese. If she had, Elise wasn't sure she would have been able to keep it down.

"I shouldn't have agreed to your terms." A flash of something very close to hurt passed over his expression. *Oh, no. I can't hurt him. I can't.* Panicked, Elise reached for him with both hands. She twisted his shirt in her fists and rushed to explain, "Cal, listen. When I agreed, I didn't realize the extent of your... of what you'd been through. I never would have agreed to it if I knew. You deserve a home and love and all the things we talked about not as a *deal,* but because it's your right as a sapient being. I can't stomach the idea of being someone who gives that to you for the first time, only to rip it away as soon as our transaction is done. You deserve better than that."

Just the idea of sending this poor soul packing the moment the book was finished made her ill. It was all fun and games when she thought he was just socially awkward or inexperienced, but this was different. What kind of monster *was* she?

Cool hands cupped the sides of her neck. Cal's grip was firm; his thumbs pressed hard into the line of her jaw. Elise stared up at him with wide eyes as he clearly struggled to find the words for something. To tell her off? To shame her for what was so clearly a terrible mistake?

"No." His voice was louder, harder, than she'd yet heard it. This was no murmur. It was a stone cold demand. "No, I do not accept this. I want our deal. I'll have it, Elise. I *will.*"

"Cal—"

His mouth crashed down on hers. She yelped, surprised by the flash of pain caused by her lips hitting her teeth, but she didn't pull away. Cal angled her head back and leaned into her until all she could see and smell and feel was him.

The pressure on her lips softened as he molded his mouth to hers, seeking something he clearly didn't know how to find. Elise's heart lurched in her chest. She was his first kiss. One hundred and thirty-nine years old, and he had only ever kissed *her*. No wonder he felt so desperate as he slid his lips against hers, a needy sound rumbling in the back of his throat.

Cal was starving for affection. She'd callously dangled hers in front of his nose, only to snatch it out of his reach by backing out of their deal.

Elise felt something in her crumble. The last clinging remnants of any professionalism were swept away with her rejection of their deal. Perhaps he wouldn't let her back out of the deal, but that didn't mean she had to actually go through with it. If she was going to do this, it wasn't going to be a transaction. It occurred to her that he may not feel comfortable interacting with her *outside* of the structure of a deal, and that was unacceptable. She couldn't let him go.

Elise would keep up the facade of their deal, but it wasn't going to be because she wanted something from him. She wouldn't be another in a long line of *takers*.

Fierce possessiveness and the overwhelming desire to protect this incredible, damaged being swept through her, scouring her doubts like a bitter wind.

For once, Cal was going to know what it was like to *receive*.

Elise untangled her fingers from the hem of his shirt and smoothed them upward, over the trim expanse of his stomach and the sweep of his chest. Curling her arms around his back, she stroked the muscles bracketing his spine with careful slowness. He shuddered, lips stilling their frantic movement against hers. His breaths puffed in harsh exhales against her cheeks.

She hummed a soft, soothing note and leaned into him, guiding the kiss into something softer, deeper. Her lips parted and she very gently swept her tongue over his bottom lip. The noise of hungry surprise that escaped him made her stomach muscles tense. A pounding heat took up residence between her thighs.

It didn't take him long to realize what he'd been missing. Cal was a voracious kisser. He let her lead, but she got the sense that it was only because he was learning, figuring out what he liked. As soon as he realized he could *taste* her, Cal kissed her like the starved creature he was.

Elise's blood was molten with desire. The magic between them was saturated with it. Even the fog obscuring the interior of her apartment began to crackle with the neon pink and teal sparks of her energy. Every slide of his tongue against hers, every soft groan of pained pleasure he made, every unconscious rock of his hips into hers made her pulse throb with a deep, achy rhythm between her thighs. Gods, she *wanted* this man more than she'd wanted anyone in her life.

Moving her hands back around to press against his chest, Elise tore her mouth away with a ragged gasp. She had to go slow. He was new to this, and making sure he was comfortable and *ready* for intimacy was essential.

Cal made to follow her retreat, chasing her lips with his own, but she turned her head away. "Cal, we need to talk about—"

His lips, wet and swollen from her kisses, trailed over her cheekbone to press against the shell of her ear. "Don't take this from me, witch," he rasped, mistaking her protest for a rejection. "A deal is a deal."

He paused, breathing hard, before he begged in a broken whisper, "Please don't take this from me."

Elise squeezed her eyes shut. How in the gods' names could she refuse him? If it was a deal he wanted, then she would just have to give it to him — in her own way.

CHAPTER FIVE

FROM THE DESK OF ELISE SASINI, AN EXCERPT
FROM THE MANUSCRIPT *THE SHROUDED CITY:*

He calls himself Calamity.

The word is derived from the ancient Latin term 'kadami-tas', meaning loss or defeat, and later, more recognizably, 'calamitas', meaning disaster, damage, or great misfortune. The word took a winding route through medieval French — 'calamité' — to finally settle in the crowded bed of fifteenth century English as 'calamity'.

When I first met Cal, I was taken aback by the implication of such a name. Of course, knowing the only clear facts about his history available to the public, I thought I knew what it referred to, but I was still surprised.

Did he name himself? If so, why would he choose a name that called back to a disaster that took the lives of over three thousand people?

Knowing him as I do now, with the intimacy and constant, pleasant surprise of a mate, I am no longer reminded of the grim events his moniker immortalizes. Like everything else in his life, Calamity was forced upon him. When I hear it, I am reminded

that he is a man who has grown into his own agency, despite the
world attempting to take it at every turn.

He is Calamity. He is a force of nature more powerful and
vast than our government would comfortably admit. He is all-
consuming. He is an act of godly wrath made flesh, and by some
miracle, he has chosen to be kind to us.

He is Calamity. He is mine.

OVER THE NEXT FEW WEEKS, THEY SETTLED INTO LIFE
together. It was no small task, considering Cal had never lived in a
home before, let alone alongside another person. Routines had to
be established, habits reorganized, and questions answered. Cal
learned to use the stove — though he mostly preferred the greasy
takeout the rare times he actually ate — and Elise got used to his
constant coming and going.

Though she'd hinted at the conversation several times, testing
the waters, Cal refused to let her out of their deal, so Elise stuck to
her plan.

Cal held strictly to the terms she'd foolishly agreed to, but, after a
sleepless night of internal debate and recrimination, she decided that
there was no harm in letting him think they were still exchanging
favors if he wanted to. For her part, there was no deal to speak of.

When he drifted into the apartment after long stretches of
what he called his *vigil,* Elise did the job he expected of her: she
listened to him tell his story, asked questions at the appropriate
times or when things needed to be clarified, and wrote. He didn't
need to know that she had no plans to publish the manuscript. As
far as she was concerned, it was a way to get to know him and a
handy excuse to keep him near. That was all it needed to be.

The more she learned, the more certain of her feelings she
became. What began as a plan to find the truth behind the man in
the fog became a carefully constructed artifice covering up a
campaign of warlike affection.

Cal was taciturn and abrupt. He didn't like not knowing how

to navigate a situation, and some days she only saw him in snatches, or as a low-hanging mist curling around her ankles. Elise discovered that, when he felt particularly grouchy or confined, he preferred to dematerialize. She didn't mind it, though the habit had finally forced her to unpack her boxes, lest the cardboard absorb any more moisture and simply dissolve onto her floor.

He wasn't an easygoing man, but the more time they spent together, and the more of his story he laid bare before her, Elise knew she'd made the right choice. Beneath the angry, confused man was a being aching with loneliness. What began as a consuming need to know his story quickly morphed into a different kind of desire and a possessiveness that took her breath away.

Elise knew she was probably headed for heartbreak. Courting a man who didn't even realize what was happening was a disaster in the making. She had no assurances that he would not be completely happy to up and leave her as soon as he thought their exchange was complete, but she firmly pushed that thought aside.

Their time together was distraction enough. It was easy to forget about the tenuous ground they stood on when her days and nights were filled with Cal. They watched feeds together, though he was mostly bemused by them. They went on long, winding walks together, swapping stories about their lives in the city. They ate and drank together. She taught him the joys of a hot bath and he showed her gorgeous, hidden alcoves in the rough coast. They lay together in the cool, black sand under the Marin side of the Golden Gate and they danced slowly in her kitchen when a slow song came on the Met.

The look of intense concentration and amazement he wore when he stroked her skin, the sounds he made when she set aside her tablet to straddle his lap and kiss him breathless, the expression of confused delight he wore when she asked to braid his hair — all of it gave her that delicious swooping sensation in her stomach that the thrill of chasing a story gave her. Loving on Cal was a greater high than any undercover work or corruption scandal or cold case.

Elise knew she had to be careful with him. She was ever-conscious of his inexperience and of how very fragile he could be. Perhaps she was even more aware of it because he didn't seem to realize what dangers could await him if he got in too deep with an arrangement like the one he *thought* they had. Protectiveness thrummed through her every time they discovered some new, heartbreaking thing he had been deprived of.

So she handled him with the utmost delicacy and did her best to navigate the thorny brambles of his past, all the while pretending like she *needed* to write his story down.

That part was no hardship either, really. The words flowed out of her even when he wasn't lingering in her home, inspecting gadgets or curling up behind her on the couch. Cal's story was an incredible one. It was perhaps the most interesting and moving thing she'd ever heard, let alone written.

It was a shame that no one would ever see it, but Elise didn't mourn too much. Instead, she took the opportunity to step back from professionalism. She wrote not just the stories Cal relayed to her, but her impressions of him, her admiration for him, and about the cliff's edge of her feelings she could feel creeping closer every day.

It was a beautiful, raw book chronicling their time together. It was, at its heart, a love letter to Cal himself.

~

FROM THE DESK OF ELISE SASINI, TEXTS RECEIVED FEBRUARY 15th 2045:

MOM - 12:15 PM: ur coming 2 dinner tonight, right??? We haven't seen u in weeks!!! I MISS MY DAUGHTER

ELISE - 12:17 PM: Will there be cake? I demand tribute for the gift of my presence, mother

MOM - 12:17 PM: My love for u is better than cake!!!!!

ELISE - 12:18 PM: False.

MOM - 12:18 PM: I can't believe I raised u

ELISE - 12:19 PM: xoxo see you tonight! Oh, also, I'm bringing a guest. Hope that's okay byyyyyye

"I don't come here often," Cal mused. He tilted his head back to examine the huge trees looming over them. The air was spicy in this neighborhood. Almost peppery.

Elise squeezed his hand. Her voice was full of warmth when she told him, "Those are old growth eucalyptus trees. Don't they smell nice?"

"They do." Although they weren't his favorite scent. That belonged to the woman strolling next to him, her golden hair shining in the late afternoon light. When she glanced up at him, the sun caught her eyes and made the green flecks in her irises glow.

Hazel, he thought for the thousandth time. *Her eyes are hazel.*

Cal hoarded every little thing he knew about Elise with the rabid acquisitiveness of a dragon. If he could have turned what he knew into pearls, he would have kept the color of her eyes, the scent of her hair, the story behind the scar on her knee, and the way she sighed when he kissed her throat in the palm of his hand always.

He wanted all the pearls. He wanted the pearls to overflow from his hands, countless and infinitely precious, until they were all he could see and feel. He'd wondered if he would get bored by her by the end of their first week together, her novelty rubbed off like fog on glass, but it didn't happen. Not the first week. Not the second.

By their third week together, Cal was certain that he'd never tire of collecting those precious pearls, nor of kissing her, listening to her, *being* with her.

Always on the hunt for more, he asked, "You grew up here?"

"Yes. My parents moved here after the war ended, when they were still rebuilding a lot of downtown. Dad was a war correspondent, but after the charter was signed, he got a job at *The Light* and married my mom." Her eyes moved over the neat homes lining the quiet streets, a fond expression softening her face. "My sister Joanna came first, then my brother Liam." Her lips quirked in that sardonic smile he loved so much. *"I was a surprise."*

He could barely comprehend life in a family, let alone one as crowded as hers seemed to be. "Is it bad to be a surprise?" he asked, brow crinkling. He didn't like the idea of her being punished by the circumstances of her birth, no matter how hypocritical that was.

Elise gently bumped his arm with her shoulder. The end of her light scarf, a pale pink number with tassels on the end, lifted with the cool breeze. "Nah, but it is a running joke in the family. My brother is ten years older than me. They weren't expecting to have anymore kids, so it made for an interesting dynamic. My siblings were too old to be my playmates, so I mostly hung around my dad. He called me his kid reporter."

Cal looked down at her and felt a familiar, deep pang of hunger in his chest. Gods, he *wanted* this. Making the deal with Elise was both the best and worst thing he'd ever done. He couldn't imagine going back to a time when he didn't know the pleasure of touching her skin or feeling the radiance of her smile when he pleased her, when he gave her parts of himself he thought were worthless, when he ate the broccoli she hated or brought her small treasures from the ocean.

He wanted to walk under trees and hear about her family and feel her fingers intertwined with his every day for the rest of his life. Too bad he'd put a time limit on the greatest thing to ever happen to him. When the book finished, so too would they.

Cold dread trickled into his veins, as it always did when he thought about the words spilling across the screen of her monitor and what they represented.

She'd wanted to terminate their deal, and perhaps he should

have let her. Maybe if they stopped this thing that day in her kitchen, he wouldn't feel like his whole world could be ripped out from under him at any second.

But, if the option presented itself, he knew he wouldn't change a thing. If he had to choose between heartbreak and a lifetime of frigid loneliness, he would choose heartbreak every time. At least now he knew what it felt like to be loved, to *live*.

"You don't have to worry about my parents," Elise assured him, misinterpreting his sudden silence for nerves. She gave his fingers a squeeze. "They're good people. Mom's a school teacher, so she's nice to pretty much everyone except my Uncle Chris — but that's because he's a bigot. Dad will probably grill you about where you're from, but only because he's obsessed with the city. If you let him ramble about history for a while, he'll think you're *great.*"

They took a left at a roundabout and passed a small park. Children and pets ran around the field and a small, colorful play structure, watched over by a group of eagle-eyed caregivers standing off to one side. One of the children had gauzy wings that caught the light and, upon closer inspection, he was fairly certain that wasn't a dog running with the small group, but a young coyote.

Elise caught him watching the scene with open curiosity and laughed. "Aren't they cute? This neighborhood used to be mostly arrants, but a lot of new families have moved in since they lifted that travel embargo." She nudged his arm and pointed across the street.

Cal turned his head and squinted at the brick house. The driveway was empty, and the small yard was impeccably maintained. A sloping path led from the sidewalk, through a fence with no gate, to a door with a symbol emblazoned on its face. It was a hand, palm forward, with an open eye in the center. He knew what it was, even if he'd never had the need to go to a place like it before. *A Healing House.*

"See? We even got a new healer recently. All the way from the

Collective. I haven't met her yet, but my dad has been to see her a few times and says that she's managed to cure both his gout *and* his sweet tooth." She snorted. "Pretty sure he's using that to cover up the fact that he's sneaking sweets in his car again, but I'm not about to narc on him."

They passed the park and the Healing House before they turned right, onto another quiet street. Elise pointed again, this time at a small, white paneled home on a slight rise. Large, flowering hedges lined the driveway and where the lawn met the sidewalk. As they walked up the driveway, Cal caught sight of the sign above the door.

No solicitors. No crooks. No murderers — unless you're here for an interview.

He let out a low, raspy laugh. Of course Elise grew up here. He couldn't imagine her coming from anywhere else.

Following his stare, Elise explained, grinning, "An anniversary gift from my mom."

They stepped onto the porch. Cal felt a small burst of nerves — this was only the second time he was invited into a home before — but his curiosity quickly pushed them aside. "Anniversary? What's that?"

Elise waved her hand over the sensor on the door. A moment later, a chime sounded inside the house.

"Oh, it's what you call the day you got married or got together," she explained, looking up at him thoughtfully. "People like to celebrate how many years they've been together by giving each other gifts or doing something nice. Dad goes all out for their anniversary. Last year he took Mom on a river cruise through Eastern Europe. She came back raving about all the dragons she saw."

He heard a voice on the other side of the door, but he couldn't tear his eyes away from her face. Something pulled tight in his chest when he asked, "What will our anniversary be? The day you summoned me?"

Her eyes moved back and forth across his face as if she were searching for something. "I'm not sure," she answered, suddenly quiet. Watchful. "Having an anniversary usually means you're together for years, Cal. It's a... well, it's a sort of celebration of permanence."

That tight band across his heart pulled even tighter. *Right,* he thought bitterly, *and I set a fucking time limit on our relationship.*

Cal opened his mouth to inform her he had no intention of letting her go even after she finished the damn book, to tell her he wanted this kind of life with her, to say how desperately he wanted her, but he didn't get the chance. The front door swung open, forcing him to swallow the raw emotion bubbling up his throat.

Elise's parents were not what he expected. Her father was a small, compact man with thick glasses and a dense, salt and pepper mustache. He wore a flannel shirt tucked into wrinkled khakis and had what appeared to be permanent frown lines etched into his forehead.

Her mother was taller than her father. Willowy, with the same athletic frame as her daughter, she had a long, kind face and a cap of short, silvery curls. He could feel the magic radiating off of her almost immediately. It was a stormy, chilly sort of power that he knew well.

Both, he noted, had a small, long-healed sigil burned between their brows.

"Oh, goodness gracious, baby," her mother exclaimed, laughing nervously. "You didn't tell me you were bringing a supermodel home for dinner! I would have put on something other than my old jeans."

Cal glanced down at Elise to find her cheeks flushing a familiar dark red. "Mom, Dad, this is Cal. Cal, these are my parents, Bob and Rachel."

He didn't know what to do, so Cal defaulted to his usual habit of keeping quiet. Squeezing Elise's hand, he gave them both a small nod.

After a moment of awkward silence, Bob put his hands on his

hips and barked, "Quiet one! Gonna have to find that voice if you want to be Elise's boyfriend, kid. She needs someone with a spine!"

Elise and her mother wore identical expressions of mortification. "Dad, please do not—"

"I am not her boyfriend," Cal calmly explained. He didn't like talking to people, but in this he wanted there to be no confusion or room for doubt. Holding eye contact with her father, he announced, "I am her *mate.*"

"You're going to tell me why you didn't mention that you'd found a mate in the most strikingly attractive man on the planet *soon*, right?"

Elise was impressed by her mother's restraint. She'd held her tongue all throughout the awkward, pre-dinner smalltalk phase and even through dinner itself. Only now that she stood alone in the kitchen, packing the leftover cake her father shouldn't have into a to-go container did her mother pounce.

"It's complicated, Mom." Knowing that wouldn't satisfy her — or anyone, really — Elise snapped the lid on the container and added, "We just met a few weeks ago. Things are new."

Her mother leaned her hip against the old kitchen island and crossed her arms, her expression skeptical. "Uh-huh. Is that why that elemental looks like he'll die if he doesn't touch you every five minutes? Seems like he's pretty certain about things."

"Well, yeah. I'm his first relationship."

Elise kept her eyes down, afraid that if her mother looked too closely, she would see how well and truly fucked her daughter's heart was. No, she didn't intend to just give Cal up, but he also hadn't said anything about the future beyond the book she was supposed to be writing. If he wanted to stick around, he would have said something. Cal was *always* direct, which was why she was having this conversation with her mother in the first place.

He said *'I'm her mate'*, but with him that could mean anything. She didn't know if elementals had permanent, monogamous relationships or if Cal even truly wanted one. She did her best to push the thought of him leaving her aside, but it was getting harder and harder to do so. Perhaps that was the real reason she hadn't yet made it clear that their deal meant nothing to her. Without it, she would be forced to face the truth: Cal might not actually want to stay.

Her mother's warm hand slid down her back. Dropping a kiss to the crown of Elise's head, she said, "I don't think that means as much as you probably think it does, sweetheart."

Tears threatened, but Elise stubbornly refused to let them fall. If she started crying out her heartache and worry now, her mother would never let her leave the house.

Instead of weeping like she was sixteen and just got stood up on homecoming night by Daniel fucking Kerber again, she leaned into her mother's embrace with a grateful hum. "We'll figure it out," she promised them both.

"I'm sure you will." Her mother straightened and brushed the hair out of Elise's eyes. "Well, if it makes any difference, I like him. A little grim, maybe, but I think that's good for you. It'll keep you out of too much trouble."

Elise let out a watery laugh. "I don't know what you're talking about. I never get into trouble."

"Uh-huh. And that's how you've ended up with a mysterious, brooding elemental for a boyfriend, right?"

She winced. "Fair enough."

Goddess help her if her mother ever found out what she'd done to get Cal's attention in the first place. They had agreed it was best for this first meeting to go without the explanation of who exactly Cal was, but the moment the truth came out, Elise was certain her mother would put the pieces together.

Smiling her wide, beautiful smile, her mother gave her back another gentle rub before shooing her out of the kitchen. "You should go rescue him from your dad's lecturing by offering him a tour of the annex."

Elise frowned. "But what about the dishes?"

"It's Bob's night to do the dishes." Her mother shrugged. "Not my problem."

They shared an impish smile. "Did you plan on having us over on his dish night so you wouldn't have to do it?"

"I admit to nothing." Her mother waved a hand towards the door. "Shoo! Go get that pretty, pretty man!"

~

FROM THE DESK OF ELISE SASINI, A NOTE IN THE MARGIN OF THE MANUSCRIPT *THE SHROUDED CITY*:

I am so totally fucked.

~

By the time Elise found her father and his silent companion, her stomach was bunched up in a series of tight knots. They didn't loosen until Cal's eyes snapped to hers. He stood up abruptly from the old leather guest chair in her father's office, cutting off whatever Bob had been going on about. The crime rate in the 1930's, probably.

"Hey Dad," she greeted, pushing her hair behind her ear and avoiding Cal's hard, penetrating stare, "Mom says it's your dish night."

Her father let out a deep sigh that ruffled his mustache and slowly levered himself up from the chair behind his old, cluttered desk. After an awkward start, he'd warmed up to Cal. She suspected it had a lot to do with the fact that Cal wouldn't think to stop him from rambling even if he went on for hours and hours. He was a damn good listener.

"We'll finish this later, Cal," Bob assured him. "Next time, I can show you the maps I mentioned. We know where all six boats are sunk in the—"

"Dad."

"Fine, okay!" He threw up his hands and, squeezing past where she stood in the doorway, he dropped a kiss onto the side of her head.

She watched him walk down the hall and, once he disappeared around the corner, listened to the familiar sounds of him and her mother chattering at one another. An unfamiliar ache bloomed in her chest. Would she have something like what her parents had? Someone to always come home to? Someone who knew her better than she knew herself?

Elise had been so busy chasing her career for so long, she'd never given it much thought. She *did* want that, though. She wanted someone to sit up with her as she pieced a story together late in the night, to worry about her when she chased a lead. She wanted to squabble over who got to eat the last slice of cake and the best temperature setting on the thermostat. She wanted someone to tease her and keep her on her toes.

She wanted that person to be Cal.

A cool hand cupped her cheek. Elise looked up to find Cal staring down at her, his expression unreadable. Her brow wrinkled. She supposed Cal *was* broody, but her mother was right. Tonight, he didn't just look aloof. He looked downright grim. She'd been so in her head during dinner that she'd barely noticed his tension.

"Hey," she whispered, leaning into the hard, sleek lines of his body, "I bet you're feeling pretty overwhelmed with all this attention. Why don't we go some place quiet before we take the m-lev home?"

Cal was quiet for a moment, his eyes an impenetrable liquid black, before he answered, "Show me."

Elise took his hand and led him down the hall and through the back door, into the fenced in garden. Large hedges stood taller than the fence, giving the area a quiet, isolated feeling. Her mother's vegetable garden stretched along the pebbled path leading to the small building at the far end of the yard. Sprouts were just beginning to poke through the rich brown soil.

"What is this?"

"We call it *the annex,*" she explained, using the ancient thumb scanner to unlock the door. They had no reason to bother updating any of the tech in the little building, since it stood more as a monument to her childhood than a usable space. She had to actually flip a switch to turn on the lights when she stepped inside. A pink lamp on the table next to the bed turned on, as well as an electrician's nightmare of snarled and carelessly draped string lights.

Stepping inside, she let Cal in before she closed the door. His eyebrows rose.

"It's a lot of pink and purple, I know," she laughed. "This was my play house, since there wasn't much room for kiddy stuff in the house by the time I came along, and then when I was old enough, they converted it into my room." She took a sweeping look at the soft pink walls and the gaudy, shimmery curtains. The building itself was tiny — more of a shed than anything — but she wouldn't change a thing about it.

Growing up in a house where everyone was so much older and beyond her reach hadn't felt quite so isolating when she had her own special space to just be as silly and carefree as she wanted to. Besides, it was the place where *The St. Francis Chronicle* was born. She was pretty sure that if her parents tried to change it into a yoga studio or a deluxe garden shed, the historical society would sue their pants off.

At the very least, she would be terribly disappointed.

Elise started to tell him about the greatest accomplishment of her childhood, her beloved paper, but stopped as soon as she noticed the low mist beginning to circle the fuzzy purple carpet.

"Cal?"

He stood in the center of the small space. His back was to her, but she could tell something was wrong by the stiffness of his shoulders and the way his hair swayed back and forth like an angry wave.

His low voice was like a whip cracking through the silence when he said, "How come you didn't tell them I am your mate?"

She blinked. Had that been bothering him the whole night? She'd assumed his chilly reserve was caused by the unfamiliar company, not *that*. "Cal..." She struggled to come up with the right words. Ones that wouldn't give away how much she desperately wanted to keep him and ones that wouldn't push him away, either. Relationships were so new to him, she couldn't bear to influence him one way or the other. And, if she were being honest, she was scared to the bone that giving up the act would put an end to their relationship.

But she couldn't lie to him, either, so instead she said, "You and I are just starting out. I wasn't going to put that kind of pressure on you."

Cal spun around and pinned her with a dark look. "You are my mate. That was the agreement."

A spark of annoyance firmed up her spine. She wanted nothing more than to forget about that stupid, stupid deal, but he wouldn't *let her!* It hurt that he seemed to only care about their relationship in the context of the deal, and that hurt came out in her voice. "Well, what was I going to say, Cal? *This is my mate, but only until after I finish writing a book?* There was no way I was going to explain that to my parents!"

Cal was in front of her in the blink of an eye. Fog billowed around the room, obscuring every bit of pressed glitter and hot pink decor. The string lights twinkled through the gossamer mist, creating a dreamlike quality that was at odds with the tension between them.

He bore down on her with an expression of pure hurt when he hissed, "No anniversary. No telling them you're my mate. What's next? I told you I wanted *everything*, Elise. This is not everything. This is some... some *half* thing, and I don't want it."

Guilt twisted the knots in her stomach tighter. She'd been so careful with him, trying to show him that she cared and that it wasn't *really* about the book or the deal or any of that nonsense, but she'd also kept from mentioning the future for fear that he would tell her he had every intention of leaving her.

But that was selfish. The only real way to keep from hurting Cal was to cut him off at the beginning, before he got too deep into something he couldn't wrap his head around yet. He couldn't comprehend the mess they could make of one another, but she did. It was her responsibility to keep control of things. Instead of sticking to her guns and ending things before they began, she'd let him convince her to make an even bigger mess because she didn't actually want to stop.

Her throat was thick with withheld tears when she asked, "Do you want to end things, then?"

Cal went very still. "End things?"

She sucked in a shuddering breath. Damn, she'd done this to herself, but that didn't make it any easier to take. "This is confusing and obviously painful for you, which is what I worried about when we... started. I don't want you to be hurt, Cal." Her voice broke on his name, but she pushed ahead anyway. "If you want to end things now, then—"

Cal cut her off with a brutal, breath stealing kiss. His hands circled her waist and drew her close enough to plaster them together chest to thigh. One hand came up to curl into her hair, holding her still as he pressed one desperate kiss to her mouth after another.

"No, no, no," he panted against her lips. "I'm not ready to let you go. I can't do it. I *won't* do it."

Elise's will crumbled to so much dust, as it always did when she felt the ache in him. Gods, she couldn't leave this man. She didn't want to. She needed to just tell him she didn't care about the book or the deal and that she wanted him to *really* be her mate. Once that was out of the way, they could move forward — one way or the other.

Cal didn't give her the chance.

He slid his tongue along the seam of her mouth and then past it, stroking hers with a possessive caress. She didn't think anyone liked kissing as much as Cal did. Certainly, no one she'd ever kissed did it half as well as he did.

The hand on her waist slid under the hem of her shirt and up the bare expanse of her back, sending a new and exciting ripple of sensation down her spine. The shock of feeling his bare skin on hers made her gasp.

So far, she'd been very careful not to go past kissing with Cal. She knew he was eager for more — it was hard not to notice when the man eschewed clothing most days — but Elise was the one with the experience. She knew it was her responsibility to make sure he didn't go too far, too fast, and overwhelm himself. She'd always been careful to watch his cues, looking for signs that he was ready to move onto the next step, but he'd never shown any.

Not until now, anyway.

Desire wiped away her tension, the urgency she felt to just *tell* him. Unfulfilled, it had only gotten darker, sweeter as the weeks wore on. When Cal moved his hand to slide his fingers under the cup of her bra, Elise leaned into his touch. When he groaned, low and throaty, at the feeling of her tight nipple between the pads of his fingers, she dropped her hands to the waistband of his jeans.

When she popped the button and carefully pulled down the zipper, he hissed and pulled back from their kiss. Panting, he rasped, "What are you doing?"

Elise cupped his cheek with one hand and slid the other under the elastic band of his briefs, her eyes on his, watching for any sign of hesitancy or discomfort. When she brushed her fingertips over the silky skin of his shaft, he sucked in a ragged gasp that nearly unwound her. She clenched her thighs, assailed by a relentless, brutal desire.

"You said you wanted everything," she whispered, kissing the corner of his mouth with the utmost care. "Baby, I haven't even *started* giving you everything yet."

She curled her fingers around him and squeezed gently. His

hips jerked. The hand in her bra spasmed, pinching her nipple sharply. A streak of pleasure raced down her spine to join the aching beat between her legs.

Gods, he felt like heaven in her hand. Heavy and silky, with all that perfect, pearlescent skin flushed *almost* pink. Elise had exactly zero doubts that he'd taste like heaven, too.

Cal stared down at her, lips parted and slick. His chest moved up and down with every deep inhale and exhale. "I want it," he breathed, voice hoarse with lust. "I want it all, witch."

CHAPTER SIX

FROM THE DESK OF ELISE SASINI, AN EXCERPT OF THE MANUSCRIPT *THE SHROUDED CITY:*

...on the subject of elementals as a whole, there is not much I can write. There is not much anyone can say for certain, as a matter of fact. Research in the subject is painfully lacking, but I cannot say I blame elementals for their circumspection. Perhaps, like the elves, they prefer to keep their secrets, their weaknesses and their wants, just that: secret.

Cal tells me that they are generally solitary, but he has only met a handful and cannot be entirely certain. He does not know if they mate for life or if they typically eschew permanent familial bonds. He doesn't know if they can have children, or if they all eat food, or if they sleep.

What he can tell me is his personal experience, and, I am ashamed to say, it is only his experience I am concerned with.

Fascinatingly, he confessed that, although he gained his physical form that disastrous morning in 1906, he'd actually achieved a level of sentience long before then. Wandering over the Earth as an amorphous cloud of magic, he remembers his first thought as, "Well, what are they all doing down there?"

I wonder, do the m-weather scientists know that the clusters of magic they study might actually be studying them back?

As an aside, I asked Cal whether this made him 139 years old, or many thousands. He thoughtfully replied, "Depends on whichever you like more."

Gods, I love him.

CAL KNEW WHAT SEX WAS. HE'D NEVER *DONE* IT, obviously, but one didn't hover in back alleys and linger around windows in a city like San Francisco for a hundred years *without* learning a thing or two about sex.

On the whole, he'd always considered it gross.

What were people thinking, plunging their tongues and fingers and genitals in places they didn't rightly belong? He understood the concept of copulation as well as its purpose, but as someone conceived by nothing other than magic and fate, Cal felt no compulsion to explore what Kaz playfully called *the carnal delights.*

Now, though, Cal wished he hadn't tuned out his friend when he tried to explain the joys of sex and intimacy all those years ago. Perhaps if he'd listened, he wouldn't be standing there, staring agog at his mate as she slowly lowered herself to her knees before him.

Doubtful, he thought wryly. In all likelihood, he would still look at her like she'd hung the moon. Even if he'd slept with every willing being in the city, this moment would still feel special. *Important.*

Elise slid her free hand under his shirt. Her palm pressed against the clenching muscles of his abdomen as she gave his cock a long, slow stroke. "Is this okay?" she asked, petting his stomach in time with her strokes. His heart swelled with the strangest mix of tenderness and borderline painful arousal he could imagine.

He wanted more.

"Yes." Cal felt her breath ghost over the sensitive head of his cock and groaned, low and long. He was so damn hard, he could

feel his heartbeat throbbing against the softness of her palm. "I've never done— *this*. I want to."

Gods, he wanted to do *everything* with her. Cal just never knew where to start. He loved kissing her more than he loved anything, but he knew there were more steps to the dance she had only begun to teach him. Was he supposed to do something to show he wanted to do *more* or was that something she needed to do? Was he missing some signal? Did he need to wait for her to tell him explicitly that they could go ahead with whatever it was that came next?

He had been on the verge of breaking down and seeking out Kaz for advice, but now that seemed unnecessary. Cal wasn't entirely certain what his witch had been waiting for, but that was a conversation for later. *After.*

It wasn't like he had any plans to let her go, anyway. Screw the terms of their deal. He'd find a way to keep her. They would have plenty of time to discuss this new facet of their relationship.

Even when he slid his fingers into her hair and felt the sweep of her tongue down his shaft in every single nerve ending, Cal felt the low hum of fury, of possessiveness in his blood. It wasn't easy keeping his shape together, and he had no control over the fog that billowed out to fill the tiny annex, obscuring the sight of them from anyone looking through the windows.

Do you want to end things, then?

Gods, he felt his heart stop when she said that. He wasn't ready for this to end. He wasn't ready to go back to how he was before. He wasn't ready to not see her every day, to not hear her voice, to not kiss her whenever the mood struck him. He wouldn't ever be ready.

Cal wasn't sure if elementals had mates. Not every race did. Humans, certainly, didn't seem to have some ingrained compulsion to stick with one partner for all time. Elementals were solitary. They didn't do packs or families. They came into the world alone and they died alone.

But he wanted more than that. She taught him that he *deserved* more than that.

He wanted Elise Sasini, the woman on her knees before him, her lips running down the length of his cock in a reverent caress, and he intended to have her. *Forever.* He was prepared to fight her tooth and nail to make it happen.

He watched her with unvarnished hunger. Elise was beautiful and smart and kind and she was *his.* Her lips were flushed a bright cherry red. They looked even more lush, more human, when they were pressed against his pearly white skin.

Cal shifted his stance, moving his booted feet so she could have more room. Wanting to see her face, he gathered her hair in one fist and held it back. It was a soft, heavy weight in his hand, and he relished the feeling of it.

"Tell me if you want to stop or if you're uncomfortable," she murmured, sliding her hand slowly back up his length to press the pad of her thumb against the underside of the flushed head. Elise kept her eyes on his as her tongue darted out to lick up a gleaming drop of pre-come.

Cal's fist tightened around her curls. *Gods save me.*

"Deal?"

He got his answer out through gritted teeth. "Deal."

Her smile was beautiful. Cal never got tired of seeing it. He'd been the subject of many grateful, nervous, or vacant smiles throughout his lifetime, but he'd never seen a grin like Elise's. It was huge and radiant; a smile that took up her whole face and crinkled her eyes until they were just little slits of glittering hazel. Whenever she blessed him with one, Cal felt like the weight of a century fell off of his shoulders. Her joy made him feel *new.*

And when she beamed up at him from her position on the floor, her cheeks flushed and her magic calling out a siren song to his, he discovered a new appreciation for it. There was an entirely new world of satisfaction to discover in the joy she took in the task at hand.

Cal's breath quickened as she began to press one achingly

tender kiss after another along his shaft, her eyes locked on his. He didn't know what to do with his other hand, so he settled for cupping her cheek.

Another wave of pleasure crashed over him when he realized he could *feel* her jaw and tongue work as she showered him with touches. It was made even more clear — and arousing — when she finally took him into the slick heat of her mouth.

"Elise!" Cal's spine stiffened as she slowly closed her lips over him. The slick, velvety pad of her tongue stroked the underside of his cock as she drew him in.

Stars exploded behind his eyes. Cal gasped, head dropping back, and held on for dear life as Elise began to move forward and back. Her lips and tongue created a maddening suction and heat, while her hand moved in time, taking over whatever she couldn't reach with her mouth.

There was something dangerously erotic about feeling her cheek hollow out under his palm. He didn't need to *see* her to know exactly what she looked like. He could feel it and hear it.

Cal rocked his hips in time with her. He knew enough to keep himself from letting go completely, but he was shocked to discover his restraint wearing away under the onslaught of plea-sure. He had no idea it could *do* that. Sure, he assumed sex felt good — why else would so many people go to such great lengths to do it? — but *this...*

It was like she was taking him apart piece by piece with nothing more than the heat of her mouth and her wicked fingers. He thought he knew carnal pleasure when they kissed for the first time, but it was *nothing* compared to this. Gods, would he ever be able to look at her mouth the same? Or would he forever see his pearlescent skin sliding between her flushed lips, taboo and beautiful and everything he never knew he needed?

Pressure began to build at the base of his spine, pulling every single one of his muscles taut. Cal made a choked sound in the back of his throat and gave her hair a gentle pull, telling her he needed her to stop. If she kept going, he was certain he'd come apart at the seams. It was too much.

Elise withdrew her head, but kept her fingers wrapped firmly around his cock when she asked, husky and breathless, "Are you okay, baby?"

Gods, her voice was rough. He'd heard it like that before, after he'd kissed her breathless. It'd done things to him then, but *now,* with his cock in her hand, it did a whole lot more.

Cal tilted his head down to look at her and groaned again. She was so fucking beautiful it nearly killed him. Did she honestly think he could live the rest of his life without her now? Without *this?* He'd wither away into senseless, formless mist without her. He'd *want* to.

"I'm— it's too much," he rasped. "It feels…" He didn't even have the words to finish the sentence. It felt fucking incredible, but even that was inadequate.

A slow, sultry smile curled Elise's wet lips. "Are you close?"

Cal blinked. "Close?"

She tightened her grip and gave his cock a slow, torturous pull. Cal made a noise of pained surprise as he watched another milky drop of pre-come slide down the tip. Before it could run over her fingers, Elise's tongue snaked out to swipe it away with careful, deliberate slowness. He watched it melt on her pretty pink tongue. Her gaze never left his face.

Tempest take me to the depths. This woman is going to kill me.

"Orgasm, baby," she explained, eyes crinkling with her smile. "Are you close to orgasming?"

Cal felt like he couldn't get enough air in his lungs. He felt like every nerve had been shot with electricity. He felt like every drop of blood in his body now belonged in his cock. He felt like he would die if she stopped and like he would *definitely* die if she continued.

"I… don't know," he managed to get out. "I've never— This isn't something I've—"

It was Elise's turn to look surprised. Sitting back a little, she used her free hand to rub soothing circles over his hip bone. "Oh, Cal. You've never had an orgasm before? Not even on your own?"

He shook his head.

"Oh, *baby.*" Elise leaned forward to press a tender kiss to his stomach. Her tone was achingly gentle when she said, "That's okay. This is all normal. Do you *want* to keep going?"

Cal swallowed hard. He was overwhelmed, but he knew he wanted this. He wanted her. "Yes."

She kissed him again. Pride glowed in her flushed face and made his heart ache. "Do you trust me?"

"Yes." He trusted Elise in ways he'd never trusted anyone. Never, in all of their interactions, had she shown anything other than care and affection for him. Even when he was angry and confused and lonely, she *cared* for him. Always patient, always funny, always practical. She was the steady ground on which he stood, the only thing that made sense to him in the world. She was his *home.*

Elise gave his cock another slow, reverent stroke. He rocked his hips and let out a small whine. The pressure had only abated temporarily. Every time she moved or even *breathed* near his sensitive skin, Cal felt like he was going to explode.

"Good," she breathed, peppering his stomach with kisses. She'd rucked up his plain black shirt and seemed to find it pleasurable to trace the contours of his abdomen with her lips and tongue. He couldn't complain. Having her mouth on him *anywhere* was bliss.

Resting her chin on his stomach for a moment, she looked up at him with an open, tender expression that stole what little breath he still had. "You're going to be okay, baby. It's going to feel like a lot, like you're going to come apart, but you can trust me. It will be good. If not, we never have to do this again, okay? I'm right here with you."

His fist tightened in her hair. "Do you promise?"

Moisture glittered in those pretty hazel eyes. Her smile softened. "Yes, Cal. I promise."

Only when he nodded did she finally dip her head back down. He let out something close to a shout when her lips closed over him again. Her left hand drew comforting patterns on his stomach and side as she sucked, gently at first, then harder and faster, her right hand working in tandem with her mouth with a pulling, twisting motion.

His blood rushed with a pulsing beat. It was a roar in his ears, overpowering his own involuntary moans and the slick, erotic sound of her mouth on him. That pressure returned with a vengeance. It pulled and pulled and pulled, curling his toes in his boots and forcing a raw, terrifying noise from his throat.

And then the tension snapped.

Cal cried out, hips bucking hard, and grasped the sides of her head to still her movements as bursts of pure pleasure rocked him to the core.

When there was nothing left of him, he felt his muscles unlock, his shoulders sagging and his eyelids falling shut as he finally, *finally* got some air back in his lungs.

The feeling of soft, warm fingers gently tucking him back into his briefs and then rubbing soothing circles over his hips and thighs brought him back to the present.

Cal blinked hard, dispelling the little white lights that danced across his vision, to see Elise grinning up at him. As he watched, dumbstruck, her tongue snaked out to catch a drop of come from escaping the corner of her mouth. She winked up at him.

"Gods, I love blowjobs," she murmured, "but that has got to be the single best sexual experience of my fucking life." Her eyes glittered. "And next time it will be even *better.*"

He dropped to his knees. There was nothing else he could do. His legs certainly wouldn't support him anymore. He wasn't even sure they were fully corporeal. Not that he cared. If she asked it of him, he would have even *crawled.*

Cupping her cheeks, Cal leaned forward to breathe against her swollen mouth, "You're going to kill me, witch."

She bumped her nose against his, playful and sweet and too

good for him. Too bad he was past worrying about that. He was a murderer and a monster and he'd rot in the mud of Grim's riverbank, but he was fucking *hers*.

Elise pressed a soft kiss to his lips. He felt her smile against them when she said, "Well, death's not really what I'm after—"

A powerful, percussive wave knocked them both to the ground. Cal threw himself over Elise as trinkets and baubles began to rain down from the shelves around the room. His ears rang with a single, high note as he curled his arms around her, blocking any shards of glass from reaching her fragile skin.

A series of smaller explosions rent the air, one after another; several distant booms that shook the annex's thin walls. In total, it only lasted a minute or two, but with the fear for Elise coursing through his veins like ice water, it might as well have been a lifetime.

Only when he was sure that it was over did Cal cautiously lift his head to examine the room. Elise pushed at him, wiggling to be let up, but he needed to know that the roof wasn't about to fall on her before he allowed her out from under him.

When a cursory scan found only minimal damage to things not bolted to the walls, he reluctantly let her crawl out from under him. "Watch the glass. You'll cut your hands," he warned.

"My hands! Screw my hands!" Elise shook her head and surged to her feet. Two strides took her to the door. "Was that an *explosion* or some insanely massive bolt gun shots? Gods, I have to go check on my parents!"

Cal followed her mad dash back through the garden and into the house. The afterglow of their time in the annex was wiped away by the sight of a living room full of glass — all from the broken windows, which had apparently blown *inward* — and Rachel attempting to help Bob up from where he knelt on the floor by the couch.

Elise rushed over to help. Putting a shoulder under her father's arm, she asked, "Are you guys okay? What happened?"

Frowning, Cal gently extracted her from under her father and took her place. Using his greater strength, he managed to get Bob onto the couch with minimal jostling.

Rachel stood by the armrest and shook her head. She looked shaken, but unharmed. Bob didn't look much worse, save for a small cut to the side of his head and a muttered complaint about his bum knee. "I don't know!" Elise's mother answered. "We were just turning on an entertainment feed when the windows shattered."

Elise grabbed a fistful of the back of Cal's shirt and leaned around him to peer out the window. The flush in her cheeks died away. "Oh, fuck me," she breathed, "there's a fire! Gods, I *told* the association that those old gas lines needed to be removed."

Cal straightened, his mouth settling into a grim line. They shared a look.

Elise sucked in a deep breath and nodded once, firmly, toward the door. She gave him a gentle shove. "Go."

FROM THE DESK OF ELISE SASINI, A TRANSCRIPT OF AN AUDIO RECORDING DATED FEBRUARY 8th 2045:

ELISE: Can— can we circle back to... back around to what you said before. About your vigil.

CALAMITY: What about it?

ELISE: I'm wondering why you do it. What it really entails. Also, I guess, how it plays into what you told me about people trying to use you over the years. Thaddeus in particular.

[PAUSE] [FABRIC SOUNDS] [CHAIR LEGS SCRAPING]

ELISE: Oh! Cal, I don't think—

CALAMITY: I will answer your questions, but only if I get to hold you while I do it. This is part of the deal.

ELISE: ...Right. Comfy?

CALAMITY: Yes. Here are the answers to your questions: I

do it because it's my penance. It usually means I keep watch over the city and its surrounding area for danger. I save every life I can — from drowning, assault, house fires, car accidents. It's all the same. [PAUSE] Lay your head on my shoulder. Yes. I like it when you do that.

    [FABRIC SOUNDS]

    ELISE: [SIGH] Go on.

    CALAMITY: The Mad Sovereign was no different from anyone else, except that he actually had the power to force my hand. For a while, anyway. He wanted me to be a part of his shadow Patrol. In his eyes I would be the perfect assassin and spy. Most people who seek me out think the same. Usually they try to offer money, sex, influence. When that doesn't work, they resort to threats, then violence. He was the only one who got close to beating me into it. I've never felt pain like what that man gave me before or since.

    ELISE: Oh, Cal...

    CALAMITY: [MUFFLED] Shh, witch. All's well. He lost his head. My only regret is that I wasn't the one to take it from him.

There was no saving the Healing House. Cal knew it the moment he shed his clothes and his physical form to spread himself out to catch the air. He didn't need to go far to find the blaze.

The Healing House was only about a block down from Elise's childhood home and it was burning down to its foundations. As he watched, hovering over the blaze, the damaged roof caved in with a crash and a roar of hungry flame. If there were people inside, they were already dead.

Feeling the tight knot of guilt that never let him go, Cal searched the area around the building for survivors before he committed himself to helping extinguish the blaze.

A lone figure lay prone on the brick path leading to the door.

Her pastel colored coat stood out starkly against the smoke and debris. Relief surged through him. Not all was lost. He could save one person, at least. It didn't scrub any marks from his soul, but it didn't add another one, either.

Cal made to swoop down, intending to pull the woman out of harm's way, but reared back in surprise when black, faceless shadows melted from the gaps between the houses. One of the black-clad figures — broad shouldered, with a smoky glamour disguising any distinguishing features — knelt by her side and briskly checked her for injuries. More figures knelt down beside her and others stood watch, their backs ramrod straight and their obscured faces turned toward the road.

Sovereign's Guard.

He could hardly believe what he was seeing. A full squadron — six elves, trained to work in seamless pairs — of the most highly trained, dangerous military force in the UTA were crowded around the fallen woman. No one but the sovereign commanded the Guard. That meant that, whoever the woman was, Theodore Solbourne ordered her surveillance personally.

Cal watched as they relayed information to one another with quick, efficient hand signs, then the figure who had checked for injuries lifted a hand to his ear.

Over the roar of flames and the distant wail of sirens, Cal heard, "Explosion at the Healing House. No combatants. Healer down but alive. Do we extract?"

People were beginning to exit their homes. Terrified neighbors peeked out of doorways and called out to one another from across the street. Somewhere, the wails of distressed pets were joined by a baby.

In a moment, people would begin to venture out in earnest. Already, Cal could hear the fire squad closing in. Would the Guard stay? They were supposed to work in the shadows, never seen except for at the sovereign's elbow. A full squadron being caught surveilling a Healing House had to be high on their list of things to avoid.

The glamoured voice of the guard was crisp and emotionless when he replied to whoever he spoke to. "Understood. Awaiting further instructions."

With a sharp gesture, the elf sent the rest of the squadron back into the shadows. Long, loping strides allowed them to disappear in the few seconds it took for the only guard left to gently lift the unconscious woman and deposit her at the farthest end of the path, nearly on the sidewalk. It was far enough away to keep her out of immediate danger from the burning building, but close enough to look as though she landed there on her own.

Carefully, like she was made of something more fragile and precious than spun glass, the guard laid her head on a patch of grass. With a flick of his matte black claw-caps, he made sure her skirt and coat were arranged around her legs in a way that concealed the most possible skin before he too stood and raced back to the cover of shadows.

In all, the entire bizarre scene took less than a minute.

If Cal had his physical form, he would have shaken his head. He never could make sense of the elves or what they wanted. Why not take the woman out of danger entirely? Why arrange her like they did? Why have a full squadron of elite soldiers watching her in the first place?

It didn't sit right with him, but he didn't have the time to consider what it all might mean. As a human neighbor raced over to help the fallen woman, Cal turned his attention to the burning house. He'd seen enough over the years to know that flames had a mind of their own, particularly in a magic saturated city like San Francisco. They could jump and weave and come back to life without any warning. If the blaze wasn't handled soon, it could consume the entire neighborhood, if not the whole city.

Thinking of Elise's childhood home and her little annex, Cal pulled his magic inward before releasing it in one big burst. Immediately, fog began to coalesce in the air, pulled from every bit of moisture he could get his incorporeal hands on. He couldn't put out the flames entirely, but he could help dampen them until the fire squad arrived.

As people poured out into the street and the battered woman was escorted away by two neighbors, Cal pressed himself as close to the flames as he dared. He was impervious to most damage in his dematerialized form, but heat could burn him as surely as it could if he were flesh and bone. It was the one weakness Thaddeus had been able to exploit, and it had taken him decades to get past the terror flames inspired in him. Only his need to save lives had pushed him past the pain of his memories. Of course, the process was helped along by a heaping helping of spite for the dead madman, too.

A thick layer of fog rolled over the neighborhood to blanket what was left of the Healing House. By the time the fire squad arrived, the flames were hissing and popping under the onslaught of moisture; smothered to death beneath a blanket of unnatural fog.

Cal worked in tandem with the foam-throwing squad, though they didn't know it. It took fifteen minutes for them to get the blaze under control. By then, Cal felt it was safe to let the professionals handle what was left of the smoldering building.

Curious, he lingered over the street and watched as first the alpha of the local coyote shifter pack arrived with his second, and then, in perhaps the most bizarre turn of events he could imagine, the sovereign himself stepped out of a sleek black car.

He'd never met Theodore Solbourne and didn't care about the man one way or another, but even Cal felt a ripple of disquiet at the sight of his furious expression and flexing claws. Kaz, of course, was close behind him.

The orc didn't follow his brother over to the small knot of people sitting on the curb in front of the ruined house, but stayed a discreet distance away, half hidden in the shadow cast by a tree. One glance upward told Cal he knew he wasn't alone.

"Long time no see, Cal."

Not wanting to draw attention to himself, Cal half-materialized in the deepest shadows under the stooping tree. "What's going on?"

Kaz shifted his stance. He was ever-so-slightly bowlegged — something that only made the massive orc look bigger than he was. Leather-clad arms crossed over his wide chest, he dryly answered, "Family shit."

Cal glanced across the street, where it looked like a stand-off was happening between the alpha and the sovereign. Why? Because of the little red-headed woman? He couldn't imagine what the Solbourne family had to do with the healer, or even the coyote shifter, for that matter. "What's so special about that woman?"

"She's family." It was a short, implacable answer. Nothing in Kaz's tone or expression hinted that he was open to more discussion on the topic. Not that Cal really cared or needed to know. A life had been saved and a neighborhood left relatively unscathed. His job was finished.

Shrugging, he eyed his only friend curiously. "I've been meaning to track you down."

Kaz shot him a quick, amused look. "You know where you can find me, fog man."

True, but Cal didn't care to waste any of his time with Elise checking Kaz's usual haunts. He shrugged. "I've been busy."

"With what?" It was more of a grunt than a question, but Cal didn't take offense. Kaz's direct, dry nature was one of the main reasons they were able to get along. When the newest regime took power, they were right to send their half-orc sibling to make contact with Cal. They were both emotionally stunted and brusque, making miscommunication almost non-existent.

"I met a woman."

The orc jolted. Tearing his eyes away from his brother, his head swiveled to pin Cal with a look of outright disbelief. "A woman? *Really?*"

"Yes," he answered, a bit defensive. "I have a mate now." He lifted his chin. "She is incredible. *No one* has a mate as good as mine."

Kaz's eyes widened. His brows, two inky black slashes, rose high on his forehead. "A mate."

Cal scowled. Was it so hard to believe that he'd found a mate? Given his history, perhaps the skepticism could be forgiven, but he still didn't like the shock on his friend's face. "That's what I said."

"When did this happen?"

"Almost three weeks ago." Cal shifted, the mist that was his lower body swirling with impatience. Truly, he didn't want to be standing there talking to Kaz. He wanted to be back with Elise, who would kiss him and fuss and needle him about every little fact he could recall about the events he witnessed.

Gods, he loved it when she spent hours and hours getting information out of him. He soaked up her attention like a damn sponge.

Still, he needed to talk to Kaz. He needed to know how to make their mating permanent, and the orc was the only person he trusted to give him good information on the subject.

"Damn. You've been mated three weeks and you wait until *now* to tell me?" He made a small sucking sound with his teeth, muttering, "Gotta get you a damn mating gift too, I guess."

"Yes, and I need to get back to her," Cal announced, waving a dismissive hand at whatever was going on across the street. "I only came to help with the fire. But I've been meaning to talk to you. I need information on mating."

Impossibly, Kaz's eyebrows crawled higher. "If you already have a mate, why—"

Impatient, Cal interrupted him to say, "Because she thinks it is only temporary, but it isn't. I need to know how to keep a mate and make sure she never leaves me."

"Only... temporary?" Kaz's eyes darted between the tense scene by the smoldering Healing House and Cal. Confusion was written in every line of his pretty orcish face. "That's not how mating works. Just what in Glory's name have you gotten yourself into, Cal?"

"I'm not sure. This is *why* I need your advice," he ground out.

Kaz shook his head. Long black hair, thick and wavy, swept back and forth over the back of his beaten leather jacket. "I'm not mated, Cal. I wouldn't know the first thing about it."

"But you know people who *are* mated," Cal pressed. "You know how it's supposed to work."

"I... Well, sure, I guess, but—"

Cal made a frustrated sound in the back of his throat. "Please, Kaz. I need help. You are my only friend. I trust you."

"Ah, fuck," the orc muttered, kicking a pebble at the tire of his parked car.

When he took too long to answer, Cal added, "She is all I've ever wanted. I can't lose her, Kaz. I won't survive it."

"Shit. Picked a real fucking time to fall in love, fog man." Kaz scrubbed his scarred knuckles over his jaw, his eyes on his brother's back. Theodore was leaning down to talk to the small woman, one gloved hand wrapped around the back of her neck in a possessive hold even Cal recognized.

Arching his brows, Cal glanced around to find more elvish shadows moving around the street. Residents were being ushered back into their homes, and a clean up crew had already begun to wipe all evidence of the incident from the street. By morning, he guessed that even the damage done to the surrounding homes would be fixed. No evidence left behind.

His eyes swung back to the sovereign and the woman he held. She didn't seem pleased to see him, but she wasn't trying to free herself from his hold, either. Petite and breakable looking, she still managed to stare up at the sovereign boldly, her fists clenched at her sides. Whatever it was the Solbournes were up to, Cal had a feeling that the healer wouldn't bend to their machinations easily.

"Fine." Kaz sighed, drawing Cal's attention back to important things. "But I'll need your help with something in exchange. Deal?"

For Elise, Cal would do anything. No questions asked. "Deal."

"Meet me at the bar. Midnight."

Cal nodded. Their business done, he let the rest of his form dematerialize once more.

Finally, he thought, catching the air currents that led back to Elise, *I'm going to get some answers.*

CHAPTER SEVEN

ELISE STAYED WITH HER PARENTS WELL INTO THE night, citing the need to help them clean up and make sure they were all right. Cal didn't mind, though he would have preferred they were both back in her apartment. He'd adapted to having a home quickly. Rather than feeling confined like he thought he would, he'd only grown more possessive of the space and of the woman who resided there.

He couldn't say the same thing about her childhood home, though. Even after Bob and Rachel retired to their room, he felt uncomfortably restricted in the unfamiliar space. Cal was sure that part of it was due to the fact that things were oddly tense between Elise and himself.

There was too much to say, too much emotion roiling between them, and her family's home was not the place to safely work through the minefield between them. By silent agreement, they didn't bring up their previous conversation, nor the way Elise had completely shattered his world in the annex.

When he stood by the open back door, half-dematerialized and ready to escape the confines of his flesh and his frustrations for a while, they shared a look heavy with understanding.

"I'll see you at home," she whispered, stretching onto her tiptoes to brush a kiss across his lips.

Cal felt that peculiar pressure building again. It was an ache in his chest, like an acute longing for her had metastasized into real pain. He kissed her more firmly, always hungry for her, and reassured himself that, come tomorrow morning, he would have the tools necessary to renegotiate their deal. He would make her his. There was no other option.

The terms had changed. He didn't want a temporary mate. He wanted *forever*, and he'd go to any lengths necessary to get it.

FROM THE DESK OF ELISE SASINI, AN EXCERPT FROM THE MANUSCRIPT *THE SHROUDED CITY*:

Cal won't tell me about what exactly happened during his year in Solbourne custody. I don't blame him. My father was a war correspondent for nearly sixty years. After the war ended, he worked full time for The Light. *Being a journalist in the 1980's through the 2000's was a dangerous venture. Thaddeus II's crackdown on the press reached its peak then, and my father was one of many journalists to find themselves in the bowels of a Solbourne dungeon.*

My father was held for three months after writing an article about a series of disappearances around the city. He was bold — or foolish — enough to outright speculate that they were politically motivated, and he paid the price for it. My father won't talk about his time with the shadow Patrol, either, but it haunts him.

Like with Cal, I can see the truth that can't be spoken. My father's knee has never been the same, though he blames his pain on gout, and he hasn't taken his shirt off in front of anyone but my mother in forty-five years. Cal won't go near an open flame if he can help it, and I've started taking longer routes on the m-lev to avoid having to take him underground. He's never said a word, but when we glide through the tunnels, I can feel his fear sticking to me like a second skin.

I'm not sure if it's the abhorrence of pity or a desire to forget about their trauma that makes them reluctant to share the details of what happened to them. Maybe it's a protective urge to save their loved ones from knowledge that can only hurt them. I don't know.

Cal is open about other things, though. When I asked him how he feels about the current regime, he simply shrugged. He doesn't seem to hold any ill-will toward Theodore Solbourne or any of the Solbourne family. He is more forgiving than I am.

Cal's eyes, swaths of inky black, are placid when he explains, "They are not their father. I don't hold his sins against them anymore than you hold the sins of my birth against me, even if I think you should."

He is a tangle of contradictions, my mate. He is an eminently practical being, and as such, he is aware that his guilt is illogical, unfounded. When he says things like that, I am reminded again of his complexity — as well as my desire to throttle a select few people.

Guilt thrives in him, eating away at a soul that is good to its deepest foundations. If I could carve the guilt out of him with my hands, I would. I can't, though. Perhaps someday he will let me replace his oldest companion with something softer, kinder, but it is not today, nor tomorrow.

For now, all I can say is, "Tell me more about the people you've saved, Cal."

Kaz's favorite bar was a shithole called *The Broken Tooth*. Deep in the seediest part of the Tenderloin neighborhood, it was as unassuming as the shattered glass in the gutters. At four AM, a cleaning bot would sweep away the sins of the night from the street, but the bar would remain, and its patrons would simply replace what was swept up. Sometimes it was glass, usually it was cigarette butts, and occasionally it was blood. Even in the capital of the squeaky clean Protectorate, filth and violence would always have a foothold.

Cal understood why Kaz picked this particular dive bar as his favorite haunt. In the middle of a web of underground Markets — where black market goods, drugs, and desperate people passed from hand to hand — it was the perfect place for the head of the Solbourne's intelligence force to keep his eye on the pulse of the EVP.

Not many people knew that Kaz was perhaps the single most dangerous man in the territory, nor that he controlled a vast underground network of informants and spies. Even fewer knew that he was not just an orcish mercenary hired to keep the sovereign safe.

He was Theodore Solbourne's half brother, and despite his outward appearance, he was every bit as elvish and single-mindedly ruthless as the rest of his family.

When Cal stepped into *The Broken Tooth's* hazy interior, he found Kaz sitting at the far end of the sticky bar, a green bottle of beer clasped loosely around the neck with two clawed fingers. Cal peered closely at his friend's hands, more curious about them than he'd ever been before.

Now that his focus had shifted to being mated, he was terribly curious about the subject on the whole. He only knew the bare minimum of orcish mating habits and nothing at all about elves, since they kept everything secret. That never bothered him before, but now he felt compelled to know more. Perhaps there was some secret to their success he could uncover if he dug far enough.

Sliding onto the stool next to his friend, Cal asked, "When you find your mate, your hands will turn black, yes? Like your claws?"

Kaz grunted and lifted his beer to his lips for a harsh swig. His claws, naturally glossy black, looked extra sinister against the glass of the bottle.

A staticky blues song played over the sound of low chatter. A hunched figure was smoking in a far corner, gaunt face turned toward an old feed screen showing the latest arena fight. With just a glance to his right, Cal could immediately tell that the three vampires sitting in a booth by the grimy window were having a *very* serious discussion. A look to his left took in the were woman behind the bar, her mismatched eyes keen and her face lined with age, as well as the patron she spoke to, a fellow were with shaggy brown hair and a pale, sweaty face.

Turning his attention back to Kaz, Cal thought, *The Solbournes don't even need me anymore.*

Truly, what use did they have for him when Kaz could blend in so well with the shadows and the people who dwelled there? No one in the bar would ever think he was half a step away from the Protectorate's throne.

The Solbourne family's enemies wouldn't think to be wary of one single, intimidating orc in elvish territory. By the time they realized their mistake, it would be too late.

Lowering the bottle back onto the scratched bar top, Kaz curtly answered, "Yeah. Hands and feet. Why?"

Cal looked down at his own hands and scowled. "I want something like that. Then she would know every time she looks at me that I'm hers."

Kaz let out a low, weary rumble. "It's not all it's cracked up to be, you know."

"What do you mean?"

"The fated shit." Kaz's voice was its usual sonorous purr, but there was an edge of bitterness in it that Cal had never heard before. "The biological imperative bullshit. A lot of people revere it, but it's not like we're given a choice." He lifted his left hand and made a sharp, dismissive gesture with his fingers. "See this hand? It could take the kohl for anyone. I wouldn't get to choose, or decide I'm ready. One day, I'll walk into the wrong room or breathe in a scent from across a park and it'll just happen. Choice? Gone."

Cal drummed his fingertips on the bar top. His hair swirled over his shoulders as he worked through his confusion. "But doesn't that make things easier? If you know that person is your mate, there is no talking or deciding or negotiating. No *deals.*"

Kaz arched a dark, winged brow. "Deals?" He shook his head. "You think it's a simpler way, but it's not. Neither fate nor biology give a shit about anyone. You know what the kohl brought my mother? Fucking Mad Thad, a bastard, and an early death." Kaz paused to take another sip of his beer. Muttering into the rim, he added, "If I stay unmated for the rest of my life, it'll be a gods-damned blessing."

It was hard to argue with that, even though Cal heartily wanted to. Now that he new the comforts of a mate — the feeling of knowing he never had to be alone again, the bone-deep contentment of her nearness, the roar of lust when he was blessed with her touch — he thought that he might have a better grasp on the benefits than his friend did.

Of course he also understood the risks. He wasn't sure what it would be like to live your life knowing you could, at any second, have your health and happiness tied to a stranger. Cal counted himself extremely lucky that the only woman he'd ever desired was a good, compassionate, intelligent witch. It was entirely possible that Kaz would not be so lucky.

Of course he won't be as lucky as I am, he thought, sitting up a little straighter on his stool. *The best mate is already taken.*

"Well, whether you want a mate or not, *I* do," he said, firmly steering the discussion back where he needed it to be. "I need to know how to make Elise mine forever."

Kaz barked out a husky laugh. "You and every other lovesick motherfucker." He tipped his beer in Cal's direction and grinned. Large upper and lower fangs gleamed against the jewel tone of his skin even in the dim, smoky bar. "Tell me the story and I'll see if I can help."

When the bartender walked over to ask if he'd like something, Cal turned her down. He didn't eat or drink much at all. A meal every other month usually did the trick, and he preferred the taste of saltwater to any of the bottled bile Kaz loved to drink. Besides, if he did want to consume something, he vastly preferred to be with Elise when he did it.

When his friend had a fresh beer and the bartender walked back to the other end of the bar, Cal asked, "First, what do you want from me?"

It was a familiar game between them, this dance of negotiation and exchange of favors. It was how they came to be friends in the first place, though neither could pinpoint exactly when it happened with any sort of certainty.

Kaz ran his claws through his loose hair. He looked tired. "Lot going on back home," he explained. "I need you to keep an eye out for anyone talking about what happened at the Healing House tonight. Any word about a bomb, or someone looking to hire someone for a job. Anything, and I mean *anything*, about it or Margot Goode."

"Margot Goode?" Cal frowned. He knew who the Goodes were, but he'd never heard the first name before. "Who is that?"

His friend snorted, but Cal couldn't figure out what was funny about his question. "She was the healer in residence. The redhead who almost died tonight." He leaned in close and dropped his voice until Cal could barely hear it over the music. "She's family."

"You said that before." The longer he stared at Kaz's grim expression, the more a suspicion niggled at him. "She's not an elf, so she's..."

The orc inclined his head, his eyes hard. He looked pissed, and Cal finally began to understand why. "Teddy's."

Cal leaned back and blinked hard, absorbing the information. At the other end of the bar, the shaggy-haired were stood up and hustled out, his hands shoved into his pockets and his head down. The bartender darted out after him, a towel thrown over her shoulder, as she called, "Roger, wait! You can't just—"

They disappeared out the swinging door. Cal watched them

go before he turned his attention back to his friend. "Someone tried to kill her?"

"Looks like."

Well, that cleared up the mystery of why the Sovereign's Guard were watching her house. If that little woman was Theodore Solbourne's mate, he pitied whoever tried to hurt her. Elves weren't exactly known for their mercy, nor their tolerance for threats. He would know.

"I'll help you however I can," he promised. He would have agreed to almost anything if it helped him keep Elise, but now that he was fighting for his own mate, he discovered a newfound kinship with the sovereign. If it were *his* mate in danger, he'd do far worse than ask for help from a friend.

Kaz reached back to clap him on the shoulder. The blow would have knocked a human man off of his stool. Cal wasn't human, but it still came close. "Thank you, fog man. We won't forget it." The orc gave his shoulder another wallop. "Now tell me about your mate."

"Her name is Elise Sasini," he proudly explained. "She's a *writer.*"

"Sasini?" It was Kaz's turn to lean back on his stool, his eyebrows arching high. "Daughter of Robert Sasini, the crime writer? International bestselling author of *A Golden Land,* the not-so-flattering history of how the elves took over this territory? *That* Elise Sasini?"

Cal flicked a floating tendril of white hair out of his eyes and answered smugly, "Yes. She's *my* mate."

Kaz looked like he almost didn't believe him. "How the fuck did you swing that one?"

"She wanted to write a book about me," he answered, lips curling into a rare smile. "Apparently, she's wanted to do it all her life. You should see her home. It's covered in pictures of my fog." And she'd been tickled to learn that at least a handful of those photos actually *did* have Cal in them, though no one but him would ever know it. "She figured out that I visit the Aerie sometimes, so she booked a pilgrim's stay and summoned me."

"You still go to the Aerie? What for?" A deep frown settled into the grooves of Kaz's mouth and forehead. "Do you need help? I thought we figured out how to get you things when you need them, Cal."

He shrugged, not meeting his friend's searching gaze. Instead, he looked at the rows and rows of bottles behind the bar when he answered, "I don't really know why I go there, after everything. Sometimes I just need something familiar." He cleared his throat. "But I don't have any reason to go there anymore. I have a home now."

"With Elise?"

Cal's smile crept back onto his face. "Yes."

"Good," Kaz grunted. "Better a story-sniffing writer than the assholes who tried to brainwash you."

"Agreed. Elise is a much nicer alternative." He had trouble imagining anyone better, if he were being honest. "And our deal was painless. She wanted to write a book about me and I wanted to know what it was like to have a mate. Simple."

Kaz stared at him for several long, silent seconds before he said, "...Uh-huh?"

"What? Why are you looking at me like that?"

"S'nothing." Kaz took a long pull from his beer. His eyebrows seemed to have permanently adhered themselves closer to his hairline. "Just... ah, that's quite the deal you made, fog man. I'm surprised she went for it."

Cal clenched his jaw and fought off the urge to snap at his friend. "Why? Because I'm a murderer?"

"No, you prissy fuck, because there's no *pretending* to be mates. You either are or you aren't. Trying to fake it is a recipe for disaster and I'm willing to bet she knows that." He eyed Cal warily. "I'm guessing you've been on some dates? Met up to talk about the book, maybe? She probably let you hold her hand or something, right? And now you're head over heels for the first woman to—"

"No," he snapped, "it's not like that."

Kaz's dismissive tone sent a roar of anger through Cal. He hated the way he alluded to their relationship like it was some passing fancy, or like Elise was merely indulging him. It was more than that. Cal felt it in every damn cell of his body.

"She brought me to her home, and when she learned that people usually only want to take advantage of me, she tried to back out. She said she didn't want to hurt me." Even now, weeks later, he felt a stab of panic at the thought. "I wouldn't let her back out."

"Why? Sounds like she has a bit of good sense."

Cal curled his hands into fists on his thighs. "Because she's my mate. I don't care if she uses me. She's mine. I wasn't going to give her up."

"Uh-huh. And how'd she take that?"

He lifted his chin. This part, at least, he knew he got right. "She *kissed* me."

Kaz looked both impressed and dismayed. "Yeah? And after?"

"What do you mean *after?*"

"I mean what happened after that? Has she kept to the deal? Are you still seeing her?" Kaz blew out a breath. "And what *exactly* were the terms of that deal you made?"

Cal leaned an elbow on the bar top and smiled. "Of course I'm still seeing her. We've been living together for three weeks. That was the deal."

The orc sputtered, choking on a gulp of his disgusting beverage. When he'd cleared his airways enough to speak, he wheezed, "Wait, you're *living* with her? She let you into her nest?"

"Yes." Cal took in Kaz's stunned expression with a pinch of unease. "Why? Does that mean something?"

It meant something to *him* to be allowed into her home, but that was because he'd never set foot in one before. It never occurred to him that it might mean something to her, too.

Kaz let out a huff that was somehow both disbelieving and amused. "I mean, if she were orcish it would mean a fuckload, but I'm guessing she's not, if you're here complaining about not being permanently mated. An orcish woman doesn't let *anyone* into her nest except her mate and babies. Not even family." His eyebrows pinched thoughtfully as he swirled the last of his beer around the bottom of his bottle. "Still, though— *Living* with a woman. Yeah, that's..." His eyes crinkled at the corners. "That's a different thing, fog man. What else have you done?"

"We spend most of our time together." Except for when he felt the itch to be out of his skin and his duty to watch the city came up, they were inseparable. Where she went, he did. "We go to the beach. Sometimes she likes to dance with me. We watch entertainment feeds and cook together. I met her parents."

Kaz put his bottle down on the bar with enough force to send a crack through the glass. "Well fuck me, you should have led with that!"

"Why?"

"Goddess help me." Kaz released his beer long enough to rub the heels of both hands into his eyes. "Cal, if you move in with a woman *and* she takes you to see her parents *and* you spend all your time together, you aren't temporary anything. You're *mated.*"

"No," he pressed, heart beating faster, "she's sticking to the deal. She hasn't said anything about staying together after she finishes the book. In fact, tonight she tried to *end* things."

"Did she say why?"

Cal's stomach curdled when he remembered the stark look on her face, the marrow-deep fear he felt when he thought she was sending him away. His voice was hushed and just a little raw when he explained, "I got angry with her for not introducing me to her parents as her mate. She said she was worried about putting pressure on me, that what we were doing was hurting me, and asked me if I'd like to end things."

Kaz's sharp-eyed gaze lingered on Cal's pained expression.

"Fog man... she asked *you* if you wanted to end things. She didn't say *she* wanted to."

"She wouldn't have said it if she didn't want it!"

Kaz rolled his eyes. "Don't be a dipshit. She was trying to take care of you. My bet is she knows this is your first relationship and is working overtime trying to make sure you never feel overwhelmed or cornered. *Especially* if you've already moved in together, for Glory's sake."

"But—"

"No buts!" Kaz snagged his cracked beer bottle and pointed an accusatory finger at him all in one movement. "I don't know shit about mating, but I know plenty about women. I was raised by a damn clutch of them. That does *not* sound like a woman running from commitment to me, Cal." He made a swirling motion with his finger. "Now tell me what happened next. What did she do when you said no?"

Cal ran a hand through the length of his hair and leaned slightly away, his throat bobbing with a hard swallow. Gods, the memory of her hot mouth and soft, sure hands made him hard all over again. "She... ah... We didn't talk much after that."

"D'you fuck?"

"I'm not answering that." Cal wasn't particularly modest or prudish, but he *was* possessive. He had no intention of sharing their most private, sacred moments with anyone other than his mate.

Kaz laughed and shook his head. "I'm going to go ahead and take that as a yes. And if not, then you got close." He finished off his beer with a long, drawn out sigh. Eyes slanting toward Cal, he announced, "Congrats, fog man. You're mated. Now get the fuck out of this shitty bar and go home."

Cal's chest seized, hope wrapping around his heart like a vice. Still, he needed to be sure. He couldn't risk messing things up any more than he already had. Living without Elise was not an option.

"How do you know she wants to keep me?" he pressed, hands

flattening against the sticky bar. "How do you know it's not just the deal?"

Kaz groaned and rolled his shoulders. "Let's see... Did your deal specify that she spend all her time with you?"

"Not exactly, no." He demanded they see each other often, but it was true that his wording was vague. If she'd wanted to, she could have spent far less time with him than she did and he probably wouldn't have known enough to complain. Without knowing her routine or responsibilities, any number of excuses would have simply flown over his head.

"And did your deal specify that she introduce you to her parents?"

"No."

Kaz narrowed his eyes. "Did it specify that she provide sexual favors?"

"No," he gritted out. "I told her that's not what I meant."

Even *he* knew he didn't want sex from someone fundamentally unwilling, even if it was part of a deal she agreed to.

"So..." Kaz began to tick points off on his clawed fingers. "You moved in with her. You're having a sexual relationship with her. You spend all your time together. She introduced you to her parents. When you got upset, she offered you an out, but didn't take one herself." He wiggled his fingers. "You're mated, man."

It was suddenly hard to keep his physical form together. Cal nearly vibrated with excitement, with the urgency to fly across the city and back to the willing arms of his mate.

"How do I know it's permanent?" he rasped.

"Well, I guess you'll just have to ask her," Kaz answered. "Women are all about being *asked*, Cal. They are way more forgiving of a stupid question than an assumption. Don't ever work on assumptions. That way lies sharp claws, poisoned coffee, and nights on the couch."

A cold, crawling fear made its way into his exhilaration. "What if she says she doesn't want me?"

Kaz shrugged. "Then you keep trying until she sends you away. Simple."

Simple. Cal had begun to hate the word. Nothing about his relationship with Elise had been simple.

It was worth it, though. He knew that the moment she let him into her life, and he'd clung onto the deal because he was terrified of letting her go. But Kaz was right. He had to trust Elise to give him the truth when he asked for it. So far, she'd never given him any reason to believe she wouldn't.

Kaz's heavy hand landed on Cal's shoulder. Giving him a hard shove, the orc said, *"Go,* Cal. You've got a mate waiting for you."

He stood up from his bar stool on unsteady legs, his heartbeat a thundering rhythm in his ears. He thought of all the intimate moments they'd shared; how she fell asleep with her head in his lap and how she kissed him whenever he came home from his vigil. He thought of her magic coursing through his fog and the way she brought him into her family's home, wreathed in smiles. He thought of her tears when he told her his story and the long, hot looks she gave him when she thought he wasn't looking.

Gods, was he fucking *blind?*

I have a mate.

I have a mate waiting for me.

Suddenly, nothing else mattered. He needed to be with her. He needed to know, with no hint of doubt, that they were not going to end now or any time in the future. He needed his mate like he needed *air.*

In an instant, Cal dematerialized. The bar's other patrons exclaimed with surprise or consternation as the space was suddenly filled with thick, rolling fog. Kaz's voice rose above the din as he cursed. "Fucking— Damn it, Cal, you can't just drop your clothes in the middle of the bar!"

If he had shoulders, Cal would have shrugged. He didn't give a shit about his clothes. All that mattered was his mate, and she wasn't in *The Broken Tooth.* She was waiting for him at home.

He would be damned if he made her wait a moment longer.

FROM THE DESK OF ELISE SASINI, A PAGE FROM HER NOTEBOOK DATED FEBRUARY 15th 2045:

Reasons to spend the rest of my life with Cal:

1. I love him

2. He's the most beautiful man in the world, bar none

3. I really love him

4. He's an insanely powerful elemental whose magic meshes with mine like we're a damn PB and J.

5. I don't think I can live without him

Reasons to not spend the rest of my life with Cal:

[PAGE IS BLANK]

CHAPTER EIGHT

ELISE COULDN'T SLEEP. SHE KNEW THAT THERE WAS NO reason to stay up and wait for Cal. He would be home when it suited him, as he always was, but her mind refused to turn off.

What was he doing? Was he safe? Did he regret what they'd done in the annex?

She shifted restlessly in her bed. Fisting a handful of her blankets, she turned on her side and stared out at the sea of lights visible through her bedroom window — unlocked, just in case he decided to blow in sometime during the night.

Anxiety mingled with a dreadful, unfulfilled arousal.

Gods, but she loved the taste of him. Elise had always been a sexual being, but sex with Cal was *different*. Everything he did — every little sound, every shift of his muscles, every involuntary, stuttering breath — thrilled her to the core. He made her feel powerful and in control. There was nothing more intoxicating than guiding him through his first sexual experiences.

The ache between her legs hadn't diminished even after the explosion. It persisted as she helped her mother clean up the living room and gave a faceless Patrol officer her statement. It didn't let up even after she got home and took a cleansing shower.

It was a good sort of ache, of course, but Elise couldn't shake the concern that she overwhelmed Cal. They'd fought and then he had what she was astonished to learn was his first orgasm. Neither were followed up with a talk or a check-in to make sure he was all right.

Is that why he left?

Elise rolled over again. Her eyes stung. Instead of staring at her closet and wall of framed articles, she forced herself to try and sleep.

But the worries came at her from all sides, robbing her of rest.

She pictured Cal out there, dematerialized and enmeshed in fog as he drifted over the water. Was he angry at her? Did he feel guilt or shame for what he'd done? She knew he still struggled with much of what Loft's acolytes tried to indoctrinate him with. Did he think they'd done something wrong?

Whatever it was that bothered him, she was certain they could work through it. The problem was that he had to *be* there to do that.

Elise curled her legs closer to her chest, a bloom of hurt taking root in her heart. She hated the idea that he might be out there confused and hurt and alone. She hated being without him. For all that he'd never slept in her bed, she felt it was cold and barren without him.

Part of loving Cal was understanding that he did not just belong to her. No matter what her possessiveness said, he was a force of nature. He was *wild*. He could not be held in one place any more than he could stay in his physical form indefinitely. He had to roam because it was his nature. He had to do his vigil because it was his duty.

She understood this. As a weather witch with an unbridled awe for the wildness of the world, she even respected it.

But the part of her that was a woman in love had to come to terms with the fact that he would not always be home at night. He would never sleep beside her, nor would he take her out to dinner and a show.

She didn't begrudge him those things. Cal was who he was.

Elise wouldn't want him any other way. Part of loving someone was trusting them to come back to you — even when they were the physical embodiment of something as ephemeral as *fog*. If she wanted a boring, five-in-the-evening-to-eight-in-the-morning kind of guy, she could have one.

Cal spoke to her soul. She didn't and never would want anyone like she wanted him. But that didn't mean she couldn't worry.

It was an exhausting night. First, the nerves that came with introducing Cal to her parents. Then their fight. Then the rush of going down on him for the first time. *Then* the explosion. Elise felt like she'd lived a year of her life in less than eight hours.

Sleep pulled her down, though her worries fought it every step of the way.

~

FROM THE DESK OF ELISE SASINI, AN EXCERPT FROM THE MANUSCRIPT *THE SHROUDED CITY:*

I've loved before. My first boyfriend was Jeremy Ackerman, a wolf shifter, in the fifth grade. I loved him.

I dated Dan, a fellow journalism student, for three years. I loved him, too. I've loved strangers on the m-lev and I've loved men who never loved me back.

I've loved before, but I've never loved like I love Cal.

Maybe it's something base and fundamental in our magic that draws us together. Maybe it's just chemistry. Maybe it's whatever unseen hand that people like to believe guides these things. I don't know.

All I know is that Cal is wild, and beautiful, and strange, and sometimes hard to get along with. He is broken and he is proud and he is carrying scars I can't even see. Every day I look at him and I see a deep, dark pool of secrets desperately trying to get out — and I see a man who wants to be held and yet does not have the words necessary to say so.

I see my whole future in a single, mercurial being, and if the gods truly exist, then only they can appreciate the scope of my devotion to him.

The feeling of cool air on her arms and face roused her from a fitful dose, but it was the feeling of chilly hands that *really* woke her.

Her eyes popped open. Elise sat up with a start, but it took her a few confused moments to understand what she was seeing. Fog was everywhere. Even her furniture seemed to have disappeared under the waves of pillowy white that poured in through her open window. Only the faint green glow of the emergency light by the bottom of her bedroom door managed to break through the cloud of condensed moisture. Magic skated over her skin, adding to the otherworldly sense of disorientation.

"Cal?" she whispered, seeking out his form beneath the swirling water vapor. Elise braced her weight on one elbow and squinted into the strange, shifting mass in the darkness of her bedroom. Relief quickly bled into her confusion.

Cool hands framed her face. In the span of a few heartbeats, he melted out of the fog. Elise didn't think she would ever tire of seeing the miracle of his existence recreated every single time he materialized in front of her.

One moment there was only the sense of him in the mist; the next water and air and magic compressed to make a living, breathing man so beautiful she sometimes wondered if he was truly real.

Cal's expression, when it appeared, was intense. His brows were drawn tight over his black eyes; his soft lips pressed thin. The hands cupping her face were gentle but firm, unyielding, and the weight of his body settling on top of hers was both comfortable and erotic. Elise would have enjoyed it more if the look on his face didn't send a dizzying sense of dread through every nerve.

She cupped one of his hands with her own and tried to swallow the lump in her throat. "What's wrong?"

Was this it? Was he here to tell her he was done with whatever their relationship was?

Gods, let it be anything but that. Elise would have taken almost anything rather than Cal finally deciding to end his experiment in intimacy with her.

His voice was its usual low murmur, but there was a distinct raw edge to it that raised her hackles when he said, "I need to ask you a question."

Slowly scooting up into a sitting position, she scanned his face for any hint of what was bothering him. Nothing in his expression screamed that he was upset over what happened in the annex, but Cal's moods were mercurial. She never really knew what was going on just below the surface, and it was something that thrilled her. He was full of surprises.

Elise normally appreciated that about him, but not this time.

Pressing his hand more firmly into her cheek, she answered, "Ask me whatever you want, baby."

Cal shifted in front of her, though the fog made it hard to see exactly what he was doing. It moved restlessly around the room to swirl in dense eddies. Usually that meant he was agitated, and that knowledge only made Elise's stomach drop even further.

Please don't let this be it. Already her eyes had begun to water. The moment he actually said the words, she feared the dam would break completely.

His hands slid down from her cheeks to cup her neck. Goosebumps prickled her skin. Cal ran much cooler than she did, and when he touched her, it felt like the kiss of sweet, fresh water on overheated skin.

Firming his chin into a stubborn angle, he asked, "Are we permanent?"

Bracing herself for the worst, Elise could only blink, stunned. "I... what?"

In the dark, with the fog blocking most of the reflected light of the city, Cal's eyes were too unbroken pools of black ink. They might have looked menacing, if only she didn't know exactly how much he gave of himself every single day to every person in their ignorant city — if only she didn't love him so damn much.

Cal pressed closer, until he was practically straddling her. "Are we *permanent?*"

Her heartbeat picked up its pace. She wanted to tell him *yes,* of course they were permanent, but Elise knew that not everything was as it seemed with Cal. His question could come from the desire to *make* them permanent, or it could just as easily spring from a desire to get as far away from commitment as possible.

Not that I really think Cal's terrified of commitment, she thought, recalling his visceral fear and anger in the annex, *but you never know. Someone like Cal could change their mind in a heartbeat.*

He was, after all, *weather.* One moment he could be as placid as a sunny day, and the next he could be a raging storm. Respecting him, *loving* him, meant understanding the nature of his being, so Elise knew she had to forgo any assumptions. Like always, she needed to be careful.

"Explain, please," she said. Reaching out to smooth her hands down his naked chest, she added, "Tell me what you mean by *permanent.*"

Cal scowled impatiently. "I spoke to Kaz tonight and he told me we are already mates, but if I wanted to be sure that we are mates *forever,* I needed to ask you. So I'm asking you."

"Wait— Kaz? Who's Kaz? Is that your friend?" He'd mentioned having a friend a few times, but Cal had never given her a name before. Something about it sounded familiar, though she couldn't put her finger on why.

Making an impatient sound in the back of his throat, Cal leaned in until he was nearly nose to nose with her. His breath washed over her face in cool, sweet-scented puffs. "Don't think about Kaz. Think about me. Are we permanent mates?"

Elise grappled with her answer, but couldn't come up with anything better than, "Do you *want* to be?"

Cal reared back, his expression outraged. "Do I *want* to be? You're *my* witch. Of course that's what I want!"

She stared up at him, lips parted with surprise. No, she couldn't just take that at face value. Cal didn't necessarily understand what he was saying, what he was *asking* for. How could he really know? He'd only been in a relationship for three weeks. She at least had the experience of being with other people around which she could frame her feelings for him. Cal didn't have that luxury.

When she could find her voice, she rasped, "Cal, I know you think that's what you want, but you haven't had enough time—"

"Do *not* say that I can't know what I want because I'm inexperienced," he growled. "I know now that you've been cautious with me, taking care of me. I don't need that. I just need to know that you want me as much as I want you."

Elise's throat felt scraped raw. Her heart beat so fast and hard, it felt like it might break through the cage of her ribs, leaving nothing but splinters behind. This was what she wanted, but she still warred with herself.

Gods, she wanted to love this man until the breath left her body for the last time, but the fear of somehow taking a natural choice from him was excruciating.

Cal deserved a life and choices. He deserved every experience, every joy, but those things were stolen from him. To count herself as one of the many who simply *took* from him without regard for what was healthy or right made her feel sick to her stomach.

And yet, when the seconds dragged by without her response, Elise realized something else: By not being honest with him, *she was doing exactly that.*

Cal's expression had begun to drain of its intensity, leaving nothing but a stark, beautiful mask. There was nothing left of his vibrant, difficult personality — just staggering pain. Even his fog went still as he took her silence for a rejection.

He released her neck with a quick, jerky movement and recoiled, the edges of his form already fading from view as he retreated into the safety of his other form.

"No, Cal!" Elise lunged, freeing herself from her tangled blankets to tackle him back onto the bed. She knew instinctively that if she let him dematerialize and drift back out of her window, she would never see him again.

And that wasn't a *fucking* option.

"No, no," she said, straddling his waist. Cal's hands snapped up to cup her backside as she leaned down. Her hair fell in a messy blonde curtain around their heads when she whispered against his stiff lips, "I want you, Cal. I don't want to go a day of my life without seeing you. I want to kiss you and hold you and deal with your brooding for the rest of my life. I've known it since the day you walked into my apartment."

Cal's fingers flexed, pressing hard against soft skin covered in thin sleep shorts. His voice was a raw murmur when he asked, "The deal?"

"I threw it out of my head that same day." She pressed her hands to his naked chest. His heartbeat was just as fast as hers, a thunderous rhythm against her palm. Elise touched her forehead to his and whispered, "All I cared about was keeping you around, Cal. I don't even care about the book."

"But..." She could feel his brow crinkle. "I saw you writing."

She felt herself flush. "Well, it would have been weird if I didn't at least *pretend* to write something, wouldn't it?"

Cal's hands slid down her thighs. His palms left her shorts to skim down her bare skin, sending a low pulse of heat through her body. "So you didn't actually write anything down?"

"No, I wrote something," she amended, sitting up a little so she could get a good look at his face. Cal was spread out beneath her, his mane of white hair haloed around his aquiline face and his eyes half-lidded. His fingertips dug into the soft flesh of her thighs, dimpling her skin.

Perhaps sensing her hesitancy, he demanded, "Tell me what you wrote."

Elise licked her lips and tried very hard not to be distracted by the beautifully naked man lying beneath her. "I... It's more of a love letter, if I'm being honest. I wrote down what you told me, but I also wrote a lot about... well, about how I feel. About what I think of you. All of it."

Cal stared up at her with a familiar, hungry expression. "And how do you feel?"

She tried to shake off the bizarrely sentimental urge to cry. Elise wasn't normally a weepy sort of person, but the relief she felt was so intense, it was like her body needed some cathartic release to process it all.

In a watery voice, she answered, "I'm stupidly in love with you, Cal."

Infuriatingly, all he said was, "So... we're permanent."

It was her turn to scowl. Sitting back so she could look down her nose at him, she muttered, "I sure *hope* so, or else I'm going to be very upset, very soon."

He was still beneath her for several awful seconds before a heartstopping smile broke out across his face. Cal so rarely smiled in earnest, but when he did, it damn near knocked Elise's world sideways.

Nodding to himself and looking very pleased, he said, "Kaz was right. Stupid questions *are* better."

A laugh bubbled up and out of her throat. *"What?"*

Cal slid his hands back up to curl around her waist. His eyes gleamed when he asked, "If you love me and we're mates, does that mean you're not going to be careful anymore?"

Elise sucked in a sharp breath when he gently pushed her down onto the swiftly hardening erection trapped between them. Desire, pushed back by worry, came roaring back in an instant. She wanted nothing more than to chase away the ache with a quick strip and slow, sensual ride.

Still, she had to ask, "Are you sure, baby? That's a big step."

"Will it be like the annex?" His voice was rough as he slowly began to move her hips back and forth, dragging her against him in a torturous rhythm.

Elise felt him through the damp seam of her sleep shorts and bit back a moan. "Better," she breathed. "It'll be better."

She watched, transfixed, as the muscles of Cal's lean stomach bunched and released with every slow stroke against her. "Show me," he demanded. "I want *everything,* witch."

Finally.

There would be no more holding back. No more tip-toeing. No more worry. Cal wanted everything, and Elise was desperate to give it to him.

Grasping the hem of her sleep shirt, she didn't hesitate to tear it up and over her head. It landed in a heap somewhere on the floor, though she couldn't see where through the dense, roiling layer of fog obscuring everything except Cal.

The presence of his fog gave an already intimate act an even more private, sacred feeling. In this moment, there really was nothing except the two of them and their combined, complimentary magic. It filled the room with the sharp, metallic scent of power and fresh water — blood and life and weather's rage and deep, scalding desire.

It took her only a moment to sit up and wiggle her way out of her sleep shorts, but she was breathing hard by the time she threw her leg back over his waist and settled her weight down. They both groaned when her liquid heat finally met his cool skin. Cal gasped — the sweetest godsdamned sound she ever heard — and tossed his head back against the mattress.

"Tell me if you want to stop," she firmly instructed him. "If it's uncomfortable or too much, just say—"

"Elise," he hissed, hips kicking up to grind against her core. "I'm going to die if you don't do *something.*"

She laughed, but didn't argue. How could she? Elise felt exactly the same way.

The memory of his taste on her tongue, the way he'd unraveled above her as she gave him pleasure like he'd never known it, practically lit her on fire.

Seeing such a powerful being lie prone beneath her, desperate for the relief she could provide, made her *explode.*

Elise braced her palms on the mattress by his ears and leaned down to kiss him long and hard, her hips moving in slow circles above him. He made a needy noise and rocked his hips to match her rhythm as his tongue snaked out to meet hers.

Never would she get bored of kissing Cal. He tasted like a storm, like everything that called to the soul of a weather witch. Even their magic meshed as they moved together, sliding against one another in a sensual dance.

Cool, dry hands slid up her sides to explore the soft skin of her stomach, her ribs, her back, and her breasts. When he stopped there, apparently fascinated by her stiff nipples, Elise broke the kiss to sit back and let him follow his instincts.

"You're so warm and soft," he breathed, awed, as he gently rolled her nipples between his fingertips. Elise sucked in deep breath as streaks of pleasure flashed down her spine to settle into a deep pool between her thighs. It was only made richer, sweeter, when he asked, "I get to have you forever?"

Taking one of his hands off of her breast, she brought it up to her lips for a slow, reverent kiss. "Yes," she whispered against his palm, "as long as you'll have me."

"Forever, then." His tone was suddenly implacable, hard as granite. Cal's hips canted upward with one hard thrust, as if to make his point. "I want forever with you, Elise. You're *my* mate."

She gasped, back bowing. "Yes, Cal, I am. *Yes.*"

His hand went back to her breast, squeezing gently, as she reached between them to align their bodies. He was thick and hard in her palm. Even in the darkness, she could *just* make out the pearly sheen of his skin. It just wasn't fair. How was it that even his damn *cock* was gorgeous?

"You're mine too," she said, reminding them both as she slowly lowered herself down onto him. It was a tight fit, but the delicious kind that sent a cascade of sparks across every nerve. It was so good, even her toes curled.

All around them, sparks of her magic danced through the fog, lighting up their naked bodies with bursts of pink and teal and bright, saturated yellow.

Cal made a strangled sound and dropped his hands to grip her hips. Every muscle in his body went rigid as she took him all the way to the hilt. She held still, panting, as she adjusted to the perfect fit, the feeling of him soothing that deep, empty ache even as it burned muscles she hadn't used in a while.

"You okay?" she asked, the words barely registering in her own ears.

His fingers flexed hard on her hips as he gave one, then two experimental thrusts upward. The sounds of their skin meeting echoed strangely in the fog, enhancing the feeling of otherworldliness, the profound intimacy of the moment. Pleasure seared away the lingering burn of the stretch as Cal's spine bowed. *"Gods,"* he gritted out, "I'm— Elise!"

"Shh," she soothed. Picking a slow, rocking rhythm, she took one of his hands and guided it between her legs. "Focus on me, baby. Touch me. And don't forget to breathe."

His fingers spasmed, as if touching her sent a shock straight through him, but Cal didn't hesitate to do as she instructed. Slowly, he followed the movement of her hips to rub her clitoris — tentatively at first, then with more confidence as she gave him soft instructions. It wasn't long before a fine sheen of sweat coated her body and her rocking turned into something more urgent.

Cal's chest moved with huge, gulping inhales as he let her ride him, his own hips stuttering beneath her. Elise gripped his shoulders and panted, "Sit up, baby. Sit up. I want to kiss you when I—"

He surged upward and would have sent her toppling over if he didn't have such a tight grip on her waist. Elise let out a bark of laughter as he leaned in close enough to bump their noses together.

"Oh, gods, I love you, you weird fog man," she wheezed, peppering his cheeks and nose and lips with kisses.

Cal smiled against her lips and wrapped his arms around her middle, holding her still as he rocked his hips up and down. "I love you, witch." Cool, wet fog kissed her overheated skin, running along her curves with purpose as he continued, "I am your mate. Permanently."

"Yes, permanently." Elise wiggled back just enough to move. Bracing her knees by his hips, she used the leverage to increase the pace. A coil of pressure and heat tightened, urging her to go faster, to chase the friction building like a fire between them. Cal met her stroke for stroke, though his movements weren't quite so fluid or practiced as hers.

It didn't matter. Sex with Cal was more than pleasurable. It was more than raw physical release. This was like everything good, and fun, and warm, and intense, and new, and thrilling she had ever felt multiplied by the thousands.

This powerful being, an act of elemental wrath made corporeal, was *hers*. Only she would know what he looked like when he came. Only she would give him pleasure. Only she would have complete mastery of his bliss.

Gods be good, it's enough to make any woman lose her mind. She would have laughed, if she had the breath for it. *No wonder love is called Tempest's Madness!*

When Cal's thrusts began to really lose their rhythm, she knew he was close to the edge. Yanking his head down, she fisted his beautiful, wild hair and pressed their lips together in a searing, open-mouthed kiss. He let out a low, broken sound as fog danced across her naked skin — and then swept between them to tease and rub her clitoris when his hand could not, sending her even higher.

I didn't even know he could do *that,* she thought, a split second before Cal came apart beneath her. Tendrils of compressed magic and water lashed at her with erratic, frenzied movements, sending her over the edge with him. Her thighs clenched, holding him there as he gave her everything he possibly could.

When the pleasure ebbed, they were both left sagging and boneless on her bed. Cal kept his arms around her, but dropped his head to nuzzle her neck and shoulder. He mumbled something into her skin, but it was too low for her to catch.

"What was that?" she asked, dazed.

His lips moved against the sweaty skin of her throat when he said, "I'm thanking the gods for bringing me to you."

Elise's heart gave a great, painful lurch. "Yeah?"

"Yeah." He kissed her throat. "You are my everything, witch."

She murmured, "Never thought I'd earnestly thank the gods for anything but orgasms, but I'm gonna say thank you, too. I never want to imagine my life without you, Cal."

"You will never have to." Stroking her hair, he added, "And just so we're clear, I'm *not* broody."

She smothered a laugh by pressing a kiss to the crown of his head. "Mm, if you say so, baby."

Slowly, in fits and starts, they repositioned themselves in her bed. Cal didn't sleep, but there was a drowsy, satisfied look in his eyes that made him content to settle down with her under her sheets. Resting her head on his chest, she listened to the strong sound of his heartbeat as she breathed in the cold, wet air.

She was half asleep when he asked, "Will you let me read your love letter?"

Her smile was so wide, it made her cheeks ache. "Yes," she whispered, kissing his chest. "But only the second draft."

FROM THE DESK OF CALAMITY, A NOTE WRITTEN IN AN ANNOTATED FIRST EDITION COPY OF *THE SHROUDED CITY*, BESTSELLING NON-FICTION TITLE AND WINNER OF THE PULITZER PRIZE - BIOGRAPHY:

Pg. 342

I am in awe of you, my mate. Every day I love you more than the day before, and every day I learn something new and precious about you.

Pg. 343

I THOUGHT WE AGREED YOU'D STOP CALLING ME BROODY.

Epilogue

October 2047 - San Francisco, The Elvish Protectorate

Cal would never like publicity. He didn't care for nosy people trying to track him down, or the throngs of folks who, for some time after *The Shrouded City's* publication, gathered on the beaches to try and catch a glimpse of him. He hadn't changed his mind about his anonymity, nor his general dislike for most people.

It was a strange thing, knowing that so many strangers read his story and felt, to no small degree, as though they *knew* him. He couldn't say he was really a fan of that.

What made it all worth it, though, was the absolute certainty he had in his claim on Elise. While he didn't enjoy the fresh scrutiny the book brought him, Cal pushed his mate to publish it on the grounds that it would show the entire world that they belonged to one another.

Not that they *needed* it, really, but Cal erred on the side of caution. He didn't feel he deserved his mate's devotion, but he was a jealous creature. If he was lucky enough to call her his, then he wanted every single being in the world to know about it.

Cal didn't have much experience in gauging the success or failure of books, but even he knew the furor around *The Shrouded City* was abnormal. The thing had only been out for a month, but it was all anyone wanted to talk about.

When he drifted past bookshop windows, he saw piles of it stacked waist-high. When a news feed alert came in on Elise's Met, it was almost always something about the book. When he was home with her, he listened to call after call, interview after interview, and made absolutely certain he was nowhere near a camera.

The only reviews and articles he cared about were the ones that gushed over their whirlwind love story — a turn of phrase that tickled Elise immensely. Everything else he ignored. Cal didn't care about the money that came in, or the upswell in public affection for him. When Kaz tried to coerce him into meeting with the Solbourne PR team, a group particularly interested in the chapters dedicated to his imprisonment and how they reflected on the current regime, he promptly dematerialized.

Cal didn't care about anything other than the public's recognition of his relationship. If Elise got acclaim for the book on top of that, then he was perfectly content to ignore the garbage that came with being suddenly *beloved* by millions of people.

"What put that scowl on your face?" Elise asked as soon as he materialized in their living room. She was curled up on the couch, a throw blanket tossed over her legs and her tablet clutched in one hand. There was a small, stemless glass of red wine in the other.

Cal closed the window with a flick of his fingers before he prowled over to his mate. When he left her in the afternoon, she'd been dolled up for a video interview, but now she was relaxed, her face clean and her thick blonde hair piled into a wispy bun. Bare toes peeked out from under the blanket.

Feeling his tension ease at the sight of her, relaxed and waiting for him, Cal grumbled, "They brought *signs* this time."

Elise snorted. Her eyes glittered with humor at his expense. "You *have* to tell me what they said!"

"No, I do not," he tartly replied, making his way over to the couch. Elise laughed and scooted to the far end, making plenty of room for him to lay down and put his head in her lap.

He still couldn't sleep, but he had grown very fond of lounging, so they upgraded their furniture. The two-seater couch changed to a behemoth that took up most of their living room, while their bed went from a queen to a California king. Cal was what Elise playfully called "a sprawler".

Not that she truly seemed to mind, of course. His mate was always ready to receive him with open arms. When he returned from his vigil, she enjoyed hearing about all that he'd done and seen in the city, while he hungrily devoured any new tidbit she offered him — how her day was, what she wrote, what strange thing had captured her formidable interest that day.

Always, she made sure to offer him contact. Rarely more than a moment went by when she was not stroking his hair or curled under his arm. Even when she cooked, Elise would make a point to brush her fingers over his skin whenever she drifted by him. Never once did she forget that he was once starved for affection, and every moment of every day she sought to shower him with it.

In return, he basked in her glow and did everything he could to encourage her rampant curiosity. Together, they explored every corner of the city and its archives. He plucked the juiciest bits from his long memory for her and hovered nearby whenever she lost herself in writing. He loved her and he was in awe of her. Cal saw it as his job to remind her just how extraordinary she was every day, lest she forget.

"Where were they this time?" she asked, setting her wine down on the edge of the small coffee table. A stack of battered notebooks took up most of the space. With her hand free, she gently nudged him until he lay in the perfect position for her to run her fingers through his long, unruly hair.

Cal closed his eyes, savoring the feeling of her blunt nails scraping gently against his scalp, and cupped her kneecap with one possessive hand. There was a small flare of magic as his fog seeped into the air, wrapping with equal possessiveness around the rest of her.

He could hardly fathom the life he lived before her, before *this*. Really, it didn't seem like much of a life at all.

"They were on the bridge," he complained. "About forty people, all of them waving signs. What in the world did they expect me to do with that? Stop to take photos?"

"Maybe they just wanted to let you know they appreciate everything you do for the city, baby."

"Yeah, well, they could be quieter about it," he grumbled.

"Poor fog man," she cooed, patting his head. "It's so hard being beloved, isn't it?"

Cal hid his smile in the blanket covering her thigh. Giving her knee a quick squeeze, he said, "Hush. This is all your fault."

"My fault? I'll remind you that *I* was the one who said we shouldn't publish the book." It was her turn to give his ear a tiny pinch. "You were the one who pushed, remember?"

"Yes, because I wanted everyone to know how much you loved me," he smugly replied. Turning his head, he looked up and found her grinning down at him, the skin around her hazel eyes crinkling. Cal lifted a hand to stroke the freckles on her cheek, a sigh of contentment on his lips. "Read that part to me again," he playfully demanded. "You know the one."

Elise blushed, as she always did when he asked her to read to him. "Didn't we just read that bit last night?"

"Yes. I want to hear it again."

It didn't matter that he'd read the book a dozen times, nor that she read excerpts from it whenever he asked her to. Cal would never get tired of seeing the words, *hearing* them. And for all that Elise blushed and grumbled, he saw the smile that tugged her full lips up and knew that she enjoyed it as much as he did.

"Fine," she sighed, using her thumb to scroll through the files on her tablet. When she found the right one, she settled her free hand on his brow and began, *"He is Calamity. He is a force of nature more powerful and vast than our government would comfortably admit. He is all-consuming. He is an act of godly wrath made flesh, and by some miracle, he has chosen to be kind to us."*

Cal closed his eyes. His chest felt too small to hold in everything he felt for her, how grateful he was to be hers. All he could do was wrap his arms around her middle, holding her tight, in the vain hope that it could express even some small amount of his love for her.

Elise's voice was soft and sure when she continued, *"He is Calamity. He is mine. The first time Cal kissed me, I knew it like I knew my magic, my heart, my hands. The kind of knowing that is instinctive and soulful even when it is new and terrifying."* She caressed his cheek with the backs of her fingers, her voice dropping to a whisper. *"He is mine and I am his. Forever."*

THE END

A SNEAK PEEK OF CONSORT'S GLORY...

Margot Goode was a practical sort of person — particularly when it came to her death.

Healers were no strangers to Grim's tithe, nor to suffering. The clasped hands of life and death belonged to the same being, after all, and healers could no more separate the two than they could change the inexorable current of time.

Even so, Margot's death took her by surprise.

It didn't come for her in the shape she always feared it would. It didn't come for her in the smothering dark, reeking of madness, piercing with claws and teeth. It came slowly, first through the tips of her fingers and then upward, over slopes of muscle and rigid bone, to steal her life before she got the chance to live it.

Burn out. The affliction all witches of her caliber suffered late in life, when the magic coursing through their veins began to damage its host beyond its ability to repair itself. It came for her too soon, and every day it got harder and harder to hide the symptoms.

What began as fine tremors after a long healing session

became hard shakes and frequent migraines. Fatigue. Lack of appetite. A peculiar sense of vertigo, like the world was slipping out from under her feet at a steep angle.

Cold practicality finally pushed her to leave the Coven. It compelled her to put in the transfer request to the Healing House in a sleepy, well-to-do San Francisco neighbourhood. That clear knowledge that her death pressed closer every day and a compulsion she just *couldn't shake* brought her to San Francisco to look for the person who could save her life.

And it pushed her to accept the dinner invitation from the alpha of the local shifter pack, the risks be damned.

The Merced coyote pack was not the largest in California, but it was the most powerful pack in the Bay Area. They had to be both smart and ruthless to win any sort of autonomy under those who ruled the Protectorate, the swath of tightly controlled land running from Arizona to the top of Oregon.

After several healing sessions with their trouble-making teenagers, Margot knew many of the Merced pack well. Even so, the risk of stepping into shifter territory was enormous. It always was when she dealt with predator races. Not because she couldn't take care of herself — healers were the people with the most intimate knowledge of the body and how to break it, after all — but because one slip-up, one good whiff of the scent buried beneath the layers of protection she slathered on every day, and her closely-guarded secrets would be exposed.

Margot dealt with Viktor Hamiliton and his pack enough to trust them not to hurt her, but there were breathtakingly few she would *ever* trust with all of herself.

So it was a risk to join the pack for dinner at the edge of marshy Lake Merced, but even the familiar anxiety of discovery wouldn't stop Margot from going. She *wanted* to go. She liked Viktor, she liked the pack members who had taken to dropping by her house on a weekly basis, and she missed the familiar chaos of a family dinner.

And Margot was desperate.

Of course I'm desperate, she thought, tightening her hands on the steering wheel of her car. *I'm dying.*

Margot drove down darkened streets, back to the Healing House with a full stomach and covered in the scents of a dozen young, single coyote shifters eager to see if she'd feel any magical tickle, any chemistry at all, when they touched. They were eager in a way that might have made her uncomfortable if she weren't currently suspended over the knife's edge of her own mortality.

Besides, she couldn't blame them. Bonding with a Goode witch, a *real* gloriana? The curiosity of it was like an aphrodisiac to the quicksilver minds of the coyotes.

Rolling her shoulders back to relieve some of her tension, Margot decided she needed another shower. The coyotes didn't smell bad, but they weren't *right,* and it grated against her nerves to have the scents of so many strange men in her pores, rubbing that niggling compulsion in the back of her mind the wrong way.

None of them were the reason she felt so compelled to step out of the safe stranglehold of the Coven to move to San Francisco. She knew it in her bones. She knew *he* was out there somewhere, but not in the Merced pack.

They were attractive, certainly, with their wide coyote grins and lean, powerful bodies. They generally leaned toward cheerful humor and quick to ignite and even quicker to die tempers. But not even the alpha of the pack, the razor-sharp Viktor, who'd managed, against her best efforts, to become a friend, inspired so much as a twitch in her magical *or* romantic instincts.

Viktor was gorgeous, intelligent, and clearly a man who cared about the people under his charge more than he cared about personal power. Even if he didn't have lush, sandy blond hair, skin of burnished copper, or baby blue eyes, she would have been drawn to his air of responsibility, his quick tongue, that easy smile.

She *liked* him. They were friends — could have even been more if only her damn magic would *cooperate.*

Why? Why can't it be one of them? Any of them?

Margot unclenched her hands on the steering wheel, fighting the tremors that came with so much more force when she was alone.

No one else has this problem. No one else needs to be so selective. Why can't I just choose?

But no one else hit burn out so young, either. And no one was what *she* was; could explain how the differences would change things, how her body might react if it didn't get what it needed. She was a witch, but she was also more.

That *more* was killing her.

She was supposed to have time. Years to figure herself out. Decades, maybe even a century. Years to settle down, date, find the right one in her own time, just like every other gloriana.

Her own grandmother didn't start feeling the symptoms until she was nearly *one hundred and fifty,* and by then, Sophie already had Noni Tula, so there was no question about who she would bond to, nor who would carry the weight of Sophie Goode's considerable magic when it turned on her.

It fell in line with Margot's consistently shitty luck that she barely made it past twenty-five before her body turned against her.

Exiting a roundabout with a tastefully lit, burbling fountain at its center, she drove with her windows down to let in the cool, eucalyptus scented air. Luckily for distracted witches everywhere, the entire Protectorate had an m-grid, allowing the sigil-lined, exhaustless engines of even the oldest vehicles to lock onto the streets and nearly drive themselves. It brought the chances of a collision to nearly zero.

Passing large, mostly arrant-owned houses with their sprawling lawns and huge, old growth trees made into silhouettes by the dark, Margot considered just how much time she had left.

Six weeks at maximum, her healer's training helpfully supplied. *With symptoms first appearing last year and increasing in severity approximately every four to five weeks, I'm looking at total burn out in two months — if I'm lucky.*

There was no use wondering what would become of her then.

She was a gloriana, the most powerful caliber a witch could be born into. If she were only a minor witch, a brightling or a brilliant, she might have just suffered permanent nerve damage or the crushing loss of her abilities.

But she wasn't, and that meant there was only one way things could end: Nerve damage. Internal bleeding. Loss of neurological function.

Death.

The only way to save her pitiful, squandered life was to find a bondmate, someone to filter her power through to diffuse the damage done to her cells every second of every day; a sort of magical dialysis that would bind her very soul to another. It was a bond that would save her life and make her partner incredibly powerful in return.

If only I could find *him.*

So far her search only revealed what Margot always feared: her bondmate couldn't just be *anyone.* There would be no hasty, ill-thought out, shotgun bonding for her. Margot Goode's bondmate would be one man and one man only.

Unfortunately, the compulsion to find him, that prickly sense of knowing, pulled her towards San Francisco for nearly a year, but gave her little else to go on. She was certain he lived in the city, but so did nearly a million other sapient beings.

Even if she had all the time in the world, the chances of running into her bondmate were slim to none.

Margot pulled into the driveway of the Healing House and killed the engine of the zippy little m-car, a thing that, like the house, belonged to the neighborhood. The Healing House and its amenities belonged to the people it served. It, along with everything within and without, wouldn't miss her when a blood vessel popped in her brain and the lights simply... went out.

Feeling suddenly, immeasurably tired, Margot let out a long sigh and leaned her forehead against the steering wheel.

I'm running out of time. And... damn it, I miss my family.

She knew it was foolish to keep her impending death from her grandmother, to lose precious time with her family. Sophie Goode wouldn't be able to fix Margot's problems, but she would do everything in her power to try. Even before Margot left Washington, the matriarch of the Goode family had begun shoving eligible men in her direction — young and mature, powerful and less powerful, witch and shifter, hybrid and even an arrant or two.

But that was why she took the job in San Francisco — that urge to *find him,* to satisfy that clawing need to hunt him down and clutch him to her chest and never, ever let him go. Even if she could explain it, Margot wasn't sure her family would understand that the normal rules didn't apply to her and never had. They couldn't. They weren't like her.

No one was.

They would never understand the compulsion to be exactly where she was, and if she confessed about her condition, she feared they would hog tie her and drag her back to the Coven to force the issue of her bonding to the first willing partner.

Because they love me, and my death will hurt them in ways I can't imagine. Uncurling one hand from the steering wheel, Margot rubbed at her stinging eyes. *Get home. Get in shower. Get to bed. You aren't giving up right now, in this stupid tiny car.*

Forcing herself to move, Margot popped open the door and swung her legs out into the chill of the February evening. Her light jacket and floral print dress did little to seal in warmth, so she hustled up the path through the small garden, through the traditional iron gate, and up the low ramp to the covered stoop. Like always, the slight bounce of her steps surprised her.

Every time she thought she was used to the way magic settled into the sidewalks and soil of San Francisco, she had to consciously adjust her gait once more. The sponginess of the ground tended to change day by day, hour by hour, like the temperamental weather the city was so famous for. It was just another quirk of the old, strange city, like the sentient fog and water teeming with bloodthirsty waterfolk.

Natives had no trouble changing the way they walked at a moment's notice, giving them the famous *San Francisco Gait,* but Margot still occasionally struggled with the loping, bouncing movements necessary to walk down the street on a magic-heavy day.

Stepping lightly toward the door, Margot didn't need to fish for keys in her purse or pocket. The doors to a Healing House were always unlocked, even when the resident healer wasn't in.

The Allied Charter listed all Healing Houses as sacrosanct. Not even the lowest criminal would stoop to stealing from one, not simply because doing so was the quickest way to spend a lifetime in a miserable, sigil-lined prison, but because they were declared holy sites after the Great War nearly wiped out healers altogether.

The gods Glory, Grim, *and* Blight claimed healers for their own. To harm one, even indirectly, was blasphemous in the extreme.

That was why Margot didn't think to check her home for intruders when she stepped through the door and dropped her purse onto the little entryway table.

Only her bedroom was warded against outsiders, her sigilwork painstakingly etched into the walls and door frame to keep out anyone who might wish her harm. A normal healer would never think to take those kinds of precautions, but Margot wasn't anywhere close to normal.

Moving to close the door, one hand extended to flick on the light. The hair on the back of her neck, exposed by her neat chignon, rose with sudden, prickling tension.

Margot turned her head slowly, her senses on high alert as she scanned the entryway and the darkened rooms that made up her living room, as well as the sterilized clinic just beyond it.

Her hearing was better than the average human's, but she heard nothing. No squeaky floorboards, no foreign breathing. There was a thread of scent, something sharp and chemical, but this was the city, not her home in the lush forest of the Pacific Northwest, and that wasn't necessarily unusual.

The only thing she could sense was a low-level hum of magic in the air. Not so strange with neighbors so close, but—

The blast hit her in a single, percussive wave, throwing her back into the yard. The heavy front door followed, its splintered bulk sailing over her in a wide arc to land with a crash against the iron gate.

Margot landed hard on her side against the smooth brick path that led to her home, her head cracking against it with a teeth-rattling crunch.

Blackness, filmy and terrifying, engulfed her.

Want a bonus epilogue for Paloma and Artem?

You can read a slice of life short story featuring Paloma, Artem, and the Pineridge's new healer on the Works by Abigail Patreon!

About the Author

 Abigail Kelly is a writer and illustrator of alternate histories, love stories, and women with drive. Her work is heavily influenced by both her modest family roots and her passion for history. She is a bookseller at an independent bookshop where she gets to badly influence impressionable young minds and put her favorite books in eager hands. She is also the host of the Kingdom of Thirst podcast, a show all about romance novels and why they matter.

Her favorite authors are Shirley Jackson, V. E. Schwab, Ursula K. Le Guin, Kresley Cole, Nalini Singh, and just about anyone who writes about the weird and wonderful. She lives in San Francisco with her dog, Babs, who remains stubbornly illiterate.

Glossary

PLACES

United Territories and Allies: What we would consider the continental USA. A loose federation of sovereign states established after the Great War. The UTA capital is United Washington, in the Neutral Zone.

The Elvish Protectorate: Also known as the EVP. Stretches from Oregon to New Mexico. Capital city is San Francisco. Led by the elvish sovereign Theodore Thaddeus Solbourne.

The Coven Collective: Also known as the Collective. Encompasses Washington state. Capital city is Seattle. Led by a large coalition of witch covens, with Sophie Goode acting as their leader.

The Orclind: Encompasses much of the Midwest. Led by the Iron Chain, a close-knit government made up of orcish clans and family groups. Capital city is Boulder.

Shifter Alliance: Takes up a section of the midwest and all of the south. (Unfortunately includes Florida.) Run by a very, very loose alliance of shifter packs from three capital cities — Minneapolis, Oklahoma City, and Atlanta.

The Draakonriik: Also known as the 'Riik. The second smallest territory, it takes up all of the Great Lakes region and stretches to New York. Led by Taevas Aždaja, the *Isand* (ee-zand) of the dragon clans. Pronounced: *dra-kon-reek*

The Neutral Zone: Also known as the New Zone. Technically it is held by a coalition government consisting of representatives from the UTA, but in reality it is run by a syndicate of feuding vampire families. It is a small strip of land squeezed between the Draakonriik and the Shifter Alliance.

GODS

Light & Darkness: The primordial gods who created all the others. Also known as The Lovers and First Union. Both are generally represented as female.

Loft: God of the sky and creator of flying beings. Twin sibling to Tempest. They know no gender. Also known as the Boundless One.

Tempest: God of the ocean and creator of all water beings. Also known as the Hungry God and the god of love.

Burden: God of the Earth, creator of all beings who live within it — most notably the orcs. Husband of Glory.

Glory: Goddess of sunlight, magic, and creator of elves. Worshipped by witches for giving the gift of magic to humanity.

Blight: God of forested places and disease. He works in partnership with his daughter Grim and shares her dominion over demons and all reviled creatures.

Grim: Goddess of death. Known as the Merciful One and the Brilliant Lady. She is widely beloved.

Craft: God of change, newness, and messengers. Creator of humanity and viewed warily by non-worshippers as the Chaos Maker. They change their gender frequently, but generally is referred to using he/him pronouns.

TERMS

Arrant: someone born without m-paths, or the ability to channel and use magic.

Dragon: a person with a dual form. In their bipedal form, they have claw-tipped wings, horns (males only), and a tail. In their quadrupedal form, they are roughly the size of a standard SUV and can fly at extremely high altitudes for weeks at a time. They come in a variety of extremely saturated colors that shift with the time of day (light to dark). They breathe cold blue fire and can see the Earth's magnetic field. Identifying mating feature is marked change in behavior, including the overwhelming urge to nest.

Elemental: a being created by a spontaneous magical eruption. They often take on the attributes of whatever weather they happen to be born into, *i.e.* a lightning storm might produce a lightning elemental, or a blizzard might make a snow elemental.

Elf: someone born with jewel-toned skin, claws, pointed ears, and four fangs. Very secretive and considered apex predators who require a strict hierarchy to function. Average height of 6-7ft. Identifying mating feature is the retraction of claws.

Fey: a person with nearly vestigial, insect-like wings, small fangs, and claws. Usually live in large groups. Identifying mating feature is bioluminescence.

M- : M- is frequently used as shorthand to denote when something is infused or otherwise combined with a magical element.

Met: acronym for *magically enhanced tech.* A branded home assistant that can do everything your Alexa can, as well as small, low-level magic to help around the house.

M-siphon: a containment device used to imprison a magical being and siphon off their magic. Highly illegal.

R-siphon: also known as *reverse siphon.* New technology that redistributes magic away from the siphon instead of into it.

M-lev: a play on *maglev,* meaning a high speed train that levitates using magnets. In this case, magnets *and* magic.

M-weather: magic weather. Very common, but can result in "clusters" or storms that wreak havoc if not properly contained. In rare circumstances, it can also produce a sapient being known as an *elemental.*

Orc: a person with green, gray, russet, or blue skin, two fangs, and claws. Widely renowned for their strength and beautiful voices. Identifying mating feature is "the kohl", or altered, dark pigmentation of the hands and feet developed after meeting their mate.

Pixie: a small, winged creature with compound eyes with about the same level of intelligence as a rat. In the wild they live in trees and in burrows, but have adapted to living in walls, pipes, mailboxes, etc.

Shifter: a person who can shift into an animal form. They can partially shift (changing only parts of their bodies at will) and often take on characteristics of their other half. Famous for their strength and tenacity, as well as their dual-voiced "shifter purr" which many people find deeply attractive. Usually found in packs.

Sigil: a symbol used to channel magic. Western countries use the alchemical alphabet formally codified in the 1800's, though many, many variations are used all over the world.

Vampire: a person who drinks blood to survive and cannot go out in sunlight. Vampirism can only be "caught" with the exchange of fresh blood, and as of 2045 is much more widely spread through procreation. Vampires can only breed with their *anchors.* Identifying mating feature is marked change in behavior, including overwhelming desire and need for total isolation.

Were: a person infected with the were virus, a much mutated strain of the vampirism virus, resulting in altered physiology and magical ability. They can be identified by their heterochromia, or different colored eyes. They are the newest magical race and viewed warily by the general public for a variety of earned and unearned reasons. Identifying mating feature is marked change in behavior, including highly increased territorial instinct and the urge to nest.

NAMES OF IMPORTANT CHARACTERS IN THIS BOOK

Artem: ahr-tem (rolled *r*)

Aždaja: ash-DIE-ah

Calamity: kuh-lam-ity (prefers *Cal*)

Charlotte: shar-let

Domhnall: doh-noll (goes by *Dom)*

Elise Sasini: uh-leese sah-see-nee

Kaz: kaz

Paloma Contreras: pah-low-mah kon-treh-rahs

Taevas: tay-vahs

CONTENT WARNINGS

#376: parental abandonment, experiences of war, kidnapping, violence, mating seasons, and sexual situations with non-human characters.

Astray: parental death, illness, potential violence, potential weather disasters, mild anxiety disorder, and sexual situations with a non-human character.

Weathering: mass causality events, imprisonment, violence, isolation, religious themes, virginity, and sexual situations with a non-human character.

www.ingramcontent.com/pod-product-compliance
Lightning Source LLC
Chambersburg PA
CBHW072337020726

47506CB00004B/911